THE JUDICIARY COMMITTEES

This book is printed on 100 percent recycled paper

The Ralph Nader Congress Project

A Study of the House and Senate Judiciary Committees

Peter H. Schuck, DIRECTOR

The Ralph Nader Congress Project

Grossman Publishers
A DIVISION OF THE VIKING PRESS
NEW YORK   1975

THE
JUDICIARY
COMMITTEES

Contributors

Peter H. Schuck, Project Director and Editor
A.B., Cornell University (1962); J.D., Harvard Law School (1965); LL.M., New York University (1966); M.A., Government, Harvard University (1969)
Director, Consumers Union Washington Office

Mark J. Green
A.B., Cornell University (1967); J.D., Harvard Law School (1970)
Director, Corporate Accountability Research Group

Martha Joynt Kumar
A.B., Connecticut College for Women (1963); M.A., Columbia University (1965); Ph.D., Political Science, Columbia University (1972)
Assistant Professor of Political Science, Towson State College, Towson, Maryland

Irene Till
A.B., Syracuse University (1928); M.A., Radcliffe College (1929); Ph.D., Columbia University (1937)
Economist, Corporate Accountability Research Group

Michael E. Ward
A.B., Dartmouth College (1969); VISTA (1969–1971); J.D., Stanford University Law School (1974)

Researchers:
Michael Massing
Senior, Harvard College

Leonard Lane
A.B., University of Wisconsin (1966)
Economic Consultant, Sierra Club

Contents

I OF OLD MEN IN NEW TIMES

II SENTRIES OF MONOPOLY

Foreword

The Judiciary committees of the House and Senate are by far the largest and in many respects the most far-reaching legislative committees in America. Yet the two committees have somehow managed to elude description and analysis during their long and illustrious histories. In large part, this remarkable freedom from public and academic scrutiny simply recapitulates the much larger theme of congressional opacity. It is a fundamental premise of this book, and of the Congress Project as a whole, that the obscurity of the most representative branch of the national government is profoundly dispiriting to the democratic enterprise. At a minimum, the public must know and care about Congress and its "little legislatures" (as Woodrow Wilson described the committees) if it is to be restored as the lifeblood of the American body politic.

To some extent the Judiciary committees, like all units of Congress, have remained closed institutions because the members have wanted it that way, and an uninformed public has acquiesced. Justice Brandeis observed that sunlight is the best disinfectant, yet Congress has preferred the artificial light of the locked caucus room, where intrigue and an inbred, protective morality flourish.

The press and the academic chroniclers of political life must share much of the blame. The former, knowing that much, if not most, committee activity is tedious, slogging, undramatic work, has generally preferred to cover the more glamorous, but ultimately insignificant, surface of legislative events—floor debates, roll call votes, and the signing of bills. The academics interested in Congress have gone to the other extreme. Abandoning the lay but literate public as an audience, and deprecating institutional description and prescription as unworthy endeavors, too many social scientists have chosen to write for and speak to themselves alone. They all too often practice a professional virtuosity whose principal products are an obsession with pseudoscientific methodology and observations that oscillate between cosmic generality, on the one hand, and trival minutiae, on the other.

This book, the first extended treatment of the Judiciary committees ever published, cannot but help to fill this yawning void. But much, much more remains to be said about these committees. This study, like all studies, was constrained by limited resources. Difficult choices had to be made and priorities had to be set, often arbitrarily. Certain areas of Judiciary jurisdiction, such as public immigration legislation, have been omitted altogether. Judiciary's shockingly inadequate oversight of the Immigration and Naturalization Service, one of the Justice Department's most troubled agencies, is not mentioned here; space limitations account for the omission. Judiciary oversight of the Federal Bureau of Investigation receives precious little attention here, for the very simple reason that there has been precious little of it. This nonfeasance by the committee may be rectified by the newly established FBI Oversight Subcommittee, but as this book went to press, little had yet occurred to justify that hope. The dimension and significance of this failure by the Judiciary committees is only now, in the wake of the Watergate revelations, becoming apparent to the committees and the public.

Senate Judiciary scrutiny of presidential appointments to high Justice Department positions, a major responsibility of the committee, is only briefly considered here. We particularly regret this omission, for in its handling of the nominations of Richard G. Kleindienst, Elliot L. Richardson, and William Saxbe to be attorney general, and of L. Patrick Gray and Clarence M. Kelley to be FBI director, and in its oversight of the appointment and firing of Archibald Cox as Watergate Special Prosecutor, the committee has shown encouraging—if limited—signs of independence, imagination, and energy in the discharge of this aspect of its constitutional "advise and consent" function. A thorough exploration of the lackluster performance of the Senate Judiciary Committee in investigating the International Telephone and Telegraph affair is also much needed, but we content ourselves with the knowledge that this fascinating chapter of Judiciary history will not long remain unchronicled. In both cases, the events either occurred too late to be fully researched or simply could not be adequately analyzed with our very limited research capability. For the same reason, the preimpeachment investigation of President Richard M. Nixon by the House Judiciary Committee is only touched upon here—a gap that will surely be filled by legions of others. As explained in the chapter on judicial nominations, Senate Judiciary consideration of recent Supreme Court nominations is omitted not because it is not significant—again, it shows the committee pursuing its independent constitutional role with unaccustomed vigor and responsibility—but because it has been described in admirable detail elsewhere.

This study focuses on the Judiciary committees in the Ninety-second Congress, and most of the basic research was conducted during the summer of 1972. Nevertheless, we have, to some extent and with the exceptions noted, also sought to document the major developments in the committees during the first fifteen months of the Ninety-third Congress, that is, through April 1, 1974. The Senate committee is discussed at considerably greater length than the House committee. For reasons discussed in detail in Part I— including a far larger budget, somewhat broader jurisdiction, greater prestige, and a more creative approach to the legislative process (there are, of course, exceptions to this generalization)— the Senate committee is considerably more active and visible than its counterpart in the House, except in a few areas such as civil rights and private legislation. The coverage in this study is weighted to reflect these differences.

This study, then, is far from being exhaustive of the protean activities or jurisdictions of the Judiciary committees. Indeed, one objective of this initial effort is to spawn others; in the files, transcripts, and collective memory of the Judiciary committees and their members lie buried the raw materials for enough dissertations to occupy an army of graduate students in social science and journalism.

An essential ingredient of any foreword, it seems, is the observation that the book could not have been written without the help of others. That commonplace is particularly true of this book, for its preparation was in very real sense a joint effort. My debts are many. Special gratitude is owed to Michael E. Ward, a gifted, indefatigable researcher who managed to make sense of the sprawling criminal and constitutional jurisdiction of the committees, and Dr. Martha Joynt Kumar, who imaginatively and energetically researched the areas of private legislation, judicial nominations, and full-committee activities. Two talented specialists in their fields, Mark J. Green and Dr. Irene Till, graciously contributed the materials on antitrust and on patents and copyrights, respectively. Others who smoothed our way were Michael Massing, Lee Lane, Barbara Lloyd, Congress Project staffers Robert Fellmeth, Faith Keating, and Beverly Wexler, and Grossman editor Carol Weiland. Ralph Nader provided inspiration and financial support, two invaluable resources.

The responsiveness, willingness to teach, and patience of the congressional staff members assigned to the Judiciary committees— the true *cognoscenti* on the subject—can hardly be exaggerated. They spent countless hours with us, and we only hope that the accuracy of our description of the committees redeems their perception and generosity. Special thanks are due to Burton Wides, Tom Hart, Howard Eglit, James Meeker, Ron Meredith, and others who preferred to remain anonymous, all of whom commented on drafts of this study. We, of course, take full responsibility for the observations and conclusions in this book. Many members of the committees, as well as professional Judiciary watchers around Capitol

Hill, were also generous with their time, their files, and their insights. All unattributed quotations in the text are based on interviews conducted with present and former subcommittee staffs and others between June 1972 and April 1974, and held confidential at the request of the person interviewed.

Finally, there are my wife Marcy and son Christopher, who endured this effort with the worst of evenings and weekends, and the best of humors. My daughter Julie was *in utero* at the time, and felt no pain.

Peter H. Schuck
Washington, D.C.
April 1, 1974

Introduction

If Congress, as it has been said, is the heart of our democracy, then the House and Senate Judiciary committees are its lifeblood. These committees provide perhaps the clearest measure of the success or failure of Congress in protecting and advancing the public good. If Congress is to assert itself as a vital organ of our political and moral life, as a counterweight to a presidency grown swollen with power, as an energetic and passionate advocate for long-ignored public interests, the Judiciary committees will have to play a leading role.

These committees are uniquely suited to perform this creative function. From the earliest days of the Republic, Congress has vouchsafed to the Judiciary committees its highest constitutional responsibilities. The definition and protection of constitutional rights; confirmation of members of the federal judiciary, including the Supreme Court; amendment of the Constitution; impeachment of the president and other federal officials—these are awesome tasks, requiring the highest degree of integrity, independence, and initiative.

Both committees consist entirely of lawyers, men and women whose professional responsibilities are expected to be tied to the cause of justice and the rule of law. If they permit the law to become an instrument of oppression or a shield for the status quo, there is little hope for facilitating self-government. If they fail to exercise vigilant control over the Department of Justice and the instrumentalities of the legal system, the tyranny of the bureaucrat will soon corrode that system. They can infuse the law with vitality and a capacity to respond to the needs of our rapidly changing society, or they can preside over the law's ossification and desiccation.

The Judiciary committees, moreover, enjoy unparalleled jurisdictions and unrivaled resources relative to other committees of Congress. They literally write the rules of the democratic game, whether that game be antitrust, criminal justice, or constitutional law. If the deck is stacked in favor of the traditional players, the vested economic interests, these committees must bear the major responsibility. The grandeur and high drama of the presidential impeachment inquiry, in which the House Judiciary Committee played so prominent a part, should not blind us to the importance of the more prosaic, routine, but ongoing activities of the Judiciary committees in their vast legislative domains.

In this volume, the first of a series on the key domestic committees of Congress, Peter Schuck and the study group that he directed scrutinize the performance of the Judiciary committees, detailing their solid triumphs (as in the work of the Separation of Powers Subcommittee) and their abject failures (as in the areas of judicial nominations, oversight of the Department of Justice, and antitrust). These findings are cause for serious public concern —and for some hope. For the dominant pattern of legislative torpor, abdication of responsibility to the executive branch and private groups, preoccupation with trivia and special interest legislation, hostility to the rights of racial minorities, women, and consumers, occasionally gives way to aggressive investigation of executive branch abuses and ventilation of important issues. The dignity, vigor, and sense of public responsibility with which the House Judiciary Committee recently conducted its impeachment investigation is notable in part because those qualities have been so rarely observed in either chamber. Perhaps it augurs well for the future.

It is a sad commentary on civic education in America that no such study has ever before been done. While shelves of books have been written on such subjects as voting behavior and presidential campaigns, not a single analysis of the Judiciary committees—certainly the single most broad-ranging legislative organ in our political system—exists. We hope that citizens, scholars, and journalists will begin to pay as much attention to these and other congressional committees as the lobbyists for the powerful have always done. Until they do, the Congress will remain an anachronism, an affront to the constitutional scheme that the Founding Fathers created less than two hundred years ago.

Ralph Nader

Members of the
Judiciary Committees

SENATE COMMITTEE ON THE JUDICIARY, NINETY-SECOND AND NINETY-THIRD CONGRESSES

Majority:

James O. Eastland, Chm. (Miss.)
John L. McClellan (Ark.)
Sam J. Ervin, Jr. (N. C.)
Philip A. Hart (Mich.)
Edward M. Kennedy (Mass.)
Birch Bayh (Ind.)
Quentin N. Burdick (N. Dak.)
Robert C. Byrd (W. Va.)
John V. Tunney (Cal.)

Minority:

Roman L. Hruska (Neb.)
Hiram L. Fong (Ha.)
Hugh Scott (Pa.)
Strom Thurmond (S. C.)
Marlow W. Cook (Ky.)
Charles McC. Mathias, Jr. (Md.)
Edward J. Gurney (Fla.)

Subcommittee on Administrative Practice and Procedure

Majority:	*Minority*:
Kennedy, Chm.	Thurmond
Hart	Mathias
Bayh	Gurney
Burdick	
Tunney	

Subcommittee on Antitrust and Monopoly Legislation

Majority:	*Minority*:
Hart, Chm.	Hruska
McClellan	Fong
Ervin	Thurmond
Kennedy	Gurney
Tunney	

Subcommittee on Constitutional Amendments

Majority:	*Minority*:
Bayh, Chm.	Fong
Eastland	Hruska
Ervin	Thurmond
Byrd	Cook
Burdick	Gurney†
Tunney	Scott*

* Indicates addition in 93rd Congress.
† Not a member of subcommittee in 93rd Congress.

Subcommittee on Constitutional Rights

Majority:	*Minority*:
Ervin, Chm.	Hruska
McClellan*	Fong
Kennedy	Thurmond
Bayh	Scott†
Byrd	Gurney*
Tunney	

Subcommittee on Criminal Laws and Procedures

Majority:	*Minority*:
McClellan, Chm.	Hruska
Ervin	Scott
Hart	Thurmond
Eastland	Cook
Kennedy	
Byrd	

Subcommittee on Federal Charters, Holidays, and Celebrations

Majority:	*Minority*:
McClellan	Hruska, Chm.

* Indicates addition in 93rd Congress.
† Not a member of subcommittee in 93rd Congress.

Subcommittee on Immigration and Naturalization

Majority:	*Minority*:
Eastland, Chm.	Fong
McClellan	Thurmond
Ervin	Cook
Kennedy	
Hart	

Subcommittee on Improvements in Judicial Machinery

Majority:	*Minority*:
Burdick, Chm.	Hruska
McClellan	Scott
Hart	Gurney
Ervin	

Subcommittee on Internal Security

Majority:	*Minority*:
Eastland, Chm.	Scott
McClellan	Thurmond
Ervin	Cook
Bayh	Gurney
Byrd†	

† Not a member of subcommittee in 93rd Congress.

Subcommittee to Investigate Juvenile Delinquency

Majority:	*Minority*:
Bayh, Chm.	Cook
Hart	Hruska
Burdick	Fong
Kennedy	Mathias

Subcommittee on National Penitentiaries

Majority:	*Minority*:
Burdick, Chm.	Cook
Hart	Mathias
Bayh	

Subcommittee on Patents, Trademarks, and Copyrights

Majority:	*Minority*:
McClellan, Chm.	Scott
Hart	Fong
Burdick	

Subcommittee on Refugees and Escapees

Majority:	*Minority*:
Kennedy, Chm.	Fong
McClellan	Mathias
Hart	

Subcommittee on Representation of Citizens' Interests*

Majority:	*Minority*:
Tunney, Chm.	Cook
Ervin	Mathias
Bayh	

Subcommittee on Revision and Codification

Majority:	*Minority*:
Ervin, Chm.	Scott
Hart	

Subcommittee on Separation of Powers

Majority:	*Minority*:
Ervin, Chm.	Mathias
McClellan	Gurney
Burdick	
Byrd*	

Subcommittee on FBI Oversight*

Majority:	*Minority*:
Eastland, Chm.	Hruska
McClellan	Scott
Ervin	Thurmond
Hart	Gurney
Byrd	

* Indicates addition in 93rd Congress.

HOUSE COMMITTEE ON THE JUDICIARY, NINETY-SECOND CONGRESS

Majority:

Emanuel Celler, Chm. (N.Y.)
Peter W. Rodino, Jr. (N. J.)
Harold D. Donohue (Mass.)
Jack Brooks (Tex.)
John Dowdy (Tex.)
Robert W. Kastenmeier (Wis.)
Don Edwards (Cal.)
William L. Hungate (Mo.)
John Conyers, Jr. (Mich.)
Andrew Jacobs, Jr. (Ind.)
Joshua Eilberg (Pa.)
William F. Ryan (N. Y.)
Jerome R. Waldie (Cal.)
Edwin W. Edwards (La.)
Walter Flowers (Ala.)
James R. Mann (S. C.)
Abner J. Mikva (Ill.)
Paul S. Sarbanes (Md.)
John F. Seiberling (Ohio)
James Abourezk (S. D.)
George E. Danielson (Cal.)
Robert F. Drinan (Mass.)

Minority:

William M. McCulloch (Ohio)
Richard H. Poff (Va.)
Edward Hutchinson (Mich.)
Robert McClory (Ill.)
Henry P. Smith, III (N. Y.)
Charles W. Sandman, Jr.
   (N. J.)
Tom Railsback (Ill.)
Edward G. Biester, Jr. (Pa.)
Charles E. Wiggins (Cal.)
David W. Dennis (Ind.)
Hamilton Fish, Jr. (N. Y.)
R. Lawrence Coughlin (Pa.)
Wiley Mayne (Ia.)
Lawrence J. Hogan (Md.)
William J. Keating (Ohio)
James D. McKevitt (Colo.)

Subcommittee No. 1 (Immigration)

Majority:	*Minority*:
Rodino, Chm.	Dennis
Dowdy	Mayne
Eilberg	Hogan
Ryan	McKevitt
Flowers	
Seiberling	

Subcommittee No. 2 (Claims)

Majority:	*Minority*:
Donohue, Chm.	Smith
Waldie	Sandman
Flowers	Railsback
Mann	
Danielson	

Subcommittee No. 3 (Patents, trademarks, and copyrights)

Majority:	*Minority*:
Kastenmeier, Chm.	Railsback
Conyers	Biester
Ryan	Fish
Mikva	Coughlin
Drinan	

Subcommittee No. 4 (Bankruptcy and reorganization)

Majority:	*Minority*:
Edwards (Cal.), Chm.	Wiggins
Conyers	Sandman
Jacobs	Keating
Waldie	McClory
Edwards (La.)	

Subcommittee No. 5 (Antitrust)

Majority:	*Minority*:
Celler, Chm.	McCulloch
Brooks	Poff
Hungate	Hutchinson
Jacobs	McClory
Mikva	
Abourezk	

HOUSE COMMITTEE ON THE JUDICIARY, NINETY-THIRD CONGRESS

Majority:	*Minority*:
Peter W. Rodino, Jr., Chm. (N. J.)	Edward Hutchinson (Mich.)
Harold D. Donohue (Mass.)	Robert McClory (Ill.)
Jack Brooks (Tex.)	Henry P. Smith, III (N. Y.)
Robert W. Kastenmeier (Wis.)	Charles W. Sandman, Jr.
Don Edwards (Cal.)	(N. J.)
William L. Hungate (Mo.)	Tom Railsback (Ill.)
John Conyers, Jr. (Mich.)	Charles E. Wiggins (Cal.)
Joshua Eilberg (Pa.)	David W. Dennis (Ind.)
Jerome Waldie (Cal.)	Hamilton Fish, Jr. (N. Y.)
Walter Flowers (Ala.)	Wiley Mayne (Ia.)
James R. Mann (S. C.)	Lawrence J. Hogan (Md.)
Paul S. Sarbanes (Md.)	William J. Keating (Ohio)
John F. Seiberling (Ohio)	M. Caldwell Butler (Va.)
George E. Danielson (Cal.)	William S. Cohen (Me.)
Robert F. Drinan (Mass.)	Trent Lott (Miss.)
Charles B. Rangel (N. Y.)	Harold V. Froehlich (Wis.)
Barbara Jordan (Tex.)	Carlos J. Moorhead (Cal.)
Ray Thornton (Ark.)	Joseph Maraziti (N. J.)
Elizabeth Holtzman (N. Y.)	
Wayne W. Owens (Utah)	
Edward Mezvinsky (Ia.)	

Subcommittee on Immigration, Citizenship, and International Law

Majority:	*Minority*:
Eilberg, Chm.	Keating
Waldie	Railsback
Flowers	Wiggins
Seiberling	Fish
Holtzman	

Subcommittee on Claims and Governmental Relations

Majority: *Minority*:
Donohue, Chm.   Butler
Mann   Froehlich
Danielson   Moorhead
Jordan   Maraziti
Thornton

Subcommittee on Courts, Civil Liberties, and the Administration of Justice

Majority: *Minority*:
Kastenmeier, Chm.   Railsback
Danielson   Smith
Drinan   Sandman
Owens   Cohen
Mezvinsky

Subcommittee on Civil Rights and Constitutional Rights

Majority: *Minority*:
Edwards, Chm.   Wiggins
Waldie   McClory
Sarbanes   Butler
Drinan   Lott
Rangel

Subcommittee on Monopolies and Commercial Law

Majority:
Rodino, Chm.
Brooks
Flowers
Seiberling
Jordan
Mezvinsky

Minority:
Hutchinson
McClory
Sandman
Dennis

Subcommittee on Crime

Majority:
Conyers, Chm.
Sarbanes
Rangel
Thornton
Owens

Minority:
Fish
Keating
Cohen
Froehlich

Subcommittee on Criminal Justice

Majority:
Hungate, Chm.
Kastenmeier
Edwards
Mann
Holtzman

Minority:
Smith
Dennis
Mayne
Hogan

I

OF OLD MEN
IN NEW TIMES

NOTE: This part was prepared by Peter H. Schuck, Dr. Martha Joynt Kumar, and Michael E. Ward.

1

From Business
to Busing

"JUDICIARY COMMITTEE VOTES IMPEACHMENT OF PRESIDENT
NIXON"

Headlines like this have thrust the Judiciary committees before
the public eye as never before. Most people now know that
articles of impeachment are voted on by the House, and that it is
the Judiciary Committee, under the chairmanship of Peter W.
Rodino, Jr., in the Ninety-third Congress, that must investigate
President Nixon and report its findings to the full House.
But consider some other headlines:

"GOVERNOR WALLACE SHOT BY MAN WITH HANDGUN"
"SIEGE OF ATTICA PRISON LEAVES THIRTY-SEVEN DEAD, INCLUDING
NINE GUARDS"
"CORPORATE CONCENTRATION ON THE RISE"
"RIOTERS OVERTURN SCHOOL BUSSES/OPPOSE FORCED BUSING"
"ANOTHER TEENAGER FOUND DEAD OF OVERDOSE"

The issues behind these banner headlines constitute the routine, daily work of the Judiciary committees and, in the aggregate, probably have a far more profound effect upon the nature and quality of American life than even the impeachment of a president. Consider the ordinary fare of the Judiciary committees:

- whether your grade-school child will be bused to a distant school;
- under what circumstances officials may tap your telephone;
- whether reporters must reveal their information sources;
- how much "speed" or other drugs your teenager will be able to find on the market;
- whether an eighteen-year-old shall have the right to vote;
- whether to outlaw the snub-nosed handgun known as the "Saturday night special";
- whether your employer can check with the Federal Bureau of Investigation and other law enforcement computer data banks to obtain intimate details of your life;
- what to do about prison riots;
- what shall be the scope of patent and copyright monopolies;
- what shape will the "war on crime" take;
- whether women and minorities will enjoy equal opportunity;
- whether the American economy is to be more competitive or more concentrated;
- whether to permit "blue movies" to be exhibited;
- who shall sit on the Supreme Court of the United States and other federal courts.[1]

The committees are charged with exercising oversight (review) functions over agencies as powerful and pervasive as the Department of Justice (including the FBI), as arcane as the U.S. Patent Office, and as trivial as the American Revolution Bicentennial Commission.*

* For the statutory duties of the Judiciary Committees, see Appendix 4.

The Judiciary committees of the House and Senate are in many ways quintessential legislative bodies, the energy centers of their respective chambers. Explosive issues like wiretapping and abortion are routine for Judiciary. In the Ninety-second Congress, they considered, among other issues, the president's pocket-veto power; drug abuse; the reform of the electoral college; obscenity and pornography; voting rights; and the separation of powers among governmental branches. No other unit of American government—with the possible exception of the Supreme Court—has more to say about the laws that define America's legal, institutional, and moral climate than the Senate Judiciary Committee and, to a somewhat lesser extent, its House counterpart. Positioned at the center of legislative power, they literally write the rules of the democratic game. Of all bills and resolutions introduced in the Senate during the Ninety-second Congress, 36 percent were referred to the Senate Judiciary Committee; 25 percent of those measures introduced in the House of Representatives were similarly channeled. One-fourth of *all* reports on legislation by all Senate committees were filed by the Senate Judiciary Committee.

Presiding over these powerful committees in the Ninety-second Congress were two formidable politicians. A study in contrasts, these men shared one characteristic: age. One was sixty-eight at the close of the Ninety-second Congress; the other was eighty-three. Like all chairmen in Congress, they won their gavels by virtue of seniority (and it was seniority that finally brought one of them down).

The chairman of the Senate Judiciary Committee was a courtly, conservative* Southern cotton-grower who was at the center of

---

* The terms "conservative" and "liberal," when used to describe political views, are obviously imprecise, often misleading, and occasionally meaningless. Nevertheless, these terms do generally convey a popularly understood, if vague, meaning to the public mind; they are used promiscuously by politicians and their aides in the halls of Congress, by Congress-watchers, by the media, and doubtless by the readers of this book. A brief but obviously unsatisfactory rendering of this popular understanding is that "liberals" are thought to be receptive to the use of governmental programs

that chamber's power elite. An exemplar of the traditionalism of
the Senate, generous and scrupulously fair in dispensing autonomy, funds, staff, and other perquisites to his colleagues on
Judiciary, he was steadfastly opposed to the extension of civil
rights and civil liberties principles.

The chairman of the House Judiciary Committee was an
urban liberal, a Jewish lawyer from Brooklyn, the architect of the
landmark Civil Rights Act of 1964 so ardently opposed by his
Senate counterpart. Yet he ran his committee as his personal
fiefdom; he was a willful potentate who was not generous with
funds and staff, and who ran roughshod over the ambitions of his
colleagues.

James O. Eastland, senior Democrat in the Senate chamber,
has been a member of that body for thirty years; Emanuel Celler
served in the House for half a century, longer than anyone else
in history.

---

to actively seek changes in social and economic conditions, while normally
opposing governmental restraints upon the civil liberties of citizens, including suspected criminals. "Conservatives" are thought to take the opposite
position. It is in this popular, colloquial sense, then, that the terms are
used throughout this study.

2

The Senate
Judiciary Committee:
Graveyard for
Liberal Legislation

James Eastland's Judiciary Committee in the Ninety-second Congress consisted of sixteen senators. The Democratic majority (in order of seniority) was Eastland, John L. McClellan (Ark.), Sam J. Ervin, Jr. (N.C.), Philip A. Hart (Mich.), Edward M. Kennedy (Mass.), Birch Bayh (Ind.), Quentin N. Burdick (N.D.), Robert C. Byrd (W. Va.), and John V. Tunney (Cal.). The Republicans were Roman L. Hruska (Neb.), Hiram L. Fong (Ha.), Hugh Scott (Pa.), Strom Thurmond (S.C.), Marlow W. Cook (Ky.), Charles McC. Mathias, Jr. (Md.), and Edward J. Gurney (Fla.). The same men sat on the committee in the Ninety-third Congress.

All of them are lawyers. All of them have ignored the law when they found it irksome.* The committee is, in one sense, a microcosm of the Senate: it includes several putative presidential candidates (Kennedy, Bayh); the senator voted as having the most integrity (Hart); an acknowledged constitutional law expert (Ervin); a would-be future majority leader (Byrd); a member who once proposed reserving a seat on the Supreme Court for mediocrity (Hruska); the minority leader of the Senate (Scott); the last of the unreconstructed segregationists (Eastland, Thurmond); and at least one member under criminal investigation (Gurney).†

The Mississippi Planter

But in Congress, it is the chairman whose politics and character determine much of what the committee does—or does not do. James O. Eastland usually sports a big smile, a big cigar, and a low profile. Aristocratic, complex, rarely showing the harried manner of many of his colleagues, he coolly monitors his empire with the complacency of a cat in a milk factory. His political

---

* Title I of the Legislative Reorganization Act of 1946 and Section 130 of the Legislative Reorganization Act of 1970 require the committee to hold regular meetings, and to publish their rules in the *Congressional Record* by March 31 of each year. Both requirements are systematically ignored by the Senate Judiciary Committee.

One member, Hugh Scott, had steadfastly refused (as of April 2, 1974) to sever ties with the law firm with which he was connected before coming to Congress, despite frequent criticism of this affiliation. According to his administrative assistant, Scott is listed as "of counsel" on the firm's letterhead, although he is not actually a partner and receives no income from the firm.[1] The American Bar Association's Code of Professional Responsibility states: "A lawyer who assumes a judicial, legislative, or public executive or administrative post or office shall not permit his name to remain in the name of a law firm or to be used in professional notices of the firm during any significant period in which he is not actively and regularly practicing law as a member of the firm, and during such periods other members of the firm shall not use his name in the firm name or in professional notices of the firm." (Disciplinary Rule 2–102[B])

† On July 10, 1974, Senator Gurney was indicted on multiple counts of accepting bribes from Florida builders in return for favored treatment by federal housing officials, and lying to a grand jury. This was the first indictment of an incumbent senator in fifty years.

dexterity is obvious: after nearly twenty years on the Judiciary Committee, he retains the acquiescence, if not the admiration, of committee members.

Eastland is one of the most conservative members of Congress.* The son of a prosperous district attorney in the rich delta country of Mississippi, Eastland was first elected to public office —the state House of Representatives—in 1928, and has served in the United States Senate since 1942. In the Ninety-fourth Congress, with the retirement of George Aiken of Vermont, he will become the dean of the Senate.

Like all senators, he has been a fierce defender of his state's parochial interests. Unlike most, he has voted against his national party more often than with it.† Eastland has been a hawk on Vietnam and a staunch supporter of Pentagon spending; he voted to allow prayer in the public schools; he has voted against federal gun-control legislation and reduced penalties for marijuana use; he has frequently opposed federal spending for health and education facilities; he voted against unemployment compensation for migrant laborers, against manpower training, and against food stamps.

One of the Senate's strongest opponents of civil rights legislation, Eastland once boasted to his constituents that he had managed to defeat 127 civil rights bills during his Senate tenure.[4] In 1948 he deserted the Democratic party, which had endorsed a civil rights platform, to support Judiciary colleague Strom Thurmond's Dixiecrats. In 1954 he campaigned for the Senate on a platform of opposition to that year's Supreme Court decision requiring school integration, and he continued to lead attacks on the Warren Court (which he viewed as pro-Communist) throughout the 1950s and 1960s.

---

* He received a cumulative rating of 73 percent from the conservative Americans for Constitutional Action, and a cumulative rating of 16 percent from the liberal Americans for Democratic Action.[2]

† In 1971, Eastland supported the Nixon administration in three out of four votes and the Democratic majority in about one out of three; he supported the conservative coalition of Republicans and Southern Democrats on 99 percent of roll-call votes he answered.[3]

Eastland's adamant resistance to civil rights for blacks inspired a rarely repeated resourcefulness on the part of Senate liberals bent upon circumventing his Judiciary Committee. The Civil Rights Act of 1964, one of the most important pieces of legislation of the century, was enacted without Senate committee consideration of the House-passed bill. The Senate voted as a body to simply bypass the Judiciary Committee. The 1965 Voting Rights Act and its extension in 1972 were sent to the Judiciary Committee under instructions by the full Senate that the bills be reported out within a certain period of time; failure to comply would automatically bring the bills to the floor of the Senate without the committee's views. Both pieces of legislation did, in fact, reach the floor this way. When Eastland failed to call a meeting before the deadline, Senators Hart and Scott issued committee majority views in a formal report, even though the chairman did not file it.[5]

The nomination of the eminent civil rights lawyer Thurgood Marshall to the United States Court of Appeals for the Second Circuit shows Eastland's obscurantism in the civil rights area. Marshall's nomination was sent to the Senate as a recess appointment in the autumn of 1961. As we shall see, other judicial nominations for district and circuit positions customarily race through the committee, averaging all of six minutes of hearings. For Marshall, however, six days of nomination hearings were held, spaced over a four-month period. Eastland did not chair the hearings; instead Olin Johnston (D., S.C.), an Eastland ally, did. A committee staffer questioned Marshall at interminable length concerning professional and personal associations extending back to his youth in a crude effort to show that some of those associates had had leftist leanings.

Committee liberals were infuriated by the committee's treatment of Marshall. The late Senator Thomas J. Dodd (D., Conn.) criticized the drawn-out hearings:

It is known that Judge Marshall was nominated for the U.S. Court of Appeals almost a year ago and since last October, he has been serving under a recess appointment. It is known that he came to the court with one of the most brilliant legal careers in the history of the bar. It is known that since assuming his post on the Federal bench, he has served with greatest distinction. It is also known, Mr. Chairman, that the reason for the unconscionable delay in his confirmation has nothing to do with his legal competence or with his qualifications for the post. I believe, therefore, that it is not the qualifications of the Judge Marshall that are on trial, but rather the qualifications of the Judiciary Committee.[6]

Senator Kenneth B. Keating (R., N.Y.) also seemed exasperated by the committee's handling of the nomination:

The last nomination of Judge Marshall was submitted to the Senate on January 15, 1962, after his having served for an interim term and it seems to me there has been more than ample time for any inquiry which this subcommittee might have desired to make.

On January 23, 1962, 8 days after his nomination was sent here, the President submitted the nomination of Robert J. Elliott to be a U.S. District Judge for the middle district of Georgia. Judge Elliott is now sitting on cases which have arisen from Albany, Georgia.

We were able at that time to complete action on his nomination within 2 weeks after its submission to the Senate. The action on [this] nomination it seems to me has been delayed beyond any reasonable doubt . . . it will be necessary for us to initiate a move in the full committee to discharge this subcommittee from further consideration unless action can be completed in this nomination and a resolution reached one way or the other very promptly.[7]

Committee members grew increasingly restless with Eastland's remote-control manipulation of the nomination. Approval of the nomination was a certainty, but Eastland was still willing to harass the nominee and delay the appointment by proxy, never making himself visible during the sordid proceedings. A year after his nomination, Marshall was finally confirmed.

Colleagues are quick to point out that such heavy-handedness on Eastland's part is rare—except where civil rights are concerned.* Eastland is philosophically opposed to legislative activism, and he has not often needed to force his will on the Judiciary Committee. His committee is dominated by a comfortable majority of seniority-rich conservatives, and Eastland has been content to see bills die a natural death on the Judiciary vine, rather than stooping to pluck them off.

Despite his long tenure with the committee, and the wide range of subjects over which it has jurisdiction, Eastland has not developed a strong interest in many of its issues. This may be one reason why his committee's record of legislative oversight is quite scanty. One person close to committee operations said of the chairman: "Eastland . . . only cares about two things: reelection and cotton."† (One might add civil rights—or opposition to it—to that list.)

The effects of the chairman's passivity may be seen in the committee's informal *modus operandi* and the relative autonomy of its subcommittees.

Committee Procedures

The Legislative Reorganization Act, as amended in 1970, specifically requires that each standing committee hold regularly scheduled meetings and publish its rules in the *Congressional Record*. The Senate Judiciary Committee observes none of these requirements: it has no published rules; there are no regularly scheduled meeting days; meetings have no circulated agenda. In the entire Ninety-second Congress, the full committee met in executive session on twenty-seven occasions, but only at the call of the chairman. Eastland refuses to give much advance notice of committee meetings.

---

* Antitrust issues, particularly in connection with the drug and soft drink bottling industries, have also occasionally energized Eastland's powers. See Chapter 4.

† As has often been noted, Eastland's family is one of the largest beneficiaries of the cotton subsidy program.

The committee does, however, follow certain generally accepted informal procedures of the Senate. One is the "seven day" rule: this allows a week's hiatus to study a piece of legislation; any senator who wishes to do so may invoke this rule. Another is the right to unlimited debate; in theory, any member can simply talk to death any legislation that he intensely dislikes. Since filibusters hold up the meetings that are convened, the mere threat of filibuster generates strong pressures to reach informal accommodations, often on terms having little to do with the merits of the particular issue.[8]

The chairman handles his committee in a style of avuncular amiability. The committee atmosphere is very informal and free-swinging, as befits a very famous and very exclusive clique within America's most famous and exclusive club. In so grand, unstructured, and glamorous a setting, the imaginative, visible, or inspired senator can glitter; the more lackluster "workhorses" are often eclipsed.

Eastland has a reputation for fairness. Senators and staffers who differ on virtually every issue that comes before Judiciary seem to agree on one thing: "Jim Eastland is very fair to us." "He is an accommodating chairman." "He is not the ogre he is made out to be." Senator Charles Mathias relates that when he first came to the Senate and was appointed to the Judiciary Committee, he met former Attorney General Nicholas DeB. Katzenbach in a Senate corridor. The sophisticate confided to the neophyte: "You have the fairest chairman around here."

This reputation seems largely justified. With a few notable exceptions, he generally fills vacant subcommittee seats in order of seniority;* assigns bills to particular subcommittees primarily

---

* There are differences in ideological composition of subcommittees having more than five members. The Antitrust and Monopoly and the Criminal Laws and Procedures subcommittees are decidedly conservative, and most of the Judiciary liberals serve on the Administrative Practice and Procedure or Juvenile Delinquency subcommittees. Nevertheless, such a pattern may simply reflect the preferences of members, and Eastland is not generally perceived as having contrived these differences.

In at least one recent potentially far-reaching case, however, Eastland

on the basis of precedent and subject matter; does not normally seek to hold bills in the full committee or assign them to *ad hoc* committees of arbitrarily selected members;† rarely exploits his perquisites as chairman to require extra hearings or investigations; and rarely delays legislation approved by a subcommittee, even when he opposes it. But Eastland is often criticized for his refusal to issue much advance notice of committee meetings.

When members wish to extend full-committee hearings, as in the case of deliberations regarding the confirmation of Richard G. Kleindienst as attorney general, the chairman graciously accedes. In that case, hearings were extended at the urging of the committee's liberals, and they were ultimately terminated by a vote of the full committee, not by the chairman's fiat.

Eastland's handling of the Kleindienst–International Telephone and Telegraph (ITT) hearings did arouse some heavy

---

jettisoned the seniority principle. In July 1973, after the Watergate hearings had laid bare the extent to which the FBI had become an instrument of partisan politics under President Nixon, Eastland established a special *ad hoc* nine-member subcommittee to exercise oversight over the FBI. Eastland named himself chairman. He then named Senator Byrd to this subcommittee, although Senators Kennedy, Bayh, and Burdick have more Judiciary seniority than does Byrd. Although it is true that Byrd has strongly urged that the committee begin to exercise oversight over the FBI and has given the issue public prominence, it is equally true that Kennedy, through his Administrative Practice and Procedure Subcommittee, has long shown an interest in FBI-related issues, particularly those affecting civil liberties. In another departure from the seniority principle, Eastland named the conservative Senator Gurney to the subcommittee despite liberal Senator Mathias's greater seniority. Several Judiciary staffers view Eastland's chairmanship of the subcommittee and the exclusion of Kennedy, Bayh, Burdick, and Mathias in favor of Byrd and Gurney, as an ominous portent that FBI oversight by the subcommittee may be less than vigorous, particularly on issues affecting civil liberties. Its meager budget—$20,000 for the 93rd Congress—augurs very little activity by the new subcommittee. As of April 1974, it had held only one day of hearings—on a bill (S.2106) to create a ten-year term for the FBI director.

† The chairman has, however, created an *ad hoc* subcommittee consisting of Eastland, McClellan, and Hruska, three hard-core conservatives, to consider every federal district court and circuit court nominee. Bankruptcy and redistricting problems have, on occasion, also been assigned to *ad hoc* subcommittees, as have some private claims bills.

criticism of his tactics, which reflected his (and hence the committee's) diffidence and restraint in investigating abuses by the executive branch. First, Eastland failed to provide members with advance notice of the witnesses to be heard. Second, he unilaterally gave the notorious Dita Beard memorandum to the Justice Department, which itself was the subject of Judiciary Committee investigation. Third, he refused to use his influence to insist that the Justice Department permit either members of the committee or their staffs to examine the settlement files or the Securities and Exchange Commission (SEC) files which had become central to the conduct of the investigation. When an aide to one of the liberals on Judiciary tried earnestly to parse out the tortured legal arguments contained in the letter in which the Justice Department had, with Eastland's acquiescence, refused to permit members access to the documents, the member smiled knowingly at his aide. "Bob," he said, "you just don't understand. Justice is telling us to go to hell." Eastland, however, didn't seem to mind the affront.[9]

Eastland's refusal to fight the Justice Department on behalf of the Judiciary Committee members' right to get at important documentary evidence critical to its legislative and oversight functions contrasts sharply with the less restrictive practice of the Senate Foreign Relations and Armed Services committees, in which even committee staff often have access to sensitive documents. Yet most members of Judiciary have dutifully tolerated Eastland's acceptance of this policy of nondisclosure. During the L. Patrick Gray–Clarence M. Kelley nomination hearings for the FBI directorship, and the William D. Ruckelshaus nomination hearings for the post of deputy attorney general, Judiciary staff were not permitted to examine crucial FBI reports at all, while committee members could only view the files briefly—and then only with an FBI agent present in the room. Senators could not take notes and could not even talk to other senators about the files! Constraints such as these are utterly inconsistent with rigorous, probing committee investigative work, as Eastland was presumably well aware. His willingness—some say eagerness—to submit to the

Justice Department's self-serving secrecy may account in part for past Judiciary failures in exercising oversight of the FBI and in conducting an exhaustive ITT investigation.*[10] Small wonder, then, that when Kleindienst, Henry Petersen, and other top Justice Department officials returned in mid-1974 to testify before the committee on the controversial nomination of Watergate prosecutor Earl Silbert to be U.S. Attorney for the District of Columbia, their scorn for the committee was only thinly concealed. "We are a paper tiger," one top staff aide confided, "and they know that better than anyone else."

Eastland's sense of timing is legendary. John Holloman III, the full committee's chief counsel through most of 1973,† who sat in on all executive sessions, described Eastland's procedure: "He has a sense of when both sides have fired away long enough and are ready to sit down and compromise." In a committee meeting on the Runaway Youth Act, for example, Senator Bayh, whose subcommittee had reported the legislation, was preparing to renew his arguments, and Senator Hruska his rebuttal, when Chairman Eastland called for a vote. The bill passed, a fact that Eastland seemed to sense well before Bayh.[11]

Subcommittees

"By most tests, Judiciary Chairman James O. Eastland has run as decentralized a committee as any in the Senate," political scientist George Goodwin concluded.[12] One of the most distinctive

---

* Recent disclosures in the press, particularly the memo from former presidential aide Charles Colson concerning extensive and coordinated White House manipulation of Judiciary's ITT-Kleindienst inquiry, tend to confirm the opinion of one Judiciary staffer that the committee was "badly bamboozled" on ITT by the Justice Department and the White House. The extent of Eastland's responsibility for this state of affairs remains unclear.

† Holloman returned to private law practice in Jackson, Mississippi, during the fall of 1973. His successor as chief counsel is Peter Stockett, formerly on the full committee staff and an Eastland man. According to one liberal on a member's staff, "We could have done a lot worse. By Mississippi standards, Stockett is a moderate."

features of the Senate Judiciary Committee is its plethora of sub-committees—fifteen,* for sixteen men—each with an extraordinary degree of autonomy. Each of the independent subcommittees —"satrapies," one staffer called them—is defined largely by the personality and motivations of the individual chairman. The average committee member, however junior, serves on as many as *six* of these Judiciary subcommittees, a situation unparalleled else-where in the Senate. As a result, senators can choose where they wish to concentrate their energies. All majority members (Demo-crats in recent years) are given at least one subcommittee chair-manship after only two years on the committee.† With little restraint or direction from the full committee, the subcommittees are freed to hold hearings, process legislation, scrutinize executive agencies—in short, to garner power and influence in the Senate.

Judiciary subcommittees hold hearings when and if they like, on whatever subjects fall within—and sometimes without—their jurisdictions.

Subcommittees, like the full committee, do not hold regularly scheduled meetings. The Immigration and Naturalization Sub-committee, which Eastland chairs, last conducted a hearing *almost eight years ago*—in March 1967. Moreover, it has apparently not met as a subcommittee in years. Its House counterpart, in contrast, meets quite frequently.

Because senators have so many subcommittee assignments, the subcommittees depend for the conduct of business not upon executive sessions but rather upon an informal system of "polling" or "circulating." They often process legislation without confront-

---

* In the 93rd Congress, two new subcommittees were added. Senator Tunney now chairs the Representation of Citizen Interests Subcommittee, a subcommittee that plans to investigate, among other things, legal fee structures and prepaid legal insurance plans. Senator Eastland became chairman of the new FBI Oversight Subcommittee created in the wake of Watergate revelations.

† The only Democrat on Judiciary who does not hold a subcommittee chair-manship in the 93rd Congress is Senator Robert C. Byrd. Byrd is fully occupied, however, with his duties as Assistant Majority Leader of the Senate.

ing one another in person. Normally the subcommittee chairman circulates legislation to the members. The members' personal staffers then contact the subcommittee staff and relate their senator's views or objections. Legislation could win approval by a bare majority, but subcommittee chairmen, anxious to avoid fights

TABLE 1.

Public Bills Assigned to Subcommittees of the Senate Judiciary Committee, 92nd Congress, as of June 30, 1972

Subcommittee	Bills assigned	Days of hearings relating to assigned bills	Days of hearings not related to assigned bills	Bills reported out of subcommittee	Bills reported out of full committee	Bills remaining in full committee	Public Laws (bills passed by Senate and House)
Administrative Practice and Procedure	6	0	10	1	0	0	0
Antitrust and Monopoly	21	17	36	0	0	0	0
Constitutional Amendments	38	2	0	2	2	2	2
Constitutional Rights	25	17	6	2	2	1	1
Criminal Laws and Procedures	71	2	10	2	2	1	1
Federal Charters, Holidays, and Celebrations	143	1	0	24	16	3	17
Immigration and Naturalization	17	0	0	0	0	0	0
Improvements in Judicial Machinery	58	9	0	9	7	1	4
Internal Security	16	3	2	1	1	0	1
Juvenile Deliquency	22	21	9	4	4	1	1
Patents, Trademarks, and Copyrights	3	3	0	12	12	1	6
National Penitentiaries	14	9	5	1	1	1	1
Refugees and Escapees	1	0	4	0	0	0	0
Revision and Codification	0	0	0	0	0	0	0
Separation of Powers	7	12	4	6	1	1	0

SOURCE: U.S., Congress, Senate, Judiciary Committee, *Legislative Executive Calendar*, 92nd Cong., 1st sess. (June 30, 1972). Figures compiled by Martha Joynt Kumar.

at the full-committee level, seek unanimity: they tend to work out disagreements by accommodation, except on matters such as the approval of staff reports. As a result of the "polling" procedure, few subcommittees, except Constitutional Amendments, met formally at all during the Ninety-second Congress.

Subcommittees are under little pressure from the full committee to report legislation. With respect to those bills that *are* reported, however, the determinations of the subcommittees are accorded great respect by committee members, and the bills are routinely approved. By June 30, 1972, of the sixty-four public bills (including twenty-four coming from the Federal Charters, Holidays, and Celebrations Subcommittee) reported by Judiciary subcommittees in the Ninety-second Congress, forty-eight were approved by the full committee. (See Table 1.) In another eight cases, House bills were substituted for bills reported by the Federal Charters Subcommittee.

The freedom accorded the subcommittees has its virtues, as we shall see, and it makes Judiciary a choice assignment. Nevertheless, subcommittee autonomy has its critics. Former Senator Joseph Clark of Pennsylvania, once a Judiciary Committee member, observed:

> Once you get a separate staff and a separate appropriation, then in my judgment, you get empire building and, with all due deference to the Judiciary Committee of the Senate, that committee is the worst possible example of empire building where year after year the separate appropriations have been built up. You go around the Committee quarters and they are just like a bunch of rabbit warrens—a subcommittee here, a subcommittee there. They all have an elaborate staff, and a separate appropriation. What do they produce? Very little in my judgment.[13]

Clark's harsh view finds some support in the statistics; for despite the enormous volume of legislation assigned to it, and despite resources unmatched by any other committee, Judiciary's legislative output is quite small and of uneven quality.* In the entire Ninety-second Congress, the full committee reported only 113 public bills—a substantial portion of which were purely ceremonial —to the Senate floor.[14]

Many Judiciary bills addressed issues, such as crime, that are inherently intractable and resistant to legislative solution. Others, such as amnesty, women's rights, and busing, are incendiary problems that do not always cool during the course of deliberation. Yet others concerned issues, such as abortion and gun control, for which interminable discussion, rather than decisive action, conveniently liberated members from the necessity of taking political risks. (With some issues, of course, inaction may be the more politically hazardous course. Obscenity and busing legislation are examples.)

Another reason the committee reports relatively few public, nonceremonial bills is that each of its members has heavy time commitments. Senator Hart, for example, sits on *seventeen* Senate subcommittees. Senator Byrd is majority whip of the Senate and chairs subcommittees on the Rules and Appropriations committees. Senate Judiciary Committee members in the Ninety-second Congress averaged 2.56 committee and 12 subcommittee assignments. The Democrats on Judiciary chaired an average of three subcommittees.

In the Ninety-second Congress, moreover, much of Judiciary's time and resources were consumed by several extraordinary hearings. The Kleindienst nomination hearings and several Supreme Court nomination hearings doubtless contributed to the limited legislative output of the committee.

Perhaps the principal reason for the committee's low productivity relative to workload, however, is the yawning ideological chasm between members. "Splintered?" asked a former counsel to one of the subcommittees. "Listen, the only appropriate analogue for the Senate committee is the patient whose brain hemispheres have

* See, for example, the discussion of Judiciary's handling of LEAA, pp. 283–305.

been surgically split, so that his right hand literally does not know what his left hand is doing."

Special interest groups, such as the Americans for Constitutional Action (ACA) and the Americans for Democratic Action (ADA), which have examined the senators' voting patterns, place few Judiciary members in the "vital center." Indeed, even the party affiliation of Judiciary members is a poor predicter of their ideological leanings. The nine Democrats split in a wide gulf. The ADA rated four of them—Eastland, McClellan, Ervin, and Byrd—at thirty points or below, and five—Hart, Kennedy, Bayh, Burdick, and Tunney—at eighty-five points or above. The seven Republicans are quite conservative: only one member—Mathias—scored over sixty in ADA ratings, and only one other—Cook—more than thirty (see Appendix 1).

The most important full-committee divisions, then, proceed along principled, rather than partisan, lines. During the Ninety-second Congress, the four conservative Democrats tended to align with five of the Republicans (Thurmond, Gurney, Hruska, Fong, and Scott) in a stable majority, while the five liberal Democrats voted together, leaving the two remaining Republicans (Mathias and Cook) "swinging" between these coalitions according to the issue. During the Ninety-third Congress, Senator Byrd has frequently voted with the five liberal Democrats and Senator Ervin has been detached from the conservative voting bloc, becoming a "swing vote" and sometimes voting with the liberals. Senator Cook, however, has tended to move from his "swing" position to vote with the conservatives. The liberal contingent now thinks of itself as numbering seven, and occasionally eight, on many issues.

The conservative dominance on the full committee and on most subcommittees means that even those liberal bills that emerge from subcommittee will rarely make it to the more hospitable environment of the Senate floor, while conservative bills are often sent to the Senate floor, only to be rejected there by the liberal Senate.*[15]

* For interest-group ratings of the Judiciary Committee as a whole, see Appendix 2. For selected committee votes, see Appendix 5.

This situation necessitates resort to some special techniques in order to advance liberal legislation. Two are common: a senator may write a bill that, although generated as a result of hearings held by a Judiciary subcommittee, can be referred to another, more hospitable Senate committee. Alternatively, a senator may persuade colleagues to seek a "time-limit" provision on the Senate floor. This technique allows the bill to be referred elsewhere or reported to the floor if the full Judiciary Committee sits on it for a certain time. All new civil rights legislation of the past decade has been enacted only through use of this latter legislative device. Chairman Eastland, the chief target of this strategem, has characterized the procedure as "legislative lynching."[16]

Some of the subcommittees seek to exert influence without writing legislation. The Administrative Practice and Procedure Subcommittee, for example, scheduled hearings on sex discrimination in employment, focusing on the Department of Labor's guidelines on hiring. When the department, under pressure from Senator Kennedy, issued stronger guidelines, the hearings were called off. The subcommittee report describes how such a strategy can obviate the need for hearings and legislation:

> The attention to the Ash report [President's Advisory Council on Executive Organization], the accelerated work of public interest advocates, and the increased congressional emphasis on federal decision-making processes all contributed to an atmosphere in which federal agencies were extremely attentive and sensitive to criticism of their practices and procedures. Thus the subcommittee frequently found that the initiation of a preliminary investigation, the dispatch of an inquiry through correspondence, or the announcement or holding of hearings was sufficient to bring about swift changes in agency practices and procedures.[17]

Another strategy is the use of hearings to educate and arouse an apathetic public rather than to formulate legislation. The Antitrust and Monopoly Subcommittee, chaired by Senator Hart, has used this method with particular skill; his subcommittee held more hearings in the Ninety-second Congress than all other Judiciary subcommittees combined. Hart has observed that his subcommittee is so conservative that he could "never get the Sherman Act through it," and statistics bear this out: it reported *no* legislation in the Ninety-second Congress. The two bills that did emerge early in the Ninety-third Congress were indeed milder than the Sherman Act. The subcommittee reported—unanimously —bills reforming the consent-decree process and conferring an anti-trust exemption on the soft-drink bottling industry. Thus Hart's liberalism, thwarted in the legislative arena, has been sublimated into a remarkable series of educational hearings on the automobile repair industry, the life-insurance industry, distribution practices in gasoline marketing, the drug industry, and other anticompetitive abuses. His staff work is a model of how to transform political necessities into virtues.

Full-Committee Legislation

The full committee matches the leaden pace of the subcommittees. Of the 1,716 bills and resolutions referred to Judiciary in the Ninety-second Congress, 1,018—or almost 60 percent—were pending at the end of the Congress. And of the 698 bills and resolutions that Judiciary *did* manage to dispose of, over 81 percent were private bills (which, as we shall see, require little or no work by the members.)[18]

Although the subcommittees unquestionably fuel the Senate Judiciary Committee's lethargic legislative engines, the full committee does not simply ratify their work. In only the first six months of the Ninety-second Congress, a total of thirty-eight public bills were not referred to specific subcommittees but remained in the full committee. The public bills constituted a curious legislative pastiche: bankruptcy legislation, interstate compacts, school busing, congressional redistricting, drugs, the genocide convention, equal rights, criminal-record information, granting land to Texas, and a legal services corporation. While bankruptcy legislation, redistricting bills, and interstate compacts generally do remain with the full committee, the others usually do not. Similar bills were in fact referred to subcommittees during the Ninety-second Congress.

By the end of June, 1972, eleven school-busing bills had been referred to the Senate Judiciary Committee. The first of the bills was referred to the Constitutional Amendments Subcommittee, but the other ten (some of which also provided for constitutional amendments) remained in the full committee. Constitutional Amendments is chaired by Birch Bayh, a liberal opposed to the busing amendments. Chairman Eastland, an implacable foe of court-ordered busing, can keep busing legislation in the full committee and retains the right to conduct hearings if Bayh fails to do so.*

Problems of overlapping subcommittee jurisdictions occasionally arise. In the past, jurisdictional problems have been amiably worked out by the full committee's chief counsel. Sometimes, however, more than one subcommittee chairman feels intensely about considering a piece of legislation and the bill remains in the full committee until a compromise is forged. In the Ninety-second Congress, Senator McClellan, chairman of Criminal Laws and Procedures, and Senator Ervin, chairman of Constitutional Rights, both wanted jurisdiction over legislation regarding the exchange of information on criminal records between the attorney general of the United States and state and local law enforcement officials.[19] Each senator knew that the other would handle the bill differently. Senator McClellan is strongly committed to facilitating the apprehension of criminals through exchanges of information between different levels of government. Senator Ervin, on the other hand, vehemently opposes federal data banks as a threat to personal privacy. The quantity and kinds of data gathered and distributed about ordinary Americans and the safe-

---

* In the spring of 1973 Eastland began antibusing hearings in the full committee.

guards provided against abuse will ultimately depend largely upon the outcome of this contest of wills.*

A telling example of such a conflict occurred just before Christmas 1972, when the Supreme Court approved new rules of evidence for the criminal justice system, as advocated by the United States Judicial Conference.† The new rules generally followed Senator McClellan's philosophy.‡ The first ever drafted, the new procedural rules were supposed to go into effect on July 1, 1973, unless Congress vetoed or changed them within ninety days. The rules would permit husbands to testify against wives and doctors (except for psychiatrists) against patients; eliminate any privileged status for communications between news reporters and their sources; and create a new "secrets of state"§ classification to keep certain government papers private.

The new rules of evidence escaped much public notice until conservative Senator Ervin stopped them in their tracks. He was quickly joined by a newly elected liberal, Elizabeth Holtzman, in the House committee. Both introduced bills (now Public Law 93-12) early in the Ninety-third Congress to prevent the new rules from taking effect without a review by, and the consent of, the Congress. Ervin gained the unanimous consent of the Senate for his challenge, asserting that the high court was encroaching on Congress's "right to legislate." Holtzman, denouncing the steady erosion of individual rights, feverishly lobbied against the rules. One old man and one young woman, they effectively forestalled what could have been a momentous diminution of liberty, acquiesced in by an uninformed, unconcerned Congress.

* Senator Ervin's subcommittee has apparently won this dispute; it held hearings on the bill (S.2963) early in 1974.

† Justice William O. Douglas was the lone dissenter.

‡ He was not really satisfied when "changes" (occasioned by outside critics) in the conference rules were offered in draft form in the summer of 1971. On August 5, on the Senate floor, he threatened to introduce legislation removing the drafting process from both the conference and the Court. The "changes" were modified on Sept. 28, 1971, to satisfy the senator—and never circulated for outside comment.[20]

§ The term was nowhere defined in the rules.

Men and Munificence

Judiciary's budget is by far the largest in Congress.[21] Of the total authorized expenditures for all Senate committees in the Ninety-second Congress—$27,213,975—the Senate Judiciary Committee accounted for well over one-fourth—$7,589,000.[22] The next most well-endowed standing committee—Government Operations—received $3,398,500, well under half of Judiciary's authorization.[23] Only six of the sixteen standing committees in the Senate (Appropriations; Banking, Housing and Urban Affairs; Commerce; Government Operations; Labor and Public Welfare; Public Works) received over $1 million, which was far less than each of *two* Judiciary *subcommittees*—Antitrust and Monopoly, and Internal Security—received.[24] In 1973, the first session of the Ninety-third Congress, Judiciary's budget rose to $4,128,600, so its budget for the entire Ninety-third Congress will almost certainly exceed $8 million.

The bounty is not shared equally among the subcommittees. During the Ninety-second Congress, the Antitrust and Monopoly Subcommittee and the Internal Security Subcommittee had the largest budgets—$1,491,600 and $1,152,500 respectively—while all others received less than $650,000. Table 2 shows the budgets and staff allotment for Judiciary subcommittees.

The two subcommittees with the largest authorizations—Antitrust and Monopoly and Internal Security—were among the least productive in terms of legislation reported.* The criteria used in establishing subcommittee budgets are opaque. Each subcommittee develops its own, based in theory upon what it believes it "needs," but based in fact upon the time-honored principle of "incrementalism":† as Table 3 suggests, the budget requests of

---

* The Antitrust and Monopoly Subcommittee reported no legislation in the Ninety-second Congress, while Internal Security managed to report only one bill (S.592, to repeal the Emergency Detention Act of 1950) and one resolution (S.Res. 204, on the refusal of Robert S. Williams to testify before the subcommittee).

† In its adherence to this principle, the Judiciary Committee's budgetary procedure is similar to the "incrementalism" which Professor Aaron Wildavsky found to characterize budgetary policy in the executive branch.[25]

TABLE 2.

Budget and Personnel of Subcommittees of the Senate Judiciary Committee

Subcommittee	Authorization (Dollars)			Number of employees, 91st Cong., 1st sess.
	91st Congress	92nd Congress	93rd Congress	
Administrative Practice and Procedure	456,000	644,400	755,600	16
Antitrust and Monopoly	1,279,300	1,491,600	1,534,000	30
Constitutional Amendments	304,700	451,500	591,700	11
Constitutional Rights	455,000	569,000	599,800	17
Criminal Laws and Procedures	297,000	405,500	431,200	10
FBI Oversight	—	—	20,000	—
Federal Charters, Holidays, and Celebrations	19,000	23,000	31,000	1
Immigration and Naturalization	413,500	473,500	445,000	10
Improvements in Judicial Machinery	439,200	466,900	458,000	15
Internal Security	1,070,000	1,152,500	932,500	26
Juvenile Delinquency	507,500	620,300	688,400	19
National Penitentiaries	40,000	134,800	167,000	4
Patents, Trademarks, and Copyrights	237,000	273,000	345,000	7
Refugees and Escapees	243,900	315,500	354,500	11
Representation of Citizen Interests	—	—	270,800	6
Revision and Codification	108,700	125,500	127,100	3
Separation of Powers	235,000	382,000	513,000	13
Totals[1]	6,135,800	7,589,000	8,166,600	199

[1] Routine full-committee authorizations ($30,000 in 91st Congress, $60,000 in 92nd, $70,000 in 93rd) and employees (17 in 93rd Congress, 1st Session) are not included.

SOURCES: U.S., Congress, Senate, Committee on Rules and Administration, *Expenditure Authorizations for Senate Committees* (Washington, D.C.:Government Printing Office, January 3, 1974), Part II, pp. 63–68; U.S., Congress, Senate, Committee on Rules and Administration, *Senate Inquiries and Investigations*, 93rd Cong., 2nd sess., Mar. 13, 1974 (Committee Print no. 3).

TABLE 3.

Budget Requests and Authorizations for Subcommittees of
Senate Judiciary Committee, 93rd Congress, 2nd Session (in dollars)

Subcommittee	Amount Requested	Difference between 1973 authorization and 1974 request	Amount reported by Rules Committee	Amount authorized by Senate
Administrative Practice and Procedure	453,300	+75,500	377,800	377,800
Antitrust and Monopoly	797,600	+30,600	767,000	767,000
Constitutional Amendments	291,000	+51,300	252,000	252,000
Constitutional Rights	245,000	+34,800	221,000	221,000
Criminal Laws and Procedures	345,000	+45,100	299,900	299,900
FBI Oversight	20,000	+20,000	20,000	20,000
Federal Charters, Holidays, and Celebrations	16,500	+2,000	16,500	16,500
Immigration and Naturalization	205,000	−35,000	205,000	205,000
Improvements in Judicial Machinery	255,500	+32,500	235,000	235,000
Internal Security	663,000	+130,500	400,000	400,000
Juvenile Delinquency	393,400	+58,000	353,000	353,000
National Penitentiaries	88,000	+9,000	88,000	88,000
Patents, Trademarks, and Copyrights	188,000	+19,000	178,000	178,000
Refugees and Escapees	245,000	+72,500	182,000	182,000
Representation of Citizen Interests	192,000	+71,300	150,000	150,000
Revision and Codification	64,800	+2,500	64,800	64,800
Separation of Powers	315,000	+65,000	263,000	263,000
Totals	4,778,100	754,600	4,073,000	4,073,000

most subcommittees increase steadily, though not dramatically, over their budgets during the previous Congress.

Subcommittee budget requests are rarely denied by the Judiciary Committee. As Table 3 shows, the Senate Rules and Administration Committee did pare those requests down considerably in the Ninety-third Congress, and in every case its actions were approved by the Senate.

Perhaps the most notorious of the Senate Judiciary wastrels is the Internal Security Subcommittee, created during the McCarthy era to investigate subversives and chaired by Senator Eastland. With a whopping budget of $1,152,500 in the Ninety-second Congress, the Internal Security Committee dwarfed not only all other Judiciary subcommittees except Antitrust and Monopoly, but almost two-thirds of the *full* committees of the Congress as well.

What do the American people have to show for this extraordinary generosity? Very little, unless one considers shelf upon shelf of turgid prose about the Communist menace in America to be a valuable legislative product. The reactionary chief counsel of Internal Security, J. G. Sourwine, is a Capitol Hill figure of mythical proportions. Haughty, secretive, contemptuous of outsiders, Sourwine plays the irascible curmudgeon, ruling the subcommittee as a personal preserve, with only occasional advise and consent from his friend and patron, Chairman Eastland.

Internal Security, with its huge staff, legendary indolence, and interminable red- and pink-baiting, has increasingly become an embarrassment to the Senate, though not to the Judiciary Committee leadership. Even a member of the subcommittee, Marlow Cook, agreed that its budget was "just too darn large," while another Judiciary staffer fumed, "The whole thing is just a sinecure for a bunch of old guys. It's a hell of a big staff and they are paid a lot of money for doing practically nothing." In March 1972, in an extraordinary challenge to the powerful Eastland, the Senate Rules and Administration Committee slashed Internal Security's budget request by 11 percent, and the full

Senate agreed. In the Ninety-third Congress, Internal Security's budget is "only" $932,500.

But this instance of frugality, while a hopeful portent, remains most uncharacteristic of the Senate, and particularly of the Judiciary Committee. Even the Revision and Codification Subcommittee, which had *no* legislation referred to it and which held *no* hearings in the Ninety-second Congress, received $125,500 during that Congress (increased slightly in the Ninety-third)—and managed to spend $115,371.94 of it. By contrast, the FBI Oversight Subcommittee received a grand total of $20,000 in the Ninety-third Congress. It is generally believed that Revision and Codification's swollen budget is largely a means of enabling the chairman, Senator Ervin, to maintain one of his legislative aides (formerly Bob Smith, now Bill Pursley) on the payroll to supplement Ervin's personal staff.[26]

The Judiciary Committee staff is far and away the largest in Congress. At the end of 1973, there were 216 employees, 199 as subcommittee staff. The other committees were far behind: the closest, Government Operations, employed 93 staff persons. Most other committees had well under 50.[27] Staffing patterns suggest pervasive sex discrimination* and use of the subcommittee staff by members for their own, rather than subcommittee, purposes.†

P. J. Mode, then chief counsel for the Constitutional Amendments Subcommittee chaired by Senator Birch Bayh,‡ said that he

---

* Although there are about the same number of women and men on the full committee staff, there is a sharp disparity in their salaries. High-salaried staffers are invariably men. (Three-fourths of the Judiciary staffers earning over $1,000 a month and forty-two of the forty-five earning over $2,000 per month were men.) It is perhaps not surprising that some of the most vigorous opponents of the equal rights amendment were members of the Senate Judiciary Committee.

† A check of a December 1971 Judiciary subcommittee payroll against the telephone directory for the Senate revealed where staffers are physically located. Subcommittee personnel work in the offices of members, and some are even listed as working for the senator without mention of the subcommittee at all. This practice is of dubious propiety, but is quite widespread.

‡ In early 1973, Mode left the subcommittee to resume private law practice in Washington, D.C.

often asked himself: "Do I work for Birch Bayh or the committee?" He concluded, "I believe I work for Birch Bayh." Most other staffers resolve their conflicting allegiances in the same manner. Outside the committee (and often inside as well), subcommittee staff are regarded as part of a particular senator's entourage, gears in his political machine. One committee staff person remarked, "If Roman Hruska were to get hit by a truck tomorrow, the unemployment rolls in Washington would be swollen." Senator Hruska is not atypical of his colleagues.

3

The House Judiciary Committee: Celler's Legacy

Casting his shadow across the House Judiciary Committee in the Ninety-second Congress, as in decades past, was the diminutive, stooped figure of the octogenarian chairman, Emanuel Celler of Brooklyn.

Moses on the Potomac

"Dealing with Celler is like dealing with Moses himself," a former colleague once tartly observed. Emanuel Celler, chairman of the House Judiciary Committee from the Eighty-first through the Ninety-second Congress, is admired by many for his fighting spirit, his peppery pugnacity, and his perseverance against high odds. Any impartial assessment of his colorful half-century-long career (he cosponsored and floor-managed no less than four constitutional amendments) must conclude that Celler rendered distinguished service.

"Manny" Celler, the tough-minded lawyer and raconteur from Brooklyn, first entered Congress in 1922. As early as 1932, according to his files at the Library of Congress, he had become the person to see on the House Judiciary panel if one had an interest in antitrust. His focus on and expertise in the industrial economy remained an individual effort for some two decades, however, since an antitrust subcommittee in the House was not created until 1949 —after his namesake law, the Celler-Kefauver Act, had been deliberated. It was then that Celler ascended by seniority to the chairmanship of the House Judiciary Committee.

Celler's most creative and enduring legislative contribution was his central role in the enactment of civil rights legislation, particularly the Civil Rights Act of 1964. The chairman not only served as perhaps the leading proponent of civil rights legislation in the Congress, he was its architect, initiator, and promoter. Along with the ranking minority member of the committee, William M. McCulloch (R., Ohio), Celler navigated the landmark 1964 Civil Rights Act between the shoals of a conservative-dominated House and a timorous White House. Rather than accept the mild bill that the Kennedy administration was submitting to the Congress in early 1963, Celler informed the President that the Judiciary Committee wanted stronger legislation. Kennedy's original bill sought to encourage southern school districts to desegregate by offering them monetary inducements. Celler and McCulloch, however, were thinking in far broader terms, envisioning legislation prohibiting discrimination in public accommodations and employment as well. Only after several dramatic events, such as the bombing of a Birmingham church in which several young children were killed, did Kennedy broaden his request, in line with what Celler had been advocating, to include public-accommodations provisions and authority to withhold funds from school districts maintaining segregated facilities. Yet President Kennedy still wavered, and in October 1963,

Attorney General Robert F. Kennedy appeared before the House Judiciary Committee to request a bill weaker than Celler's. Celler and McCulloch held firm, however, and the bill ultimately passed in its present form.*

The two old friends also labored together on the Civil Rights Act of 1967, which prohibited racial discrimination in housing. Celler and McCulloch refused to weaken the bill on the floor of the House, even though it was brought up shortly before the 1966 election. After House passage, however, it failed in the Senate. During the next session, unwilling to endanger their troops needlessly, Celler and McCulloch waited until the Senate had acted favorably and then obtained House passage.

Emanuel Celler spent 1972, his last year in the House, grappling once again with civil rights legislation. He used his considerable talents—and his even more considerable powers as chairman—to defeat a constitutional amendment prohibiting busing to achieve school desegregation. Constituents exerted enormous pressure for support of legislation or a constitutional amendment to bar the practice. Many members of Congress responded to this pressure and sought remedial legislation. When the surge of public opinion against busing grew, Celler and McCulloch waged their last civil rights battle together.

In four months of hearings, Celler and McCulloch bravely attempted to defuse the explosive busing issue. John Herbers of the *New York Times* described the atmosphere as the hearings began:

> Emanuel Celler of Brooklyn, the Chairman, and William McCulloch of Ohio, the ranking Republican, the two men most responsible for the civil rights performance of the House, faced a row of members angered by what they called excessive busing to achieve school integration and by the mounting complaints of their constituents.

---

* The subsequent failures of both Judiciary committees to exercise oversight of the act's enforcement is discussed below, pp. 189–203.

Mr. Celler will soon be eighty-four years old. Mr. Mc-
Culloch, seventy, is retiring from Congress at the end of this
year because of poor health. Both are frail, and they were
clearly on the defensive in the busing controversy.

The two old civil rights warriors gently lectured the
younger House members who lined up to demand that the
committee approve one of some thirty antibusing amendments that have been introduced.[1]

Angered by the delaying tactics of Celler and McCulloch, 140
members signed a petition to discharge the House Judiciary Committee from further consideration of an amendment sponsored
by Norman F. Lent (R., N.Y.) which provided that "no public
school student shall, because of his race, creed, or color, be
assigned to or required to attend a particular school." Celler held
lengthy hearings at which *all* nonadministration witnesses
opposed the Nixon proposals on busing. By April, the discharge
petition had 160 names. And on August 1, in a rare move, the
House Rules Committee discharged the Judiciary Committee from
further consideration of the constitutional amendment.[2] Ironi-
cally, two of the last few times this procedural device had been
used, Celler had also been the target. But Celler's defeat was not
decisive. For even with the discharge, the amendment never
reached a vote on the floor of the House.

Celler's extraordinary record was not altogether consistent. In
his younger years, Celler had exerted genuine, vigorous leadership in legislative matters, particularly in the antitrust field.
But his vision of the legislative role of the House Judiciary
Committee, except in civil rights, grew myopic as the years wore
on. Under Celler's leadership, the committee became simply a
passive instrument for processing legislation created elsewhere,
not in fashioning or building support for new legislation. Whereas
the Senate Judiciary Committee often uses hearings to educate
the public—especially where legislation has no chance of being
passed—the House committee generally has not done so. Bess
Dick, staff director of the House committee until early 1973,

regarded this as a virtue: "We are a sober committee. We don't seek publicity or headlines."[3]

One notable exception was the 1964 school-prayer hearings. In that instance, Celler perceived a threat to the integrity of the Constitution by the proposed constitutional amendment to allow voluntary prayer in public schools—a response to the Supreme Court decision specifically barring this practice. While the hearings themselves were certainly useful, Celler's attempts to block passage of the amendment demonstrate that cynical manipulation of the powers of the chairmanship of a major committee is by no means confined to conservatives. Representative Frank Becker (R., N.Y.), who led the prayer forces in the House, initiated a petition to discharge the Judiciary Committee from further consideration of the amendment. When 160 of the 218 members necessary had signed the petition, Celler announced that he would hold hearings on the legislation. At the hearings, constitutional lawyers were called upon to testify about the difficulty of drafting legislation that would retain the First Amendment's guarantees intact while permitting prayer in the schools. As a result, pressure from the public gradually subsided and the amendment became moribund.

The Committee

The stark contrast between the background, ideology, and operating style of their chairmen was richly symbolic, for the House Judiciary Committee shares little with its Senate counterpart, other than its name and much of its jurisdiction. Indeed, the two committees are as dissimilar in workload, membership, ideological inclination, structure, and legislative style as any two congressional committees responsible for the same subject matter can be.

The House Judiciary Committee, one of the oldest of Congress's standing committees, is rich in history. Its alumni have included three presidents, a Supreme Court justice, and the non-pareil legislator, Daniel Webster. In the Ninety-second Congress, its roster, while somewhat less luminous, boasted great variety. It included a convicted felon,* a Jesuit priest (Robert F. Drinan), an urban black (John Conyers), and the scion of an aristocratic Eastern family which had sent four generations to Congress (Hamilton Fish).

Members of the House Judiciary Committee in the Ninety-second Congress, in order of seniority, were: Celler, Peter W. Rodino, Jr. (N.J.), Harold D. Donohue (Mass.), Jack Brooks (Tex.), John Dowdy (Tex.), Robert W. Kastenmeier (Wis.), Don Edwards (Cal.), William L. Hungate (Mo.), John Conyers, Jr. (Mich.), Andrew Jacobs, Jr. (Ind.), Joshua Eilberg (Pa.), William F. Ryan (N.Y.), Jerome R. Waldie (Cal.), Edwin W. Edwards (La.), Walter Flowers (Ala.), James R. Mann (S.C.), Abner J. Mikva (Ill.), Paul S. Sarbanes (Md.), John F. Seiberling (Ohio), James Abourezk (S.D.), George E. Danielson (Cal.), and Robert F. Drinan (Mass.), Democrats; William M. McCulloch (Ohio), Richard H. Poff (Va.), Edward Hutchinson (Mich.), Robert McClory (Ill.), Henry P. Smith III (N.Y.), Charles W. Sandman, Jr. (N.J.), Tom Railsback (Ill.), Edward G. Biester, Jr. (Pa.), Charles E. Wiggins (Cal.), David W. Dennis (Ind.), Hamilton Fish, Jr. (N.Y.), R. Lawrence Coughlin (Pa.), Wiley Mayne (Ia.), Lawrence J. Hogan (Md.), William J. Keating (Ohio), and James D. McKevitt (Colo.), Republicans. (For committee membership in the Ninety-third Congress, see p. xxx.)

The striking behavioral differences between the two committees reflect their distinctive memberships. While the sixteen Senate Judiciary members, as we have seen, tend to polarize at fairly rigid ideological extremes, the thirty-eight members of the House committee in the Ninety-second Congress clustered at the center of the political spectrum. Six Democrats on the House

---

* John Dowdy was convicted on Dec. 31, 1971, on charges arising from accepting a bribe, conspiracy, and perjury. He retained his seat for the second session of the 92nd Congress, and, despite a recommendation asking him to refrain from voting and taking part in committee work, actually did cast proxy votes three times on another committee.

Committee held ADA ratings of between thirty and eighty, while *none* on the Senate committee did. Similarly, six Republicans on the House committee held ADA ratings of thirty or over, while only one Republican did on the Senate committee.* These differences reflect the fact that while the South and the Midwest regions were "overrepresented" on the Senate Judiciary Committee, the House committee membership favored the East and the South. (The West was quite unrepresented in proportion to the number of members that the region has in the House.)[4] These ideological and regional configurations, then, have made the House Judiciary Committee a far more liberal body than the Senate committee.†

All members of the House committee, as in the Senate, are lawyers. Fully *half* the members of the House committee retain their affiliations with law firms, probably reflecting the relatively short tenure and insecurity of a House seat. House members who retained membership in law firms late in the Ninety-second Congress included: Coughlin, Dennis, Donohue, Edwin Edwards, Eilberg, Keating, McCulloch, Mann, Railsback, Rodino, Sandman, Smith, Waldie, Danielson, McClory and Mikva.[5] (The last three were still receiving funds from work they did with their firms but were no longer formally affiliated.) This pervasive practice contravenes recommendations issued by the American Bar Association.[6] Antitrust, criminal, patent, and private legislation are all considered by the committee, and the clients of members' law firms often have an obvious economic stake in how these laws are shaped. Chairman Celler, who headed the subcommittee handling antitrust legislation, was simultaneously a senior and named partner of a major law firm handling cases for clients such as the Schenley company,[7] a firm that has been charged with violations of the antitrust laws.

The House committee, while considered by congressmen to

---

* For ADA and ACA ratings of members, see Appendix 1.
† For interest-group ratings of the Judiciary Committee as a whole, see Appendix 2. For selected votes, see Appendix 5.

be a good assignment, is not as prestigious as the Senate committee. Judiciary ranked behind seven other House committees* in committee attractiveness, as measured by transfer rates of members on and off of the various committees. Senate Judiciary ranked fourth in the same survey.

There are several reasons for the House committee's lesser appeal, and they tell us much about the committee's deficiencies. First, the House committee has fewer legislative responsibilities; neither judicial nominations nor internal security matters fall within its jurisdiction. And the House committee does not maneuver to add major new legislative areas (as the Senate committee did, for example, in the case of no-fault auto insurance).† Indeed, in recent years Celler had encountered some difficulty in husbanding his committee's existing authority, much less expanding it. The chairman spent so much of his time on administrative matters rather than legislative leadership that he relinquished issues by default.

Organized crime, for example, was simply not being dealt with at all, and the House responded by establishing a select committee outside of Judiciary, headed by Claude Pepper (D., Fla.), to do investigative (nonlegislative) work on the problem. When the Select Committee on Crime drafted legislation, as it frequently did, the legislation would be referred to another committee for processing. Congressman Railsback expressed the belief that, because of the Select Committee's limited role, it did not trespass on the Judiciary Committee's jurisdiction.[8] Counsel for the Select Committee stated that every effort was made to avoid duplication of effort, and that in any event, criminal legislation was not solely within the jurisdiction of the Judiciary Committee; some criminal legislation on drugs, for example, might go through the Commerce Committee.[9] Some believe that the Judiciary Com-

* Rules, Ways and Means, Appropriations, Foreign Affairs, Armed Services, Internal Security and Interstate and Foreign Commerce were the seven leaders.

† Eastland, by contriving to have the no-fault bill referred to Judiciary at the last hour in the 92nd Congress, ensured its death for that Congress.

mittee needlessly surrendered jurisdiction to the Select Committee on Crime, but conflict is purely theoretical now, for the Select Committee's authorization expired in the Ninety-third Congress. In 1973, House Judiciary established a Subcommittee on Criminal Justice to deal with an avalanche of anticrime bills —one contained the recommendations of a national commission, a second came from the Senate Criminal Laws and Procedures Subcommittee, and a third was introduced by the Nixon administration. Many of the bills call for sharp—sometimes radical— changes in federal criminal law. Early in 1974, the Subcommittee on Courts, Civil Liberties, and the Administration of Justice (formerly Subcommittee No. 3) held a day of hearings to receive the Select Committee's recommendations.

In February 1972, Celler also had to defend his committee's jurisdiction against an attack by Congressman Cornelius E. Gallagher (D., N.J.), who wished to establish a select committee to study invasions of privacy by government and industry. Celler won this time, arguing that his committee was already dealing with the issue. Gallagher's resolution was defeated, 216–168. The old man prevailed again when the investigations subcommittee of the Government Operations Committee, scheduled to open hearings in New York on the illegal-aliens problem, was restrained by Chairman Chet Holifield (D., Cal.) at Celler's insistence.

Even where the House committee does have unchallenged legislative jurisdiction, however, it often exhibits institutional inertia; antitrust and oversight of the Justice Department are areas of particular passivity, as will be seen below.

House committee members lack the independence and responsibility routinely granted to even their most junior counterparts on the Senate side. In the Ninety-second Congress, with more than seven times as many members as subcommittees, the seniority rule hung heavy on House Judiciary. Where Senate Judiciary members quickly acquire subcommittee chairmanships, House Judiciary members must have the patience of Job and the political endurance of Emanuel Celler.

Even subcommittee chairmen have little control over their

subcommittees, for staff and budget are tightly controlled by the committee chairman. This centralized control, only slightly affected by Celler's departure, is in dramatic contrast to the pattern in the Senate committee.

Finally, assignment to the House committee can easily become a legislator's graveyard. House members must select committee assignments with exquisite care. On the average, House Judiciary members in the Ninety-second Congress served on only 1.6 committees (fifteen House committee members served on *no* other standing committee). They also sat on an average of only 2.4 subcommittees (including Judiciary subcommittees) of standing committees. Senate Judiciary members, with multiple subcommittee assignments—they average *twelve* (including Judiciary subcommittees)—are in an excellent position to pursue varied interests, but a junior House member can easily draw a dull subcommittee assignment which may also be his or her only one. Senators take no such risks. For the unlucky House committee neophyte, Judiciary membership may be a dreadfully unhappy experience.

The risks to junior House Judiciary Committee members of unappealing assignments were traditionally heightened by Celler's practice of arranging subcommittee jurisdictions so that the most interesting issues were taken up by Subcommittee No. 5, of which he happened to be chairman (see Table 4). Junior members were not normally assigned to Subcommittee No. 5 but must have first served long apprenticeships on the other four subcommittees. If they performed there to the satisfaction of Celler and ranking Republican William McCulloch they might be assigned to No. 5. But because there are so few subcommittees on the House committee and because Subcommittee No. 5 was relatively attractive, a vacancy on No. 5 would elicit many applicants, with Celler deciding among them. Although subcommittee chairmanships were determined on the basis of seniority, the selection of subcommittee members ultimately depended on the chairman's will. (On the Senate committee, in contrast, vacancies are filled on the basis of seniority.) In this respect, as in so many

TABLE 4.

Public Bills Assigned to Subcommittees of the House Judiciary Committee, 92nd Congress

Number of Bills

	Referred to subcommittee	Bills on which hearings were held	Reported favorably to full committee	Reported adversely to full committee	Reported to House	Passed—House	Pending—House	Pending—Senate	Enacted into law
Subcommittee 1 (public)	257	105	12	0	12	11	2	8	2
(private)	2142	NA	92	NA	NA	88	14	13	67
Subcommittee 2 (public)	81	37	25	5	25	23	2	2	22
(private)	609	NA	116	93	116	105	11	19	86
Subcommittee 3	216	83	15	40	15	14	1	1	13
Subcommittee 4	431	131	10	0	9	74	1	15	38
Subcommittee 5	297	186	11	58	11	10	1	1	9

SOURCE: U.S., Congress, House of Representatives, Judiciary Committee, *Summary of Activities*, 92nd Cong.

others, Celler's power fed upon itself, for the value to members of assignment to Judiciary was very much a function of his or her relationship to the chairman.

The Subcommittees: Fluid and Flexible

Like everything else about House Judiciary, subcommittee struc- ture—and even nomenclature—in the Ninety-second Congress was an artifact of Emanuel Celler's long-nurtured craft: the creation of mechanisms to augment his personal influence. Unlike the Senate committee, which had fifteen named subcommittees (increased to seventeen in the Ninety-third Congress) with reasonably distinct jurisdictions to which bills were routinely referred, the five House Judiciary subcommittees in the Ninety-second Congress were merely numbered. Certain jurisdictional traditions had grown up about each of them, and they acquired vague descriptive titles, but the chairman also claimed and exercised great discretion in selecting—on whatever basis he wished—the subcommittee to which he would refer a particular bill, or indeed in deciding whether to refer a bill at all. The numbering system assisted him in maintaining this flexibility.

Subcommittee No. 1 (immigration). This unit handled all public and private immigration and naturalization legislation. In the Ninetieth Congress, the subcommittee received 6,278 private bills. Most of them (4,846) were still pending at the end of the Congress. When Peter W. Rodino, Jr. (D., N.J.) (now chairman of the full committee) became chairman of Subcommittee No. 1 at the beginning of the Ninety-second Congress, he resolved to shrink this backlog. Rodino's predecessor, Michael Feighan (D., Ohio), had evidenced little interest in public immigration policy,* concentrating the subcommittee's efforts on private bills. Rodino introduced several changes to reorient the subcommittee's efforts and demonstrated considerable interest in

---

* Feighan and Celler had strong antipathies for each other; they disagreed on virtually everything, barely maintaining civility.

the reform of immigration policy. He discontinued Feighan's practice of holding public hearings on private bills, except where a member sought reconsideration of an adverse report. Rodino also enhanced the effectiveness of Subcommittee No. 1 by establishing a warm relationship with Chairman Celler, who had helped Rodino obtain his original assignment to Judiciary. As soon as Rodino became chairman of the subcommittee, Celler began to refer legislation other than immigration bills to No. 1.

Subcommittee No. 2 (claims). Presided over by lethargic Harold D. Donohue, this subcommittee considered private claims bills and little else. In the Ninety-second Congress, a few bills dealing with other matters were referred to the subcommittee, including counterfeiting of postal money orders, state lotteries, and U.S. attorneys for Puerto Rico. The subcommittee spent a good deal of time on a bill to compensate industrial users of cyclamates.

Controversy also surfaced—through no fault of the subcommittee—on the proposed extension of the American Revolution Bicentennial Commission.* A series of three articles in the *Washington Post* by an investigative reporter indicated partisan political bias in the commission's operations and documented many commission failures. The subcommittee was obliged to have the bill, which it had already casually approved, pulled from the House calendar because of the new facts brought out in the *Post* articles. As this example suggests, oversight by Subcommittee No. 2 was very limited.

Subcommittee No. 3 (patents, trademarks, and copyrights). Chaired by Robert W. Kastenmeier, this group had jurisdiction over patents,† trademarks, and copyrights, as well as corrections legislation. The subcommittee also handled some other legislation in the Ninety-second Congress, including an interstate compact

---

* The commission, after three and a half years of work, still had no acceptable plans for the nation's 200th birthday celebration, according to the *Washington Post* (May 16, 1973).

† The subcommittee has had little impact upon the Patent Office. See Chapter 5.

dealing with the New York–New Jersey Waterfront Commission, the repeal of the Emergency Detention Act, and a Juvenile Justice Institute bill.

Under Kastenmeier, this subcommittee was far more active in the Ninety-second Congress than in the Ninetieth, dealing with almost three times the volume of legislation in the first session alone. The subcommittee's work increased partly because of the sudden popularity of prison reform. In the Ninetieth Congress, there were no bills dealing with correction issues; more than fifty such bills were introduced in the first session of the Ninety-second Congress, several of them important reforms.

Subcommittee No. 4 (bankruptcy and reorganization). This subcommittee, in the Ninety-second Congress, experienced a significant change in the kind of legislation with which it dealt. After Don Edwards replaced Byron G. Rogers (D., Colo.) as subcommittee chairman in the Ninety-second Congress, the subcommittee was given oversight jurisdiction over the civil rights laws. The subcommittee also considered legislation concerning bankruptcy and reorganization, judicial administration, narcotics, criminal laws, and federal holidays and celebrations. Because of the many ceremonial bills referred to the subcommittee, such as one to declare a National Square Dance Week, it received the heaviest volume of public legislation of any subcommittee.

In the Ninety-second Congress, this subcommittee held hearings on proposals for a constitutional amendment and for statutory changes to secure equal rights for women. In addition, the subcommittee held seven days of hearings on various narcotics bills and conducted about fifteen days of hearings on the Voting Rights Act and discrimination in federally assisted housing.

Subcommittee No. 5 (antitrust matters). In addition to its antitrust jurisdiction, Subcommittee No. 5, which was chaired by the full-committee chairman, wrote civil rights legislation. In the Ninety-second Congress, the group extended the authorization of the U.S. Civil Rights Commission. The subcommittee did not hold hearings relating to crime legislation during the first session, as it had often done in prior years, despite a large volume of bills dealing with the subject. Many of the crime bills (including nine of the bills to repeal the Gun Control Act of 1968) were not referred to subcommittees but instead remained with the full committee, with no action taken on them. In the Ninety-second Congress, the subcommittee also considered the constitutional amendment to lower the voting age to eighteen, congressional districting legislation, legislation to create an administrative assistant to the Chief Justice of the Supreme Court, and legislation relating to the president's pocket-veto power.

The subcommittee's workload diminished considerably when Chairman Celler began to temper his long-standing practice of referring the "glamour" legislation to Subcommittee No. 5; the workload was somewhat more evenly distributed in the Ninety-second Congress, and all of the subcommittees received at least some bills outside of their previous jurisdictions. Nevertheless, Subcommittee No. 5 received a disproportionate share of the important legislation referred to Judiciary.

In the Ninety-third Congress, under new leadership and considerable pressure from members, the number of subcommittees was increased to seven; they received formal designations; and their jurisdictions were modified.* Subcommittee No. 1 became the Subcommittee on Immigration, Citizenship, and International Law. Now chaired by Joshua Eilberg, this unit still considers all public and private immigration and naturalization legislation, as well as other matters as referred. Subcommittee No. 2 became the Subcommittee on Claims and Governmental Relations. Still chaired by Harold Donohue, this subcommittee continues to handle all claims bills, as well as legislation involving the American Revolution Bicentennial. Subcommittee No. 3 is now the Subcommittee on Courts, Civil Liberties, and the Administration of Justice. It is still chaired by Robert Kastenmeier and considers a great variety of issues, including amnesty, capital punishment, certain constitutional amendments, corrections, courts, criminal proce-

---

* The circumstances leading up to these changes, and their significance, are discussed in detail in Chapter 16.

dure, judicial procedure, patents, trademarks, and copyrights, pornography, electronic surveillance, and other bills as assigned. Subcommittee No. 4 became the Subcommittee on Civil Rights and Constitutional Rights. Don Edwards remains the chairman. Its jurisdiction includes general legislative and oversight jurisdiction with regard to civil rights, constitutional rights, and constitutional amendments, as well as bankruptcy and reorganization, federal charters, and holidays and commemorations. Subcommittee No. 5 became the Subcommittee on Monopolies and Commercial Law, still headed by the full-committee chairman, now Peter Rodino. Its jurisdiction includes antitrust, constitutional amendments, federal court reform, the Law Enforcement Assistance Administration, and other matters over which the chairman wishes to retain control.

Two new subcommittees were added. Early in the Ninety-third Congress, prior to the subcommittee reforms, a Subcommittee No. 6 was created with general jurisdiction over bills as assigned and special jurisdiction over "revision of the laws" (a routine function of classification and codification of statutory law). In June 1973, it became the Subcommittee on Crime, chaired by John Conyers. Despite its title, it has jurisdiction over a variety of miscellaneous and largely unrelated legislative subjects, while most criminal legislation is referred elsewhere. Finally, a Subcommittee on Criminal Justice was established, chaired by William Hungate, with jurisdiction over various matters relating to the criminal justice system.

The subcommittee reforms of June 1973, as will be seen, did not significantly diminish the chairman's traditional power over the referral of bills. This centralized power in the Judiciary chairman has long been exercised so as to fragment the committee's jurisdiction among its subcommittees in a wholly irrational fashion. During the Ninety-second Congress, for example, civil rights matters were divided between two subcommittees, with legislative jurisdiction in one (No. 5) and oversight of administration of the civil rights laws in another (No. 4). Constitutional amendments were spread out over three subcommittees (Nos. 1,

4, and 5), as was legislation dealing with the federal court system (Nos. 2, 4, and 5). Criminal Justice legislation also went to three subcommittees (Nos. 3, 4, and 5). During the Ninety-third Congress, this fragmentation has not been significantly reduced; indeed, in the criminal justice area it has been exacerbated, with *five* subcommittees considering such legislation.

While some flexibility in jurisdictions of particular subcommittees is certainly desirable, dividing discrete subject-matter areas deprives the committee and the Congress of expertise which has been or can be developed by subcommittee members and staff, expertise sorely needed on the Hill. Yet Celler did not consider expertise and accustomed jurisdiction as particularly important in his referral of legislation to House Judiciary subcommittees. While Subcommittee No. 4 often dealt with the question of representation for the District of Columbia, this made little difference in the Ninety-second Congress—the legislation was assigned instead to Subcommittee No. 1, which customarily exercised jurisdiction over immigration and naturalization matters and had no expertise in the area of representation. Even Subcommittee No. 5, with its familiarity with the complexities of the representation and congressional districting problems, would have been a more appropriate forum.

Celler peremptorily bottled up important legislation in full committee during the Ninety-second Congress, including some with widespread support. He failed to refer *any* of the three abortion reform bills, the six amnesty bills, the thirty public prayer amendments, and ten labor-court bills (even though one bill had twenty-four cosponsors). Indeed, only about half of the public bills coming to the committee (1,282 out of 2,536) were referred to subcommittees. The remainder languished in the full committee without action.

Most of these were bills which the chairman evidently felt should not be enacted. In the Ninety-first Congress, Celler refused to refer the Equal Rights Amendment to subcommittee or to hold hearings, and the bill eventually had to be liberated from his clutches by means of a discharge petition. The amendment passed the House by a vote of 350 to 15. The amendment, which has been introduced every year since 1923, failed to pass the Senate in 1970. When it was reintroduced in the Ninety-second Congress, Celler did refer it to Subcommittee No. 4, which held hearings and favorably reported it to the full committee, where changes were added exempting women from the draft and preserving the applicability of special "health and safety laws" (which have often been used to deny employment to women).

One committee staffer explained, "The chairman is willing to take the brunt. If he passes them on to subcommittee, he is passing on the responsibility." Celler may have been stopping undesirable legislation that subcommittee chairmen might not have been strong enough to halt,* but at the same time, one man—and a man in his eighties at that—was making the final determination on the merits of over a thousand pieces of legislation, many of them (like those mentioned above) clearly controversial.

In the Ninety-third Congress, the full committee became the focus of high drama and delicate deliberations. Following the surprise resignation of Vice-President Spiro T. Agnew on October 10, 1973, the committee launched an apparently exhaustive staff investigation, utilizing the confidential files of many federal agencies. In November, the full committee held lengthy hearings on the nomination of minority leader Gerald Ford to become Vice-President of the United States, a procedure authorized by the Twenty-fifth Amendment and never before invoked. After having heard thirty-six hours of testimony, the committee

---

* The staff regards many, if not most, bills not referred to subcommittees as nuisance legislation introduced only in order to satisfy constituents. Many unassigned bills do indeed conform to that pattern. One example is House Concurrent Resolution 459, introduced by John Rarick (D., La.) to enshrine the song "Dixie" in American history by permitting its playing at all public functions or gatherings. In earlier years Celler refused to refer bills introduced by Rarick which would have repealed the Civil Rights Act of 1964, the Voting Rights Act of 1965, and the Gun Control Act of 1968. The first two of these acts, of course, were largely Celler's own handiwork.

reported the nomination favorably, the House agreed, and Ford assumed office in December.

But the committee's ascent into history was only beginning. Late in 1973, Chairman Rodino began to assemble an investigative staff to consider the impeachment of the President of the United States. Rodino moved with deliberate—some called it irresponsible—slowness, and it was not until January 1974 that special majority and minority counsel, John Doar and Albert Jenner, were named to head the impeachment inquiry. By April 1974, as a result of a series of constitutional contretemps with the White House and its impeachment counsel, James St. Clair, over access to information and the role of St. Clair in the impeachment inquiry, the full committee was meeting frequently, often once or more in a week. On April 11, 1974, the committee, by a vote of thirty-three to three, decided to issue a subpoena to President Nixon covering various tapes and other memoranda of presidential conversations. This vote constituted the first and only such subpoena ever issued by Congress, clearly a constitutional precedent of historic dimension. Yet just as clearly, the most arduous and delicate labors of the committee lay ahead.

Procedure by Rules

Although the House Judiciary Committee is rather amorphous in terms of the substantive content of its subcommittee jurisdictions, it does follow definite procedural rules (see Appendix 3), unlike its Senate counterpart. The full committee has a prescribed meeting day, Tuesday. At least two days before the committee has its meeting, an agenda is sent to all members designating the bills and subjects to be brought up. Other bills can be brought up only if more than two-thirds of the members desire to do so.

The rules pertaining to voting sometimes affect the outcome of decisions. In accordance with the Legislative Reorganization Act, the House committee limits proxy voting to written authorizations for specific measures; the proxy cannot be a general one. (In the Senate, a tacit policy on proxies permits unwritten proxy voting only on a particular item and only when the vote cannot be decisive.)[10]

All House Judiciary subcommittees have rules prescribing when the subcommittee will meet, whether the meetings will be open, and what bills will be considered. Weekly meeting dates can be canceled by the chairman if there is little business. Having a definite date means that meetings tend to be held more frequently than otherwise.

The House subcommittees' rules facilitate expeditious handling of many matters coming to them. The two subcommittees that handle most of the legislation (in terms of quantity) coming to Judiciary, Subcommittees No. 1 and 2, prescribe by rules what kinds of private bills the subcommittees will handle and under what circumstances.* The claims subcommittee (No. 2), for example, will not consider certain categories of bills, such as bills concerning injury or damage resulting from service in the National Guard, any claim that arose before 1956, or claims for retirement benefits, compensation, pension, or gratuities under the Railroad Retirement Act. The immigration subcommittee (No. 1), unlike its Senate counterpart, will not request reports of the attorney general (which would have the effect of suspending deportation proceedings) with respect to aliens who entered the United States as nonimmigrants, stowaways, or deserting crewmen, or otherwise surreptitiously. These rules also prescribe how members are to submit information in support of private bills.

Full-committee prescription of subcommittee rules in the House Judiciary has had some unfortunate consequences. There has been little experimentation. New methods of operation or other rules changes must be approved by the full committee with or without the concurrence of the subcommittee affected. Until the Ninety-second Congress, for example, all subcommittees had to hold their markup† sessions at meetings closed to the public. Television coverage of their hearings was not permitted unless

---

* See Chapter 11.

† Committee negotiation of the precise provisions of a bill.

full committee permission was granted. Since networks normally cannot decide very far in advance which hearings they wish to cover, the "permission" becomes purely theoretical, for networks cannot, as a practical matter, avail themselves of it.

Some changes were effected in the Ninety-second Congress. As noted above, jurisdictions were broadened somewhat. In addition, more latitude was permitted in operations. For example, subcommittee chairman Robert Kastenmeier won the right to hold open markup sessions on prison-reform legislation.

One is struck by the extent to which the rules of House Judiciary reflect and reinforce the power and operating style of the full committee chairman, while the absence of formal rules in the Senate Judiciary Committee nourishes the independence and power of the subcommittees and their chairmen. Rule structures depend for their effects upon the underlying configuration of power in the committee. And in the House Judiciary Committee, rules, like everything else, have simply been levers for the exertion of the chairman's weighty influence.

Parsimony and Preference

The hopper at the House Judiciary Committee groans under the massive volume of bills placed in it. By the end of the Ninety-second Congress, the House committee had 5,289 bills and resolutions referred to it, while the Senate committee received only 1,763 items—reflecting its smaller membership and the more frequent Senate practice of cosponsorship of bills.*[11] And while the Senate workload has remained roughly the same for several Congresses, the House committee is experiencing a dramatic reduction in workload—in the Ninety-first Congress, it had considered 8,443 bills and resolutions,[12] primarily because of the decreasing number of private bills.

Although the committee handled well over a third of the legis-

* In the House, for example, thirteen different bills for the compensation of those suffering losses from the cyclamates ban were introduced.

lation introduced in the House of Representatives,* it had one of that chamber's lowest budgets. In contrast to the Senate committee's lavish and unrivaled funding, Judiciary actually ranked *twelfth* in committee budgets in the House. In the Ninety-second Congress, House Judiciary received an authorization of $800,000—all that Chairman Celler requested. This authorization was lower than even that of its own offshoot, the Select Committee on Crime ($1,145,000), less than the moribund Internal Security Committee ($1,045,000), and less than the inactive and phlegmatic Post Office and Civil Service Committee ($1,056,000).†[13]

Celler's frugality had many consequences, most of them perverse. Staffing is chronically inadequate. Thirty-six employees served the thirty-seven congressmen in the Ninety-second Congress, while the Senate Committee staff numbered 204, almost six times larger. The disparity is perhaps best illustrated by the numbers of House and Senate aides dealing with highly intricate concerns of the antitrust subcommittees: *one* House staffer, contrasted with over thirty staffers in the Senate. House Judiciary subcommittees do not hire consultants and rarely hold hearings outside of Washington, D.C.‡

One result of Celler's parsimony may be crudely measured by

---

* A large number were private bills.

† In the 93rd Congress, Chairman Rodino requested and received a considerably expanded budget, but most of this increase reflected the requirements of the impeachment investigation. And part of the supplemented budget threatened to be held hostage to the pique of crusty Wayne Hays, the irascible chairman of the House Administration Committee. In early April 1974, Hays encountered several youths in a House elevator whose behavior offended him. When they told him they worked for the Judiciary Committee impeachment investigation, Hays castigated them as "arrogant little jerks" and expressed some pleasure in the fact that "you are coming before my committee next week asking for another million dollars."

‡ Subcommittee No. 1, with jurisdiction over immigration and naturalization, did hold one set of hearings in several cities, but the subcommittee's staff was so inadequate that little advance work was done, even in briefing witnesses.

contrasting the days of hearings held in the Ninety-second Congress by the Senate Antitrust and Monopoly Subcommittee with the complete absence of antitrust hearings held by Subcommittee No. 5. Celler, like an imperial suzerain, had seized so many legislative jurisdictions for No. 5 in addition to antitrust that it could not possibly oversee all or even most of them. No subcommittee, particularly one so woefully understaffed, could adequately handle antitrust, civil rights, the federal judiciary, congressional redistricting, and constitutional amendments. (The Senate committee considers legislation in these areas through *four separate subcommittees* with vastly more staff.) Given the enormity of the House committee's jurisdiction, Celler's adamantine refusal to recognize and meet the monetary needs of the Judiciary committee can only be characterized as irresponsible.

There is no question that the House Administration Committee would have willingly authorized virtually any budget that the powerful Celler had submitted to it. That he requested so little in the face of the committee's awesome jurisdiction and responsibilities (responsibilities, in the view of liberals, made even more critical by the conservatives' dominance of most powerful House committees and the Senate Judiciary Committee) testifies to Celler's truncated vision of the committee's legislative role. If the committee's paltry budget has meant that it cannot hold valuable hearings, employ expert consultants, maintain adequate staff, or generate independent sources of information or ideas, and if these limitations have contributed to the flow of influence and function away from the House to the Senate and the executive branch, Emanuel Celler must bear a significant measure of the responsibility.

Celler eloquently, if not persuasively, explained why he thinks members should not have to give up outside income-producing activities:

> The average length of a congressman's tenure is eight years. If he is going to divest himself of his calling as a farmer or a banker or a lawyer, what is going to happen to him when he

is defeated or resigns? He is bereft, he no longer has his profession, he no longer has his job, he no longer has his wealth, he is like a rudderless ship on a sea without a shore.[14]

Celler often brushed off criticism of his law-firm connection by asserting, in the spirit of the late Adam Clayton Powell, that his constituents knew what he did and were alone capable of judging him. They have indeed judged him, and harshly. For the first time in fifty years, Emanuel Celler is once again a private citizen,* defeated by Elizabeth Holtzman, a thirty-one-year-old lawyer, in the 1972 Democratic primary. Like many senior members of Congress, especially committee chairmen, Celler had lost touch with his constituents and his district. His office was not even in his Brooklyn district; it was in Manhattan, an hour's trip by subway for many of his constituents, and in the same building as his law firm, Weisman, Celler, Allan, Spett, and Sheinberg. His law-firm connections and potential conflicts of interest (his law office had two doors, one including Celler's name and one without it),† the lack of an office in his district, his age, and his high absenteeism‡ were lively campaign issues.

Celler said in 1971 in an interview: "Don't judge me in part, judge the whole me."[15] In judging the whole of Mr. Celler's long congressional career, one must conclude that it was one of distinction. And he was sorry to be leaving it:

Well, frankly, I shall sorely miss being here. The grace of serving in Congress is the putting aside of self, it is the dwelling in the world of ideas, without the isolation that generally accompanies such pursuits. It is the give-and-take in daily encounters. It is comradeship, it is challenge, it is excitement in the planning and execution of legislative

* He now represents his law firm in Washington, D.C.

† Representative Celler was not entirely alone in this questionable practice. In May, 1969, fifty-six congressmen reported that their names were still on the doors of the law firms where they practiced upon entering Congress. Another nineteen admitted to practicing law while in office.

‡ Celler had the highest absentee record of any Democratic member of the New York delegation. During the first session of the 92nd Congress, he missed 107 out of 313 roll-call votes.

battles, it is a life of service. But the compensations are more than amply rewarding. I am grateful I have had 50 such years, yet it is well that the old order changes, yielding place to the new.[16]

The New Chairman

Peter Wallace Rodino, Jr., the chairman of the full committee in the Ninety-third Congress, has none of his predecessor's pugnacity or habituation to power. First elected to the House in 1948 from Newark, New Jersey, at the behest of the notorious Essex County machine, Rodino has hung on for over a quarter of a century, slowly amassing seniority and practicing the art of ethnic politics to the evident satisfaction of his predominantly Italian, working-class constituency.

The diminutive Rodino is a man of quiet irony. A gentle lover of opera and poetry, his voice evokes the rough edges of the immigrant's son. A fierce spokesman for Italian causes, he has been at the forefront of civil rights struggles in the House. The product of malodorous Essex County courthouse politics, he has never been tainted by personal scandal. Virtually unknown outside the precincts of the House until 1973, he has been suddenly thrust onto center stage by the drama of presidential impeachment.

He senses the improbability of his position. "If fate had been looking for one of the powerhouses of Congress," Rodino has remarked, "it wouldn't have picked me."[17] As chairman of Subcommittee No. 1, Rodino had acquired considerable influence over public and private immigration legislation, but this was a power base of decidedly limited dimensions.

In the Ninety-third Congress, however, he acceded not only to the full committee chairmanship but to one of its prerogatives —the chairmanship of the important Subcommittee No. 5, renamed the Subcommittee on Monopolies and Commercial Law. And it soon became clear—from his successful cooptation of the subcommittee reforms,* to his garnering from the House of wide-

* See Chapter 16.

ranging subpoena and investigatory powers for the impeachment inquiry, to his careful cultivation of bipartisanship on delicate impeachment issues—that during those twenty-five years of obscurity, Rodino had actually been busy studying Emanuel Celler's political artistry with the careful eye of the talented epigone.

II

SENTRIES OF MONOPOLY

4

Monopoly Capitol:
The Antitrust Subcommittees

Oil, drugs, coffins, cars, steel and baseball, books and milk—are diverse commodities with one thing in common. At some point in the past twenty years, each has been carefully studied by congressional subcommittees whose mandates are the preservation and enhancement of a competitive American economy. There is an urgency in their deliberation—because monopoly overcharges transfer an estimated $23 billion annually from consumers to producers;[1] because economic concentration shrinks the Gross National Product by some $48 billion annually;[2] and because monopolies contribute to maintaining the highly skewed distribution of wealth in America.[3] How much a consumer pays for a car and how much a housewife can put in the bank are intimately affected by industrial structures that convert consumer dimes into nickels—and wooden ones at that.[4]

NOTE: This chapter was prepared by Mark J. Green.

61

But the structures of these industries are not noticeably different in the past two decades by reason of the efforts of the congressional antitrust subcommittees. Like gymnasium bicyclists pedaling furiously away on their stationary vehicles, the congressional subcommittees frequently seem to be going nowhere. In a Congress that roughly mirrors a society grown dependent on business—big business—it is unlikely that congressional subcommittees dealing with antitrust will be permitted to include even a few of the handful of Capitol Hill critics of corporate power. Most congressmen are simply reluctant to challenge powerful corporate interests whose support they need. Many congressional conservatives are committed to states' rights and are unwilling to cede greater antitrust powers to the federal government. And even those lawmakers who ostensibly champion the antitrust cause seem more absorbed in other issues; no one has yet become a presidential contender by brandishing the antitrust banner.

Not yet, anyway. But as problems of inflation, foreign trade, growth, consumerism, corporate responsibility, and wealth/income distribution converge, the common remedy of antitrust policy—long the lonely *cri de coeur* of the populist—may be forced upon a resistant Congress. And if it is, a focus of antitrust attention in Washington will inevitably be the antitrust subcommittees of the Senate and House Judiciary committees. Their activities and passivities, the play of their personalities and politics, and their unique educational function, could help shape the future course of the American economic and political systems.

THE SENATE SUBCOMMITTEE

The Early Years

In the beginning, there was the Sherman Antitrust Act of 1890,[*] but it was not until 1953 that the Senate had an antitrust subcommittee. The handful of laws dealing with antitrust in the

---

[*] The Sherman Act makes illegal any "contract, combination or conspiracy, in restraint of trade."

intervening six decades had been handled on an *ad hoc* basis by a variety of congressional committees. As the American economy grew and interest in antitrust issues accelerated, especially after passage of the 1950 Celler-Kefauver Act (see below), this random procedure proved unsatisfactory.

It took a Senate maverick to launch the committee. The Senate Antitrust and Monopoly Subcommittee was opened for business in 1953 by Judiciary Committee Chairman William ("Wild Bill") Langer, a dynamic Republican populist from North Dakota. Denied official sanction and appropriations by the Senate, he ran the subcommittee initially out of his own office and with his own office funds. The Senate Rules Committee finally officially recognized the new committee on March 18, 1955, when Senate Resolution 61 allocated up to $200,000 for an antitrust subcommittee, since "no attempt has yet been made by the Congress to survey the entire field of antitrust laws with a view toward a comprehensive revision and coordination of these [antitrust] laws."

From the outset, the subcommittee regarded facts and publicity as its most effective weapons. By exposing the conflicts of interest swirling around the Dixon-Yates contract, which allowed a private firm to build a power plant to supply the Tennessee Valley Authority, the subcommittee spurred the Eisenhower administration in 1955 to cancel that controversial agreement. Publication in 1956 of the subcommittee report *Bigness and Concentration of Economic Power: A Case Study of General Motors Corporation* presaged in title and content its future preoccupation with economic concentration.*

But it was not until January 22, 1957—when Senator Estes Kefauver, having finally shed his ambitions for national office, took over as subcommittee chairman—that the subcommittee's personality finally took shape. Kefauver's reputation preceded

---

* This report led to the first piece of subcommittee legislation to become law, the "Auto Dealer's Day in Court" act of 1956, which gave auto dealers the right of court review for the alleged failure of manufacturers to act in good faith in reviewing or terminating a franchise.

him: campaigns for the Democratic presidential nomination and investigations into organized crime had won him wide notoriety. As early as 1946, he had held hearings for a subcommittee of the House Select Small Business Committee, to "reverse the trend toward economic concentration." This effort ultimately led to the Celler-Kefauver Act of 1950, the seminal antitrust law of this century, which plugged up the loophole in the 1914 Clayton Act that had tolerated anticompetitive asset acquisitions.

The subcommittee and Kefauver appeared to be the fortuitous wedding of a willing instrument (Kefauver had a "magnificent working majority," said a staff economist of that era) and a talented artisan. Despite his background in southern gentry and corporate law,[5] Kefauver's reputation and militant antitrust views so frightened Senate conservatives that, in his first year as chairman, they moved to cut appropriations to the antitrust subcommittee by more than 30 percent. Critics, led by Republican leader William F. Knowland of California, complained—with some justification—that the subcommittee produced no legislation and functioned merely as Kefauver's antibusiness forum. Aided by an unexpected defense from the late Senator Everett M. Dirksen (R., Ill.) ("I think the work the subcommittee does is important, even though I disagree so generally with my able and affable friend from Tennessee"),[6] Kefauver and his allies easily defeated Knowland's motion. But the critics had a semblance of a point: the Antitrust and Monopoly Subcommittee was, and would continue to be, a sounding board rather than a legislative machine.

For example, Kefauver launched hearings in 1957 on "administered prices"—i.e., prices set by a few leading firms in concentrated industries. The hearings, which articulated and dramatized the problems of industrial structure, were organized by Dr. John Blair, Kefauver's chief economic aide, and were based on the approach of economist Gardner Means who argued in the 1930s that administered prices distorted the economy. Between 1957 and 1963, hearings on administered prices in the steel, automobile, bread and drug industries, among others, were to fill twenty-nine volumes and more than 18,000 pages. "Before the subcommittee made its record, it was possible for policy-makers to ignore the structure of industry," *Washington Post* reporter Bernard Nossiter later wrote. These hearings established the fact that "corporate, and union, pricing power is a phenomenon with which every administration must cope, either openly or covertly."[7] But—in a pattern that was to be repeated up to the present day—no legislation ever resulted.

There were many other hearings during these early years; one was instrumental in unraveling the intricate and massive collusion of electrical equipment manufacturers in sales to the Tennessee Valley Authority. This probe ultimately led to the largest criminal antitrust case in the history of the Sherman Act. Twenty-nine corporations and forty-five executives were charged with price-fixing, bid-rigging, and market-splitting; eventually twenty individuals received suspended sentences, seven others served jail sentences, and total fines of $1,954,000 were assessed.

But "magnificent working majority" or not, Kefauver assembled a slender legislative record on antitrust during his six years as chairman, largely due to a Judiciary Committee and Senate uncommitted to a vigorous antitrust policy. Only two antitrust bills became law.* All other efforts failed, including Kefauver's proposals to increase criminal antitrust penalties and to require business to notify the government prior to mergers in concentrated industries.

The most important subcommittee bill to become law in this period involved health and safety, not antitrust. The so-called Kefauver-Harris Amendments of 1962 provided for premarketing review by the Food and Drug Administration (FDA) of the efficacy of new drugs and for seizure of drugs when there was an imminent hazard to public health; drug advertisements had to indicate adverse side effects and cite the drug's generic name, i.e., the chemical name and not the brand name. But the law was

---

* S.726 in 1959 provided that orders issued by the Federal Trade Commission under Section 11 of the Clayton Act "shall, if not appealed, become final by mere passage of time"; and S.167 permitted the Justice Department to subpoena pertinent documentary material from a firm under investigation.

only a shadow of what Kefauver had intended it to be. His original bill had sought to reduce the "extraordinary" prices of patented drugs by making certain anticompetitive patent agreements illegal, by requiring compulsory licensing under specified product patents, and by giving the Department of Health, Education, and Welfare authority to establish simplified generic names for drugs. Some members of his subcommittee and Judiciary Chairman James Eastland, however, stripped the drug bills of these provisions in secret meetings with industry lobbyists, which occurred without the knowledge or presence of Senator Kefauver.[8] That the drug amendments passed with even as much substance as they had was less a result of Kefauver's "clout" than of the thalidomide tragedy, when sale of this drug to pregnant women in Europe and Japan caused about ten thousand horribly deformed babies.

Kefauver's travail over his drug bill was only one in a train of events diminishing his influence. In 1962, both he and House antitrust chairman Emanuel Celler sent out "cost" subpoenas to the steel industry at the direct behest of President Kennedy, then jousting with Big Steel. After the presidential battle had ended, "Celler was smart and canceled his investigations," said a former Kefauver aide, "but Kefauver was bullheaded and went ahead." Four of the twelve firms refused to cooperate with the subpoenas, and in what was considered a senatorial rebuke, the Senate Judiciary Committee refused to enforce Kefauver's subpoenas.[9]

By 1962, Senator Eastland, who is normally receptive to the recommendations of his subcommittee chairmen when vacancies occur on their subcommittees, began to ignore Kefauver's preferences for new subcommittee members. Instead of the liberal Democrats Kefauver wanted, Eastland named conservatives, and by 1962, Kefauver found himself hamstrung in his own subcommittee.[10] That year, Kefauver heard that conservative Democrat John McClellan was about to get the subcommittee seat of defeated liberal Democrat John Carroll. "He was terribly upset," recalls an aide, since the Tennessean had not even been consulted. When Kefauver angrily called Judiciary

Chairman Eastland to complain, Eastland advised him to calm down, since the selection had not yet been officially announced. They would talk about it later, Eastland said. They didn't. The McClellan appointment was formally announced that afternoon.

Then a new subpoena controversy erupted in 1963—and this time the subcommittee itself was balking. Kefauver wanted to issue subpoenas in early May to American drug manufacturers who were allegedly interfering with the marketing by other drug houses of low-priced generic drugs in South America. But an informal head count made it apparent that the subcommittee would not support him in this effort. Kefauver was spared this final humiliation. Before the issue came to a vote, Senator Estes Kefauver—of whom the *New Republic* had once said, "What George Norris was in the public power field, Estes Kefauver is in the field of antitrust enforcement"[11]—died of coronary complications on August 10, 1963.

Hotspur to Hamlet

Senator Philip A. Hart of Michigan—former war hero, former head of the Michigan Securities Commission, and ex-officer and (through marriage) director of the Detroit Tigers and Lions—was next in line for the chairmanship. He was unsure whether he wanted the position, said a former aide. "Hart agonizes over any major decision . . . and he did over this. . . . The press was appalled that he waited at all." He went to Senator Hubert H. Humphrey, admitting his doubts and soliciting advice; the Minnesotan told Hart to seize the influential position. Finally, on August 19, 1963, reluctant but resigned, Hart took over as chairman.

The nine-day period of indecision was pure Hamlet—and pure Hart; it reflected a sharp departure from the style of his predecessor. Deliberate where Kefauver had been decisive, personally modest where Kefauver had been brash, Hart told *Time* magazine, "When you get on the Monopoly Subcommittee, the feeling develops that you're out to change the economic system. That's not me."[12] And it wasn't. "He just wasn't interested in muckraking," says a former Kefauver loyalist. (This person recalled how, years later, Hart cut off an aide's hard-hitting cross-examination of some Blue Cross witnesses because, said Hart, "it sounded too much like Kefauver!")

Hart immediately ordered an end to the drug hearings on the premise that the subject was exhausted. Since the Parke, Davis and Upjohn companies had their homes in Michigan, this move depressed the more cynical staff, and some unkindly began calling him "Chicken Hart"—an initial hostility that Hart's obvious intelligence, fairness, and sympathy to antitrust soon overcame.

More difficult for Hart was a decision on Kefauver's drug subpoenas. If the subcommittee refused to support the subpoenas, Jerry Cohen, then the subcommittee's staff director, recalls, "that would have screwed Hart right away." At six or seven executive sessions on the matter, Senator Dirksen was one vote shy of quashing the subpoenas. Each time it was Senator McClellan who would say, according to one participant, "Well now, Everett, let's not be too hasty. Maybe we can work this out." McClellan was not eager to undermine senatorial subpoenas, since his own Permanent Investigations Subcommittee used them so often; and since he personally liked Hart, he did not want to humiliate him. The deadlock was finally and cunningly broken on December 11, 1963, when the subcommittee sent its files over to the Justice Department, which issued its own subpoenas.

As Senator Kefauver had been, Senator Hart was a minority chairman. For Hart inherited a conservative majority of three Republicans plus three Democrats, all prepared to oppose antitrust advances. Within a year after Kefauver's death, the subcommittee was composed, on the Democratic side, of Senators Hart, Thomas Dodd, Edward Kennedy, Russell B. Long, McClellan, and Sam Ervin; on the Republican side, there were Senators Dirksen, Roman Hruska, and Kenneth Keating. Thus, although many observers of congressional antitrust politics accept it as conventional wisdom that Judiciary Chairman Eastland "stacked" the Antitrust Subcommittee against Hart after Kefauver's death, in fact its composition was established well before Hart's succession. And this "balance" has been delicately maintained over the past decade by Eastland (who, when asked how he decides appointments, said, "I consult a little with Hart and Hruska, but I appoint!").[13] In 1963 Hart could generally depend on support from three of nine members (Dodd, Kennedy, and himself); in 1974 he can still only count on three supporters out of nine (Kennedy, John Tunney, and himself). The other members are McClellan, Ervin, Hruska, Hiram Fong, Strom Thurmond, and Edward Gurney, who, for reasons both philosophic and self-interested, do not seem interested in promoting antitrust policy. (Senator Gurney, for example, received significant campaign contributions in 1968 from large Florida bankers, businessmen, and corporate lawyers. While senator, Roman Hruska has: leased a Lincoln Continental from the Ford Motor Company for $750 per year, although the regular charge was $3,480; received a salary as chairman of an insurance firm; and, says columnist Jack Anderson, aided the business clients of his former law firm.) There are some predictable consequences for a subcommittee chairman on the short end of a six-to-three lineup: tough subpoenas are rarely issued; committee reports are not written; and bills are not reported out—except those that carve out new exemptions from the antitrust laws.

The Gentlemanly Trustbuster

The subcommittee, at the senatorial level, *is* Philip Hart. Day in and day out, year in and year out, it is he who assumes the Sisyphian role of pushing the antitrust rock to the top of the legislative mountain.

Senator Hart is a widely respected and well-liked member of the Senate. He is patient and polite to all witnesses, a model of fairness and decorum. Senator Ervin has remarked that "There is no one in the Senate with whom I disagree more often, nor for whom I have more respect, than Senator Hart." In a world of overblown egos and self-promoting posturing, he displays a disarming charm, a certain candor mixed with whimsy. When there were rumors in 1968 that Hubert Humphrey might select him as a vice-presidential nominee, Hart's comment was characteristic:

"I would be a good vice-president, but I would only take the job on condition the first guy promises never to die in office." Nor can it be doubted that Senator Hart is a hard-hitting and committed advocate on paper. His speeches bristle with passages like the following:

> I am convinced that in the long run economic concentration and democratic institutions cannot survive side by side. . . .[14]
> What our corporation executives desire is not competition, but security; not the discipline of the marketplace, but the anarchy of unrestrained pricing. In Professor Galbraith, they have found their apologist; in the federal government, I fear they have found an accomplice. . . .[15]
> I would estimate that easily 30 percent of all consumer spending is wasted. And, I would not say "nay" if someone theorized that the percent was as high as 40. . . . In other words, 174 to 231 billion [dollars which] consumers spend each year may buy no product value.* [16]

Hart also has the courage of his convictions. It was far from inevitable that a senator from Detroit would be an outspoken critic of the auto oligopoly, which is like tossing kindling on the political firefights back home. Yet Hart is that, despite his ownership of 315 shares of General Motors stock, which he discloses annually with his other stockholdings. His anti-industry positions, however, have provoked neither the auto firms nor the United Auto Workers to oppose him formally.

Despite political pressures, Hart will stand by his staff once they take a position with which he philosophically concurs. After it was announced that the Antitrust Subcommittee would hold hearings into the oil industry's projected exploitation of federally owned shale land in Colorado, Hart's staff feared that the

---

* This speech was an imaginative effort to tally the cost of all perceived anticompetitive and wasteful practices. Perhaps too imaginative. The numbers cited on waste do not add up to 30 to 40 percent. Hart's estimate that criminal price-fixing can boost prices "15 to 35 percent" is accurate, yet his apparent application of this overcharge to the *entire* economy is far-fetched; price-fixing is widespread but surely not universal.[17]

House Interior Committee might retaliate by tabling a major project in the senator's home state—the conversion of the Sleeping Bear Sand Dunes into a national park. At a meeting of Senate and antitrust staff, Hart's personal aides urged him to call off the hearings; Hart then turned to ask Jerry Cohen why the hearings should be held. Cohen said, "The only reason is that, if you don't do it, no one will." Hart said, "Well, that's reason enough for me." The hearings went forward.

But for all his respect, speeches, and courage, for all his moral leadership, Hart ultimately fails as an advocate. The militant speeches are written by his staff and delivered almost apologetically, without vigor or passion. "He talks a great game," said one Washington reporter who has covered the subcommittee, "but what do they have to show for it? . . . . The killer instinct just isn't there." Hart is a very temperate, studious, judicious and mild-mannered man, wary of oversell because he does not want to be considered, in his words, "a common scold."

Hart's self-deprecation is appealing, to be sure, but it also can make it hard to take him seriously. At a packed 1972 press conference on his Industrial Reorganization Act, a reporter asked him a question about nonferrous metals, one of seven industries covered by this bill. Hart paused and then said, "To tell you the truth, I don't know what the hell nonferrous metals are." ("I almost died when he said that," a staff aide said later.) And during a Senate debate on the Lockheed loan, he held forth ably, drawing upon a paper prepared for him by his subcommittee lawyers and economists. Then, to the surprise of his staff, Hart added that he wasn't all that familiar with what he was talking about, but happily he had a very able staff.

Yet there may be a method to his mockery: he is really not too interested in antitrust. Hart seeks out a vast range of areas which are, according to him, "people-oriented"—from pollution to pensions. While many issues tug at his time, "civil rights is the closest to his heart," observes subcommittee editorial director Pat Bario. He has difficulty connecting the arcane world of antitrust with the problems of the American underclass. "The economic concentration hearings drove him nuts," commented a former subcommittee lawyer close to Hart. Not that Hart doesn't believe in antitrust; he does. But his interest and record are due to his position and his staff, not to spontaneous enthusiasm. "He likes everyone and can understand everyone's problems and arguments," said a Senate friend, "which makes him a lousy advocate." "He's a bad advocate, but a perfect judge," said another antitrust lawyer. The effects of Hart's temperament are not limited to antitrust alone. After fifteen years in the Senate, a sort of ennui seems to have settled in. According to one Hart watcher and ally:

> I love him as a human being, and there's no one in the Senate closer to a saint. But he's developed this melancholy about everything. He gets and gives the impression that nothing he does can change anything. He himself has said, "If I knew twenty years ago what I know today, I would have walked in front of a bus then." . . . Also, so many people come to him for so much that he's tired: antitrust, the environment, civil rights. He's batted his head against so many walls for so long that he wonders if it matters anymore.

Consider Senator Hart's approach to the problem of economic concentration. By late 1970, after six years of hearings and volumes, no report had been issued and no legislation had been introduced. Why? Says Howard ("Buck") O'Leary, the present subcommittee staff director, "Hart's temperament is cautious and judicial, and you always carry the burden of persuasion with him . . . . But you turn him off if you yell at him about General Motors." When Ralph Nader sent Senator Hart a letter in 1970 to urge, among other things, that General Motors be broken up,[18] the response was negative.[19]

Chairman Hart did eventually alter his position, proposing his Industrial Reorganization Act a year later. But his cautiousness and disinclination to generic solutions are a paradigm of Hart's approach. All of which may be, in a way, beside the point. One present staffman put it well: "Hart is too good to become a

Proxmire, and Proxmire is too good to become a Hart." Each does well what the other cannot—Hart, the reflective, impartial and universally respected spokesman; Proxmire, the passionate, aggressive, and fact-filled advocate. Neither, in the eyes of this staff person, could possibly change his stylistic stripes.

The Senate as Staff

When it is fully understood that the majority of the subcommittee's members oppose vigorous antitrust policy and that its chairman has other priorities, the *real* antitrust subcommittee begins to become apparent: it is the majority staff—talented, committed, and apolitical.

Both Kefauver and Hart have relied heavily on this staff. The Tennessee populist leaned especially on his brilliant and irascible chief economist, Dr. John Blair, who choreographed the six years of hearings on administered prices for Kefauver and then did the same for Hart's six years of hearings on economic concentration. Blair could not only organize complex, academic hearings—he was himself a noted economist—but was adept at investigative hearings. It was Blair, for example, who deduced from pieces of scattered information that a world quinine cartel probably existed; it was he who sent out subpoenas, which verified his hunch.

Hart, somewhat less conversant than Kefauver with the nuances of antitrust, depends even more on his subcommittee aides. He chose Jerry Cohen as staff director and chief counsel in 1963. Cohen's sense of detail (he is now practicing law in Washington) and literary style (he co-authored the best-selling *America, Inc.*) provided Hart with both a good cross-examiner at hearings and a good speechwriter. He also had Hart's total confidence, presenting *faits accomplis* for Hart's ratification. As one former staff lawyer said admiringly, "Cohen could convince Hart to do anything no matter whose nuts were cut off. Hart would do it and the big people would pour in. . . . He really manipulated Hart well." Wasn't Hart uneasy at this? "No, because he never really got burned."

Buck O'Leary succeeded Cohen—who wanted to try his hand at private practice—in 1969. Because O'Leary desired his own chief economist, he encouraged Blair to leave—which Blair did with some bitter recriminations. O'Leary became, and remains, the unchallenged authority on the subcommittee and the sole conduit between the subcommittee staff and Hart. He increased control over the daily activities of the staff by requiring more reports and clearances. And, reflecting his background as a trial attorney, he became more punctilious than his predecessors about standards of proof in the subcommittee's hearings. "He's going to court [in hearings] in terms of evidence and cross-examination," said a colleague approvingly.

O'Leary, now thirty-four, met Hart when he volunteered to work in the 1964 senatorial race. Immediately after graduation from law school, O'Leary became Hart's campaign chauffeur. A few years as an assistant U.S. attorney followed, until Cohen offered him the post of staff director and chief counsel. Upon meeting Hart, O'Leary said, "You're crazy. I don't know anything about antitrust." To which Hart replied, typically puckish, "Don't worry . . . I don't know anything about it either; let's learn together." Since then, the two have worked well and closely together, in no small measure because of their evident similarities. Like Hart, O'Leary is candid, modest, self-deprecating, slow-paced, slow-talking, slow to anger, and undogmatic. Both have learned antitrust by assignment if not affection; and both are intuitively skeptical of the kind of zealous, Kefauver-like populists who populate the field.

Under O'Leary are five attorneys and two economists, including chief economist David Martin, an insightful institutional analyst from the University of Texas. The minority staff of five professionals consists of four liaisons to minority members who do little antitrust work, and Peter Chumbris, a diligent though not entirely effective counterpoint to the majority-staff view at hearings. "We have so much trouble with the senators—can you imagine our problems with a really tough minority?" a member of the majority staff commented with some relief. In all, there were thirty full-time professional and clerical staff on a $1,491,600 budget in the Ninety-second Congress.[20] While the budget has ballooned from a mere $225,000 in 1956, the increase has gone into higher salaries; the number of staff members has not changed appreciably. At one time under Kefauver, there were as many as forty-four on the staff. But Hart has been steadily reducing the staff by about one per year since 1963 because, says Buck O'Leary, "Hart's embarrassed by the size of the staff." In fact, in his budget-request letter to Senator Eastland of January 22, 1973, Hart carefully and with some pride points out this decline:

> Since 1964, the first full year of my chairmanship, staff has been reduced from 40 to 30 members, a 24 percent reduction. Taking into account pay raises previously voted by Congress, this represents a real savings of $229,998. During 1972, the subcommittee has, with some sacrifice, reduced the staff by two professional positions, at a savings of $52,224.*

What does the staff do? They answer letters (some seven thousand a year), field phone calls (two to three hundred a day, we were told), and spend an estimated "5 to 10 percent of the time consulting or listening to businessmen who either have problems or who seek to make [Senator Hart] aware of positions on issues."[22] (Said one staff representative of this lobbying, "We

---

* But lest Hart think his antitrust staff is still too bloated, editorial director Pat Bario lobbied him to the contrary in a staff memorandum:

"While we grant the subcommittee budget is impressive in size—as is the staff—perhaps a bit of perspective would be helpful.

"The Federal Trade Commission has a staff of 1,200. The Antitrust section of the Department of Justice has a staff of 575. In relationship to the gross national product—which President Nixon not too long ago proudly told us is $1 trillion—our budget is six one-hundred thousandths (.0006) percent. In relationship to other staffs on Capitol Hill, you have approximately 19 on your personal staff, Senator Javits has 28, Senator Scott, 31. And the Commerce Committee—which also has the economy as its jurisdiction—has a total of 44."[21]

listen, but that's all.") But much of their time goes into hearings (at least 40 percent, according to Pat Bario) and commentary on pending legislation. Chief counsel O'Leary is especially proud of the way his staff will comment on scores of non-antitrust-committee bills—an estimated thirty to forty in 1973.

But handicaps beset the staff. Foremost is the complaint of lack of access to Hart. The staff understands that this is due to Hart's extraordinarily busy schedule and to his detached manner. Second, the subcommittee's senators, alternatively apathetic and antagonistic, do not inspire much creative work at the staff level. On the Industrial Reorganization Act, for example, some of the staff argued for the most radical bill possible. The idea was to at least articulate the issues sharply, since there seemed no hope of passage; under O'Leary's influence, however, a more moderate bill was proposed. Third, the difficulty in issuing a successful subpoena dampens vigorous probes. The subpoenas issued are usually requested by witnesses for their own protection, and are not demands for data from the country's largest corporations. Fourth, ranking minority Senator Roman L. Hruska, as a matter of policy, regularly objects to staff reports, and Hart accedes. Hruska fears that such reports, not signed by senators, are attributed to a panel's senators anyway and give the staff too much uncontrolled power. Fifth, many of the staff are frustrated at their fireman's role, frequently working on *ad hoc* emergency projects to the detriment of long-range substantive work. While Hart has been paring down the staff, they feel overworked.

Finally, there are the conflicts between Hart's personal staff, politically interested in his continued survival in Michigan, and Hart's subcommittee staff, ideologically interested in promoting antitrust everywhere. The two goals are not always compatible. According to one subcommittee lawyer:

> The state guys have to explain things back home. From their perspective, all we give them is grief. For example, if some constituent wants some favor done, the personal staff

says, "Sure, okay," but the antitrust staff, if it's an anti-consumer issue, will kill a bad idea. Like, when the Michigan broadcasters wanted Hart to support Pastore's bill guaranteeing the permanence of their licenses, we said "No" from the antitrust standpoint and sent them a mean letter. The personal staff thought we were crazy to tell the big Michigan broadcasters to shove off.

In another conflict, Senator Hart's personal staff favored the attempt by Michigan Consolidated Gas Co. to secure exemption from the 1935 Public Utility Holding Company Act in order to build low-income housing in Detroit. What mattered to them was not who built these units but that they were built. Hart agreed and submitted a bill to this effect in 1970. The antitrust staff found this out and wrote Hart a stinging letter in opposition, supporting the principle of the 1935 act to keep such giant utilities from moving into other fields. Hart agonized over the conflict, and then split the difference: he resubmitted the bill in 1971 but with a series of amendments to ensure against antitrust problems.

The Legislative Record: 1963–1974

As Senator Hart said in an interview, "You could do a lot of things, if you had the votes." He doesn't. Reviewing his antitrust subcommittee's legislative record in the last ten years, it is easy to understand Hart's lament and why one subcommittee staffer called the record "a disgrace." The only bills reported out of the subcommittee in the past decade have been an amendment to the Expediting Act; an increase in criminal fines; reform of the consent-decree process; and antitrust exemptions for the bank, newspaper, and soft-drink-bottling industries. Six bills in ten years —and three of them *reduced* the reach of antitrust enforcement.

It was no great loss to the antitrust movement when the first two proposals approved by the subcommittee failed, in their initial efforts, to become law. The 1903 Expediting Act permitted antitrust cases to be appealed directly from district courts to the Supreme Court. Because of a supposed Supreme Court case overload (although in the last forty years it handled an average of only 3.56 antitrust cases a year, 30 percent of which were disposed of *per curiam*, i.e., by an abbreviated procedure), a proposal sought to have these cases go first to the Court of Appeals. This would have significantly delayed already drawn-out cases, would have opened an intentionally vague and malleable Sherman Act to eleven varying jurisdictions, and would have kept many cases from their most historically congenial forum.[23] A bill to do just this passed both chambers, but died in conference committee in 1970. Conferee Emanuel Celler refused to accept the Senate's version because it failed to allow the attorney general to certify the most timely and important cases from the district court to the Supreme Court.

A well-meaning reform to increase the maximum Sherman Act fine for a corporation from $50,000 to $500,000 was considered. Such fines, however, simply do not deter trust-builders. Judges very rarely impose the maxmium, and even a $500,000 top fine would be worth the cost of the violation to many big firms.[24] But even this mild increase in sanctions proved too much for the Judiciary Committee. Although Senator Hruska originally cosponsored the bill in the antitrust subcommittee, he successfully opposed it in the full committee. In the intervening time, contended Hruska, the 1969 Tax Reform Act prohibited the deductibility of two-thirds of a treble damage payment if it followed a successful government prosecution. This was assumed to be sanction enough, despite the fact that there has hardly been a single case obtaining full treble damages since the early 1960s (although some cases have recouped single damages).

Shortly after the 1972 Kleindienst-ITT hearings, Senator John Tunney, a relative newcomer to the subcommittee, introduced a bill to reform antitrust consent decrees.* Tunney energetically

---

* The consent decree—a device that resolves more than 80 percent of all government antitrust civil cases—requires that a defendant promise never to do again what the government alleges, although most defendants claim they never did anything wrong in the first place! It is a process whose frequency is matched by a secrecy and invisibility that raise suspicions about political influence on enforcement decisions.

promoted his proposal, which, to make consent decrees less secret, (a) required the Justice Department to offer "a public impact" statement explaining every proposed consent decree; (b) encouraged intervention in court by critics of a consent decree; and (c) required antitrust defendants to log all contacts with any government agency concerning their antitrust cases. The bill, formally cosponsored by Senator Edward Gurney, also included the Expediting Act amendments and increases in criminal fines.

In the summer of 1973, in what may be the most stunning legislative *volte-face* of the decade, the Senate Antitrust and Monopoly Subcommittee *and* the Senate Judiciary Committee *and* the Senate all *unanimously* passed this measure—despite the fact that the Justice Department opposed most of the consent-decree reforms. What is unclear, however, is whether this alignment is an augury or merely a unique congressional backlash to ITT's arrogance and the Watergate revelations.

Two exemptions to the antitrust laws were approved by the subcommittee and became law during the last decade. The first was the Bank Merger Act of 1966. In 1963 the Supreme Court shocked the banking and regulatory community in its *Philadelphia Bank* decision by holding that bank mergers approved by federal banking agencies were not immune from antitrust prosecution.[25] Whatever the benefits to the community, the Court reasoned, Section 7 of the 1950 act proscribed all anticompetitive mergers. This case, plus the then-pending suit against the Manufacturers-Hanover merger and "the prospect of splitting that $6 billion institution in two . . . led to the passage of the Bank Merger Act of 1966."* [26] Kenneth Elzinga, recently the resident economist at the Antitrust Division of the Department of Justice, criticized the political maneuverings behind this exemption:

---

* In the legislative history, Congress "forgave" bank mergers (other than those "attempting to monopolize") consummated prior to June 17, 1963, the date of the *Philadelphia Bank* decision. The act permitted the regulatory agencies to condone mergers which might lessen competition *if* "the anticompetive effects . . . are clearly outweighed . . . [by] meeting the convenience and needs of the community to be served."

This bill was in direct response to antimerger activity directed against banking—and specifically nullified three court divestiture orders! Even those who have resigned themselves to the role of strong lobbies and powerful special interest groups in a democracy cannot help but be somewhat disturbed by the determined and successful efforts of the banking interests to ram this bill through Congress.[27]

The second exemption to become law involved the newspaper industry. In 1967 and 1968 the Antitrust and Monopoly Subcommittee held forty days of hearings and produced seven volumes on Senator Carl Hayden's (D., Ariz.) Failing Newspaper Act, S.1312.[28] The act provides for an antitrust exemption for joint operating ventures of competing newspapers where one is "failing," overruling the Supreme Court's seven-to-one decision in a 1969 case (the *Tucson* decision), which found that such pooling arrangements violated the Sherman Act. The subcommittee used its hearing to document the kind of anticompetitive conduct that should have warranted prosecution, not exemption. They uncovered unreasonable territorial exclusives for syndicated material, price discrimination in the sale of newsprint, obstructions to obtaining newswire service, cross-subsidization from other media, predatory practices to injure competitors, and an increase in concentration of media ownership.

Was it really necessary for major metropolitan dailies in twenty-two cities to fix prices in order to avoid bankruptcy? The public record cannot answer that question because the publishers gave profit-and-loss figures to Senator Hart's antitrust subcommittee only on the basis of a promise of secrecy; they claimed that disclosure might compromise them in negotiating with future competitors and labor unions and in defending future antitrust suits. The publishers were requesting an exemption based on financial need but refused to document that need publicly. Former Representative Abner Mikva, who, as a member of the House Judiciary Committee, did see the confidential financial data, said that it "shows more black figures than red."[29]

In 1969 the Newspaper Preservation Act easily sailed through all committees and chambers to become law. The passage of this "poverty program for the rich," as Senator Hart called it, was achieved by vigorous lobbying. Led by the American Newspaper Publishers Association (ANPA) on the outside and by Senator Dirksen on the inside, Congress learned firsthand the intimate relationship between politics and publishing. Legislators wanted to "collect IOUs," according to Mikva, to exchange for future endorsements from local publishers. Representative Clarence J. Brown, Jr., of Ohio, among others, complained that he had received considerable pressure from "reporters acting on behalf of their chains."

This political action generally succeeded. The *National Journal* studied the votes of congressmen and senators from districts and states with joint agreements. Of thirty-eight such senators, only two voted against the bill: Gaylord Nelson of Wisconsin and Robert Byrd of West Virginia. Of the twenty-seven congressmen voting from districts with joint ventures, *all* voted in favor of the bill.

The subcommittee's sixth bill of the decade, another one that weakens enforcement of antitrust, is the so-called bottlers' bill, reported out of subcommittee unanimously (Hart, Ervin, Hruska, Thurmond, and Gurney voting). The measure, passed by the Senate in 1973, aims to permit territorial restrictions in the soft-drink industry where the trademarked product is in "substantial and effective" competition with other soda bottlers.

Exclusive territorial arrangements restrict sellers of certain products to a geographically limited area. This reduction of *intra*brand competition (Seven-Up bottler vs. Seven-Up bottler, for example), artificially boosts the price to consumers of the trademarked product. The Federal Trade Commission (FTC) estimates an overcharge of $250 million annually in the $5 billion soft-drink market alone.

The "bottlers' bill" was formulated in response to an FTC case in July 1971 that attacked this system of territorial restrictions. Lobbyists for the National Soft Drink Association swarmed over

Capitol Hill seeking relief. "It was a tremendous lobbying job; the best I've ever seen," said a subcommittee staff lawyer. "They saw *every* congressman and senator. And they had a hell of a big kitty. The National Association assessed all its members on the number of bottles they produced."

Proponents of the bill argued that territorial exclusives were needed to protect small bottlers from their bigger competitors. In fact, the major beneficiaries of this proposal would be the larger multiplant bottlers who were the targets of the FTC action. The percentage of industry sales controlled by large multiplant bottlers has steadily increased from 43.3 percent in 1958, to 50.9 percent in 1963, to 62.5 percent in 1967.[30] To cite two examples: in an area in which 41 million Americans live, Pepsi-Cola brands are bottled exclusively by Pepsico; Westinghouse (a conglomerate) has exclusives for Seven-Up bottling in areas with a total population of 32 million people. Without such territorial restrictions, food retailers and wholesalers could shop among many bottlers to find the lowest price. With them, there is only one source for any brand—which is why courts have considered similar territorial restrictions as palpably anticompetitive.*

But the Senate and its antitrust subcommittee have treated S.978 with affection. The lobbyists' success has been impressive even for antitrust annals: by 1973, various versions of bottlers' bills had forty-one Senate cosponsors and nearly half the House. Even so, the bill's sponsors and the industry are not taking any chances. Although the Antitrust Subcommittee considered the bill in the Senate, it will be handled in the House by the Interstate and Foreign Commerce Committee—a forum considered more favorable to antitrust exemptions than the House antitrust subcommittee. This is a switch that, though not unprecedented,

---

* According to United States v. Arnold, Schwinn & Co., 388 U.S. 365, 379 (1967): "Under the Sherman Act it is unreasonable for a manufacturer to seek to restrict and confine areas or persons with whom an article may be traded after the manufacturer has parted with dominion over it. . . . Such restraints are so obviously destructive of competition that their mere existence is enough."

is rare. At the same time, the bottlers continue their energetic, if not overzealous, politicking.*

In the Ninety-third Congress, the antitrust subcommittee has pending one of the most important antitrust proposals of the past two decades. S.3832, the Industrial Reorganization Act (or IRA in subcommittee parlance), is the long-awaited dividend from Senator Hart's economic-concentration hearings. The bill would create an Industrial Reorganization Commission to study seven major industries over a fifteen-year period and determine whether they illegally possess monopoly power as defined by the act. The industries are chemicals and drugs; electrical machinery and equipment; electronic computing and communication equipment; energy; iron and steel; motor vehicles; and nonferrous metals. S.3832 establishes a rebuttable presumption of monopoly power if (a) corporate profits exceed 15 percent for five consecutive years of the most recent seven years; (b) there is no substantial price competition in a line of commerce for three consecutive years out of the most recent five; or (c) four or fewer firms account for 50 percent or more of sales. Firms so charged could defend themselves by proving that their monopoly power was based on valid patents or legitimate economies of scale. Because the bill could restructure a considerable segment of our corporate economy, industry is wildly hostile to the idea, although subcommittee staff have succeeded in getting conservatives like Federal Reserve Chairman Arthur Burns and economist Pierre Rinfret to say some favorable things about it. Still, prospects for its passage are slim. What chance does Buck O'Leary think it has? "We're so far from winning it's hard to evaluate." Pat Bario speculated that "it will be a minimum of four years before we even take it to a vote in committee"—and Jerry Cohen called even this estimate "optimistic."[33]

---

* Part of the bill's hearing record is entitled "Materials Relating to Allegations of Intimidation of Federal Witnesses."[31] This section discusses the way big bottlers threatened small ones who had opposed the various bills, such as the bottlers "who came forward to say they didn't want protection—only the chance to compete."[32]

While its own record of affirmative legislation is, to be charitable, unimpressive, the antitrust subcommittee majority staff has nevertheless achieved some substantial successes. First, there are the bills that didn't become law in part because the subcommittee staff mobilized support and expertise against them. Most of these proposals were considered by other subcommittees although they had some antitrust components. They include the "Scott Amendments" to legitimize a variety of illegal patent practices (see next chapter); a proposal by Senator Robert P. Griffin (R., Mich.) to permit auto manufacturers to collaborate on antipollution research and development despite an Antitrust Division consent decree forbidding such a combination; a measure sponsored by Senator Warren G. Magnuson (D., Wash.) to overrule three Supreme Court decisions and permit the El Paso Natural Gas Company to retain its acquisition of the Pacific Northwest Pipeline Corporation; and Senator Daniel K. Inouye's (D., Ha.) Export Expansion Act of 1971, which would have encouraged export cartels unless they would "materially lessen competition within the United States" (as decided by the Commerce Department). When there are so many pressures to whittle the antitrust laws down to a sliver, these negative successes are not insignificant.

The second group of legislative achievements are those bills that are planted by the antitrust subcommittee but germinate elsewhere. Chairman Hart and the subcommittee staff at times will develop an idea and perhaps hold hearings on it, but then draft a bill in such language that the Parliamentarian (who decides such matters) will channel it to a more sympathetic committee. When Senator Kefauver let Hart chair hearings into packaging and labeling problems in 1961 and 1962, the eventual result was the passage, through the more hospitable Senate Commerce Committee, of the truth-in-packaging law of 1966. The no-fault automobile insurance bill, which was passed by the Senate in the Ninety-third Congress, also came from the antitrust subcommittee. Finally, under the supervision of former staff counsel Donald Randall, the antitrust subcommittee held sixteen days of hearings and generated over four thousand pages of transcripts on the automotive repair industry. The record culminated in the "Motor Vehicle Information and Cost Savings Act of 1972," which among other provisions encouraged the federal government to establish diagnostic testing centers for auto repairs and delegated to the Department of Transportation authority to require more crash-worthy car bumpers. This bill was also sent to the Commerce Committee and was one of the only consumer bills to become law in the Ninety-second Congress.

Hearings: Blaring the Trumpet

The subcommittee's educational record is as broad as its legislative achievements are narrow, fulfilling Woodrow Wilson's adage that "the informing function of Congress should be preferred even to its legislative function." "Those guys can stop us from getting legislation," said a staff member about the subcommittee's senators, "but they can't stop us from holding hearings."[34] The consequence has been described as a "publishing house of some dimension."[35] Since 1955, there have been some 1,400 days of hearings, producing about 200 volumes and more than 100,000 printed pages.* Although there has been something of a drop in hearings recently (1965–1968 saw a yearly average of 51 hearing days, while in 1969–1972 there was a yearly average of 36 days), the subcommittee's compiled hearings provide the best assessment of our industrial economy since the Temporary National Economic Committee (TNEC) hearings of the late thirties.

Introducing the economic-concentration hearings in 1964, Chairman Hart said:

---

* Hearings also inspired, or form the basis of, a series of popular books on antitrust and related subjects: Kefauver's *In a Few Hands: Monopoly in America* (Pantheon, 1965); Richard Barber's *The American Corporation* (Dutton, 1970); Morton Mintz's and Jerry Cohen's *America, Inc.* (Dial, 1971); John Blair's *Economic Concentration* (Harcourt Brace Jovanovich, 1972); and Don Randall's and Arthur Glickman's *The Great American Auto Repair Robbery* (Charterhouse, 1972).

> In July 1964, the subcommittee began a broad scale in-
> quiry into the concentration of economic power. . . . The
> subcommittee had focused its attention on *effects* of con-
> centration in its administered price hearings. In contrast,
> this new inquiry is concerned with underlying *structural*
> aspects—the level, trend and causes of concentration.[36]

Six years, 11 volumes, and 4,400 pages later, the subcommittee
had exposed the extent of market and aggregate concentration,
the negative correlation between bigness and innovation, the
secrecy of conglomerates, and the pattern of new technologies
permitting *smaller* scale (not larger) production. In other
words, as Morton Mintz and Jerry Cohen later described it in
America, Inc., "a gigantic industrial and financial complex functioning much like a sovereign government."[37]

These hearings built a necessary foundation for Hart's deconcentration proposal, but they dealt with the complex esoterica
of microeconomics, which is not exactly Hart's bent. Other hearings, while lacking the ultimate importance of the economic-
concentration hearings, raised antitrust issues in more specific
contexts and in ways more meaningful to consumers:

• Hearings in 1964, inspired by Jessica Mitford's *The American Way of Death*, exposed the practices of the funeral industry[38] (although no legislation resulted). "Hart was a tiger on that
one," said Jerry Cohen, recalling that this was an issue where the
victim was apparent and the bilk understandable. "This involved
taking advantage of people at the time of death." The committee
chairman learned that while deaths were up 18 percent between
1936 and 1962, the amount spent for funerals rose 224.7 percent. Price did not seem pegged to cost. "In one funeral home,
for example, if a casket costs $52.50, the funeral charge is $298; if
a casket costs $95.50, the funeral charge is $715; and if the casket
costs $388, the funeral charge is $1590."[39] In 1963, Americans
spent $1.8 billion for funerals, or an average $988 for each one,
according to the Department of Commerce. There are two reasons for this extravagant cost: one is the determination of the

National Funeral Directors Association, the industry's trade association, that price advertising and "prearrangement" plans are unethical. The other is that bereaved consumers are especially vulnerable to unfair practices, and uninterested in price shopping. Senators Dirksen and Hruska angrily dissented from this analysis, castigating it as a "theoretical, preconceived, and biased economic and legal philosophy of the funeral profession as developed by the subcommittee staff."[40] This drew a testy riposte from Hart, who repeated his charges against what he called the "high cost of dying."

• In 1966, the subcommittee looked into the "alleged price-fixing of library books,"[41] revealing the collusion between publishers of the library editions of children's books and book wholesalers to fix the prices charged to schools, libraries, and government agencies. "When procurement officials ask for bids to get a competitive price," said Hart at the start of the hearings, "the prices are not competitive but identical."[42] As a result, prices paid for these purchases ballooned one-third to one-half above normal. These hearings provoked the Antitrust Division to file complaints (which resulted in consent decrees) against eighteen book publishers, which accounted for some 40 percent of the children's textbook market.

• A 1967 investigation into the worldwide prices of quinine and quinidine, which are used by an estimated quarter of a million people in this country alone to maintain normal heart rhythm, exposed the workings of an international cartel.[43] A tip by an industry insider, as well as well-placed subpoenas, produced the minutes of seventeen secret meetings held by the conspirators in 1959 to 1962. According to John Blair in the subcommittee's report, the cartelists "entered in a series of restrictive agreements designed to control prices, distribution, and production in every aspect of the quinine industry." A key objective was "the elimination of competition among the various producers in securing the U.S. stockpile." The cartel successfully raised retail prices for quinidine 300 to 600 percent in 1964–1965. "I cannot continue to pay these high prices," complained an elderly citizen to the

Hart panel, "yet my doctor tells me I cannot live without it." The subcommittee's hearings led to antitrust action by the Common Market, which resulted in a fine to the conspirators of more than a million dollars and a still pending Justice Department prosecution.

• In 1969–1970 the subcommittee investigated the petroleum industry. Hart's opening remarks were characteristically understated:

> These hearings have been prompted by suggestions that various forms of governmental intervention in the market mechanisms of the petroleum industry have had the effect of impairing the ability of a variety of industries, trades, and regions to compete effectively. . . .[44]

But he then proceeded to chair eighteen days of hearings into the way the government underwrote the oil industry's domestic cartel: oil import quotas (which Hart said cost consumers between $30 and 50 billion during the 1960s); "market-demand prorationing" by Texas and Louisiana (whose purpose was to "preserve the high price of domestic oil by restricting supply"); the oil-depletion allowance; the tax treatment of foreign royalties; and Department of Interior leases of oil and gas lands on our outer continental shelf. This prescient inquiry predated by four years an "energy crisis" which would lead later Senate and House committees over similar ground.

Auditing the Agencies

In inspiring the Antitrust Division of the Justice Department and the Federal Trade Commission to file important cases they would otherwise ignore, the subcommittee has had some successes: the electrical cases, library-book cases, quinine case, and, according to the staff, even the conglomerate cases of 1969. But the subcommittee has conspicuously failed to audit the work of the Justice Department and regulatory agencies failed to push and prod them to better performance by exercising vigorous oversight. One former staff lawyer gave what he considered the prevailing view: "Hart just doesn't like to review the agencies. He hates telling them, 'Why didn't you do x, y, or z?' He is more prone to say, 'Well, you made a judgment and it was an honest judgment.' " Buck O'Leary confirms this view. "The boss assumes that the Antitrust Division is better equipped to make the decision. So you really have to carry a hard burden of proof in this area. We do very little auditing of this type, although maybe we should." In an interview, Hart confirmed that he didn't want to "second-guess" law enforcers.

In 1971, Ralph Nader suggested that Hart (and Emanuel Celler in the House) begin a full-fledged inquiry into the Antitrust Division of the Justice Department.[45] Hart brushed aside the suggestion. "Every once in a while, as I'm sure you know, someone suggests oversight hearings on why the Department of Justice did or did not act in an area. In the past, I have resisted these hearings simply because, while I know they made good headline fodder, I'm not convinced they put dents into economic problems."[46] Nader's reply articulated the need for such oversight hearings:

> At present the Antitrust Division is unaccountable, enforcing the laws—or not—largely free from public or Congressional scrutiny. The only time the Division has to answer for its performance is in executive session before the House Appropriations Subcommittee. And those hearings, even when published, make no effort to study the substance and impact of enforcement, doting instead on the number of cases brought and the amounts of fines collected. Any oversight effort by your Subcommittee, therefore, would have invaluable incremental benefit. The . . . failure to perform this mission is most deplorable.

This is not to say that the Antitrust and Monopoly Subcommittee will never nudge an agency. If it accomplished nothing else, the ITT affair of 1972 demolished the view that the antitrust agencies could arrogate all wisdom unto themselves. In the last few years, Hart and the majority staff have, among other efforts: campaigned against a 1964 Internal Revenue Service ruling which permitted treble damage payments to be deductible as "ordinary and necessary" business expenses; asked Transportation Secretary Alan Boyd in 1967 to obtain data from the auto manufacturers justifying increased prices for added safety equipment; protested President Nixon's cutbacks of Pacific airline routes which had the effect of eliminating "pressures which might lower prices and improve service"; persuaded the FTC in 1970 to determine whether the gasoline industry was violating the antitrust laws (which provoked that agency into issuing subpoenas in mid-1973 to the major oil firms); and wrote Federal Power Commission (FPC) chairman John Nassikas to protest his proposed natural-gas price hikes, urging an FTC study to determine whether there truly was a gas shortage. (When the FTC reported in 1973 that the natural gas industry was apparently underreporting reserves, at the same time that some Federal Power Commission staff had attempted to destroy some reserves data, the Antitrust and Monopoly Subcommittee actually *subpoenaed* the FPC to produce its data on reserves. It was a bold and unprecedented challenge, and the FPC reluctantly acquiesced.)

But the subcommittee's potential to monitor and stimulate the agencies on antitrust—agencies that are quick to respond to senatorial inquiries, not to mention inquiries from the chairman of the Senate Antitrust and Monopoly Subcommittee—still far exceeds its accomplishments. Antitrust Division officials, among others, understand this, and have expressed relief that they don't have to worry too much about Hart's critical gaze. For example:

• Reporter James Ridgeway complained in a 1967 *New Republic* article (entitled "Antitrust Doldrums") that Hart could have done battle against the FCC's casual acceptance of the proposed ITT-ABC merger, but didn't.[47]

• When Attorney General John Mitchell rejected his Antitrust Division's recommendation in mid-August 1971 to file an antimerger case against two steel giants, a consolidation with demonstrable anticompetitive effects, the response was hesitation, caution, and no critical letter to the Justice Department. (Celler later sent one.)

• When the International Business Machines antimonopoly case was four years old (and after IBM had participated in the shredding of key records), some of the committee staff encouraged Hart to make a public statement about the case. He initially refused, waiting on further developments. Later, after a district court judge chastised IBM for its role in the document destruction, Hart finally did go public. In an interview in the *Washington Post*, he made the important point that, if the result of a search for the subjective "intent" or "attempt" to monopolize was a dinosaur of a case like IBM, then a simplification of the Sherman Act was needed—for instance, his Industrial Reorganization Act, with its objective rather than subjective criteria.[48]

This general aversion to oversight is due in part to staff time devoted to studying seven major industries in connection with their deconcentration bill, and in part to a staff too small for the problems it could confront, a limitation self-inflicted by the chairman. In large measure, however, the subcommittee's inattention here is one of disinclination to tangle, an unwillingness to confront those who are simply not doing their job. It is easier to crank out hearings which, while impressive and valuable, perhaps make a less valuable contribution to antitrust policy than would an activist effort aimed at the agencies.

Finding (or Creating) a Constituency

It is on the issue of constituency-creation that Hart is most sensitive, and most involved. "The only time you get action on antitrust," he said ruefully in an interview, "is if—pray God we avoid it —there is economic collapse." Nevertheless, throughout the past decade, he has, in his diligent but detached way, attempted to proselytize the Senate and the public on the importance of antitrust issues. But it is difficult to arouse his colleagues. As former staff economist Richard Barber has written, "Hardly a member of the House or Senate can today be found who is seriously concerned on more than a fleeting basis with issues of antitrust."[49]

Even the members of his subcommittee tend to be either vastly uninterested in this assignment or implacably opposed to antitrust improvements through new laws. At hearings only Senators Hart and Hruska are usually in attendance. (Senator Thurmond came once, but left approximately thirty seconds later to take a phone call—and never returned.) Yet it is precisely this group of the uninterested and hostile who must be converted for the antitrust subcommittee—and antitrust enforcement—to prove successful. As one subcommittee staffer emphasized, "If you can't sell Senator Hruska on this, and all those who believe in 'free enterprise,' you just won't be successful. Hell, the socialists are against you, so it's very important to win over the conservatives." Until then, antitrust remains relegated, in the words of the late historian Richard Hofstadter, to "one of the faded passions of American reforms." The Senate subcommittee has not yet been able to rekindle that passion.

THE HOUSE ANTITRUST SUBCOMMITTEE:
THE CELLER PRESERVE

Emanuel Celler's name was synonymous with antitrust activity in the House for twenty-three years, and for good reason. He became chairman of the House Judiciary Committee in 1949, and on July 11 of that year, with H. Res. 137, created Subcommittee No. 5. While its jurisdiction came to include such matters as civil rights, the federal judicial system, and various criminal matters, its original design and ultimate concern were antitrust and monopoly. The members of Subcommittee No. 5 in the Ninety-second Congress were: Celler, Jack Brooks, William Hungate, Andrew Jacobs, Abner Mikva, and James Abourezk, Democrats; and William McCulloch, Richard Poff, Edward Hutchinson, and Robert McClory, Republicans.*

---

* The Subcommittee on Monopolies and Commercial Law took over jurisdiction on antitrust in the limited reforms of the House Judiciary Committee in the Ninety-third Congress (see p. 103 and Chapter 16). Its members were Rodino, Brooks, Walter Flowers, John Seiberling, Barbara Jordan, and Edward Mezvinsky, Democrats; and Hutchinson, McClory, Charles Sandman, and David Dennis, Republicans.

Strategies and Goals

At first it was called the Subcommittee on the Study of Monopoly Practices. Bess Dick was staff director (she stayed for all twenty-three years), and the budget was some $48,000 in its first year of operation. The subcommittee got off to an energetic start, as frequent confidential meetings were held from 1949 to 1950 to map out program and strategy. Issues to be taken up, according to an August 1, 1949, subcommittee memorandum, included advertising, government procurement, antitrust penalties, investment bankers, patents and antitrust, monopoly in communications, and "divorcement, divestiture and dissolution."[50]

An internal staff memorandum of August 23, 1949, described a ground-breaking parley at the Mayflower Hotel between, among others, Representative Celler, Senator Kefauver, economists Corwin Edwards and John Blair, and Antitrust Division lawyer John Steadman. The subject was deconcentration and divestiture proposals, and the memorandum describing the talks, like the earlier ones, read like a primer and forecaster of issues that would dominate the next twenty years of antitrust:

> Mr. Steadman said that because of the uncertainty of the data on size and efficiency . . . you cannot prove a loss of efficiency on the part of a big corporation and must, therefore, resort to a political theory that the corporation must be broken up because of its effect in tending toward socialism.
>
> Dr. Blair disagreed with Mr. Steadman, and emphasized that we must be practical because the chairman must sell a program to other chairmen, to which Mr. Celler agreed. Dr. Edwards said he thought it would be a good idea to cast upon corporations charged with monopolistic abuses the burden of proof that they are efficient though big.
>
> Mr. Celler said that while he valued political freedom above economic efficiency, he has to bear in mind that he must be political and not extreme in order to sell the program to committee members.

The subcommittee launched a series of hearings into monopoly power in 1950. The *New York Times*, with much excitement and some exaggeration, called it "the greatest full-dress inquiry [into monopoly] since the days of the Temporary National Economic Committee hearings held in the nineteen thirties."[51] The earliest hearings spotlighted the steel industry, as Celler fulminated about U.S. Steel's dominance of the market and its inefficiencies. And more:

> Nor has the United States Steel Corp. been content to rule tranquilly over the entire steel industry. It has embarked upon invasions into such various alien fields as international steamship lines, cement, sulfate of ammonia, zinc mining, production of natural gas, and prefabricated houses. . . .
> I am questioning whether this untold power should rest in the hands of a small coterie of men, no matter how able. And I am suggesting finally that the centralization of private economic power, like the centralization of political power, results in inefficiency, red tape, bureaucracy, and waste.[52]

This was good antitrust and good public relations, generating the kind of initial publicity Celler needed to launch his new subcommittee. Of course, such rough-and-tumble trust-busting did not satisfy everyone. But at least it made the right enemies. Thus the *Wall Street Journal* protested all this activity:

> If "Manny" Celler has his way—and he frequently does, with somewhat arrogant control over his committee—his group won't be content merely to study; it will recommend legislation and try to get it passed by Congress. . . . Mr. Celler favors a law against "too bigness," though he's not sure just how the term might be defined, how the law should be phrased, or when it might be passed. But he's patient.[53]

Following his steel study were probes into newspaper print, aluminum, and interlocking directorates. Nor were there only hearings. Chairman Celler appeared frequently on radio and before audiences spreading the antitrust gospel. He wrote letters

TABLE 5.

Antitrust Bills in the House of Representatives, 1949–72

Number of Bills

Congress	In sub-committee	Introduced by Celler	Reported out of sub-committee	Days of hearings	Public Laws
92nd	24	5	0	6	0
91st	23	6	2	4	1
90th	26	4	1	5	1
89th	31	4	1	0	1
88th	27	5	0	0	0
87th	36	12	2	18	1
86th	36	9	1	9	1
85th	42	8	1	32	0
84th	43	13	2	19	3
83rd	20	3	1	3	0
82nd	24	4	2	15	0
81st	26	3	4	7	0

SOURCE: Compiled from the *Legislative Calendars*, House Judiciary Committee, 1949–72. When the same bill was introduced more than once, it was counted as one bill.

to allies and opponents promoting antitrust enforcement,* and he began proposing legislation to promote economic competition. As Table 5 indicates, the subcommittee's first five legislative years were relatively unproductive: House members overall, and

---

* In 1954 he complained to the then attorney general, Herbert Brownell, that the Justice Department had filed only one antimerger case in four years under the Celler-Kefauver Act. Also in 1954 he wrote Senator Estes Kefauver a letter typical of the Celler style:

If our party wins, and I sniff victory in the air, I shall resume chairmanship of the House Judiciary Committee and you will be near the chair on your side. It will give me great comfort to work again with you against economic concentration. . . .

I have some misgivings about the forthcoming recommendations of the Oppenheim Committee. I think it will recommend weakening our antitrust laws. We must be watchful. Any bill having such an effect will earn my opposition and as House Chairman I shall hold my "fanny" firm and tight upon it.

Celler particularly, introduced little legislation; no bills became law. But educational groundwork was laid for accelerated activity from 1955 through 1962.

The Driving Years

The years 1955 to 1962 overlap with the presence of Kenneth Harkins and Herbert Maletz, two very able staff lawyers who catalyzed well with Chairman Celler. The overall number of antitrust bills introduced, and the number introduced by the chairman, substantially increased. Five bills became law, all introduced by Celler: bills to increase the maximum Sherman Act fine from $5,000 to $50,000; to amend the Clayton Act, enabling the United States to recover damages for itself under the antitrust laws; to make "final" the FTC's cease-and-desist orders; to give auto dealers more rights *vis à vis* their auto manufacturers; and to permit the Justice Department to subpoena documentary evidence (by "civil investigative demands") from firms under investigation. Celler sought to establish standards for the organization and operation of government advisory boards; also, like Kefauver, Celler wanted large firms that planned to merge to notify the FTC beforehand. And he tried to bring bank mergers clearly within the ambit of the Clayton Act. The last two measures both passed the House but not the Senate—although the Supreme Court's 1963 *Philadelphia Bank* decision[54] did what Chairman Celler's bank bill was never permitted to do.

Perhaps more significant than the legislative record of these years were the hearings held by Subcommittee No. 5. For example, beyond hearings on proposed legislation, 1955–1956 saw seventeen days of hearings into antitrust enforcement procedures, hearings that were critical of the agencies' antimerger record;[55] fifteen days on conflicts of interest within industrial advisory groups;[56] and thirty-one days into the anticompetitive habits of the regulatory agencies, especially the Civil Aeronautics Board (CAB).[57]

From 1957 to 1959 the subcommittee conducted its now-famous

investigation into Justice Department consent decrees. Its May 26, 1959, report, based on 4,500 pages of hearings and thirty-four witnesses,[58] found the following:

• The consent decree procedure at Justice was seriously deficient; the report therefore recommended more public notice and participation, a statement accompanying and explaining the consent decree, and a waiting period between the proposal of a decree and its acceptance by a court (the latter was done by Justice Department regulation in 1961).

• The 1941 consent decree in the mammoth *Atlantic Refining* case abandoned all of the original antitrust goals of divorcement and compensation, and what little it required was continually ignored by the oil industry, with the Justice Department's supine acquiescence.

• The 1956 American Telephone and Telegraph (AT&T)– Western Electric consent decree was "devoid of merit, ineffective" and a blot on the enforcement history of the antitrust laws. The original complaint had sought to divest Western Electric from AT&T, but the decree inexplicably permitted the two to remain consolidated. The subcommittee uncovered a series of secret hotel meetings between Attorney General Brownell, Justice Department lawyers, and AT&T lawyers—a situation it sharply denounced.

The Dry Decade

The subcommittee's vigor and impact, however, have ebbed considerably in the last decade. The number of bills proposed by the House and by Celler dropped; the number of legislative hearings fell precipitously; and only four bills were reported out of the subcommittee between 1962 and 1972. For although Celler did chair both the committee and the subcommittee, and exercised a control Phil Hart only dreams about, he confronted an institutional indifference in the House; when combined with his own increasingly lagging efforts, this tandem produced little legislation. In fact, only three of the subcommittee's bills became law

—and *all* were antitrust exemptions.* It was this record that Celler later called, with more bravado than accuracy, a "plethora of legislation."[59]

The frequent and hard-hitting hearings of the 1950s were gone. As evidence, one need only glance at the listings in the subcommittee's published index. For the Eighty-fourth through Eighty-seventh Congresses (1955–1962), there were an average of fourteen hearings or reports per Congress; for the Eighty-eighth through Ninety-first Congress (1963–1970), the average was five. Between 1963 and 1968, while the Senate Antitrust Subcommittee held 237 days of hearings, the House Antitrust Subcommittee held eleven.[60]

Timidity, or worse, characterized some of their efforts. In 1963, both the Justice Department and House antitrust subcommittee investigators uncovered compelling evidence of a criminal conspiracy between the Hearst and Chandler newspapers in Los Angeles.[61] The alleged conspiracy involved a division of the newspaper market to permit Hearst's *Herald-Examiner* to monopolize the afternoon market and Chandler's *Los Angeles Times* the morning one, as well as a set of three "codes"—covering advertising, production, and ethics—which fixed prices and practices between these supposed competitors. In March 1963 Celler's unit began public hearings. After four days of testimony, as the staff prepared to cross-examine the implicated executives, Chairman Celler suddenly and unexpectedly halted the hearings. He stated that pending civil rights legislation was more urgent and that he wanted to avoid covering the same ground as the Justice Department investigation.

* PL 89–175 exempts certain joint agreements between banks from the antitrust laws; PL 90–62 extends the exemption of banks from the antitrust laws to assist in safeguarding the balance-of-payments position of the United States; and PL 91–354 exempts certain joint operating arrangements among newspapers from the antitrust laws. Celler voted against the Newspaper Preservation Act on the House floor, but *not* in his antitrust subcommittee. When Ken Harkins was asked if Celler could have blocked this bill in committee, he snapped, "You can't block or defeat something which newspaper publishers want in an institution whose members have to run for public office."

The dismissal raised many questions. The Justice Department had sent out civil subpoenas before any of the hearings had begun; anxiety about overlapping jurisdiction could therefore have been raised at any time, not just as the price-fix was to be exposed. And if Celler did not want to interfere with the department's investigation, why weren't the hearings resumed after Justice decided not to file suit? In fact, the House subcommittee failed to publish a record of the four days of hearings that had occurred; its existence is nowhere evident in the *Index of Antitrust Subcommittee Publications.* In an interview before his retirement, Celler claimed that the hearings were not published because they were never completed; but they were never completed precisely because Celler had called them off. It devolved to the Senate Antitrust and Monopoly Subcommittee to print the proceedings five years later—but only after some antitrust cloak-and-dagger work. To discourage dissemination of those hearings, the transcripts were not allowed to leave their House room. So a Senate subcommittee aide asked to read parts of them in the prescribed room, and proceeded to surreptitiously photograph the transcript with a secret portable camera. "Modern technology surprised and defeated them," said a Senate antitrust subcommittee lawyer with more than a trace of self-satisfaction.

While activity slowed to a crawl, it didn't stop completely. A 1965 report, *Interlocks in Corporate Management,* was valuable, although one staff lawyer who worked on it said, "The eventual result was a shadow of the original study; I therefore refused to sign it." Celler held hearings in 1966 on a proposed merger of the two professional football leagues. Although he opposed it, the measure passed when Senator Russell Long tacked it on as a rider to a tax bill, a move Celler called "shocking . . . outrageous . . . a dirty trick."[62] A study of the monopoly problem in the electronic computer industry, especially IBM, was initiated in 1967. But it was suspended after five days "in order to permit the Department of Justice investigation to proceed without interference."[63]

In 1969 and 1970, Chairman Celler, supported by a supplemental staff, held a series of significant and revealing hearings into six major conglomerates. But the eventual report created more controversy over its publication than its contents. Although the report was sharply critical of some conglomerates, the accompanying press release went out of its way to praise these same firms and people. This, as well as its untimely release over the 1971 Labor Day weekend, led journalist I. F. Stone to charge that Celler deliberately underplayed the conglomerates report.[64] Subcommittee staff director Bess Dick hotly denies this charge, arguing that it had been scheduled to come out earlier, but the Government Printing Office had gotten its plates all wrong. "After two years and seven volumes of work," she added, "it's crazy to say that they tried to keep it quiet."

More recently, Celler was given to writing agencies about their antitrust nonfeasance: on September 8, 1971, he urged the CAB to stop airline mergers, calling the agency "a wet nurse for sick airlines"; on October 6, 1971, he wrote then Attorney General John Mitchell to protest the Justice Department's acceptance of the National Steel–Granite City Steel merger; and in a February 10, 1972, letter to Securities and Exchange Commission chairman William Casey, he called for the physical separation of customer funds and securities by broker-dealers.

Knowledgeable observers, however, agree that the House antitrust subcommittee declined. "There were months when we had absolutely nothing to do," grumbled a former staffer, echoing the sentiments of others. "For some reason, Celler went backwards on antitrust." One of the few dissenters to this view is Emanuel Celler himself, who in a 1969 newspaper interview with Morton Mintz of the *Washington Post* said twice, "I'll pit my record against the Senate's"[65]—a bit of damning with faint self-praise.

An Erosion of Faith

Why the deterioration? Part of the problem was Celler's competing interests in other Judiciary activity. When asked why he would not give up either the full committee or the subcommittee chairmanship, he answered, "Because I want to control both."⁶⁶ Perhaps a more telling reason was the size of the staff: when Celler left in 1973, the professional subcommittee staff was down to one; a second was added later. Asked in 1969 why he didn't hire more staff, Celler said, "I wouldn't want 'em stumbling all over each other."⁶⁷ It is one thing to desire a tight, lean staff, but one or two people simply cannot cope with even the minimum demands of a successful antitrust subcommittee. Celler could not blame a stingy committee chairman, for he *was* the committee chairman, and as such disbursed money to his subcommittees. Even niggardly Wayne Hays, chairman of the House Administration Committee and the person who decides who gets what, faulted Celler for seeking such a small appropriation for the Judiciary Committee. The *full* Judiciary Committee got about $350,000—less than one-half what the Senate Antitrust and Monopoly Subcommittee got at that time.

But the two basic causes of the subcommittee's anemia appear to have been Celler's age and his commitment. In 1963, he was seventy-four and in 1973, eighty-four; he simply lacked the energy and resources required to activate his subcommittee. And it is questionable that he possessed the will to do so even if he could find the way. For Celler seemed to mellow on antitrust, either because of decades of lost battles or because of an erosion of faith created by conflicts of interest stemming from his continued connection with his law firm:

• In a case involving the Burlington Watch Company in the mid-fifties, Celler's New York law firm represented Benrus, a competitor of the defendant. Benrus was unhappy with the practice of importers bringing in low-jeweled (lower-duty) watches and "upjeweling" them here. They wanted this practice included in the complaint, but Mary Gardiner Jones, then an attorney in the Antitrust Division and later an FTC commissioner, did not. The division received an official letter from Celler asking why this count was not included. Jones drafted a scathing reply, which antitrust chief Stanley Barnes chose not to send; instead, no reply at all was sent and no followup was received from Celler. Later Commissioner Jones stated that this official silence was the best way of letting Celler know that he had stepped out of line.

• A case was proposed by the Antitrust Division against Schenley Industries, Inc., producers of liquors, which was being defended by Celler's firm. Celler lobbied then Attorney General Katzenbach about it, opening the conversation by commenting on his labors for the administration's then-pending civil rights bill. He argued that the case should not be brought because the division was in error over the issue involved—whether a license to import a scotch, Cutty Sark, was an asset within the meaning of the 1950 act. He claimed that, as one of the authors of the act, he was well qualified to interpret the law in this situation. His arguments were ultimately ignored.

• In the mid-1960s, Schenley found itself in the opposite situation, urging the Antitrust Division to investigate its competitor, Seagram & Sons, for an alleged conspiracy in restraint of trade. The agency considered the evidence insufficient to call a grand jury. Celler demanded an explanation, and a high antitrust official had to be dispatched to explain the issue to him.

• Celler's "two-door" arrangement with his law firm meant that clients with business against the federal government entered through one door, which lacked Celler's name; other clients entered through a door *with* Celler's name on it. No one was fooled, least of all the clients. Robert Sherrill, writing in the *New York Times Magazine*, noted that the Celler arrangement was "one of the longest-standing and most notorious embarrassments to Congress."[68] A former top official at the Antitrust Division confirmed in 1970 that the word had gone out: "If you want Celler's support, hire his law firm."

• In August 1970 the *Wall Street Journal* quoted Celler as suggesting that a superagency be created to pass on all mergers in the regulated industries. The article urged that the Penn Central bankruptcy be probed as a case study—which might prove embarrassing, since the New York Central was a client of Celler's firm. In 1968, according to Interstate Commerce Commission records, the law firm of Weisman, Celler, Allan, Spett and Sheinberg received $51,644 in legal fees from Penn Central, which had picked up its predecessor's tab.

When asked about these conflicts in an interview, Celler denied any knowledge of them, and added a parting defense: "Your constituents are the final arbiter of any conflicts, and I'm always re-elected."

But in 1972 he wasn't, when, after fifty years in Congress, he was defeated in the Democratic primary. It is still too early to assess just what Peter Rodino, Celler's successor as chairman of the antitrust subcommittee as well as of the Judiciary Committee, will do with his new power, other than change the name of No. 5 to the Subcommittee on Monopolies and Commercial Law. At an obvious minimum, Rodino—once freed of his impeachment responsibilities—will probably reverse the recent ossification of the subcommittee. Some encouraging signs are the subcommittee's antitrust amendments to the emergency energy bill (which passed both houses but was vetoed by the President in March 1974) and hearings in March 1974 on a bill (H.R. 12528) to permit states to sue under the antitrust laws as *parens patriae* (i.e., on behalf of their citizens). On the other hand, antitrust advocates have criticized the subcommittee's reluctance to pass H.R. 9203, the Antitrust Procedures and Penalties Bill.

How much Rodino achieves depends not only on his own interest and capacity and that of the subcommittee members, but also on the antitrust environment in which he and the committee function: i.e., the whole House of Representatives, the Senate, the White House, and public opinion. For there is a reverberating dynamic among these components; if most do not care about antitrust, the House Judiciary subcommittee alone, or its counterpart Senate subcommittee, can hardly advance the ball. Consider Kefauver's example. John Blair has defended Kefauver's meager legislative record by asserting, "We passed every bill the White House supported; but we couldn't get anything passed without that support." Kefauver, it cannot be doubted, struggled diligently for reforms, but without support his efforts usually failed.

The last decade has reinforced defeatism among participants in the congressional antitrust process. But failure has been as much self-inflicted as ordained. Two unenthusiastic chairmen operated in the context of an indifferent public and a lax Justice Department. What *would* happen if, say, a William Proxmire were to head one subcommittee, and Edward Mezvinsky (D., Ia.) (an energetic freshman member of the Subcommittee on Monopolies and Commercial Law) the other? What if there were an attorney general more interested in filing tough antitrust cases than in filing them away? And finally, what if the public began to demand such efforts?

The dream is not impossible. Senator Tunney's consent-decree success in June 1973 may be just an aberration . . . or a harbinger. And incidents like the ITT brouhaha seem to be having their effects. For example, recent public opinion polls have found that 77 percent of those asked wanted the second Nixon term to be "tougher on business" (Harris Survey); 60 percent of those polled in Chicago thought that "big business forgets the public welfare" (Social Research, Inc.); and 61 percent agreed that "there's too much power concentrated in the hands of a few large companies for the good of the nation" (Opinion Research Corporation). Nearly half of the Americans in this last poll concluded, "Many of our largest companies ought to be broken up into smaller companies." Four years ago the top economic aide to Richard McLaren, then Antitrust Division chief, wrote an internal office memorandum in support of a General Motors divestiture case. In one part, he argued:

> We would have lots of public opinion on our side. . . .
> In terms of winning votes, a big automobile case might be
> worth a hundred merger cases. Conceivably, it would make
> Nixon into another Teddy Roosevelt.

Neither McLaren nor Nixon apparently heeded this advice. But it is not visionary to assume that a confluence of executive officials, senators, congressmen, committee chairmen, and subcommittee members may eventually comprehend the potential popularity of antitrust action. Then oil and milk and coffins and cars might never be the same.

5

Acres of Diamonds: Patents and Copyrights

In August 1971, the Nixon administration issued a memorandum on patent policy authorizing government agencies to grant exclusive as well as nonexclusive licenses on about 25,000 government-owned patents to private companies. The stated reason for this recommendation was to speed up the commercial use of government-financed and -owned inventions—despite the lack of evidence that useful inventions had ever failed to be commercially exploited under nonexclusive licenses. This would mark a radical departure from past policy, for government-owned patents have historically been dedicated to the public and made available for general licensing on a nonexclusive, royalty-free basis.[1] Dr. Betsy Ancker-Johnson, Assistant Secretary of Commerce for Science and Technology, characterized the potential value to industry of patents owned by the federal gov-

NOTE: This chapter was prepared by Dr. Irene Till.

ernment: "These patents," she said, "are acres of diamonds."[2] If the plan had succeeded—it was thwarted by a federal court*— Americans would have been required to foot the bill for these patents *twice*, once as taxpayers funding government research and development and again as consumers paying monopoly prices.

The stakes in patent and copyright policy are very high, as high as the mammoth profits from long-term, legally protected monopolies—which is what they in fact are. Corporations regard these monopoly rights with reverence, as Robert Gottschalk, a former reform commissioner of patents, can readily attest. In 1970, Gottschalk entered the Patent Office as deputy commissioner; in 1971, after the forced resignation of the incumbent commissioner, Gottschalk was made acting commissioner. In 1972, Maurice H. Stans, then Secretary of the Commerce Department, in which the Patent Office is lodged, named Gottschalk commissioner.

Gottschalk commenced an overhaul of the slow-paced bureaucracy of the Patent Office, streamlining its administrative operations and stiffening its search practices prior to the issuance of patents. Under present law, patents may be issued only for inventions that are both *new* and *useful*, and the increment of novelty must be more than would be obvious to anyone with ordinary skill in the art. Gottschalk's efforts were directed at improving the research tools in the Patent Office for ascertaining whether these statutory requirements had been fully met. It soon became clear to the large corporate beneficiaries of these monopoly grants that

---

* *Public Citizen, et al.* v. *Sampson*, Civil Action No. 781–33 (D.D.C. January 17, 1974). This decision ruled that the administrator of the General Services Administration had violated Article IV, Section 3, clause 2, of the United States Constitution, which provides that only Congress may dispose of public property, by offering to grant exclusive licenses on government-owned patents and inventions without congressional authorization, and that GSA's effort to do so without prior public notice—except to a selected group of industry associations—violated the requirements of the Administrative Procedures Act. The government has appealed the case to the U.S. Court of Appeals for the District of Columbia Circuit.

Gottschalk was making it more difficult to secure patents. When Stans and his successor for a brief time, Peter Peterson, departed for greener pastures, and Frederick B. Dent was appointed Secretary of Commerce in December 1972, Gottschalk became a vulnerable target.

In May 1973, Gottschalk was summoned to the office of Betsy Ancker-Johnson, formerly a Boeing official and newly appointed Assistant Secretary of Commerce. She ordered the commissioner to submit a letter of resignation within a week, and declined to give any reason for the action. A week later, Gottschalk unsuccessfully attempted to see her. The next day, as he was departing to sign a trademark treaty in Vienna, she again called him and demanded his resignation. When Gottschalk explained that he was leaving within the hour, she informed him that he could not leave the country until his letter of resignation was in her hands. Gottschalk angrily replied that she was forcing him to choose between a treaty in which he had invested much effort and giving up his job. "No matter what," she stated icily, "I'm asking for your resignation or you don't leave the country." Gottschalk hurriedly dashed off his resignation and left for Vienna. Four months later, testifying before the Senate Judiciary subcommittee on patents, trademarks, and copyrights, Gottschalk could still say, "In truth, I do not know why I was fired."

On his return to Washington, he found that the White House has posted a notice in the press room that Gottschalk's resignation had been accepted "with regret and with admiration for his splendid record as Commissioner of Patents." Subsequently, Thomas E. Kauper, head of the Antitrust Division of the Justice Department, expressed disappointment at his departure and appreciation for Gottschalk's interest in "significant patent reform, during our recent protracted efforts with respect to revisions of the Patent Code." Even the American Patent Law Association (APLA), the organization of the patent bar, said: "It's not surprising that the Federal bureaucracy fired someone who has made some important improvements and was on the road to making more."[3]

Gottschalk's experience illustrates the hazards of attempts at patent reform. Gottschalk ardently believes in the benefits to the public of the American patent system; his aim was to make the Patent Office more responsive to the legitimate ends for which it had been established. The sudden—and still officially unexplained—interruption of his efforts by his forced resignation constitutes a grave setback both to the agency and to the American public.

Under our Constitution, such valuable gems as patents and copyrights are entrusted to Congress for safekeeping. Congress has delegated this task to the Judiciary committees, and more specifically, to the subcommittees on patents, trademarks, and copyrights. In recent years, the Senate subcommittee has assumed primary responsibility in the field of patents, and House Subcommittee No. 3 has done so in the realm of copyrights. (Trademarks have received little attention by the subcommittees.) The work product of each then constitutes the subject of study and hearings in the other chamber.

This division of function evolved informally and is largely explainable by the fact that the issues in this area are highly technical in character, involving the frontiers of several scientific disciplines and the cutting edges of new technologies. Even a modicum of understanding of their import requires considerable specialized knowledge by committee members. In any event, this division is convenient for lobbyists. Over the years, the patent interests have developed close contacts in the Senate subcommittee and the copyright groups have forged similar ties on the House side.

In the distinctive illogic of congressional politics, one comes to expect that those subcommittees that dispense the greatest public largesse will be precisely the subcommittees most insulated from public scrutiny and controls. So it is with the taxing committees,

House Ways and Means and Senate Finance. And so it is with the Judiciary subcommittees on patents, trademarks, and copyrights, which are empowered to carve lucrative monopolies out of the body of our antitrust laws. The work of these subcommittees is *terra incognita* to outsiders.

Once a bill has emerged from the subcommittee, it usually secures easy approval by the parent Judiciary Committee and by Congress itself, with little additional consideration. Other members of Congress presume that the subcommittee members are expert in their field, that they have fully studied the issues, have held extensive hearings, and know what they are about. This presumption also frees most members of Congress from any attempt to understand the complicated proposals on which they are voting.

The press and the general public provide little check on the subcommittees. Except for trade journals, the media provides virtually no news coverage of the subcommittee deliberations nor analysis of the legislative proposals. The issues appear too complicated and abstruse; the testimony tends to be concerned with technical minutiae rather than broad general policy; the controversies seem too dull and remote from people's lives to arouse public interest. As a result, although hearings—and in the House subcommittee, executive sessions—are open to anyone interested, the work of these subcommittees proceeds in splendid isolation.

The subcommittees' handiwork is the patent and copyright statutes, authorized by the constitutional provision (Article I, Section 8) permitting (although not requiring) Congress to grant "for limited times to authors and inventors, the exclusive right to their respective writings and discoveries," where the purpose is solely "to promote the progress of science and the useful arts." The latter clause recognizes that a grant of monopoly rights violates the precepts of a competitive economic system and should be permitted, if at all, only for compelling reasons grounded in the public interest.

Yet out of the simple constitutional provision has evolved the erroneous concept that patents and copyrights are *rights* guaranteed by the Constitution. Patent and copyright owners—who directly benefit—are not alone in stressing this view. Even the subcommittees have focused their attention on the monopoly aspect of the grant, ignoring the constitutional requirement that a grant must serve broad social ends. They seem to forget that the constitutional provision is permissive, not mandatory; Congress may refrain from making such grants or may condition such grants as it sees fit.

Economic producer interests seeking legitimized monopoly rights find the patent, trademark, and copyright subcommittees easy marks. Armed with the funds to hire an influential and articulate corps of special pleaders,* and generous with well-placed campaign contributions, these groups work closely with the subcommittees. Their varied legislative activities are pressed by influential friends in Congress, trade associations, and the members of the organized patent and copyright bar, as well as by individual lobbyists.

The private patent and copyright bar plays a particularly strategic role. The vast majority of its members are in the service of economic interests seeking patent and copyrights monopolies—not surprising, since there is no other market for their specialized expertise. Some members of this exclusive club are directly employed as house counsel in the large corporations; others are

---

* For example, former Senator Kenneth B. Keating appeared before the House subcommittee in 1965 on behalf of the large book publishers. At that time he remarked:

> This is my first appearance as a witness before a congressional committee since taking up the private practice of law. And I say to you with the utmost sincerity that my study of this problem regarding the proposed revision of the copyright laws has convinced me that this appearance is in the nature of an extension of my public service. I am sure you will agree with me that to be paid a fee to advance what I conceive to be a public interest is indeed a fortuitous concatenation of events.

Fortuitous indeed—at least for Keating. For his brief appearance, he was reportedly paid $50,000.

in private law firms where the practice of patent and copyright law is frequently combined.

The patent and copyright bar has flourished at the federal trough. Today the federal government spends about $17 billion annually for research and development.[4] The major portion is handled by such agencies as the Department of Defense, the National Aeronautics and Space Administration, the Department of Health, Education, and Welfare, and the Atomic Energy Commission. Much of this money goes to large corporations under contract. Not only must the contract terms be negotiated, but a disposition of the patent rights must be worked out. Copyright problems must also be resolved, though such rights are often left to private researchers, who assign them to commercial publishers.

Another contingent of these legal specialists is on the federal payroll, employed in the government offices that issue these monopoly grants. The U.S. Patent Office in the Department of Commerce administers the patent law, issuing approximately 70,000 patents each year, with a backlog of 11 million applications in 85,000 subclasses.[5] The Copyright Office, part of the Library of Congress, processes the registration of copyrights. In recent years, these have exceeded 300,000 annually—almost a thousand "works of art" a day.

The viewpoint of the attorneys working on patent matters throughout the federal government tends to mesh with that of the private patent and copyright bar.* They are members of the same professional organizations; much of their working time is spent in direct daily contact with their private counterparts concerned with protecting and expanding the claims of corporate clients. The tendency to perceive problems in similar ways is strengthened, in many cases, by the lure of future employment by these same private interests. In this very real sense, the private and public patent and copyright bars are interchangeable.

---

* The marked exception is the small band of examiners in the Patent Office who are dedicated to limiting patent grants to truly new and useful inventions.

The patent and copyright bars have separate but intertwining professional organizations. The copyright lawyers are organized in the Copyright Society of the U.S.A., with headquarters in New York City. In patents, the structure is more complex. A national association, the American Patent Law Association, and a network of city, state, and regional associations of patent attorneys are joined in the National Council of Patent Law Associations (NCPLA). The NCPLA shares offices with the APLA in Washington, D.C. The Government Patent Lawyers Association consists of individual members also affiliated with the APLA and local societies.

In the American Bar Association, the two disciplines are combined in the powerful Section on Patent, Trademark and Copyright Law. The lawyers attracted to service on this ABA committee are the private and corporate practitioners in these fields. Again, because of the singular complexities of these branches of the law, the committee's recommendations on pending legislation and policy carry great weight with the bar association. Their recommendations are usually adopted by the House of Delegates of the ABA with little discussion or debate. At a later point in the process, representatives of the ABA Section on Patent, Trademark and Copyright Law change their hats. No longer representing the private interests of their clients, they now appear before the Judiciary subcommittees as spokesmen for the united view of one of the most prestigious and influential organizations in the United States.

The role of the ABA in patent matters has been aptly described by Simon Rifkind, formerly federal district judge in New York City. In a hearing on a pending patent bill before the Senate subcommittee on patents, he remarked:

> I have, myself, been a member of the American Bar Association for more years than I care to admit. I should confess to you that as individuals, I do not know a group of people with whom I would rather play and work and drink than lawyers. But once they are formed into an organized body, a group, somehow or other, they are not conspicuous, either

for imagination or for break-throughs or for bold reforms. When they meet in an aggregated body, it seems that the cautions which are, of course, characteristic of the profession, and the fears which are, of course, the attributes of a great many of the practitioners, reinforce each other so as to create a wall encompassing them with fear so that you cannot break through and make progress. Inside that wall they just worship the status quo.[6]

He was shortly followed by representatives of the ABA Section of Patent, Trademark and Copyright Law, whose testimony nicely substantiated Rifkind's point.[7]

The congressional subcommittees on patents, trademarks, and copyrights become the cynosure of these pressures, particularly since approval of measures by the subcommittees is usually tantamount to enactment. The proposed legislation is often drafted by private lawyers representing the particular corporate interests that the bill will benefit. Where private interests are in sharp conflict and have been unable to compromise in advance of hearings, subcommittee members have an opportunity to see more than one side of the issue. But even then, the issue usually surfaces as a conflict of narrow private interests, while the general public, if it is even aware of the event, looks on helplessly from the sidelines.

THE SENATE SUBCOMMITTEE ON PATENTS, TRADEMARKS, AND COPYRIGHTS

During the 1950s when Senator Joseph C. O'Mahoney (D., Wyo.), a strong antitrust advocate, was chairman of the Patents, Trademarks, and Copyrights Subcommittee, much of its work centered upon improving the practices of the U.S. Patent Office. The subcommittee published a number of reports on the patent policies of federal departments and agencies, demonstrating a vast disparity in their policies and practices concerning the disposition of government rights to public-financed inventions. It also published a series of analyses by outside experts critical of the operation of our patent system.[8] The O'Mahoney period was essentially a holding operation; corporate patent owners were unable to expand private monopoly rights while he ruled the subcommittee.

With his departure from the Senate, however, the situation changed. Since 1961, Senator John L. McClellan has been chairman. Without prior membership on the subcommittee or knowledge of the highly technical patent and copyright fields, McClellan was chosen by Senator Eastland, chairman of the full Judiciary Committee and, along with McClellan, one of the Senate's most conservative members. Today, the subcommittee reflects the McClellan-Eastland orientation. Its members are McClellan, Hugh Scott, Hiram Fong, Philip Hart, and Quentin Burdick, the two latter members constituting the liberal minority.

The annual budget of the patents subcommittee is among the lowest of the numerous Judiciary subcommittees, hovering around $150,000 for many years. In fiscal 1974, it requested $185,000. The Senate Committee on Rules and Administration, which reviews such requests, reduced the figure to $143,000. The staff of the Senate patents subcommittee is limited to three lawyers—chief counsel, special counsel, and assistant counsel—and four administrative and clerical people. Notably absent is any scientific or engineering expertise on the staff.

McClellan's accession in 1961 generated a flood of patent revision proposals, which continued through the decade. Some were designed to implement the recommendations of the President's Commission on the Patent System, established by executive order in 1965; its members were largely industry executives and patent attorneys interested in expanding private patent rights.[9] Other proposals came from private sources, including the ABA, and were directed toward the same purpose.

The Scott Amendments

By the late 1960s, a new development was changing the routine course of events. Estes Kefauver's hearings in the Antitrust and

Monopoly Subcommittee on administered prices in the prescription drug industry, held from 1959 to 1962,[10] laid bare the important role of patents and restrictive licensing agreements in maintaining the noncompetitive price structure in this industry. Copies of these agreements were made a part of the public record and were also submitted to the Department of Justice for consideration.

The Antitrust Division in the Justice Department belatedly embarked upon a campaign to eliminate these restrictive patent practices. Beginning in 1968, a number of suits were instituted against the major drug firms.[11] Particular attention was directed to a standard provision in the drug-licensing agreements which required licensees to sell products in final dosage form only. The purpose of this clause was to prevent the sale of bulk material to small drug companies—the only real source of price competition in the industry. Without access to drugs in bulk form, small firms could not market the products.

The major drug firms reacted swiftly to these suits. A group of their Washington patent lobbyists drafted amendments to the pending patent revision bill. These amendments provided sweeping immunity to the antitrust laws for all industries relying upon patents to curb competition. Companies would be free to engage in cartelization, fix prices, enter into geographical division of field agreements, force tie-in sales (requiring the purchase of unpatented goods as a condition of securing a license), or engage in package licensing (forcing unwanted patents in a package deal as a condition of securing desired patents). One provision made it virtually impossible for licensees to challenge the validity of patents under which they had been licensed; another section permitted continued royalty charges after expiration of the patent. In effect, the intent of the proposals was to reverse a long course of judicial decisions that had placed strict limitations upon restrictive practices going beyond the legitimate exercise of patent rights.

The drug companies selected Hugh Scott, ranking minority

member on the Senate subcommittee, to sponsor the amendments. Scott's Pennsylvania constituency includes a number of major drug firms. Another company active in securing Scott's sponsorship was Westinghouse Electric, with home offices in Pittsburgh. In early 1970 the Justice Department sued Westinghouse Electric under the Sherman Act for its restrictive patent agreements of over forty years' standing with Mitsubishi, a Japanese combine.[12] The suit charged that the companies agreed not to sell licensed products in each other's home country, whether or not such products were covered by patents, and that Westinghouse also forced upon the Mitsubishi group a broader license than was asked for, extending the territorial restrictions to many other products. These covered such fields as power transformers, switch-gear and distribution apparatus, industrial control equipment, refrigerators, television sets, air-conditioning equipment, and elevators. The suit further charged that specific royalty charges were agreed upon and paid even in the absence of existing patents on products, and that the effect was to greatly curtail competition in home markets and to maintain an artificial price structure.* Westinghouse's interest in the enactment of the Scott amendments, it is fair to conclude, was far from academic.

In the spring of 1971, the subcommittee held additional hearings on the patent-revision bill and the Scott amendments.[13] Most of the testimony supported the proposals. Witnesses included representatives of large corporations holding vast portfolios of patents and the National Association of Manufacturers (NAM), as well as officials of the major patent-law associations—the APLA and the NCPLA. The ABA filed a brief in general support, and also urged enactment of a provision to repeal the compulsory patent licensing provisions contained in the Clean Air Act of 1970.

Agencies of the federal government were divided. The Department of Commerce spokesman supported the proposed legisla-

* The suit is still pending.

tion,[14] and was immediately followed in the hearings by the head of the Antitrust Division at Justice, who opposed the Scott amendments. Subsequently a detailed brief was submitted to the subcommittee by Justice showing the present state of the law, as reflected in court decisions, and the extent to which the bill would overrule such decisions. The Justice Department argued that the public would be injured by expansion of private monopoly rights.[15] Still later, the department submitted to the subcommittee a confidential list of pending antitrust cases that would automatically be ended if the legislation passed.[16]

Because of the subcommittee's membership, the Scott amendments were generally expected to clear that body by a three–two vote. At this critical point, however, Senator Hart's Antitrust and Monopoly Subcommittee became actively involved in opposition. A joint protest was filed by a number of prominent law school professors, and some members of the academic community appeared at the hearings to testify against the amendments. Ralph Nader also objected.* McClellan was then involved in a close primary fight in Arkansas and seemed to be in trouble; strenuous efforts were made to persuade Fong to withhold his support.

In consequence, the Scott amendments foundered in the subcommittee. In executive sessions in October 1971, McClellan and Fong alternately shifted their positions on key proposals. One or the other joined Hart and Burdick in opposition, resulting in a three–two vote against the Scott amendments. Also defeated was a provision in the original bill that would have prohibited unauthorized importation of any product on which a process patent was held in the United States. In effect, this provision would have converted patents on processes and their improvements—no matter how insignificant and whether or not actually employed in manufacture—into product patents. Under the latter,

---

* Unaccountably, these letters of protest were not included in the record of the hearings.

a patent holder has a total monopoly on a product, no matter how made, and can bar all competition during the life of the patent.

Still at issue was the original bill, which contained some useful reforms. Whereas under existing laws an applicant for a patent has to file an oath that he has made full disclosure of the prior art to the Patent Office, an amendment offered by Senator Hart (and incorporated in the bill) would require attorneys and agents for the applicant to file a similar oath. Also, instead of the present presumption in the applicant's favor, the bill would require an applicant to establish the patentability of the invention by a preponderance of proof. The bill allowed for critical examination of the patent by the Patent Office even after the issuance. The public would be permitted to submit information showing prior art or other grounds for nonpatentability. Otherwise, the bill, without the Scott amendments, did not make substantial changes in the present law.

The stage was now set for new maneuverings. The bill was sent to the parent Judiciary Committee but without an accompanying subcommittee report. Thomas C. Brenna, McClellan's chief counsel since 1961, had prepared an advance draft of a report which presumed acceptance of the Scott amendments. Since these proposals had now been rejected by the majority, the old draft required revision. Nothing happened, however, for in the absence of an accompanying report, Chairman Eastland would not submit the bill for consideration by the full committee.

For almost a year, the various patent interests lobbied vigorously to secure a recommittal to the subcommittee for a new vote on inclusion of the Scott amendments.[17] Needing only one more vote—either McClellan's or Fong's—the patent lobby's chances looked promising. But still nothing happened. Then, in a desperate move to secure action before the close of the Ninety-second Congress, Senator Hart circulated his own draft of a subcommittee report among the subcommittee members who had joined with him to form a majority rejecting the Scott amendments. Senator Burdick signed the Hart draft, but Fong vacillated and, in the end, did not sign. Efforts were made to secure McClellan's signature to the Hart draft, but they also failed. Congress adjourned with the bill still pending in the full committee. This result apparently came as no surprise to some members of the Senate subcommittee. On September 25, 1972—some months before adjournment—McClellan and Hugh Scott sent a letter to President Nixon categorically stating that "the Ninety-second Congress will be adjourning shortly without acting on the legislation to modernize the American patent system." The letter urged the formulation of a single position within the executive branch respecting patent legislation to which all government agencies must conform. This would presumably have the effect of silencing the Antitrust Division, which earlier had mounted an effective attack upon the Scott amendments. After referring to the difficulties in securing passage of patent legislation, the letter stated:

> Our task has been rendered significantly more burdensome by the inability of the executive branch to formulate a single position on the patent revision legislation, including a proposed statutory clarification of the rights of patent owners with respect to the licensing of their inventions. The absence of an Administration position has been exploited by some who wish to weaken and discredit the patent system. . . .
>
> We, therefore, request that you direct the appropriate departments and agencies of the executive branch to undertake renewed efforts to formulate an Administration position on patent law revision. We would hope that it will be possible for you to communicate this position upon the convening of the 93rd Congress.

The letter was promptly acknowledged by Tom C. Korologos, Deputy Assistant to the President. No public announcement followed, but numerous meetings reportedly were held within the executive branch to implement the suggested strategy.

Still More Patent Lobbyists

While Congress wrestled with the Scott amendments, the corporate beneficiaries of the patent system were preparing a more intensive campaign of their own. During 1972, two new, well-financed lobbies mounted a strong offensive for favorable patent legislation. Significantly, each is headed by a former U.S. commissioner of patents. The Association for the Advancement of Invention and Innovation (AAII) is directed by Edward J. Brenner, who was patents commissioner from 1964 to 1969. Prior to his tenure as commissioner, Brenner worked for Standard Oil (N.J.) (now Exxon) in the processing and expansion of the company's vast portfolio of patents. Membership in the AAII is open to "inventors, entrepreneurs, research directors, businessmen, scientists, engineers, lawyers, patent attorneys and agents, economists and others who support the objectives of the Association."[18] Fees are $25 annually for individuals and $100 for corporations; contributions are also accepted. Brenner refused to supply any information on current membership. The organization's purposes, however, are clearly stated in its own publication:

> The Association is intended to be basically a prime mover in generating positive and constructive programs which will enhance the climate for invention and innovation and in marshalling the necessary support by individuals, companies and organizations to achieve the desired government or public action. The second major basic function of the association is to serve as an important public spokesman in support of the importance of invention and innovation to the national interest and national goals, in response to attacks thereon by critics or opponents of invention and innovation. Thus, the Association is basically in the business of government relations and public relations for the advancement of invention and innovation. Its interests extend to broad national issues which affect or are affected by invention and innovation and to government programs or legislation in the

fields of patents, taxation, antitrusts, regulation finance
and the like which have a bearing on invention and innovation.[19]

One of its immediate goals is to enhance the prestige of the
Patent Office by elevating the post of the commissioner to Assist-
ant Secretary of Commerce for Invention and Intellectual
Property.

The second organization—Intellectual Property Owners (IPO)—
is directed by William E. Schuyler, Jr., who was commissioner
of patents from 1969 through mid-1971. After working as a
patent lawyer for RCA and Sperry Gyroscope, he entered the
private practice of patent law and later became a partner in the
Washington firm of Browne, Schuyler and Beveridge. Since his
departure from the Patent Office, he has headed the Washington
patent firm of Schuyler, Birch, Swindler, McKie & Beckett. One
of his partners, Edward F. McKie, Jr., has, like Schuyler, been
chairman of the ABA's Section of Patent, Trademark and Copyright Law. In the 1968 hearings of the Senate patents subcommittee, both appeared on behalf of the ABA. In the 1971 hearings, Schuyler, then commissioner of patents, accompanied the
undersecretary of commerce in support of the bill. McKie was a
leading member of the Washington lobbying group that originally
drafted the Scott amendments. He is also on the advisory board
of Brenner's AAII.

In its initial stage, the Schuyler lobby was largely financed by
Minnesota Mining and Manufacturing (3M), which has been
sued in a number of patent-related antitrust actions and would
profit greatly by the Scott amendments. In the early 1960s,
the Justice Department had charged that the company attempted
to monopolize the market for Scotch tape by coercing its competitors, with threats of infringement suits, into entering patent
license agreements giving 3M control over their manufacture and
sale. In this manner, the suit charged, 3M dictated the products
its competitors could manufacture, the manner of making them,
the classes of buyers to whom they could sell, and the prices

they could charge. Similar charges involved aluminum presensitized lithographic plates used by printing presses.[20]

Intellectual Property Owners has engaged in an ambitious campaign to broaden its membership base. It offers various classes of membership with annual dues (deductible as a business expense) as follows: sponsor, $10,000; sustaining, $5,000; regular, $1,000; associate (nonvoting), $500; and individual, $100. Its current board of directors includes officials of Borg-Warner, Allis-Chalmers, Westinghouse Electric, Monsanto, 3M, Kaiser Industries, and Merck & Company. Like AAII, it publishes a monthly bulletin unavailable to nonmembers. In soliciting members in September 1972, Schuyler explained the function of his group:

> IPO was organized earlier this year to improve the public image of the U.S. Patent System by acquainting the interested public with the ways in which the incentives of the patent system operate in the public interest. So far, our overhead and promotional effort have been financed by a few interested corporations. . . . Now we need your help to finance a professionally organized and directed public relations campaign, designed to build a wider understanding of the patent system. We have contracted with Carl Byoir Associates, one of the largest and best known public relations firms, to undertake this campaign.[21]

The next round on patent legislation in the Senate will be fought in this intensified lobbying climate. During 1973, no action was taken by the McClellan-Scott forces. Presumably, they were waiting for the emergence of a united front in the executive branch to still the powerful opposition of the Antitrust Division in Justice to the Scott amendments.

Real Patent Reform?

In March 1973, Senator Hart boldly seized the initiative with the introduction of S.1321, the Patent Reform Act of 1973. In a letter to interested parties, he explained the purpose of his action and requested comments on the proposed bill.[22] Hart began by stating that "substantial controversy surrounded legislation intro-

duced in the last Congress, which would have substantially
limited the applicability of the antitrust laws to the licensing of
patents." Legislation in this "complex and delicate area," he
thought, was a "mistake"; resolution of conflicts should be left
to "judicial determination of specific issues on a case-by-case
basis—where two parties, with a direct financial stake, a specific
factual problem, and the best counsel they can find, argue the
limited and precise issue." Significantly, he added:

> Because I do feel this strongly, I am certainly reluctant to
> propose any legislation in this area. However, patent reform
> is now before this Congress; and exemptions of contracts
> involving the licensing of patents from the antitrust laws
> may well be discussed. If such proposals are put forth, in
> order to protect the antitrust laws, I would like to suggest
> an alternative way to cope with the problem.

Hart's bill contains a number of interesting proposals. The
Patent Office would be removed from the Department of Commerce, the official spokesman for business interests, and set up as
an independent agency responsible to Congress. Instead of secret
ex parte proceedings between patent applicants and government
hearing examiners in determining the issuance of patents, public
adversary proceedings would be used. The Patent Office would
be given subpoena and investigative powers to determine the
question of patentability in advance of the patent's issuance. To
aid impecunious independent inventors, fees would be graduated;
they would not become sizeable until after the invention was
commercially utilized and inventors could afford their payment.
Oaths from applicants would be required to the effect that all
material information that would adversely affect issuance of the
patent had been supplied promptly to the Patent Office. All of
these proposals, particularly the removal of the Patent Office from
the Department of Commerce, constitute important and desirable reforms in our present patent system.

A similar move was made on the House side. On April 17,
1973, a companion to the Hart bill, H.R.7111, was introduced

by Congressmen Wayne W. Owens (D., Utah) and Edward Mezvinsky. Both were freshmen in the House and were newly
appointed to the House subcommittee responsible for patents. In
offering this legislation, Owens also presented a critical analysis
of the operation of our patent system—perhaps the strongest ever
presented in the halls of Congress. After stating that "whatever
proposals for change that have been made by the organized patent
bar have been retrogressive, seeking to lower the standard of
invention and create barriers to effective evaluation and elimination of improper or fraudulently procured patents," he remarked:

> The patent system is very sick and perhaps failing, and the
> results are clear to see. Fully 72 percent of the patents
> litigated in the Federal courts of appeals are held invalid,
> and fewer than 20 percent of the litigated patents are upheld
> as valid and infringed. This represents an increase from a
> rate of 57 percent invalidity for the period 1953–63. Such a
> high rate of invalidity means that many more patents issue
> than are warranted. Simply put, this means that the Patent
> Office has not been doing its job of weeding out bad and un-
> justified patents.[23]

As Owens suggests, the need for a reordering of priorities in
the Patent Office itself is pressing. In the past, the office has
stressed the quantity of patent applications cleared and the speed
of processing. Official denials of a quota system for patent examiners have been contradicted privately by many of the lawyers
who actually carry on the examination work. In this kind of situation, the rigor of the examination process is the first casualty.
Patent examiners who wish to exercise great care sometimes find
themselves harassed or labeled as incompetent and inefficient
unless they meet the standards of output. The more enterprising
simply leave the agency; others, willing to adapt themselves to the
system, remain and in the course of time rise to high positions
in the Patent Office bureaucracy.

On July 30, 1973, Senator Hart followed up by introducing
S.2287, his compulsory licensing bill. Drafted as an amendment

to Section 5 of the Federal Trade Commission Act, the senator's new proposal would go far toward reducing chronic patent abuses. For example, any patent related to "public health, safety, or protection of environment" would be subject to compulsory licensing under certain conditions, i.e., production of insufficient quantities of the goods, inferior quality, exorbitant prices, or other conditions which may substantially lessen competition or tend to create monopoly. This provision, if enacted into law, would have great importance in the area of prescription drugs, where excessively high prices are due in large part to the exploitation of patent rights of doubtful validity.

Other provisions are of equal importance. Failure to utilize a patent commercially after three years from date of issuance—or four years from date of the patent application—would trigger compulsory licensing unless the failure were demonstrably beyond the owner's control. Similarly, an existent patent or portfolio of patents could not be used to block the use of a significant improvement developed by someone else. This situation is particularly prevalent in the case of product patents, which, with the denial of a license to manufacture and sell the product, can effectively preclude commercial use of the superior process of manufacture.* Compulsory licensing could also be invoked where a business firm had commercially marketed a product only to discover that a newcomer had later acquired a patent on that product and now attempted to freeze the firm out.† Or it may be employed under conditions in which a minor patent is thrown across an entire technology as a roadblock either to choke off competition or as the instrument for cartelizing the industry. The introduction of S.2287 clearly opens a new chapter in the struggle over patent policy.

In the spring of 1974, the disputants remained stalemated. In overreaching on the Scott amendments, the entrenched patent lobby had accomplished what few reformers had been able to do:

---

* This abuse has been documented in the drug industry on several occasions, including the case of meprobamate (Miltown and Equanil).
† This occurred in the automobile industry in the early 1900s.[24]

they stirred up enough opposition on Capitol Hill to call into question the normal pattern of patent legislation. If, ultimately, the Antitrust Division is silenced through the formulation and enforcement of a single administration position on the legislation, the burden of opposition will pass to others. Whether the Senate subcommittee will pick up the burden remains to be seen. But the unthinkable has occurred. Control of the nation's diamonds—the patent monopolies—may finally have become a public issue.

THE HOUSE SUBCOMMITTEE

Throughout the drama over patent legislation on the Senate side, House Judiciary Subcommittee No. 3, with jurisdiction over patents, trademarks, and copyrights, watched quietly from the wings. It had held hearings on earlier patent bills in 1967 and 1968; but until the Owens-Mezvinsky initiative in April 1973, it had simply waited for bills to emerge from the Senate and be submitted to the lower house. And according to a House committee staffer, no action will be taken on the Owens-Mezvinsky bill unless the Senate acts first. "Frankly," he confided, "no one here has taken much notice of it."

Subcommittee No. 3 had little real autonomy during Emanuel Celler's long reign over Judiciary. He controlled—through Bess Dick, staff director of the full committee—the work of his various subcommittees. The subcommittees had no independent budgets; staff hirings and work assignments were handled by the staff director; and virtually all matters regarded by Celler as important were assigned to a subcommittee which he chaired himself. The professional staff of Subcommittee No. 3 had been composed of only one counsel, who regularly spent considerable portions of his time on matters other than patents, copyrights, and trademarks. The result of this understaffing was as predictable as it was perverse. It meant an almost total reliance upon the Copyright Office and the copyright bar for information, ideas, arguments, and legislative drafting.

The limited reforms of the House Judiciary Committee in the

Ninety-third Congress (see Chapter 16) transformed Subcommittee No. 3 into the Subcommittee on Courts, Civil Liberties, and the Administration of Justice. Its new jurisdiction, along with "rights of authors and inventors," includes Department of Justice oversight, wiretapping, federal penitentiaries, capital punishment, amnesty, obscenity, and presidential succession. Robert W. Kastenmeier, who became chairman of Subcommittee No. 3 in 1969, is also chairman of the new subcommittee. Kastenmeier, a liberal, represents a district that encompasses the University of Wisconsin; his support comes from the university community and organized labor. In the 1972 election Kastenmeier retained his seat by a landslide, receiving a hefty 68 percent of the vote.

The subcommittee's membership has been radically altered. During the Ninety-second Congress, the subcommittee members were Kastenmeier and fellow Democrats John Conyers, Robert Drinan, Abner J. Mikva, and William F. Ryan. The Republicans were Tom Railsback, Edward Biester, Hamilton Fish, and Lawrence Coughlin. With the exception of Drinan and Railsback, the tenure of present subcommittee members began with the Ninety-third Congress. Democrats were Owens, Mezvinsky, and George E. Danielson. The Republican minority was composed of Railsback, Henry P. Smith III, Charles Sandman, and William S. Cohen (Me.).

Over the last several years, the subcommittee has devoted itself to a revision of the copyright law, which has been virtually unchanged since 1909. Copyrights provide monopoly rights to such private interests as book publishers, newspaper and magazine publishers, music publishers, motion picture producers, record producers, broadcasters, television stations, learned societies, song writers, performing-rights societies, composers, and authors. Each of these groups seeks to entrench its exclusive "rights" and protect them for the longest possible period. The interest of the general public, on the other hand, is in substantially free access to products covered by copyright—the elimination of monopoly restrictions to permit the free play of competitive forces in the marketplace.

Formulating legislation to revise the copyright law is difficult because the present statute embodies minute regulatory provisions rather than enunciating broad national policy. Because of the rapid pace of technology and industrial change in such areas as radio, television, community antenna systems, juke boxes, and phone-recording, detailed legislation tends to become obsolete even before it has made its way through Congress.

Toward a New Copyright Law

The 1909 law is administered by the Copyright Office, lodged in the Library of Congress. In 1955, Congress authorized the Copyright Office to conduct studies leading to a general revision of the copyright law. Thirty-four reports were published on various aspects of copyright law practice.[25] In 1961, the register of copyrights, who heads the Copyright Office, submitted to Congress a report containing recommendations for reforms.[26]

Since 1891, the copyright law has contained a "manufacturing clause," requiring printing of the product in the United States as a condition of securing a U.S. copyright. American printers, who had earlier thrived on the pirating of foreign works, exacted this protection from foreign competition as a *quid pro quo* for the international protection contained in the 1891 law. Today, these provisions, according to the register's report, are "an intricate and abstruse tangle of general requirements, exceptions, and special procedures."[27] It recommended their total elimination.

The report also proposed statutory recognition of the "fair use" doctrine. The copyright law itself makes no reference to "fair use"; this concept was fashioned by the courts to fulfill the obvious need to permit some copying without fear of infringement suits. For example, teachers need to reproduce material for classroom use, and researchers must have access to information in scientific and technical journals.* Here, the public library is the

* Courts have established no precise definition of what constitutes "fair" or "unfair" use with respect to the free copying of material protected by copyright. Account is taken of the purpose and character of the use, the nature of the copyrighted work, the amount and substantiality of the

focal point of distribution. The register recommended that only *single* photocopies be made available, and only for the researcher's exclusive use. He also recommended higher maximum penalties for copyright infringement—from $5,000 to $10,000.

Since 1909 the copyright law has contained a provision for the compulsory licensing of sound recordings of music. This was written into the law at that time because the leading record company, anticipating that exclusive rights to records would be legislated, had contracted with the major music publishers for sole rights for recording purposes. Even the maximum royalty charge —two cents per record—was written into the 1909 law, and this charge has remained unchanged for sixty-five years. The register recommended that this whole provision be eliminated: market forces should determine the fees, and there should be a one-year continuance to permit music publishers and record companies to make their arrangements.

It is clearly in the public interest that "works of art" be given maximum distribution, and thus that works become part of the public domain as soon as possible. Yet the Copyright Office recommended *lengthening* the term of the copyright monopoly. Copyright protection in the 1909 law was fourteen years; this was gradually lengthened by amendment until, by 1961, it had reached fifty-six years—an initial term of twenty-eight years with renewal rights for another twenty-eight. The register proposed that this now be increased to seventy-six years. Failing to mention the injury to the public in prolonging the monopoly, the report merely stated that the Copyright Office was "sympathetic to the view that our maximum term should be generally comparable to the term given our works in most other countries."

The register failed to address the problem of copyright rights arising out of work directly financed by American taxpayers. In recent years, the practice of making federal grants for research

---

material used in relation to the copyrighted work as a whole, and the effect of the use on a copyright owner's potential market for and value of his work.

has greatly proliferated. The recipients are diverse: individual researchers and editors, nonprofit groups, learned societies, and "think tanks," as well as large and small corporations operating for profit. In the vast majority of cases, these publicly supported parties are permitted to obtain private copyrights on the products. Normally these rights are assigned to the publishers, who engage in extensive promotion for sales purposes. One big market for such materials is the public school systems. Local school authorities— easily persuaded that they need the materials—then apply for funds from the Department of Health, Education, and Welfare to finance their purchase. As in the case of publicly financed patented research, the nation's taxpayers pay for the original work twice—once when it is researched and a second time when the public pays monopoly prices for its purchase.

The register of copyrights called for discussion and comments on his 1961 report from interested parties; these comments were published in full in a separate report in 1963.[28] In 1964 the register issued a Preliminary Draft for Revised U.S. Copyright Law, with further discussions and comments on this draft.[29] The same year, House Judiciary Committee Chairman Celler introduced a bill "for purposes of discussion and comment as a basis for the preparation of a revised bill for the Eighty-ninth Congress." Proceedings of panel discussions held by the register's office and the comments received on the Celler bill were published.[30] Finally, another draft bill, H.R. 4347, was introduced in 1965 in the House (and its companion, in the Senate). This bill was also subject to discussions and comments under the register's aegis—again all published.[31]

Subcommittee No. 3 held hearings on H.R. 4347 intermittently from May through September 1965.[32] In the twenty-two days of testimony, more than 150 witnesses appeared. The general public, however, was sparsely represented. With the exception of the representatives of the National Education Association, library groups, and educational television, the hearings were dominated by representatives of private economic interests concerned with expansion of copyright protection. Few academic experts testified on behalf of the general public; many, if not most, who appeared "moonlight" for private copyright interests as economic or legal consultants. Much of the testimony concerned detailed, technical changes in the existing law, unintelligible to the lay public. Indeed, without some background and knowledge of the trade practices of the various industries involved, it is virtually impossible to evaluate many of the proposed changes. Subsequent to the hearings, the subcommittee scrutinized this testimony in more than a hundred hours of executive sessions. An amended version of H.R.4347 was then reported out of committee but died in the Eighty-ninth Congress.

H.R.2512: A New Copyright Bill

The copyright revision bill reappeared in the Ninetieth Congress as H.R.2512. The extensive Judiciary Committee report on submission of this bill to the House in 1967 provides some insight into the legislative process concerning copyright revision.[33] The Copyright Office played a leading role in this process. According to knowledgeable observers, the entire draft of the report and the bill itself, in its final form, were largely the work of the Copyright Office. The revision procedure ordinarily started with private parties meeting informally in an attempt to compromise their differences. Where this was achieved, the subcommittee usually simply ratified the result of the negotiation with little regard for those interests not represented at the bargaining table. Where full accord could not be reached, the subcommittee tended to "split the difference."

The compromises resulted in a bill far more exploitative of the public in many respects than the original proposals of the Copyright Office in 1961. H.R.2515 extended the period of copyright exclusivity on the variable basis of "life of the author plus fifty years." Using tables of life expectancy, the subcommittee calculated that protection would generally run for seventy-six years. In discussing this change, the report stated that the register of copyrights had a change of heart respecting a fixed term, and "now regards a life-plus-fifty term as not only the distinctly preferable alternative but *as the foundation of the entire bill*" (emphasis added).[34] The doctrine of "fair use" was also written into the proposed statute—merely, according to the report, to restate the present judicial doctrine and not "change, narrow, or enlarge it in any way." But the bill was so beset with qualifications and complex minutiae that it appeared of doubtful usefulness in protecting teachers and scholars from infringement suits.

In the case of phonorecords of copyrighted music, there was no real consideration of the register's original proposal to let market forces determine the royalty charge. Instead, it ended up with a two-and-a-half-cent charge for records running for five minutes, with another half cent for each additional minute.

The subcommittee capitulated to the U.S. printing industry—including trade unions, book manufacturers, and typographers—on the "manufacturing clause." Its report stated:

> The committee concluded that, although there is no justification in principle for a manufacturing requirement in the copyright statute, there may still be some economic justification for it. Section 601 of the present bill represents a substantial liberalization that will remove many of the inequities of the present manufacturing requirement. The real issue that lies between Section 601 and complete repeal is an economic one, and on purely economic grounds the possible dangers to the American printing industry in removing all restrictions of foreign manufacture outweigh the possible benefits repeal would bring to American authors and publishers.[35]

With minor changes, the basic provisions remained intact.

Perhaps the best illustration of the subcommittee's supine posture on critical regulatory issues involved nonprofit educational television. The battle lines were clear-cut: educational interests stressed the tremendous importance of this medium, not only as an adjunct to the schools but also for adult education and the general broadening of cultural interests. These interests argued for free use of copyrighted material on their programs. The opposition insisted upon remuneration to authors and publishers. The subcommittee report stated:

> The arguments on both sides, while advanced in support of opposite positions, struck the committee as fundamentally valid and as pointing the way toward a middle course. Following the hearings, representatives of the various interests affected met together to discuss the problem and although no definite agreements emerged from the meetings, certain areas of possible accommodation were suggested. Very recently, proposals for a nationwide communications satellite system that would directly benefit educational broadcasting have underlined the need for copyright solutions that will preserve the right of copyright owners, but without impairing the growth of educational broadcasting or the important services it performs for the Nation.[36]

In fact, the subcommittee proposed a very limited copyright exemption—only to "performances of a nondramatic literary or musical work." Anything of a dramatic character would require the copyright owner's permission. Also, the exemption would only apply to transmissions encompassing areas whose radius did not exceed one hundred miles—thus limiting it strictly to local transmissions.

No attempt was made to correct what the subcommittee called a "difficult and far-reaching problem": the private copyrighting of works done under government contract with public funds. It stated:

> The argument against allowing copyright in this situation is that the public should not be required to pay a "double subsidy", and that it is inconsistent to prohibit copyright in works by Government employees while permitting private copyrights in a growing body of works created by persons who are paid with Government funds.[37]

Having made the case against this giveaway, the bill left the decision to various government agencies. The subcommittee remarked that "where the need to have a work freely available outweighs the need of the private author" for a monopoly, "the problem can be dealt with by specific legislation, agency regulations, or contractual restrictions." In other words, the subcommittee passed the buck. At the same time, the proposed bill reiterated a basic principle in the present law—that where work is done for hire, the employer is entitled to the copyright.[38] Most foreign countries make this principle applicable to hire by the government as well as by private employers. H.R.2512 did not. In this country, the interests of commercial publishers evidently outweigh those of the public.

Double Indemnity

The whole issue is starkly portrayed in a current case, *Williams & Wilkins Co. v. U.S.*[39] Williams & Wilkins is a major publisher of medical books and journals; it markets thirty-seven journals concerned with various medical specialties. Many of the articles in these publications are the result of research funded by the National Institutes of Health (NIH), an arm of HEW. The institutes are currently spending over $900 million a year for research. The National Library of Medicine (NLM), one of the world's largest repositories of medical literature, is housed on the NIH campus. In establishing it, Congress stated specifically that its purpose was "to aid the dissemination and exchange of scientific and other information important to the progress of medicine and to the public health."[40] To further this purpose, the surgeon general was delegated the function "to make available, through loans, photographic or other copying procedures or otherwise, such materials in the Library as he deems appropriate."

In response to its statutory duties, NLM has made photocopies of medical articles available to its own research staff as well as to other libraries. In each case, only a single copy is furnished, and extensive copying from a single issue of a periodical is not permitted. Furthermore, on the presumption that recent issues are available locally, NLM does not furnish copies of articles published within five years in widely disseminated journals.

In 1968, the Williams & Wilkins Company instituted an infringement suit against HEW, NIH, and NLM for unauthorized photocopying of seven articles from its journals. In each case, the research had been funded by HEW. The action for damages was the first copyright case instituted under a statutory provision that the federal government may, in the public interest, infringe private monopoly rights, but that injured parties may sue for monetary damages in the U.S. Court of Claims. This provision (28 U.S.C. 1498[b]) had applied only to patents until 1960, when Congress amended the section to include copyrights as well.

Extensive hearings were held in the Court of Claims before Trial Judge James F. Davis. In February 1972 he rendered an opinion fully supporting the position of Williams & Wilkins and finding the government liable for infringement.[41] In so doing, he ignored the statutory duties of NLM and discarded the judicially developed doctrine of "fair use."* The matter then went to the seven-member Court of Claims, a body which in the past had exhibited great compassion for private claimants in similar cases involving patents.

The case aroused wide concern in educational and library circles. If the judge's opinion were upheld, it would halt the widespread practice of limited copying of materials, even those resulting from publicly funded projects, for teaching and classroom purposes. It would also prevent the routine servicing of researchers with single copies of material out of print or not readily available from commercial sources. The possibility of being sued for infringement has loomed as a constant threat to teachers and libraries in making photocopies; under H.R.2512, maximum penalties would be increased from the present $5,000 to $20,000.

The number of parties represented in the *amici curiae* briefs

---

* After this salute to private monopoly rights, Davis resigned from the government and joined Howrey, Simon, Baker & Murchison, a leading Washington law firm defending large corporations in antitrust cases.

filed with the Court of Claims indicated the intensity of interest.*
Almost two years elapsed from the date of the trial judge's opinion
to the decision by the court itself. In November 1973, the court,
by a four–three vote, reversed the trial judge and upheld the
photocopying on the basis of the "fair use" doctrine. At the same
time, the court urged Congress to speak definitively, based upon
the "economic, social, and policy factors" involved, respecting the
extent to which photocopying should be allowed. Judge Nichols,
in dissent, lamented that libraries would now be free to exploit
copyright holders: "We are making the Dred Scott decision of
copyright law."†[42]

The Future of Copyright Reform

H.R.2512 passed the House in April 1967, but no action was
taken in the Senate. In the same year, hearings were held by the
Senate patents subcommittee on its own copyright bill but it went
no further.[43] Virtually the same bill has been reintroduced in
each new Congress since then; the version in the Ninety-third
Congress is S.1361.

According to Chairman McClellan, Senate action has been
delayed because of the "unresolved cable television question."[44]
This issue was fiercely fought over in the House hearings as well.
Representatives of the Community Antenna Television (CATV)
industry argued for copyright exemption for most of their operations. Arrayed against them were the business interests holding
copyright monopolies. Eventually, the CATV issue was sub-
merged in a free-for-all between the Congress, the Federal Com-

---

* These included the National Education Association of the U.S., the
American Library Association, the Authors League of America, Inc., the
Association of American Publishers, Inc., the Association of American Uni-
versity Presses, Inc., American Chemical Society, the American Medical
Association, Association of Research Libraries, American Association of Law
Libraries, and a host of other groups.
† The Williams & Wilkins Co. subsequently filed a petition for *certiorari*
in the U.S. Supreme Court, and the Court has agreed to decide the case
during its 1974–75 term.

munications Commission, and the Office of Telecommunications Policy in the White House. Speaking on the Senate floor in March 1973, McClellan acidly referred to this matter:

> It has been proposed that special treatment should be accorded the cable television royalty issue. The principal justification for this position is a private agreement developed by Dr. Clay T. Whitehead, Director of the Office of Telecommunications Policy. The Whitehead agreement has been generally interpreted as seeking to eliminate the Congress from any role in determining cable television royalty rates. Even though public law places copyright affairs exclusively in the legislative branch, neither the Copyright Office of the Library of Congress, nor the House or Senate subcommittees having jurisdiction in copyright matters, were represented at Dr. Whitehead's meetings.[45]

Nearly twenty years after the initial effort to revise the 1909 copyright law, success remained elusive. In early 1974 the Office of Telecommunications Policy issued its report on CATV and shortly thereafter the Supreme Court ruled that CATV systems which transmit distant signals to local subscribers are not required to pay copyright fees. Only Congress remained silent. In April 1974, the House subcommittee had not even held hearings on copyright reform; the Senate subcommittee was still immobilized by division. Meanwhile, copyright owners benefit handsomely from this delay. Resolutions have regularly passed both houses of Congress extending, in the interim, copyright protection on existing copyrights. This began in 1962 with a three-year extension in anticipation of prompt legislation; in 1965 there was a two-year extension; and since then five annual one-year extensions. A new extension for two years will end on December 31, 1974.

As a result, the fifty-six-year limitation under the present law has become meaningless. Copyrights that would have expired in 1962 or soon after have been given another dozen years of life. The intensive concern of the Senate subcommittee in protecting the interests of copyright holders is indicated by Senator McClellan in his report recommending further extension, "so that the copyright holders may enjoy the benefit of any increase in term that may be enacted by the Congress."[46]

In 1971, one dissenting voice spoke out on this issue in the House. Kastenmeier, chairman of the House subcommittee and sole remaining participant in that committee's long legislative labors, objected. He remarked that, though he had supported interim extension legislation in the past, he now thought it was a mistake.[47] In 1972, he was joined in his dissent by two other members of the subcommittee—John Conyers, Jr., and Robert F. Drinan—and also by Don Edwards, member of the parent committee. The dissenters stated:

> The most frequently heard defense of the legislation invokes compassion for elderly authors and composers whose retirement income is threatened by the expiration of their copyrights. What is lost sight of here is that we are talking about copyrights that are between fifty-six and sixty-seven years old, so that their present owners are in all but very rare cases descendents and assignees, including commercial, corporate assignees, of authors and composers rather than the creators of the copyrighted works themselves.
>
> We must remember that the national policy is to encourage free enterprise as well as authorship—not to preempt ever greater segments of the public domain, as this measure and its predecessors tend to do.[48]

Past efforts at writing copyright legislation have failed to recognize the imperatives of technological and industrial change in forms of communication, photocopying developments, data storage, computer usage, and the like. Nor have they effectively protected the interests of the general public against exploitation of monopoly rights by copyright holders. Entrenched economic interests have managed, with the acquiescense of the submissive Judiciary subcommittees and a sympathetic, attentive Copyright Office, to thwart both of these objectives, maintaining a highly profitable status quo.

A national commission to recommend a copyright policy, composed of technical experts and industry representatives balanced by an equal number of spokesmen for the general public might constitute a more hopeful approach to reform and modernization of the copyright law. Such a group might thaw the present frozen structure of private control by vested interests, as well as generate pressure for long-needed reforms. Acres of diamonds, be they copyrights or patents, are simply too valuable to be left to industry and the specialized bar for harvesting.

III

CONSTITUTIONALISM IN CONGRESS

6

Separation of Powers:
Finding the Founding Fathers

"I would trust him," said Republican Senator Barry Goldwater, "with my wife's back teeth."[1] The Senate evidently agreed, for it entrusted the same man with the most explosive political dynamite in American history—the Watergate investigation.

This man—the "only" one, according to the majority leader of the Senate, who commands the respect of the "whole Senate"— is Sam J. Ervin, Jr., the North Carolina mountain man who quotes Shakespeare and the Bible on the run, and is a master of the pithy anecdote with the poisonous bite. In a homogenized, computer-driven society that values horsepower more than horse sense, Sam Ervin is a septuagenarian holdout battling to preserve the unique and the traditional. His shield is his reputation in the Senate. His sword is his wit and his passion for the Constitution.

A former North Carolina supreme court justice, dean of the

NOTE: This chapter was prepared by Peter H. Schuck and Lee Lane.

constitutional experts in the Senate, Ervin chairs one of the most intriguing and innovative operations in Congress—the Subcommittee on the Separation of Powers. Here, erudition is entrée, hearings are seminars, consultants are scholars, and legal philosophers are kings.

On the first day that his new subcommittee held hearings, in July 1967, Ervin observed:

> It must be conceded that the efficiency of a plenary governmental power is not available to the American government. And it must be expected that this inefficiency, due in no small degree to the separation of powers, is unpopular with those who are eager to use government as an instrument of social change. I have always felt . . . one of the most salutary features of our constitution is the degree of inefficiency it imparts to the exercise of governmental power. And I have suspected that the Founding Fathers intentionally and very wisely provided for a measure of inefficiency to assure that the impulse to act and the opportunity to take action would not occur simultaneously.[2]

To some, this view is quaint and archaic, like stovepipe hats. Kevin Phillips, a syndicated columnist and former Nixon campaign aide who has earned a reputation as a conservative Republican Party theorist, has characterized the Constitution's separation-of powers doctrine as "Montesquieu's mistake," frozen in "legal concrete"; as "doing more harm than good." Phillips, lumping America's system with that of several "banana and betel-nut" republics, observed:

> Congress's separate power is an obstacle to modern policy-making. . . .
> A special inertia flows from Congress's empire of committees and subcommittees, pork barrels, personal policy dukedoms, huge personal staffs . . . all by-products of our unique separation of powers. . . .
> The "separation of powers" concept—which lives on so vigilantly in the name of Sen. Sam Ervin's subcommittee—

may in fact be obsolete: an eighteenth century theory
turned into late twentieth-century malfunction. . . .[3]

If anybody in Congress will listen to this kind of brash critique
it is "Uncle Sam," as his admirers call him. A forthright man, he
has peremptorily—with a leap of his full brows—dismissed the
President of the United States as someone "who ought to go back
to law school for a refresher course."* When the Watergate affair
began to erupt and key Senate Democrats sought a "nonpartisan"
leader with an unimpeachable reputation and a sharply honed
mind accustomed to the give-and-take of legal fencing, Ervin was
the natural choice.

The Subcommittee

Ervin's subcommittee jurisdiction is broad: his own enormous
prestige in the Senate assures its budget and perquisites. The
limiting factor in the performance of the subcommittee, in the
chief counsel's view, is "simply Sam Ervin's time." With his
assumption of the chairmanship of the Government Operations
Committee, and the press of work on the select Watergate committee, that resource became even scarcer.

During the Ninety-second Congress, the five-man subcommittee included conservatives John McClellan and Edward Gurney,
and liberals Charles Mathias and Quentin Burdick. Senator Robert Byrd joined the subcommittee in the Ninety-third Congress.
McClellan, now chairman of the Appropriations Committee and
second-ranking Democrat in Government Operations, rarely par-
ticipates in Separation of Powers work and almost never attends
hearings. He does vote, allying himself with Chairman Ervin
more than any other member. Senator Burdick's participation has
also been limited, though he attends some hearings.

In contrast, the two Republicans have been active participants

* The comment was widely reported in the media when the issue of "executive privilege" arose prior to Watergate, and President Nixon refused to
allow his aides to testify.

in hearings. Senator Mathias has not only attended, he asks probing questions. Mathias differed from the administration's position on every issue and bill taken up by the subcommittee— helping to create a nonpartisan atmosphere on the subcommittee. His relationship with Ervin is cordial and mutually respectful.[4]

Senator Gurney is intermittently active in subcommittee hearings. A former prosecutor, he is abrasive in his questioning, even with administration officials such as Caspar Weinberger, Secretary of the Department of Health, Education, and Welfare (in hearings on executive privilege).[5] Gurney's occasional votes against administration positions indicate that, though not as independent as Mathias, he has abjured the role of White House mouthpiece.

Budget and Staff

The subcommittee received a budget of $382,000 in the Ninety-second Congress, which was expended primarily on staff salaries and consultants. The budget increased substantially in the Ninety-third Congress, exceeding $500,000.

Rufus L. Edmisten, chief counsel and staff director of the subcommittee, assumed his responsibilities in 1969. Edmisten asserts that his responsibilities run only to Ervin, not to the other subcommittee members. Whatever the legal propriety of this view, Edmisten is in every way Sam Ervin's man. A native of North Carolina, Edmisten refers to himself as "Ervin's neighbor." He has campaigned for the senator and has performed legislative work unrelated to the subcommittee.* He was intent on handling Ervin's impoundment bills, for example, even though they were referred to the Government Operations Committee, of which Ervin is chairman.

Other members of the Separation of Powers majority staff in-

* Edmisten also served under Ervin as deputy majority counsel to the select Watergate committee, and is expected to become a candidate for the post of state attorney general in North Carolina, having received much TV exposure as "the young man whispering in Sam Ervin's ear."

clude three full-time professionals, a part-time law student, and three clerical workers. McClellan and Burdick provide meager staff input into the subcommittee, which reflects their minimal participation in its work. The minority staff allotment ($36,000 a year in the Ninety-second Congress) is used for two and a half staff positions. Minority Counsel Joel M. Abramson and his staff, although on the subcommittee payroll, are hired by and work for Mathias. Abramson, in fact, handles all of Mathias's Judiciary Committee work. Abramson also has official responsibilities to Senator Gurney, but he estimates that he has done very little work for Gurney. Instead, Gurney relies on his personal staff, preferring not to ask the more liberal minority counsel to prepare statements with which he disagrees.[6] In any event, Gurney accords Separation of Powers a low priority in his Judiciary responsibilities.[7]

One of the subcommittee's most fruitful innovations is the extensive use of consultants to supplement the work of regular staff. (Hiring consultants was at one time very widespread among congressional committees; the practice was mostly pork and patronage. Now prior approval by the Senate Rules and Administration Committee is required for the retention of consultants, and they are used sparingly.)

Because of his excellent relationships with the present and former chairman of the Senate Committee on Rules and Administration, Ervin has been able to finance the services of four distinguished legal scholars: Philip B. Kurland of the University of Chicago Law School, chief consultant, who has been associated with the subcommittee longest; Alexander M. Bickel of Yale Law School and the Center for Advanced Study in the Behavioral Sciences at Stanford; and Ralph K. Winter, also of the Yale Law School, are all conservatives. A recent addition is Arthur S. Miller of the George Washington University National Law Center, formerly a mentor of Edmisten. Miller, the only consultant in Washington on a regular basis, is, by his own account, the most liberal of the four. Their contributions are augmented by specialists retained to deal with specific issues: for example, Professor Preble Stolz of the University of California Law School at

Berkeley, an expert on fiscal affairs, was brought in to work on executive impoundment of appropriated funds.

Edmisten would like to use temporary specialists more extensively but cannot; Chairman Eastland requires that everyone hired by Judiciary undergo a rigorous and time-consuming security check, regardless of previous clearances. Authorization from the Rules and Administration Committee also takes time. The entire process consumes about five months, and since the normal lead-time for hearings is less than half that, the use of temporary consultants becomes virtually impossible.

Hearings

The Separation of Powers Subcommittee conducted a total of sixteen days of hearings during the Ninety-second Congress. In the Ninety-first, the subcommittee had inquired into the independence of the federal judiciary and federal court jurisdiction over unfair labor practices. In the Ninety-second, investigations centered on the pocket-veto power of the president, executive impoundment of appropriated funds, executive privilege, Executive Order No. 11605 (defining the powers of the Subversive Activities Control Board), and executive agreements.

The subcommittee charts its investigatory symposia by a kind of curriculum plan. At the beginning of each year, Edmisten writes to all consultants inquiring about pertinent issues that may be appropriate for subcommittee study. Occasionally, consultants take the initiative in suggesting topics.[8] The minority also makes suggestions for hearings (no such suggestion has yet been implemented, although they are given "serious consideration").[9] Finally, sources from within the executive branch alert the staff to situations, such as impoundments, that raise questions within the subcommittee's jurisdiction.

Staffers perform most of the background research, relying upon the consultants only for brief introductory memoranda and suggestions for witnesses. The Congressional Research Service, an arm of Congress which is available to do research for members, is not regarded as an independent informational or analytical resource. Due to understaffing, the service often provides superficial research, simply updating or revising previous studies and relying heavily upon information provided by executive agencies.[10]

Hearings center on the powerful personality of Sam Ervin. Edmisten usually drafts Ervin's opening remarks, but the staff does little else to prepare him for the hearing; unlike most senators, Ervin is not supplied with written questions by the staff, nor is he usually briefed. Instead, he listens intently to testimony and then questions the witness closely. Ervin's interrogations are usually lucid, and his disagreement rarely becomes acrimonious. Although his approach is legalistic, his formulations are folksy and allegorical, generally avoiding technical jargon.[11] The subcommittee, unlike others on the Hill, permits its consultants, as well as the chief and minority counsels, to interrogate and respond to witnesses. Typically, two or three consultants are present, and each is permitted sufficient time to develop a serious line of questioning and analysis. An unusually large portion of the hearing record is devoted to academic monographs and scholarly articles.

The Pocket Veto

Long before Watergate, Nixonian impoundments, and other presidential innovations had made strained presidential-congressional relations a fashionable legislative issue, the Separation of Powers Subcommittee had begun to plow this fertile field. One of the subcommittee's less ambitious investigations—the hearing on presidential pocket-veto power—is an example that also illustrates Ervin's ability (with the help of the media) to transform esoteric, abstract questions of constitutional law into visible, palpable national issues.

Edmisten had to put the hearing together in less than one month in January 1971 to permit the subcommittee to capitalize on President Nixon's pocket veto of a health bill in December 1970.

The basis for the pocket veto is Article I, Section 7, clause 2, of the Constitution:

> Every bill which shall have passed the House of Representatives and the Senate, shall, before it becomes a law, be presented to the President of the United States; if he approve he shall sign it, but if not he shall return it, with his objections, to that House in which it shall have originated. . . . If any bill shall not be returned by the President within ten days (Sundays excepted) after it shall have been presented to him, the same shall be a law, in like manner as if he had signed it, unless the Congress by their adjournment prevent its return, in which case it shall not be a law.

The president neither endorses nor affirmatively vetoes, but simply holds the bill in his "pocket" until Congress adjourns, thus effecting a veto by inaction. Use of a pocket veto rather than a regular veto has two advantages to the president. First, a pocket veto cannot be overridden by a two-thirds vote of both houses of Congress. Second, a pocket veto is normally less visible than a regular veto and is therefore often preferable politically.

The bill at issue, S.3418, was very popular. S.3418 authorized "grants to medical schools and hospitals to assist them in establishing special departments and programs in the field of family practice and otherwise to encourage and promote the training of medical and paramedical personnel in the field of family medicine." The bill had passed the Senate by a vote of 64 to 1 and the House by 346 to 2. The ten-day period expired during the four-day Christmas recess; this was the shortest period ever cited by a president as justification for a pocket veto.

The veto raised two key issues. First, did a mere four-day recess (for the Christmas holiday) constitute an "adjournment" within the meaning of the constitutional provision? Second, did the adjournment actually "prevent" the President from returning the bill to Congress? In other words, could the President have used a conventional veto?

Ervin claimed that the President's pocket veto of S.3418 was an unconstitutional expansion of the pocket-veto power, which was available at the end of a session, but not during an indefinite (*sine die*) adjournment. Professor Miller bolstered Ervin, pointing out that the permanent officers of the House and Senate had been instructed to receive any messages from the executive. A veto message could easily have been delivered to them.[12] Assistant Attorney General William H. Rehnquist (now a justice of the Supreme Court), testifying for the administration, flatly rejected both of these arguments.[13]

The discussion was technical, legal, and arcane, but some consideration was given to the political dimension of the problem. The subcommittee's hearings included an unusual list of participants. Dr. Donald Matthews of the Brookings Institution, speaking on the policy issues, pointed out that the President's action indicated "a gross lack of respect for congressional opinion."[14] Dr. Thomas E. Cronin, professor of political science at the University of North Carolina at Chapel Hill, suggested viewing the President's action in the broader perspective of executive-legislative relations.[15] Senator Edward Kennedy declared that the administration had a propensity for vetoing health measures.[16] None of these ideas was fully developed, however. Instead, Miller and Rehnquist debated the intricacies of the legal precedents at great—and inconclusive—length.*

Congressional opponents of the administration have used tactical approaches in the past to attempt to limit the president's pocket-veto power. In this case, Ervin and Kennedy cooperated in efforts to appropriate funds under the vetoed authorization. The money was appropriated. But the administration simply refused to spend the appropriation: it impounded the funds. Kennedy subsequently filed a court action to invalidate Nixon's pocket

---

* Even the format was academic. Conducted as a round-table discussion, this hearing, in the view of some participants, encouraged a freer exchange of opinions.[17] This format is useful, however, only when there are relatively few witnesses or participants, and the subcommittee has not used it since.

veto.* Kennedy's testimony at the hearing indicated that he was already considering the suit at that time, and it seems fair to conclude that the hearing itself did not influence his decision to do so.[18]

Ervin then introduced a bill defining the conditions under which a pocket veto may be exercised. This legislation would, in effect, prevent pocket vetoes unless the Congress had adjourned *sine die,* and it also explicitly authorizes the president to deliver veto messages to the permanent officers of the Congress during a recess.† The bill was reported out of the Separation of Powers Subcommittee by a unanimous vote, but died in the full Judiciary Committee with the expiration of the Ninety-second Congress. The bill, reintroduced in the Ninety-third Congress, was referred to the subcommittee, where it was again approved, and was reported to the full committee. On the House side, a pocket veto bill (H.R.7386) was approved by the subcommittee on Monopolies and Commercial Law (formerly No. 5) after a day of hearings, and the full House Judiciary has voted to report it to the floor.

Baiting the Red-Baiters

The Subversive Activities Control Board (SACB), created by the Internal Security Act of 1950, administers the act's provision requiring registration of Communist-action, Communist-front, and Communist-infiltrated organizations. The Supreme Court in 1965 ruled that the registration requirement violates the Fifth Amendment protection against self-incrimination.[19] The SACB was left with no raison d'être. In January 1968, Congress attempted to revive SACB as an independent agency to classify

* On August 15, 1973, the United States District Court for the District of Columbia upheld Kennedy, ruling that the pocket veto in question was unconstitutional. Kennedy v. Sampson, 364 F. Supp. 1075.

† In August 1973, Congress adjourned for a month and took the highly unusual step of delaying the presentation of several bills to the President until shortly before Congress was to return, thereby ensuring that no ten-day hiatus—and thus no occasion for a pocket veto—could be said to exist.

those organizations, but a federal appeals court ruled that public disclosure of membership (without determination that the individual member shares the illegal purposes of the organization) violates the First Amendment.[20] The Supreme Court refused to review the case. Again, SACB was left powerless.

On July 2, 1971, President Nixon issued Executive Order No. 11605, purporting to grant SACB new powers. This order ostensibly amended Executive Order No. 10451, issued by President Eisenhower in 1953, which established loyalty and security requirements for federal employees. The Nixon order conferred on SACB the authority (on petition of the attorney general) to conduct hearings to determine which organizations are totalitarian, Fascist, Communist, subversive, or advocate acts of violence and seek to overthrow the government.

In early October 1971, the Separation of Powers Subcommittee conducted two days of hearings on Nixon's executive order, Ervin having earlier introduced two bills to nullify it.* Professor Miller played the most prominent role at the hearings, serving as consultant in the first hearing and testifying as a witness in the second. The chairman was present and active throughout. He was in fine fettle.

The administration position was defended by then Assistant Attorney General William Rehnquist; John W. Mahan, chairman of SACB; and Senator Gurney. The basic argument was summarized by Senator Gurney:

> This nation has a right to defend itself, to prevent its destruction . . . the people of this nation are entitled to have the background and character of government employees thoroughly investigated. I do not believe that the taxpayers

---

* There was an initial rivalry between Edmisten and Lawrence Baskir, chief counsel of the Constitutional Rights Subcommittee—of which Ervin is also chairman—over which subcommittee would hold the hearings. Two of Ervin's three basic objections to E.O.11605 related to constitutional rights.[21] Edmisten prevailed, however, for two reasons. First, he convinced Ervin that congressional opposition to the order would be more effective if the issue was defined as one of separation of powers. Second, Edmisten got to Ervin first.[22]

of this country should have to subsidize revolutionaries under the guise of protecting the First Amendment rights of freedom of speech and assembly by employing them as "civil servants."[23]

Rehnquist cited several precedents for such a delegation of authority to an independent board or agency.[24] Mahan asserted that congressional appropriations to SACB implied congressional approval.[25] Ervin would have none of it. He maintained that the order was only tenuously related to the fitness of government employees, and was actually an attempt to amend the Internal Security Act by executive fiat, a usurpation of Congress's legislative power. He challenged the vague statutory criteria such as "subversive" or "totalitarian," and a definition of "organization" so broad that it applied, in Ervin's view, to any two Americans acting together. The senator, returning to his folksy style, ridiculed the administration's position as "sailing clear across the Atlantic Ocean when your objective is to get across the creek."[26]

Ervin also argued that the president could not delegate such responsibilities to an independent board or agency, as distinguished from department heads who are solely instruments of the president. Rehnquist objected on the ground that unchallenged executive orders had delegated authority to such agencies in the past.[27] Ervin, in a burst of alliteration (since repeated several times in the Watergate hearings), rejoined, "I would observe that murder and larceny have been committed in every generation, but that has not made murder meritorious nor larceny legal."[28]

Ervin's two bills in the Ninety-second Congress, S.2466 and S. Res. 163 sought, respectively, to (a) prohibit any board employee from carrying out any functions conferred by the executive order, and (b) express disapproval and demand revocations of E.O.11605. But rather than push his bills, Ervin concentrated his energies on ending the appropriations for SACB. He won— the second time around. Ervin first proposed an amendment to the fiscal 1973 appropriations bill for the Departments of State, Justice, and Commerce, and for the federal judiciary, which would have cut off all funds for the SACB. After meeting defeat, he tried again with an amendment to cut off funds for activities carried out to enforce E.O.11605. This was accepted, and on June 30, 1973, the SACB met a well-deserved but long-delayed death for lack of funds.

Senator Ervin decided to take no chances on SACB's resurrection. A bill to eliminate from the Internal Security Act all references to the SACB was drafted by the Separation of Powers Subcommittee staff and was introduced in the Ninety-third Congress as S.1965. Senator Eastland referred S.1965 not to Separation of Powers but to the Internal Security Subcommittee, where it now rests.

Conventions, Privileges, Other Legislation

The Separation of Powers Subcommittee has been active on other fronts as well. In the Ninety-second Congress, it reported out S.215, which carefully limits the conditions under which a constitutional convention may be convened and conducted, thereby reducing the likelihood of wholesale, precipitous amendment of the Constitution by the convention method. S.215 passed the Senate eighty-four to nothing, but stalled in the House Judiciary Committee due to Chairman Emanuel Celler's opposition. The bill was reintroduced as S.1272 in the Ninety-third Congress, was immediately reported to the Senate floor, and quickly passed the Senate by voice vote. Its fate now rests with Subcommittee No. 4 of the House Judiciary Committee, where three House bills (H.R.2937, H.R.6919, and H.R.4799) addressing the convention issue have also been introduced.*

The subcommittee also considered a bill (S.3671) introduced by Senator John G. Tower (R., Tex.) in the Ninety-first Congress to shift jurisdiction over unfair-labor-practice cases from the National Labor Relations Board (NLRB) to federal district courts —a proposal that greatly agitated pro- and antilabor interest

* The American Bar Association has also set up a special convention committee, which has issued a report to guard against the "chaos" attendant upon such a convention.

groups. The three–two vote by which the bill was reported out of the subcommittee reflects the bitter division on the issue. Ervin (who has a reputation for being antilabor) argued that the board was pro-union and hence was not a fair judge to hear labor cases. Senators Burdick and Mathias, both of whom enjoyed substantial labor support in their last elections, opposed the bill. S.3671 died in full committee in the Ninety-second Congress when Ervin decided not to push it. It was reintroduced in the Ninety-third Congress as S.853.

S.1125, Senator J. William Fulbright's (D., Ark.) executive-privilege bill in the Ninety-second Congress, illustrates the unanimity with which the Separation of Powers Subcommittee approaches issues that can be defined as conflicts over executive and congressional power. The bill required that any claims of executive privilege be supported by written authorizations by the president, and it authorized a total fund cutoff against any agency that fails to comply. It passed the subcommittee without dissent, but died with the expiration of the Congress. Reintroduced in the Ninety-third Congress as S.858, the bill was referred to the Government Operations Committee, of which Ervin had become chairman. In the spring of 1973 joint hearings were held by Senator Edmund S. Muskie's (D., Me.) Intergovernmental Relations Subcommittee, Senator Kennedy's Administrative Practice and Procedure Subcommittee, and the Separation of Powers Subcommittee. In addition, Separation of Powers cleared S.J. Res. 72, a "sense of the Senate" resolution on the same issue.

Department of Justice

In the wake of Watergate, the subcommittee is considering several bills designed to assure that the Department of Justice cannot again be manipulated by a White House intent upon concealing official wrongdoing. In March 1974 hearings were held on S.2978, Senator Cranston's bill to establish a commission to study the creation of an independent permanent mechanism to investigate and prosecute alleged official misconduct by high public officials, and S.2803, Senator Ervin's bill to safeguard the independence of the Department of Justice, providing, among other things, for a six-year term for the attorney general. Other, related bills pending before the subcommittee are S.3395, Senator Robert Byrd's bill to prohibit the president from appointing a campaign or party official to be attorney general, and S.3652, Senator Ervin's bill to create an independent public prosecutor. No final action on this legislation is expected during the Ninety-third Congress.

Adding It Up

If a handful of bills extending back into the Ninety-first Congress appear to constitute an unimpressive subcommittee product, one must consider the constitutional dimensions of their subject matters. Moreover, some of the subcommittee's earlier hearings seem likely to bear legislative fruit in the Ninety-third. In particular, Ervin's anti-impoundment bill, S.373, requiring the agencies to spend appropriated funds, passed the Senate in the spring of 1973, while a weaker version passed the House in July. As this book went to press, the bills were awaiting consideration by a conference committee.*

In any event, indications of subcommittee effectiveness, other than the number or quality of bills passed, abound. For example, in the Ninety-second Congress, the subcommittee issued an interim informational report on a bill (S.3475) sponsored jointly by Ervin and Fulbright—who chairs the Foreign Relations Committee—that would require congressional review of executive agreements. Its successor in the Ninety-third Congress, S.1472, has been approved by Separation of Powers and awaits action by the full committee, after which it must be sent to the Foreign Relations Committee for final action. Ervin's hearings and sponsorship have substantially increased the issue's appeal to many conservatives in Congress, who distrust Fulbright and his committee's work. Furthermore, Ervin's active involvement in this area was a decisive factor in convincing the administration to

---

* S.1514, a bill to reform the budgetary process, contains an anti-impoundment provision which, if adopted, would obviate the necessity for S.373.

accept a more permissive executive agreements bill sponsored by Senator Clifford P. Case (R., N.J.), in hopes of forestalling Ervin's legislation.[29]

Perhaps the critical element in evaluating the work of Separation of Powers is the value of the investigations themselves, a value not easily measured. With the exception of the hearings on the NLRB, which reflected the chairman's personal political concerns as much as the intrinsic importance of the issue to the subcommittee's functions, they have been far too abstract and scholarly to constitute effective oversight of executive agencies. But they have served an even more important function, calling public and Congressional attention to the silent but fundamental shifts in the substratum of the American constitutional system.

If there is a criticism to be leveled at the Separation of Powers Subcommittee, it must be directed not to the quality or saliency of its work but simply to the need for much more of it, particularly in the areas of congressional reform and budgetary decision-making. Given the quality of its chairman,* its ranking minority member, its staff, and its access to budget, the Separation of Powers Subcommittee has not fully exploited its potential. Yet in this cavil, there is a considerable compliment.

---

* Senator Ervin has announced his retirement from the Senate at the end of the Ninety-third Congress.

7

Constitutional Amendments: Legislating for the Ages

A leading scholar of the Constitution, the late Arthur E. Sutherland, Jr., has observed: "Few statutes, and no document as general in terms as a Constitution, can speak with enough specifics
to meet the emerging needs of a complex society. The amending
process is too inflexible to serve the needs of adaptation and
change; but the Court has been able to accomplish both."[1]

An examination of the processing of proposed constitutional
amendments by the Judiciary committees and their subcommittees both supports and casts doubt upon Sutherland's assertion.
For such an examination reveals the great strengths and virtues
of congressional leadership in the amendment process, particularly in view of its potential fact-finding and policy-analysis
resources. At the same time, it is evident that Congress is hobbled

NOTE: This chapter was prepared by Peter H. Schuck and Michael E.
Ward.

in its ability to process constitutional amendments by the extreme difficulty of overcoming the glacial pace, institutional inertia, and hostility to innovation built into congressional procedures. Yet in the area of constitutional amendments, perhaps this is as it should be. Certainly different criteria of evaluation are required. Because routine legislation must address the contemporary and short-run needs of American society, and because these needs are complex and rapidly changing, one desires legislating committees to be responsive, innovative, productive, and dynamic.

Constitutional amendments, however, properly address faults in the basic structure of American government, in the Constitution that confers legitimacy upon conventional legislation. The stability of the American system, certainly among its greatest strengths, in large part reflects the stability of the Constitution and the immutability of its underlying precepts. Changes should therefore be made only when absolutely necessary and only after the most painstaking and thorough deliberation, for mistakes, however well intended, cannot easily be remedied. Extensive hearings must develop relevant facts and values, educating members of Congress and the public about the need for, and consequences of, proposed amendments. The Constitution itself, of course, recognizes this need, providing for amendment only after various procedural hurdles have been surmounted and assuring that precipitous changes cannot easily be made. Indeed, subsequent to the adoption of the Bill of Rights in 1791, only sixteen efforts to amend the Constitution have succeeded. Senator Birch Bayh, chairman of the Senate Judiciary Subcommittee on Constitutional Amendments, notes this fact with satisfaction:

> We do not want a Constitution that can be changed at every whim, every wave of passion that sweeps over the country. . . . It should take a major effort. It should not be taken lightly. . . . We need to study all aspects thoroughly.[2]

In the area of constitutional amendments, as in so many other areas within the jurisdiction of the Judiciary committees, the Senate committee has carried the laboring oar, particularly in recent years. Under Bayh's leadership, the Senate subcommittee has pursued a careful and deliberate course, although its hearings have often lacked the balance requisite for impartial consideration of the proposals. In the Ninety-first and Ninety-second Congresses, the Senate subcommittee reported to the full committee three proposed constitutional amendments: an amendment providing for direct election of the president; the Equal Rights Amendment (ERA), prohibiting governmental discrimination on the basis of sex; and what came to be the Twenty-sixth Amendment, prohibiting the denial of the franchise to persons eighteen years of age or over on account of age. Midway through the Ninety-third Congress, the subcommittee once again approved a direct-election amendment.

Although the chairman's opinion is undoubtedly the single most important factor in the choice of amendments on which hearings are to be held, Senator Bayh has insisted that he will not prevent action on controversial or popular amendments he opposes.[3] Hearings were held early in the Ninety-third Congress, for example, on the school-prayer amendments, although Bayh vigorously opposes these measures. The senator has stated that, because of the nature of constitutional amendments, hearings should be held

> in an atmosphere free from partisan passions and inflamed emotions. I believe it is appropriate to delay hearings until such time as tempers have cooled following particular events which give rise to sudden public emotions—for example, controversial decisions of the Supreme Court.[4]

Other than Bayh, three subcommittee members appear to have considerable effect upon the subcommittee's work. Two minority senators—Marlow Cook and Strom Thurmond—are quite active.[*] Cook, in particular, has vigorously interrogated witnesses. Other minority members in the Ninety-second Congress were Hiram

---

[*] They attended, respectively, eleven and nine of the nineteen days of hearings in the 91st and 92nd congresses for which printed records are available.

Fong, Roman Hruska, and Edward Gurney. In the Ninety-third, Gurney was replaced by Hugh Scott.

Senator Bayh's most formidable foe in the subcommittee is Senator Sam Ervin, who, as a traditional conservative, is quite skeptical of constitutional innovations. Although Senator Ervin has attended only one day of the nineteen, he has been quite influential in shaping the subcommittee's product due to his reputation as the Senate's leading constitutional law expert. The other majority members, James Eastland, Robert Byrd, Quentin Burdick, and John Tunney, do not participate extensively in the subcommittee's work.

Direct Election

When the subcommittee began work on electoral reform in 1966 in response to a presidential message, Bayh was opposed to the direct-election concept. The subcommittee staff prepared a memorandum analyzing various proposals, primarily on the basis of existing legal and political studies.[5] The subcommittee then commenced several days of hearings,[6] after which the staff began to study the proposals suggested in the hearings. On the basis of the hearings and the study, Bayh determined that direct election was the best alternative to the existing electoral college system after all. The hearings were reconvened, and more witnesses were heard. At their conclusion, Bayh held a news conference to announce his conversion to full support of direct election.[7] The subcommittee held additional hearings on electoral reform in early 1969.[8] One congressional aide, not on the subcommittee staff, has suggested that these hearings were "loaded" in favor of the direct-election plan,[9] but the statistics do not justify such a charge. Opposition viewpoints were amply represented; 45 percent of the witnesses testified *against* direct election. And extensive hearings on the same subject had been held just a few years earlier.

Despite Bayh's preferences, however, the amendment that was reported by the subcommittee in May 1969 contained not a direct-election plan but the so-called District Plan, whereby electors would be chosen from single-member districts within each state and two electors would be chosen statewide. By February 1970 the full committee had still not considered the proposal; Senator Strom Thurmond had delayed such consideration through filibuster. When Bayh threatened to retaliate with a filibuster of the G. Harrold Carswell nomination for the Supreme Court, the committee finally agreed to vote on the amendment by late April.[10]

First, however, the full committee would hold its own hearings. These hearings were ordered, according to one congressional aide, at the instigation of Senator Sam Ervin,[11] who wished to retain the Electoral College and was to prove to be Bayh's most formidable foe on this issue. These hearings did indeed appear to have been "loaded." Seventy-six percent (71 percent if senators are excluded) testified against the direct-election proposal. Furthermore, Bayh was not informed of the hearings until less than a week before they were scheduled to be held, and had not even been consulted with regard to the witness list. When he finally saw the list, it contained no proponents of direct election; only through his insistence were some added.[12]

When the full committee finally did consider electoral reform, it became evident that Bayh had done his work well. To his delight, the full committee reversed the decision of the subcommittee and reported the direct-election plan to the Senate by a vote of eleven to six.[13] Exhausted by its lengthy journey, however, the amendment expired on the floor of the Senate, the victim of a filibuster. It was reintroduced in the Ninety-third Congress, some additional hearings were held, and in December 1973, the subcommittee unanimously voted to report the amendment to the full committee.

The direct-election concept has fared better in the House. In the Ninety-first Congress, the full Judiciary Committee held hearings on,[14] and reported, a direct-election amendment.[15] Committee members had begun consideration with many diverse opinions about the value of such an amendment, but strong support was expressed by groups such as the American Bar

Association and labor organizations. Committee opinion finally coalesced[16] and the amendment passed the House. It failed, however, in the Senate. The House took no action in the Ninety-second Congress, for the committee was convinced—correctly, as it turned out—that the Senate would again block action.[17]

Equal Rights

Although equal rights amendments barring governmental discrimination against women on the ground of sex were introduced in every Congress since 1923, and were reported many times in the past twelve Congresses, their last full airing was in the mid-1950s. Women's organizations approached the Senate subcommittee in the late 1960s to insist that it take a fresh look at this old subject. The subcommittee staff believed that most persons were for or against the amendment largely on emotional grounds, and that considerable study was needed to learn the extent to which present statutes discriminated against women and what effects the Equal Rights Amendment would have on existing law.

In order to document the extent of present discrimination and to destroy the many myths used to justify it, the staff worked with a number of women's groups, including the National Organization for Women (NOW), the National Federation of Business and Professional Women's Clubs, and the National Association of Women Lawyers. With respect to legal questions such as the impact of the proposed amendment on existing statutes, generally recognized constitutional scholars, such as Paul Freund of Harvard, were consulted. Many opposed the amendment, often on the ground that the Fourteenth Amendment already barred most sex discrimination. The staff then recruited other legal scholars—"new legal talent"—to research and write about ERA. The Harvard and Yale law reviews were encouraged to study the area.[18]

Hearings were held publicizing the data on existing discrimination,[19] but the women's groups lobbying for the amendment suspected that the hearings were merely a delaying tactic.[20] In reality, however, hearings were essential. For although the amendment would undoubtedly have had little difficulty on the Senate floor—it was cosponsored by seventy-six senators—considerable public support would be necessary to push the proposal through the full committee in the first instance, and to increase the chance for House passage and ratification by the states.

The principal opponent of ERA was Senator Ervin. He maintained that "constitutional and legal chaos" would be the result of such a measure; acknowledging that some state laws did discriminate against women, he characterized the amendment as "about as wise as using a bomb to exterminate a few mice." When the amendment reached the full Judiciary Committee in the Ninety-first Congress, Ervin prevailed upon Eastland to hold additional hearings.[21]

Seven hours of full-committee hearings were held chaired by Senator Cook. These were somewhat more balanced than those on electoral reform; 68 percent of the witnesses testified in favor of ERA. However, fifteen of the witnesses for the amendment—all but one—testified in one day, while one favorable witness and seven opposition witnesses had their testimony spread over a three-day period. Senator Ervin, who had requested the hearings, did not even attend on the day when the proponents of the amendment testified.

Although the Senate committee did not report the ERA, a House-passed version went directly to the Senate floor, where amendments were added to exempt women from the draft and to allow prayer in public schools. As the opponents had prophesied, the pro-ERA forces would not accept this hybrid. The amendment was "laid aside."

When the amendment was reintroduced in the Ninety-second Congress, the subcommittee approved, six-to-four, a substitute offered by Senator Ervin, and reported it to the full committee.[22] Ervin introduced nine amendments which would have "emasculated" ERA; his major substitute would have preserved legal distinctions based on "physiological or functional differences" between the sexes. As in the electoral reform dispute, however, the full committee was not convinced by Ervin's arguments, and rejected his substitute, one to fifteen.[23] The original, unqualified amendment was reported, and soon passed the Senate.

In the House Judiciary Committee, Celler had doggedly thwarted consideration of the amendment. In the Ninety-first Congress, he was seriously challenged by the strong pressure for the amendment, yet, insisting upon his prerogatives as committee chairman, he refused to refer the bill to subcommittee or hold hearings. When he saw the battle was almost lost—a discharge petition was brought up to bypass his committee—Celler assured congressmen that he planned to hold hearings the next month, a maneuver employed successfully in the past. This time, however, it was too late; his committee was discharged, and ERA passed the House 350–15. All to no avail, however, for as we have seen, the Senate took no action in that Congress.

In the Ninety-second Congress, faced with overwhelming support for the amendment in both chambers, Celler was obliged to refer the amendment to Subcommittee No. 4. Hearings were held,[24] and the amendment was reported to the floor with an amendment sponsored by Representative Charles E. Wiggins (R., Cal.), providing that ERA would not impair the validity of laws discriminating between the sexes with respect to military service or health and safety. Fourteen committee members opposed the Wiggins Amendment,[25] and the House deleted it before passing ERA. ERA subsequently passed the Senate and awaits ratification by the requisite number of states. The youthful Bayh had managed to outwait, if he could not outwit, the two ancients, Celler and Ervin.

The Eighteen-Year-Old Vote

An amendment to lower the voting age to eighteen had been introduced by Senator Arthur H. Vandenburg (D., Mich.) as early as 1942, and Senator Jennings Randolph (D., W.Va.) had been advancing such a reform since that time, first as a congressman and, since 1958, in the Senate. Hearings were held in the Ninety-first Congress on an amendment to permit persons at least eighteen years old to vote; all witnesses supported such an amendment and it was reported out of the Senate subcommittee. Consideration by the full committee was delayed, however, pending the Supreme Court decision on the constitutionality of Congress's earlier statutory effort to lower the voting age.[26] The decision, which came too late in the Ninety-first Congress for any action, upheld the constitutionality of the statute as applied to federal, but not state, elections.[27] The committee staff was concerned that the Nixon administration might attempt to block passage of the amendment in the Ninety-second Congress. The staff also recognized that the strongest arguments for the amendment were the confusion, cost, and fraud that were certain to result from the Court's decision. Working quickly, the staff telegraphed, and then telephoned and wrote to the chief election officers of every state, requesting them to analyze the dire consequences that would flow from a dual election system.[28] The replies, which generally favored the reform, were quickly consolidated in a report for the full committee,[29] which reported the amendment.[30] It passed the Senate in an atmosphere of widespread concern that only uniformity between federal and state electoral requirements would avoid chaos in the 1972 elections.

The House Judiciary Committee reported the amendment without even holding hearings,[31] and it was rapidly passed. The requisite number of states ratified the Twenty-sixth Amendment in time for the 1972 elections.

Other Proposed Amendments

The Senate subcommittee considered, without approving, four other proposed amendments during the Ninety-first and Ninety-second Congresses. Hearings were held on: an amendment to grant congressional representation to the District of Columbia;[32] a proposal lengthening to six years the president's term of office and establishing a limit of one term, thus freeing the president from political pressures of reelection;[33] a proposal for a national primary election, or system of primary elections, to facilitate the nomination of candidates for the presidency and vice-presidency;[34]

and a measure to require the reconfirmation of federal judges after a term of eight years.[35]

In the Ninety-third Congress, the subcommittee had, by April 1974, held hearings on an amendment to overrule the Supreme Court's restrictions on school prayers; the amendment to grant congressional representation to the District of Columbia; an amendment to lower the minimum age for senators and representatives by three years, to twenty-seven and twenty-two, respectively, in recognition of the reduction in the voting age from twenty-one to eighteen; and an amendment to overturn the 1972 Supreme Court decision (*Roe* v. *Wade*) prohibiting certain state restrictions on abortion. Hearings were scheduled to consider Senator Fong's proposed amendment to permit naturalized citizens to run for president after they have been citizens for fourteen years.

The House Judiciary Committee has considered two other major proposed amendments, one of which was also considered by the Senate. Subcommittee No. 1 held hearings on congressional representation for the District of Columbia; the proposals ranged from granting full representation to ceding the territory back to the state of Maryland. None was reported out of committee.[36] Subcommittee No. 5 considered various proposals to prohibit the busing of school children to obtain racial balance.[37]

Staff and Hearings

Since each of the measures considered by the Senate subcommittee has been either pending for a number of years or was recently introduced by a senator outside the subcommittee, the work of the subcommittee staff has been, rather than the development of new amendments, primarily educational: the study and documentation of the need (or lack of need) for such measures, and the social and legal consequences of their adoption. The staff may seek the assistance of outside groups in this work. Because of the varied nature of constitutional amendments, however, only a few groups are contacted with any regularity. Among these are the American Bar Association, the Association of the Bar of the City of New York, and the League of Women Voters. Law professors are also called on in efforts to evaluate proposed amendments.[38]

Other sources are used as the occasion demands, such as the women's groups mentioned in connection with the Equal Rights Amendment, or the Chamber of Commerce and the AFL–CIO in the more recent work on direct election.[39] On other occasions—the first memorandum on electoral reform and the research following the Supreme Court decision on the eighteen-year-old vote are examples—staff research may be done without much input from outside groups.

Hearings serve a number of purposes for the Senate subcommittee. They are often an important source of information, as when they convinced a skeptical Senator Bayh of the value of direct election.

They may also illuminate an issue for the public. The 1970 hearings on electoral reform, for example, were directed almost exclusively at the public, the subcommittee having gained most of the necessary information at the earlier hearings. The absence of any witnesses opposing the amendment in the hearings on the vote for eighteen-year-olds might indicate that those hearings were also for public, rather than subcommittee, benefit.

Similarly, the hearings on congressional representation for the District of Columbia were held because of public interest; they contributed no new information. Senator Bayh favored this amendment, and there was an intensive lobbying campaign for it.[40] It was clear, however, that the amendment could not command enough votes to be reported out of the subcommittee; the executive session that defeated it was so one-sided that it was described as "a joke."[41]

The composition of witness lists at the hearings on constitutional amendments in both Senate and House subcommittees leaves something to be desired. In the Senate, present and former representatives of the federal government constituted a disproportionately large portion—47 percent—of the witnesses at subcommittee hearings in the Ninety-first Congress and the first session of the Ninety-second. The proportion of government officials testifying at House subcommittee hearings on constitutional amendments was much less—5 percent. But nearly half (44 percent) the witnesses in the House were members of Congress; the figure is 23 percent in the Senate. Members of Congress have other, less wasteful means of communicating their views to the subcommittees and the public, and should be discouraged from dominating these hearings.

Academics are seriously underrepresented at hearings. Few persons are as qualified to assess the legal impact of constitutional amendments as law and political science professors, yet faculty members have constituted only 11 percent of the witnesses during the period examined. Such participation might be adequate for a subcommittee dealing with routine legislation, but not for one considering so peculiarly legal and institutional a matter as constitutional amendments. Legislators seeking to understand the historical analogues and political consequences, intended and unintended, of fundamental reforms would benefit greatly from academic insight, while an adequate appreciation of the technical drafting problems and legal context requires significant input from law professors and legal scholars. That the staff may have already talked to many of these persons, read their works, and prepared memoranda on the basis of this information is little reason to deny the subcommittee members themselves the opportunity to hear and interrogate these experts at first hand.

As we have seen, some of the hearings have also been philosophically biased. The majority of witnesses in each of the recent sets of Senate hearings have advocated the same viewpoint as chairman Bayh. In the hearings on representation for the District of Columbia, the eighteen-year-old vote, and the Equal Rights Amendment, staff members sought to justify this imbalance on the implausible ground that few opposition witnesses were available.

When legislating for the ages, the subcommittee has a particularly weighty responsibility to consider all points of view fully, even if that consideration results in some delay. For, to paraphrase Chief Justice Marshall, members must never forget that it is a Constitution that they are writing.

8

Constitutional Rights:
Acid Test for Conservatives

No jurisdictional responsibility of the Judiciary committees demands a greater measure of the legislator's wisdom, virtue, and vision than the protection of constitutional rights. These rights, conferred for the most part by the Bill of Rights—the first ten amendments to the Constitution—constitute the previous heritage of liberty under law. Yet these rights are particularly vulnerable to periodic depredations by the Congress and the executive branch, and gradual erosion due to changes in public opinion. There are several reasons why this is so.

First, the constitutional provisions that enshrine these rights were purposefully written in vague and general formulations, such as "due process of law," "freedom of speech," "equal protection of the laws," and "unreasonable searches and seizures," and do not

NOTE: This chapter was prepared by Peter H. Schuck and Michael E. Ward.

172

readily yield self-evident, agreed-upon interpretations when applied to specific situations.

Second, this vagueness permits—and encourages—citizens and politicians, patriots and demagogues, to encroach upon the traditional understanding of these rights while continuing to affirm their loyalty to them. In times of social polarization, strong efforts are frequently made to "save" the constitutional system by restricting (or, less commonly, expanding) these rights in novel ways.

Third, the guarantor of these rights has recently and increasingly come to be the federal judiciary. In the short run, of course, the courts have managed to perform the function of constitutional protector with admirable courage and prudence. But it is too much to expect that the courts, armed with great prestige and mystique but few other political resources, can hold the line for very long against an aroused and alarmed public seeking swift solutions to intractable social problems—often at the behest of politicians who should know better. Ultimately, as Finley Peter Dunne's wise bartender Mr. Dooley observed, the courts "follow the election returns"; they are frail reeds to lean upon in the long run for the protection of rights that a majority, or an intense and powerful minority, insists upon restricting.

Finally, the citizens most in need of the protection of constitutional rights tend to be the poor, the minorities, the unpopular, the unconventional, and the outspoken. Yet these are precisely the persons least capable of protecting themselves against legislative, administrative, or popular incursions on their liberties.

For all of these reasons, constitutional rights are exquisitely delicate and fragile safeguards, easily compromised or lost. The responsibility of Congress to protect, nurture, and enforce them is correspondingly great, and any failure to do so—as in the area of civil rights, as we shall see below—assumes the dimensions of a national tragedy.

THE SENATE SUBCOMMITTEE ON CONSTITUTIONAL RIGHTS: UNCLE SAM'S LOVE AFFAIR WITH THE CONSTITUTION— OR MOST OF IT

The Senate Judiciary Committee has conferred jurisdiction over "all matters pertaining to constitutional rights" upon its Subcommittee on Constitutional Rights. In the Judiciary Committee, as in the Senate itself, the acknowledged high priest of the Constitution is Sam Ervin of North Carolina, self-proclaimed "country lawyer" and formerly a judge on his state's supreme court. It is not surprising, then, that Ervin chairs this subcommittee,* nor that the Bill of Rights is always the current business of the day on the subcommittee's agenda.

Sam Ervin's subcommittee is very much a one-man band. His interpretations of the Constitution determine which investigations the subcommittee will undertake.[1] His reputation as the premier constitutional lawyer in the Senate, a reputation enhanced by the Watergate hearings, also gives the subcommittee influence far beyond its legislative jurisdiction. Other subcommittees often question the staff about the constitutionality of particular measures on which they are working.[2] Other senators, out of respect for Ervin, often make concessions on points that the North Carolinian feels raise constitutional questions.†

Ervin attracts a remarkable degree of bipartisan support for his projects. Being both a conservative southerner and a civil libertarian, he constitutes a much-needed and -valued bridge over which liberals and conservatives may often cross, even on controversial bills. This rare quality makes Ervin a unique institution in a body in which consensus and accommodation are necessary but often difficult to achieve.

Informal "oversight" by the Subcommittee on Constitutional

---

* Ervin assumed the chairmanship in January 1961.

† One example is the narrowing of permissive wiretapping provisions in the Omnibus Control and Safe Streets Act of 1968, processed in Senator McClellan's Subcommittee on Criminal Laws and Procedures.[3]

Rights reflects Ervin's view that congressional committees must closely scrutinize the federal establishment.[4] In particular, the subcommittee carefully monitors bureaucratic invasions of constitutional rights. Letters of inquiry, criticism, and recommendation are sent to federal departments and agencies, and often produce results. In response to such letters from the subcommittee, the army reversed an earlier decision and permitted the distribution of anti-Vietnam War leaflets in areas of Fort Bragg, North Carolina, accessible to the public; the Defense Department eliminated a medical form that invaded privacy; the army reduced its surveillance of private citizens; and HEW issued new regulations to prevent the use of "blacklists" and unnecessary inquiries into the personal beliefs of employees.[5]

Ervin's views on the obligation of congressmen to interpret the Constitution further augment the subcommittee's function. Too many legislators, in Ervin's view, are unwilling to render a judgment concerning the constitutionality of particular measures independent of that of the courts:

> Every Congressman is bound by his oath to support the Constitution, and to determine to the best of his ability whether proposed legislation is constitutional when he casts his vote in respect to it. In my judgment, a Congressman is under no obligation to accept as valid a constitutional decision if he personally deems such decision unconstitutional. In taking this position, I am supported by Abraham Lincoln, who expressly declared . . . that the Dred Scott decision was unsound . . . and that he refused to accept it as a rule of government of the people and that he would do everything within his power to secure its reversal.[6]

Senator Ervin might also have mentioned that he was supported in his view by Thomas Jefferson,[7] Andrew Jackson,[8] Franklin Roosevelt,[9] and Richard Nixon, all practitioners of the strong presidency that Ervin regards as a fundamental threat to liberty.

These views have the effect of negating one vital area of the subcommittee's responsibilities. For Ervin considers large parts of the civil rights legislation of the past decade—as well as Supreme

Court decisions permitting busing as a tool of integration—to be unconstitutional. For example, the senator stated in 1971:

> I still consider Title VI of the Civil Rights Act of 1964 unconstitutional under the Due Process Clause of the Fifth Amendment. . . . [It] makes every Federal Department and Agency administering federally assisted programs a prosecutor, a judge, and a jury in respect to all controversies involving alleged discrimination in the programs they respectively administer. . . .[10]

One Capitol Hill lobbyist, while expressing admiration for the senator's efforts in the civil liberties field, commented, "Nobody lobbies Ervin on civil rights matters. . . . He's unapproachable."

Some view his strict constructionism as a mask for a slick obstructionism. For instance, Ervin opposes the Consumer Protection Agency bill on constitutional grounds, attacking the proposed agency as another attempt by big government to interfere with the rights of citizens, notwithstanding that the proposed agency would have no regulatory powers whatsoever. When the bill reached the Senate floor in 1972, Ervin offered an amendment to strip the agency of its capacity to intervene in court proceedings as a legal advocate for consumers. When this was rejected, Ervin led a filibuster that killed the bill for the Ninety-second Congress, and as this book went to press he was preparing to do the same for the Ninety-third. Some of his maneuvers against civil rights legislation would make James Eastland blush. As one congressional aide put it, "There isn't anyone in the Senate who can match Sam Ervin on the Constitution, as long as you don't go beyond the Twelfth Amendment."[11]

Because of Ervin's opposition, and the domination of the Judiciary Committee by Southerners and conservatives, the only civil rights legislation referred to the committee without a time limit imposed by the Senate is either routine or unimportant. Nevertheless, Ervin's position does not strain the subcommittee staff's relationships with civil liberties groups. Indeed, when the senator is involved in efforts inimical to "equal protection" rights, the work is usually performed by the separate staff of the Subcommittee on Revision and Codification, which Ervin also chairs and which does little or no other work. A peculiar arrangement, to be sure, but a political contrivance that seems to work well.

Subcommittee Operations

Subcommittee members in the Ninety-second Congress were Ervin, John McClellan, Edward Kennedy, Birch Bayh, Robert Byrd, and John Tunney, Democrats; and Roman Hruska, Hiram Fong, Strom Thurmond, and Hugh Scott, Republicans. In the Ninety-third Congress, McClellan dropped out and Scott was replaced by Edward Gurney.

Senator Hruska, ranking minority member, generally introduces administration bills and is regarded as the Justice Department's spokesman on the subcommittee.[12] One of Hruska's staff members during the Ninety-second Congress, Malcolm Hawk, was a former Justice Department employee, and maintained close contact there.*

The only private-interest group that plays a significant part in subcommittee operations—the American Civil Liberties Union (ACLU)—is a vital information source and a subcommittee asset. The ACLU's concerns coincide substantially with those of the subcommittee. Their respective staffs are in frequent contact, and the ACLU almost always testifies at subcommittee hearings.[13] Other groups from which the subcommittee occasionally draws information include the New York City Bar Association, and, to a lesser extent, the American Bar Association. Law schools are frequently contacted.[14]

Since the subcommittee generally obtains most of its information prior to hearings through informal contacts and letters, the hearings themselves perform less of an informational role to the senators than an educational one for the public. Chief Counsel Lawrence Baskir perceives the primary functions of hearings to be public exposure and the meeting (and, it is hoped, reconcilia-

---

* Hawk later returned to the Justice Department.

tion) of legitimate criticisms of subcommittee bills and reports. For this reason, witnesses are drawn from many fields, and all viewpoints—particularly those of the Justice Department—are encouraged.[15] For example, in hearings on the extension of the Voting Rights Act of 1965, to which Senator Ervin was unalterably opposed, most witnesses advocated extension of the bill in the same or stronger form.[16]

During the Ninety-third Congress the subcommittee's legislative product has been rather meager. In large part, this reflects the chairman's preoccupation with the select Watergate committee during much of the Congress. It also reflects Ervin's practice of using subcommittee staff for his personal legislative chores. Much staff time, for example, was devoted to amendment of a Justice Department appropriations bill to repeal "no-knock" authority in the District of Columbia and for federal narcotics agents. This amendment passed the Senate in July 1974.

The subcommittee's jurisdiction is relatively broad and untrammeled—the entire Bill of Rights is its domain. Since it does not create programs or authorize particular administrative activities, the subcommittee is free to play the role of constitutional ombudsman, ferreting out threats to basic liberties wherever it finds them.

Preventive Detention: The Presumption of Guilt

The Sixth Amendment's guarantee of a "speedy trial" was one of the least controversial constitutional rights until the recent explosion of criminal court dockets threatened to overwhelm the judicial system, particularly in urban areas. Lengthy delays between arrest and trial posed, perhaps for the first time in our history, a conflict between the need for expedition and equity in the processing of criminal cases.

The Bail Reform Act of 1966 assured that accused persons in federal courts and in the District of Columbia would not be denied the opportunity for pretrial bail merely because of poverty. The act had been developed by the subcommittee in response to a survey of the criminal justice process conducted in the early 1960s,[17] and it established a hierarchy of conditions that a judge might impose in order to ensure the appearance of the accused for trial. The requirement of money bail was discouraged. Release of the accused on his or her own recognizance, after satisfying the court as to his or her roots in the community (as demonstrated by, for example, steady employment), became the preferred method of pretrial release.

The Bail Reform Act, however, met with a mixed reaction on Capitol Hill and at the White House. The Nixon administration and some members of the House and Senate insisted that the act had permitted or caused (the distinction was never made clear) additional crimes to be committed by persons already under indictment but released, sometimes for long periods of time, on their own recognizance. During the Ninety-first Congress, the administration introduced, through Senator Hruska, a proposal for a system of "preventive detention," which would deny pretrial bail to defendants accused of serious crimes and deemed both "a danger to the community" and "substantially guilty."

Hearings were held on the administration's preventive-detention bill,[18] and its many deficiencies, including a lack of legal standards, were exposed. Indeed, of the twenty-six witnesses, only four testified in favor of the bill, while two others provided factual, essentially neutral, testimony. The extent and intensity of opposition to the measure belies any assertion that Ervin "loaded" the hearings. The Justice Department, the main proponent of the bill, was given ample time to prepare for the hearings. Lawrence Baskir, chief counsel of the Subcommittee on Constitutional Rights, noted that it is usually to one's advantage to see that all viewpoints are represented; in his experience, loaded hearings often backfire.[19] The minority counsel confirmed the fact that the administration's forces on the subcommittee were free to call any witnesses they chose.

The wall of opposition to preventive detention convinced the administration that the time was not ripe for such a bill: although a bill was reintroduced in the Ninety-third Congress, the action was largely *pro forma*. Neither the Justice Department nor Senator Hruska actually expect favorable action to be taken; they have not pressured the subcommittee to do so and Ervin has let the bill languish.[20]

As part of their effort to forestall the administration bill, the subcommittee staff had quietly dusted off old "speedy trial" legislation (prepared, but not used, in the Lyndon B. Johnson years by the Department of Justice), sending drafts to judges and other persons and groups involved in the reform of the criminal justice system.[21] The resulting bill, introduced by Ervin, required federal courts to assure accused persons a trial within sixty days. If the deadline were not met, the case would be dismissed and future prosecution prohibited.

At the hearings on Ervin's speedy-trial bill, no witness opposed its basic intent, but the particular time limit was a matter of some contention. The Justice Department wanted the bill tied to a reform of federal criminal procedure which would limit the right of federal prisoners to attack the validity of their convictions by means of a writ of *habeas corpus*.[22] As a result, the bill was reported out of the subcommittee too late in the Ninety-second Congress for action by the full committee. When it was reintroduced early in the Ninety-third Congress, Justice joined forces with state prosecutors in opposition to the bill.[23] To the National Association of District Attorneys' assertion that the bill would "emasculate justice," Ervin replied that dismissal, while a harsh sanction against delay, was nevertheless the only effective one.[24] After approval by the subcommittee and the full committee, the Ervin bill was passed by the Senate in July 1974.

Privacy: Keeping Big Brother in His Place

The Subcommittee on Constitutional Rights is exceptionally responsive to queries and initiatives from the public. Its 1965 hearings on psychological testing stimulated a continuing flow of letters and visits from citizens and groups with grievances about invasions of privacy. Such unsolicited input in turn stimulated investigations, solicitations of information by the staff, publicity, and, thus, more gratuitous input.[25] The privacy-related issues studied by the subcommittee in the past decade cover a broad spectrum, including clearance requirements for consultant-scientists of the Department of Health, Education, and Welfare; privacy of employees in the executive branch; and investigations of federal data banks and army surveillance.[26]

In June 1974 the subcommittee reported to the full committee S.2318, a bill to restrict surveillance of civilians by military authorities, and to provide for civil and criminal sanctions and citizen suits against unauthorized monitoring activities. Senators McClellan, Hruska, Thurmond, and Gurney dissented, opposing the sanction provisions. In April 1974 hearings were held on the Ervin and administration bills (S.2693 and 2694) to restrict the use and dissemination by criminal justice agencies of data on individuals and organizations. The Ervin bill has been marked up by the staff and weakened somewhat in order to attract administration support. The problem of data banks generally has been explored in joint hearings with the Government Operations Committee, which is considering several bills on federal data banks.

Recent Supreme Court decisions have generated interest—and information—on activities of grand juries. Letters from prisoners have prompted a staff study of prisoners' rights. Even small incidents have prompted some subcommittee action: when a local high school group approached the subcommittee about Federal Communications Commission (FCC) rulings prohibiting radio stations from playing drug-related songs, the protest provided part of the impetus for hearings on the rights of broadcasters and listeners.[27]

The subcommittee has also responded to a recent spate of proceedings seeking to require journalists, under pain of imprisonment, to reveal their sources to grand juries and courts. In the Ninety-first and Ninety-second Congresses, the subcommittee considered a "shield" law, which would provide a legal defense to reporters who refused, under certain circumstances, to disclose their information and sources. Such a bill was again introduced in the Ninety-third Congress, but division on the subcommittee between proponents (primarily Ervin and Byrd) and opponents has created a stalemate.

CONSTITUTIONAL RIGHTS IN THE HOUSE: TRYING TO FILL THE CIVIL RIGHTS VOID

Like so many of its other jurisdictional areas, responsibility for constitutional rights in the House Judiciary Committee is divided. The principle of division is rather legalistic.

When "civil liberties"—those rights enumerated in the Bill of Rights and made applicable to the states by the "due process" clause of the Fourteenth Amendment—are involved, Subcommittees No. 4 and (occasionally) No. 3 have assumed responsibility. When the issue is "civil rights"—those rights arising from the "equal protection" clause of the Fourteenth Amendment—legislation is handled by Subcommittee No. 5 and oversight is the role of No. 4.

Civil Liberties

The activities of the liberal House Judiciary Committee in the protection of civil liberties during the Ninety-second Congress can be described briefly: it did very little—while its far more conservative Senate counterpart managed to play an active role in monitoring the operations of federal agencies affecting civil liberties. During the Ninety-third Congress, Congressman Robert Kastenmeier's Subcommittee on Courts, Civil Liberties, and the Administration of Justice (formerly Subcommittee No. 3), with an augmented staff, has been somewhat more active. In March 1974, it held three contentious days of hearings on various bills dealing with amnesty for war resisters and draft evaders. In January 1974, it held a day of hearings on voting rights for ex-offenders.

During 1973, the subcommittee held lengthy hearings on more than fifty bills dealing with the issue of privileged communications between reporters and news sources. In late March 1974, the subcommittee approved H.R.5928 and sent it to the full committee along with a package of amendments sponsored by Chairman Kastenmeier. The bill, which confers an absolute "shield" upon reporters, except at the trial stage, is extremely controversial. Indeed, H.R.5928 so divided the otherwise cohesive subcommittee that Kastenmeier sided with the minority to support the bill against the opposition of all Democrats on the subcommittee.

Congressman Don Edwards of California, chairman of Subcommittee No. 4 (Civil Rights and Constitutional Rights in the Ninety-third Congress), desires to see the committee perform more oversight of the FBI, and his subcommittee took a significant step in that direction in the Ninety-second Congress. The 1972 appropriations for the FBI included provisions authorizing the bureau to distribute arrest records to federally chartered banks. Arrest records may often go into the mammoth FBI computer—whether there is ultimately a conviction or not. Since, according to Aryeh Neier of the ACLU, one out of every two American men will be arrested at some time during his life,[28] dissemination of these records would clearly be a threat to the privacy of a vast number of citizens. Subcommittee No. 4 developed and held hearings on several bills to prohibit the dissemination of arrest records to organizations other than law enforcement agencies, and to prohibit such dissemination altogether if the record is more than two years old. The measures were still under consideration by the subcommittee in the spring of 1974.

The House Judiciary Committee dealt with two other significant civil liberties issues in the Ninety-first and Ninety-second Congresses. Subcommittee No. 3 reported out the expansion of the Criminal Justice Act of 1964, which had been processed through Ervin's Senate subcommittee and had passed the Senate. Subcommittee No. 4 held extensive hearings on preventive detention. Indeed, according to one observer, the subcommittee "heard it to death."[29] The issue was so controversial that the staff was deluged by private organizations seeking to contribute information; the American Civil Liberties Union, the Bar Association of the City of New York, and the American Friends Service Committee were among the participants—as they often are on constitutional rights questions.[30]

As is the case in much of the other work of the House Judiciary Committee, hearings on constitutional rights are burdened with excessive testimony by members of Congress. Fully 30 percent of its witnesses in the Ninety-first and Ninety-second Congress were members of the House. In part, this may reflect the fact that the busing hearings were consciously designed for the purpose of delay and thus included an exceptionally large number of witnesses from the Congress. Yet even if busing is excluded from consideration, congressmen constituted 18 percent of the witnesses.

Civil Rights

The liberal House Judiciary Committee treats civil rights with the same tender loving care that the Senate committee lavishes on civil liberties. Chairman Emanuel Celler traditionally directed civil rights legislation to his own subcommittee, No. 5, whose staff, drawing upon the resources of the U.S. Commission on Civil Rights and occasional crisis-oriented consultations with the Leadership Conference on Civil Rights,[31] had developed considerable expertise. In the past, a bipartisan spirit has prevailed in the Judiciary Committee on civil rights issues. Former ranking minority member William McCulloch was deeply committed to civil rights and worked closely with Celler in this area.[32] Moreover, the Republican minority has never hesitated to oppose an administration proposal to weaken hard-won civil rights legislation.

This bipartisan coalition was put to the test during the Ninety-first and Ninety-second Congresses.

A key provision of the Voting Rights Act of 1965 abolished the use of literacy tests as a precondition for voter registration (long used to bar blacks from the polls) in certain southern states. To ensure nondiscrimination, it required states with low minority registrations to submit to the attorney general* any new voting restrictions or apportionment changes they enacted.

* Or the U.S. District Court for the District of Columbia.

The Nixon administration had plans to change the act when the time came for an extension in 1969. It suggested that any state's changes in voting requirements be considered "presumptively valid," shifting the burden of proving discrimination to the attorney general. This was a fundamental departure from the scheme of the 1965 act. At the same time, the administration offered a carrot: the nondiscrimination law would be made nationwide, and the laws invalidating voting restrictions would be broadened.[33]

Celler and ranking minority member McCulloch balked: they and the subcommittee wanted only a simple extension of the act. A compromise was enacted, retaining the burden of proof on the states, but incorporating the administration's nationwide literacy test ban.

Mississippi (the Senate Judiciary chairman's home state) was less than enchanted. In early 1971, various counties in that state passed and enforced (without the attorney general's approval) state laws requiring all voters to reregister. The Department of Justice, then under John Mitchell, took no action; it argued that a simple affidavit declaring the new laws nondiscriminatory in purpose and effect would satisfy the requirement for enforcement.[34]

The committee, sensing trouble, mobilized forces. On May 26, 1971, Subcommittee No. 4 held its first hearings as the subcommittee specifically charged with civil rights oversight responsibilities.[35] (Chairman Don Edwards had spent several years trying to win this as a principal jurisdiction for his subcommittee.)[36] The hearings addressed Mississippi's defiance, and witnesses for civil rights groups testified in opposition to the Justice Department's policy of acquiescence. The subcommittee issued a unanimous report condemning the department for its policy, and included recommendations as to the proper standards to be used in assessing compliance with the law.[37] Civil rights activists later noted a significant improvement in the enforcement procedures of the Department of Justice as a result of the subcommittee's hearings and report.

Other Oversight Activities

The subcommittee selected very specific, manageable subject matters for its first investigations after the Mississippi case. Counsel Jerome Zeifman explained that at this early stage the subcommittee preferred areas of investigation that would set the tone and credibility of its operations for the future.[38] One lobbyist suggests that investigatory subjects are chosen for the additional purpose of educating the members of the subcommittee on the assumption that, given the right information, everyone will make the "right" judgments.[39] The bipartisan actions of the subcommittee demonstrate that it has been remarkably successful on both counts.

After the Mississippi case, Edwards' subcommittee conducted an investigation of the federal employment problems of the Spanish-speaking: specifically, the extent to which the federal civil service had made progress in overcoming prior discrimination against this group. One set of hearings in 1972 examined whether quotas and discrimination inhered in the Civil Service examination process,[40] and another studied the educational problems of Spanish-speaking people.[41]

In 1972, the subcommittee also studied whether the Federal Power Commission was authorized and/or obligated under Title VII of the Civil Rights Act of 1964 (the equal-employment-opportunity title) to require that FPC licensees not practice discrimination. The subcommittee's conclusion that the FPC was authorized to issue such regulations was accepted by the Department of Justice.[42] The department's agreement on this issue helped rehabilitate its reputation after the Mississippi debacle and cemented bipartisanship on the subcommittee.

The subcommittee's investigation of the Farmers Home Administration, a part of the larger study of federal housing programs, resulted in the adoption by that agency of a procedure by which denials of loans can be appealed. The subcommittee found that minorities suffered from the absence of such procedures and recommended specific improvements in the new rules.[43]

Subcommittee Operations

In its investigatory role, the staff maintains frequent contact with and often relies for its raw data upon, the United States Commission on Civil Rights, the Leadership Conference on Civil Rights, the Lawyers Committee for Civil Rights Under Law, the Washington Research Project, the National Urban Coalition, and the Center for National Policy Review. In most of these instances, the subcommittee has solicited information from the groups.[44] In addition, groups that specialize in a particular subject area may be called in for hearings; for example, La Raza Unida on Chicano problems, or the Voter Education Project on voting rights. Few witnesses in hearings represent organizations other than the civil rights groups and the federal government. According to Congressman Edwards, the subcommittee's efforts to encourage other private groups with particular grievances to come forward have had only limited success; the civil rights oversight function is still so new that many outsiders do not yet know of its existence.[45]

Subcommittee No. 4 has also exploited the resources of the General Accounting Office for data and field investigations. After using the GAO in other areas of subcommittee jurisdiction, such as a study of the urban drug problem, the subcommittee requested a GAO investigation of discrimination in hospitals and other facilities receiving federal funds through Medicare and Medicaid. The study failed to disclose any significant—other than *de facto*—discrimination, and no hearings were held.[46]

The subcommittee frequently requests hard data from administrative officials and other witnesses to evaluate civil rights performance. In hearings, members cross-examine federal officials vigorously when they are dissatisfied with their work.

Congressman Edwards concedes that the subcommittee has not taken on the big one—oversight over the nonenforcement by federal agencies of Title VI of the Civil Rights Act of 1964,*

---

* The subcommittee's only effort in the Title VI area—an investigation of federal housing programs—did not produce any major changes in the opera-

which prohibits discrimination in federally assisted programs. He stresses that the subcommittee's jurisdiction is limited to oversight in this area; it cannot generate and report legislation.* In order to enforce its recommendations and conclusions, in Edwards' view, the subcommittee would have to produce entirely new legislation.[47] Edwards feels that a committee or subcommittee with direct legislative jurisdiction over agencies could exert leverage by amending their authorizations. Similarly, appropriations committees could condition allocation of funds on satisfactory performance by agencies in enforcing Title VI and other civil rights laws.

But Subcommittee No. 4 could not monitor Title VI even if it devoted its entire budget to the effort. Like all House Judiciary subcommittees, it has taken vows of poverty. Three majority counsel cannot handle an enormous jurisdiction, only one part of which is civil rights oversight. As Jonathan Fleming of the United States Commission on Civil Rights has pointed out, "The Commission has over 150 people and can barely keep up with Title VI, so how can you expect three people to keep up with it?"

Congressman Edwards' efforts to obtain more staff were generally rebuffed by full committee chairman Celler.† Lack of funds also precludes more innovative techniques of investigation, such as holding field hearings, which would be more accessible to citizens and groups affected by discrimination. Such hearings were planned in at least one instance, but Celler denied the necessary funds.[48] Celler's parsimony was certainly not the result of a lack of commitment to civil rights, but reflected his belief, attested to by many congressmen and staff persons, that the committee budget should be tightly controlled—by Celler!

---

tion of the programs by the Department of Housing and Urban Development.

* Another unit studying this area, but also lacking legislative jurisdiction, is the Senate Select Committee on Equal Educational Opportunity, chaired by Walter Mondale (D., Minn.). It held a series of hearings in July and August 1970 on Title VI enforcement in the education field.

† Celler did accede to Edwards' request for permission to hire a Chicano attorney.

And there is another obstacle. Since civil rights bills tradition-ally passed through Celler's own subcommittee (No. 5), the staff of Subcommittee No. 4 still lacks experience in these issues.[49] The enthusiasm for their civil rights oversight work, however, partly compensates for this inexperience, as do Edwards' efforts to hire more, particularly minority-group, staff.

When all is said and done, the House Judiciary Committee cannot and will not fill the constitutional void created by the Senate committee's refusal to ride herd on federal agencies charged with enforcement of the civil rights laws. There is simply too much to be done. How much remains to be done may be suggested by sampling the fruits of almost a decade's experience under the Civil Rights Act of 1964.

THE JUDICIARY COMMITTEES AND TITLE VI: PRESENT AT THE CREATION; PRESENT AT THE CREMATION

In perhaps its grandest gesture of commitment to the constitu-tional principle of equality before the law, Congress enacted the Civil Rights Act of 1964. President Johnson, invoking all of the symbolism of the occasion, signed it into law on the Fourth of July. Title VI of the act prohibited racial discrimination in all federally assisted programs.

The creation of the act, and particularly Title VI, spoke vol-umes about the Judiciary committees and the protection of con-stitutional rights. For the House Judiciary Committee, it was one of the proudest moments in its long history; its chairman, Emanuel Celler, had been the act's principal architect. For the Senate Judiciary Committee and its chairman, James Eastland, the act was a crushing defeat; the committee had done everything in its power to defeat it.

Almost nine years later, it appeared that the Senate Judiciary Committee had lost the battle but won the war. In January 1973 the United States Commission on Civil Rights issued its fourth lengthy evaluation of the federal civil rights enforcement effort, and grimly concluded:

> Our findings are dismayingly similar to those in our earlier reports. The basic finding of our initial report, issued in October 1970, was that executive branch enforcement of civil rights mandates was so inadequate as to render the laws practically meaningless. . . . This latest Commission study has reinforced the findings of the three preceding reports that the Government's civil rights program is not adequate or even close to it. . . .[50]

The core provision of Title VI of the Civil Rights Act of 1964, Section 601, provides:

> No person in the United States shall, on the ground of race, color, or national origin, be excluded from participation in, be denied the benefits of, or be subjected to discrimination under any program or activity receiving Federal financial assistance.[51]

The United States Court of Appeals for the District of Columbia has summarized the enforcement provisions of Title VI as follows:

> Section 602 authorizes and directs each federal agency empowered to expand [sic] federal funds for aid . . . to effectuate the commands of Section 601 by appropriate regulations. Compliance may be effected by cutting off the flow of federal funds after opportunity for hearing has been afforded to the offending party, or by any other means authorized by law. The imposition of these sanctions are to be preceded in every case by voluntary efforts to effect compliance; and prior notice is to be given to the Congress in each case where the agency proposes to terminate funds.[52]

This, then, is the law that the House Judiciary Committee wrote and Congress enacted. A simple but noble ideal, with a mechanism for assuring compliance that could make the ideal a reality. But that is not the way things have worked out. Year after year, federal agency after federal agency has trampled upon the act—

and the legal rights of American citizens—with impunity. And Congress has stood by in splendid silence.

One could select almost any federal agency and document a massive lawlessness in the face of the requirements of Title VI. Indeed, the U.S. Civil Rights Commission has done precisely that on four separate occasions.[53] We briefly summarize here the Title VI performance of two agencies—the Department of Health, Education, and Welfare and the Department of Agriculture. Unhappily, they are apparently not atypical.*

HEW: Voluntary Noncompliance

During the congressional debates on the Civil Rights Act, the issue of greatest concern was federal funds for education administered by HEW, and it was at HEW that the first significant enforcement of Title VI took place.

By 1966, HEW Secretary John Gardner had issued strict Title VI guidelines, including a minimum percentage of black students required to be attending public schools for the schools to be considered integrated. In extreme cases, compliance was sought through fund terminations. After no fund cutoffs in 1965, HEW terminated funds to 41 school districts in 1966. From 1966 through 1970, the department terminated the funds of over 150 districts, and noticed for administrative hearings an average of over 100 districts a year.[54]

HEW's enforcement of Title VI, however, changed abruptly with the Nixon administration's accession to power. On June 3, 1969, Attorney General John N. Mitchell and HEW Secretary Robert H. Finch, appearing to abandon the termination of funds as an enforcement tool, issued a joint statement:

> To the extent practicable, on the Federal level the law enforcement aspects will be handled by the Department of Justice in judicial proceedings.

---

* In its November 1971 report, the U.S. Civil Rights Commission concluded that no agency with a significant Title VI program rated better than "marginal."

The purpose of this policy was

> to minimize the number of cases in which it becomes neces-
> sary to employ the particular remedy of a cutoff of Federal
> funds.[55]

In March 1970 Leon E. Panetta, director of the HEW Office for Civil Rights, resigned in protest against the administration's new policy. After that date, HEW commenced *no* enforcement proceedings against school districts. Between March 30, 1971, and July 30, 1972, only nine were even noticed for hearings.[56]

In abandoning the traditional enforcement approach, the Nixon administration gave up what many believe to be the most effective means of ending educational discrimination. The Lawyers' Review Committee to Study the Department of Justice noted that during the Johnson years integration was achieved more quickly in school districts acting under HEW guidelines than in those under court orders. In the seven southern states analyzed by the committee, the percentage of blacks attending integrated schools in "HEW districts" was 21 percent, while in "court-order districts" it was only 9.4 percent.[57]

The U.S. Civil Rights Commission made similar findings. In the commission's view, Congress had enacted Title VI to shift the burden of achieving desegregation from federal courts to administrative agencies.[58] The U.S. Court of Appeals for the Fifth Circuit, in *United States v. Jefferson County Board of Education*, had reached the same conclusion:

> We read Title VI as a congressional mandate for change—
> change in pace and method of enforcing desegregation. . . .
> Congress was dissatisfied with the slow progress inherent in
> the judicial adversary process. Congress therefore fashioned
> a new method of enforcement to be administered not on a
> case by case basis in the courts but generally, by federal
> agencies operating on a national scale and having a special
> competence in their respective fields.[59]

It is not clear from the legislative history of Title VI whether Congress intended to express a preference concerning the particular means to be employed by administrative agencies in seeking compliance. What is clear, however, is that Congress required at a minimum that the agency or department take *some* affirmative action. Yet HEW had not only abandoned the administrative means of enforcement, but had failed to effect the means it had chosen. Title VI requires that voluntary compliance first be sought from recipients; but this requirement obviously was not intended to permit negotiations for an indefinite period of time— which is what the Nixon administration has done. The U.S. Court of Appeals for the District of Columbia ruled in June 1973:

> Although the Act does not provide a specific limit to the time period within which voluntary compliance may be sought, it is clear that a request for voluntary compliance, if not followed by a responsive action on the part of the institution within a reasonable time, does not relieve the agency of the two alternative means [cutoff of funds or prosecution in court] contemplated by the statute. A consistent failure to do so is a dereliction of duty reviewable in the courts.* 60

By these standards, HEW has long been guilty of a monumental "dereliction of duty." Consider the following findings of fact by a federal court in November 1972, still characterized as "unassailable" by the U.S. Court of Appeals in June 1973:

1. Between January, 1969 and February, 1970, HEW concluded that the states of Louisiana, Mississippi, Oklahoma, North Carolina, Florida, Arkansas, Pennsylvania, Georgia, Maryland, and Virginia were operating segregated systems of higher education in violation of Title VI. At that time HEW requested each of the ten states to submit a desegregation plan within 120 days or less.

2. Five states, Louisiana, Mississippi, Oklahoma, North Carolina and Florida, have totally ignored HEW's re-

* The court also observed that "HEW's decision to rely primarily upon voluntarily compliance is particularly significant in view of the admitted effectiveness of fund termination proceedings in the past to achieve the Congressional objective."

quest for a desegregation plan and have never made
submissions.

3. The other five states, Arkansas, Pennsylvania, Georgia,
   Maryland and Virginia, submitted desegregation plans
   which are unacceptable to HEW. Although the submissions were made between 18 and 36 months ago,
   HEW has failed formally to comment on any of these
   submissions.

4. As of yet HEW has not commenced an administrative
   enforcement action against any of these ten states nor
   have these matters been referred to the Justice Department for the filing of suits against any of said ten states.

5. HEW has advanced and continues to advance federal
   funds in substantial amounts for the benefit of institutions of higher education in said ten states.[61]

HEW's record in enforcing Title VI against elementary and
secondary school systems was comparable. The same court found
that "as of the school year 1970–71, 113 school districts had
reneged on prior approved plans and were out of compliance
with Title VI. Some 74 of these districts are still out of compliance with Title VI." Although HEW knew of the noncompliance of most of these districts early in the 1970–1971 school
year, by June 1973 it had commenced administrative enforcement
actions against only seven districts, and of the eight cases referred
to the Justice Department, only three suits had been brought.
HEW excused its inaction on the ground that it was still seeking
voluntary compliance; meanwhile, the noncomplying institutions
received substantial federal assistance from HEW.[62]

The court concluded that "defendants now have no discretion
to negate the purpose and intent of the statute by a policy
described in another context as one of 'benign neglect' but, on
the contrary have the duty, on a case-by-case basis, to employ the
means set forth in [the act] to achieve compliance."[63] In this
case, as in so many others, the government found itself on the
receiving end of a court order in a Title VI case, a defendant
where the law contemplated that it would be a plaintiff.

The record of HEW in the enforcement of Title VI is profoundly shocking in its contempt for the act, yet it is important to bear in mind that *this deplorable record is perhaps the best in the federal government.*[64]

USDA and the Extension Service: Rewarding Racism

The Federal Extension Service is one of the oldest federal agencies, and one whose history is intimately intertwined with the development of rural America. Despite its illustrious history, however, the Federal Extension Service has also nourished some of the most traditionally racist institutions in America.

From its inception in 1914, FES, along with other USDA agencies, lavished enormous sums of money on the all-white land-grant colleges in the southern and border states for extension and research work.* In each of these states, this federal support nurtured a powerful and mutually supportive rural establishment composed of the all-white land-grant college (one per state), the segregated state extension service headquartered at the college (but with politically potent county agents throughout the state), and private agribusiness interests. Not only were blacks, who comprised a majority of the rural population in many of these states, excluded from the services provided by this establishment; FES cemented this exclusion by refusing to give any support to the "separate and unequal" black land-grant colleges established under the Second Morrill Act of 1890, which alone sought to serve the black farmer.

The state extension services were formally segregated, with federal assistance and acquiescence, as recently as 1965. Until fiscal 1968, USDA gave no research or extension money to the seventeen black land-grant colleges, and from fiscal 1968 through fiscal 1971 gave them a *combined total* of $283,000 a year (compared with over $90 million given by USDA to their seventeen white counterparts in fiscal 1972 alone). USDA justified

---

* With "integration," they are now approximately 95 percent white, on the average.

this practice on the ground that the federal statutes authorizing these grants provided that the state legislature could designate how the funds were to be divided between the two colleges in each state, and that in every state in every year the legislature had allocated *all* of the funds to the white college.

USDA had ample legal authority—and a statutory obligation under Title VI—to terminate these practices by its grantees. In 1965 Secretary of Agriculture Orville Freeman ordered an end to segregation in the state extension services. But little has changed.[65] Civil rights compliance audits conducted by USDA's Office of Inspector General,* which is independent of FES, and by the Civil Rights Commission, have consistently found extensive and continuing discriminatory practices in the extension services of eleven southern and border states. Despite these findings, USDA failed to require assurances of nondiscrimination or updated compliance plans from these state agencies until June 1970, fully six years after Title VI was enacted. Thereafter, eight states submitted assurances, of which even USDA found five unacceptable. As a result, USDA decided in September 1970 that, prior to accepting assurances, USDA would require each state extension service to conduct its own statewide compliance review, with FES also conducting reviews in each state.

The nature and quality of the state-conducted reviews has been described by the Civil Rights Commission:

> ES has 52 Title VI recipients. There are many more sub-recipients—namely, the State and county extension offices. In Fiscal Year 1972, 2,495 Title VI reviews of subre-cipients were performed. For the most part, the reviews were performed by the recipient State Extension Services. As usual, none of the subgrantees was found in noncompliance.
>
> In a prior Commission report, it was noted that compliance

---

* This is now called the Office of Audit. Its audits, which have been withheld from the public, are the subject of a long-pending suit under the Freedom of Information Act (*Schuck* v. *Butz*, Civ. Action No. 956–72, D.D.C.).

reviews performed by State Extension personnel were not reviewed by Federal personnel, raising numerous questions about the quality of the reviews. This situation continues. Staff in the Compliance and Enforcement Division of [USDA's] OEO have no way of knowing whether the State ES personnel are performing the required reviews—much less whether the reviews are of sufficient scope.*[66]

The reviews conducted by FES remain a mystery. According to the U.S. Civil Rights Commission, FES reviews were conducted between December 1971 and March 1972 in sixty-two counties in eight states for which assurances of noncompliance were not acceptable to USDA. As of July 1974, the review reports had not been made public, despite the commission's efforts to get them released. No additional FES reviews were planned for those states. The USDA civil rights staff also conducted two countywide reviews in a Southern state, but, as the commission noted, "despite the apparent success of these reviews, they have been discontinued because of lack of staff." (Several such reviews were resumed in fiscal 1974.) Four similar reviews were conducted in Louisiana parishes by a team from the Department of Justice and USDA's civil rights staff. A very critical report was submitted to USDA in August 1971, yet three years later no action had been taken on it.[67] In early 1974, USDA's civil rights staff completed several more reviews of FES compliance with Title VI. According to a top USDA official, these reviews documented "serious deficiencies":

> The typical county extension service still has *total segregation* in most of the organized clubs, (4-H, home demonstration, etc.) and virtually no service across racial lines. Some offices have separate facilities for blacks. In one instance, late in 1973, we found a separate entrance for blacks. We got immediate voluntary corrective action, but we haven't been back to check again.

* According to a USDA official, the almost complete lack of review of state compliance programs by FES or the USDA civil rights staff still prevailed as of July 1974.

These conditions, it must be noted, were found almost a decade after USDA ordered an end to segregated facilities. Yet as of July 1974 no enforcement action was in the offing.

As in the cases of HEW, USDA lawlessness has meant that black citizens have had to go to court to obtain the justice that Title VI requires USDA to provide. Consider the case of *Strain v. Philpott*,[68] a suit against the Alabama extension service (ACES) and Auburn University, the white land-grant college in Alabama which receives USDA extension and research funds. The USDA-mandated "integration" of the extension service in 1965 had resulted in the systematic downgrading of black ACES employees, their subordination to far less qualified whites, massive discrimination in the assignment and service of clientele and subject-matter areas to ACES employees, dramatic pay differentials based on race, and other grossly racist policies. According to the court:

> The stipulated and uncontroverted facts affirmatively reflect . . . that the purported merger of the ACES' dual systems in 1965 has thoroughly and effectively perpetuated and to a substantial degree aggravated the racial discrimination which existed previously.[69]

Only after the Department of Justice had exacted the plaintiffs' agreement to dismiss USDA as a defendant did Justice intervene in the suit on the side of the plaintiffs. The court finally issued extraordinarily detailed requirements for the termination of the persistent discrimination by the defendants, yet USDA continues to receive complaints by black extension workers in Alabama that the *Strain* decision is being flouted by the Alabama Extension Service. And on February 15, 1974, two and a half years after the *Strain* decision, a federal court issued a similar opinion and granted similar relief in a case brought by blacks against the Mississippi extension service.*

---

* *Wade v. United States*, No. EC 70-29K (N.D. Miss.). Similar lawsuits brought by blacks against the North Carolina and Texas extension services are still pending.

The Civil Rights Commission described the aftermath of the *Strain* decision:

> Although [FES] officials expressed a willingness to apply the legal requirements of the *Strain* decision to all States, they first requested that the Department of Justice set forth specifically what legal standards had to be met. This request seemingly was motivated less by a need for clarification than by a conscious attempt to shift the "blame" for imposing the administrative requirements from [FES to the Department of Justice].[70]

FES, ever alert for a new device to permit state extension services ever more delay, took the Department of Justice guidelines, which had been transmitted to USDA in December 1971, and asked the state extension services to submit yet another set of "affirmative action plans" on these guidelines by July 1972 and to implement them by December 1972.[71] The Civil Rights Commission notes what happened:

> The FES's proclivity for delaying compliance again manifested itself, however, in an action which moved these deadlines back to September 1972 and February 1973, respectively. These new dates clearly will be the final test of USDA's new resolve to discharge its civil rights obligations.[72]

By this test, USDA has flunked again. The implementation date was delayed again, this time to July 1, 1973. And when the plans were finally submitted to FES, most were so inadequate that even FES was dissatisfied and rejected them. The last plan was not approved by FES until early 1974.

In addition, each state extension service was told to submit a compliance report by March 28, 1973, and that failure to do so would result in Title VI enforcement proceedings. But, as the commission noted, "Given past events . . . this likelihood is remote."[73] The commission was remarkably prescient.

In fact, as of July 1974, no administrative hearings under Title VI had ever been noticed by FES, nor were any anticipated. And rather than audit compliance by the state extension services with their new plans, FES has given that responsibility—and the political heat associated with it—over to the Office of Audit. OA conducted new audits in nineteen states and found noncompliance in three of the only four southern and border states to have been fully audited by July 1974. No enforcement action has yet been taken. "FES hasn't changed its attitude at all," says one USDA staffer. "It spends more effort in subverting and corrupting the process than in trying to carry out the law." Another observed, "If FES has made any progress at all, it is because Willie Strain, Charlie Wade, and other blacks risked everything they had to force change on it."

During the decade of noncompliance with Title VI, the state extension services have continued to receive every penny of their overgenerous, ever-increasing federal largesse. With USDA and the Department of Justice enforcing Title VI, contempt for the law in rural America pays handsome dividends indeed.*

The Congressional Role in Civil Rights

The problem of racial discrimination aided and abetted by federal funds continues today in numerous federal programs. Enforcement of Title VI by the federal agencies has been episodic and often nonexistent; on the whole, the agencies have desolated the act. What meager enforcement of Title VI there has been has occurred almost entirely through the federal courts and at the instance of those whom the federal government undertook to protect when it enacted the act. The courts, however, cannot continue indefinitely to be the backbone of Title VI; they have few resources to compel the agencies to act *affirmatively* on a wide scale to enforce the law. In the long run, only Congress and the executive can do that.

Congressional oversight of agency enforcement of the civil rights laws will never be possible until certain conditions are met.

* Another shocking case of agency neglect in enforcing Title VI is that of the Law Enforcement Assistance Administration. See *Law and Disorder*, I, II, and III, an excellent series of reports by the Lawyers Committee for Civil Rights Under Law on the performance of LEAA and its grantees.

A specific locus for systematic, continuing oversight must be established outside the substantive subject-matter committees in order to give civil rights advocates a place upon which to focus their efforts, to give senators and congressmen a place to turn with their own concerns, and to permit the development of the necessary expertise. Once this unit is designated, it must be given the investigative tools to discover violations of Title VI and other civil rights laws, and to probe agency compliance activities. This requires both sufficient staff and access to information about the operations of local programs. In addition, exposure of abuse is not enough; some method of enforcement must be supplied.

Finally, the appropriations subcommittees should become central institutional levers for ensuring civil rights compliance and enforcement by the agencies. "This is where the real bite could be," says one civil rights expert, who echoes the views of many others. A recent example of the potential of the appropriations process for civil rights oversight occurred early in the Ninety-third Congress when the Treasury, Postal Service, and General Government Subcommittee of the House Appropriations Committee closely interrogated officials of the General Services Administration and the Office of Management and Budget concerning civil rights matters.

The following measures constitute one approach to these objectives:

1. House Judiciary Subcommittee No. 4 should be permitted a considerable increase in staff and responsibility to enable it to monitor Title VI compliance by the agencies. (The methods of field investigation are discussed below in recommendation number 3.) The subcommittee should also be given jurisdiction over civil rights legislation itself; the body that develops a bill, perfects it, and guides it through Congress is best able to develop the expertise necessary for its oversight.

2. A new committee or subcommittee should be created in the Senate exclusively to handle civil rights legislation and oversight. Even if Senator Ervin's opposition to most civil rights legislation is not taken into account, the creation of a new sub-

committee would seem justified. The Constitutional Rights Sub-committee is already engaged full time in the protection of civil liberties, and has developed staff with considerable expertise in that field; to impose upon it a new responsibility would diminish its present activities. Given the autonomy permitted to Judiciary subcommittees by Chairman Eastland, such a new subcommittee might well be able to function within the Judiciary Committee. If not, an entirely new committee should be established. This would not, of course, rule out concurrent oversight by commit-tees with jurisdiction over the agencies.

3. A purely investigative office should be created in the U.S. Commission on Civil Rights or the General Accounting Office to monitor civil rights compliance in federally assisted programs. It should conduct its own field investigations in response to both complaints and the directives of the subcommittees with oversight jurisdiction. Such an investigatory office should report directly and solely to the subcommittees.

4. All appropriations bill for grant-in-aid programs should be jointly referred to the Appropriations committees, and to the civil rights subcommittees of the Judiciary committees. The civil rights subcommittees ought to have the power to hold up an appropriations bill if they find an inadequate Title VI enforce-ment effort on the part of the agency in question. The subcom-mittees could also condition appropriations on specified efforts on the part of the agency or department to improve enforcement capability or performance. Needless to say, such a reform would be very difficult to effect; congressional committees are notori-ously jealous of their jurisdictions, and civil rights is not a high priority issue in Congress. Nevertheless, a national commitment to the fact, rather than simply the appearance, of racial justice requires nothing less.

5. While every effort should be made to impress upon the line agencies that Title VI enforcement is an integral part of their program responsibilities, the Judiciary committees must also strengthen the Civil Rights Division of the Justice Department as a backup enforcement mechanism when agencies refuse to

move against their program recipients. The nominations of top Justice personnel and agency personnel should not be confirmed unless and until specific assurances are made of their intention to vigorously enforce the act. Congressmen and senators should, under appropriate circumstances, bring legal actions in their own names or on behalf of constituents against the department or other recalcitrant agencies failing to enforce the laws that they have helped to write.* Where possible, program funds should be withheld by Congress until appropriate civil rights enforcement actions are forthcoming. The committees should fully exploit their ability to use publicity and investigations to compel obedience to the law.

---

* An example is *Mitchell* v. *Laird*, 488 F.2d 611 (D.C. Cir., 1973), which was a challenge by a group of congressmen to the legality of the Indochina war.

IV

OVERSEEING AND OVERLOOKING

9

Administrative Practice and Procedure: Kennedy's Fire Brigade

As heir to the Kennedy political dynasty and as a leading presidential hopeful, Senator Edward M. Kennedy is not like the other members of Judiciary or, indeed, like other senators. Nor is his Judiciary subcommittee, the Subcommittee on Administrative Practice and Procedure (APP), like other subcommittees.

APP writes no basic laws, authorizes no funds, creates no programs. Rather, it thrusts straight at the public eye and ear; its weapons are the public media; and its target is public opinion.

One expects Kennedy's pronouncements at subcommittee hearings to sound like the grandiloquent calls to arms of a presidential candidate—and they often do. During an investigation of the efficiency of presidential commissions, for example, Kennedy,

NOTE: This chapter was prepared by Peter H. Schuck and Michael Massing.

summoning rhetoric from the vasty deep of his charisma, managed to transcend the rather uninspiring subject at hand:

> When we look this week at our response to the best advice this country can muster, we are really looking at our national commitment to progress, our determination not only to face, but to face up to, the future. And if our leadership refuses to meet both the challenge and the opportunity in this advice, the task will be one for all the people, to rise as a nation and say, "We can. We shall. We must."[1]

All in the true Kennedy tradition.

The Administrative Practice and Procedure Subcommittee could not be more admirably suited to an ambitious politician's purposes. Its formal jurisdiction is essentially unlimited, as delineated in S. Res. 333:

> . . . to make a full and complete study and investigation of administrative practices and procedures within the departments and agencies of the United States in the exercise of their rule-making, licensing, investigatory, law enforcement, and adjudicatory functions, including a study of the effectiveness of the Administrative Conference of the United States, with a view to determining whether additional legislation is required to provide for the fair, impartial, and effective performance of such function.

In short, the subcommittee's sweep embraces the entire executive branch. Procedure merges imperceptibly into structure and structure into substance. It is not surprising, then, that under Kennedy's guidance, subcommittee surveillance of administrative practices and procedures has become a lever for upending the substantive policies of the Nixon administration.

On at least one occasion, Kennedy reached for the jugular—Watergate. The bugging of the Democratic national headquarters at the Watergate apartment complex in June 1972 quickly became a top-priority APP investigative project. During the heat of the 1972 election campaign, when it became clear that no other committee intended to investigate the matter, Kennedy overcame an initial reluctance and instructed subcommittee staffers to follow up reports from two investigative reporters at the *Washington Post* on the apparent "irregularities" emanating from the White House.

Former subcommittee staffer Joe Onek provides one reason why: "If committee leadership were more representative of Congress," he says, "Kennedy could have relied on these other committees to do the job." With so many congressional committees dominated by conservative or politically cautious members, however, this alternative was simply not open.

Stewart Alsop wrote in *Newsweek* that it was a case of "Kennedy or nothing."[2] According to Alsop, the House Banking and Currency Committee refused to investigate the matter because "[Chairman Wright] Patman . . . lacks a majority on the committee to grant him the necessary subpoena power." Similarly, neither the Subcommittee on Constitutional Rights nor the Government Operations Committee, headed by Senators Ervin and McClellan, respectively, deigned to become involved in what seemed at first to be little more than preelection hijinks, a "Mickey Mouse" affair.

In mid-January 1973, when Watergate was becoming a household word, the Democratic leadership decided that the investigation should be conducted by a select committee of the Senate chaired by Senator Ervin, one of the most respected members of the Senate and one whose political future lay in voluntary retirement. Kennedy readily concurred with the leadership's decision. His putative candidacy for the Democratic presidential nomination left him particularly vulnerable to charges of political maneuvering, charges that might have obscured the substance of the investigation of what is certainly "the worst political scandal of the century."[3] Kennedy, clearly relieved at being taken off the hook, dutifully turned over to Ervin all evidence which had been developed by the APP staff.

Even so, some suggest, Kennedy may not have escaped unscathed. When the administration announced formidable new budget cuts in federal military installations several months later, hardest hit in the loss of men, money, and jobs was the state of Massachusetts.

Subcommittee Operations: The Bully Pulpit

Like most subcommittees, APP is the creature of its chairman. But because of the autonomy granted to subcommittees by full-committee chairman James Eastland, and because of the large number of subcommittees to which senators are assigned, Senate Judiciary subcommittees are shaped by their leaders to an unusual degree. The chairman is the member—often the only member—with a substantial interest in the subcommittee's work. At eleven randomly selected APP subcommittee hearings, Kennedy presided, Senator Thurmond attended six and Senator Tunney two. Senators Hart, Gurney, Burdick, Bayh, and Mathias attended only one each. Such high absenteeism by other members virtually assures the responsiveness of the subcommittee to the chairman's wishes.

Kennedy's subcommittee held no executive session in the Ninety-first and Ninety-second Congresses; all activities and decisions are handled through informal polling. Kennedy writes a letter to members of the subcommittee asking their opinions on whether to report a bill or undertake a certain investigation. If there is unanimous approval, Kennedy and the staff follow through. If not, an executive session is convened. The evidence is that subcommittee members rarely disagree with Kennedy.[4]

The APP subcommittee reported out only two bills in the Ninety-second Congress. One of the bills, to fund the Administrative Conference, a federal agency monitoring the administrative practices of the government, was signed into law in October 1972. The other bill sought to restrict the use of the sovereign immunity* defense by the federal government. It died in full committee.[5]

---

* "Sovereign immunity" is the common-law doctrine that, since all law flows from the king, "the king can do no wrong." Translated into a democratic system, it is the principle that the government cannot be sued without its consent.

Early in the Ninety-third Congress, APP reported out the Bureaucratic Accountability Act (S.1421), a bill to amend the Administrative Procedure Act to end the exemptions from the act's rule-making provisions for certain categories of agency actions. The subcommittee also reported out S.2543, a series of amendments to the Freedom of Information Act which would increase the celerity and certainty of public access to government documents. In July 1974, S.1421 was still pending before the full committee and S.2543 had passed the Senate and was awaiting a conference with the House.

This modest legislative record, however, is a deceptive measure of the subcommittee's metabolism, for its activities are essentially investigative and informative rather than legislative. APP is the "publicity subcommittee" in the Senate; its "clout" is to be found not in legislation or appropriations, but in the public pressure it generates.

Commissions and Omissions

In 1971 hearings, the subcommittee investigated the practical results of various presidential commissions, including the National Advisory Commission on Civil Disorders (headed by Otto Kerner), the President's Commission on Obscenity and Pornography (William B. Lockhart), the National Commission on the Causes and Prevention of Violence (Milton Eisenhower), the President's Commission on Law Enforcement and Administration of Justice (Nicholas Katzenbach), the President's Commission on Campus Unrest (William Scranton), and several advisory commissions on medical matters.* Otto Kerner† recounted how his commission "begged and borrowed from presidential funds," a process that took up much of its time. William Lockhart spoke of inadequate financing as well as time constraints. Milton Eisenhower spoke of "almost total silence" from the executive

---

* As of May 1973, some 1,439 such commissions were extant; in 1972, tax-payers doled out $25.2 million for their activities.
† Later convicted in a racetrack scandal while serving as a federal appellate judge.

branch with regard to his commission's report, and he recommended that the White House be required to reply to a commission report within a set period of time, as in the British system. Nicholas Katzenbach criticized the Justice Department for not administering the Law Enforcement Assistance Agency according to his commission's recommendations. Father Theodore Hesburgh, chairman of the Commission on Civil Rights, spoke of commissions as a "copout," a substitute for real action.*[6]

Testimony concerning various health commissions provided Kennedy with a podium for denouncing the American Medical Association (AMA) and the Nixon administration. Noting that the AMA has opposed "virtually every major health reform in the past fifty years" (health benefits for World War I veterans, Blue Cross, equal opportunity in medical education, and Medicare), Kennedy lost no time in beating the Nixon administration with the AMA stick:

> The influence of the AMA has become more pervasive . . .
> the AMA and the administration . . . have formed a marriage
> of convenience against the public interest, made possible by
> the self-interest of an organization that puts the wealth of
> doctors ahead of the health of the people, and by the apathy
> of an administration that lacks the will to implement the
> principles it piously proclaims.[7]

Predictably, Kennedy's harsh and partisan indictment of the AMA received far more media coverage than the central subject of the hearings—national commissions.[8]

In January 1973 APP staff members began work on a bill modeled after the British procedure for responding to the reports of royal commissions. The bill would require the president to respond in general terms, within several months, to a commission's report and designate a cabinet-level official to implement recommendations. Within six months, this official would be

---

* President Nixon, according to the *Washington Post* of May 13, 1973, expressed a desire to establish a commission to study presidential campaign activities.

required to report on the extent of the government's compliance with the recommendations. One year later, the reassembled commission would receive a final implementation report.[9] The subcommittee's bill, when completed, will be sent to the Government Operations Committee for processing.

The Politics of Oil

Most of the subcommittee's investigations directly concern substantive policy issues. A paradigm is APP's investigation into the administration of the oil import program.

On March 10, 1970, President Nixon announced the imposition of the first formal mandatory quotas ever imposed on the importation of Canadian oil. By law, the Office of Emergency Preparedness (OEP) is responsible for maintaining surveillance over imports to determine whether quotas are necessary to achieve the objectives of "national security." Less than three weeks earlier, the President had established an Oil Policy Committee, headed by the director of OEP, "to consider both interim and long-term adjustments that will increase the effectiveness and enhance the equity of the oil import program."[10]

On March 20, only ten days after the President's action, Kennedy convened a subcommittee hearing on the administration of the oil import program. Why, one might ask, would a subcommittee dealing with administrative process concern itself with the nation's oil import policy? At first glance, such an issue would seem to fall outside of the jurisdiction of APP. At second glance, too. On March 3, Senator Hart's Judiciary Subcommittee on Antitrust and Monopoly had held hearings on the report of the President's task force on oil-control policy, which had recommended fundamental changes in the oil import program—only to be ignored by the president who had appointed it. That subcommittee, then, was already considering closely related matters. (Indeed, Hart held further hearings on March 26, just six days after the APP hearing, on whether import quotas were necessary.)[11]

Why, then, would APP barge into this delicate matter? According to Kennedy, the APP hearings would concern only OEP's unusual administrative practices. Kennedy enumerated the procedures to be studied:

> The procedures employed by the OEP were . . . disappointing. No hearings were held concerning this, the most important change in the import program since its inception. The Administrative Procedure Act was ignored and interested parties were given only 10 days in which to comment on the proposed rulemaking. Once again, the OEP did not explain why the traditional 30-day comment period was rejected. Neither the OEP nor the President have an adequate explanation for this startling departure from past U.S. policy. The OEP did not issue a report demonstrating why the new restrictions were necessary to protect the national security, even though such a report is expressly required by the Trade Expansion Act. Instead, we were treated to a press conference and to several misleading pronouncements about the current state of Canada's reserve capacity.[12]

But as might have been expected, Kennedy did not limit the scope of the inquiry. His interrogation of George Lincoln, director of the OEP, often strayed far from procedural issues into the sensitive policy area:

> We are trying to look beyond these magical words "national security." We have not been able to develop the national security question this morning except in the broadest kind of generalities. I still do not know how we are more secure today with a limitation on Canadian oil than we were before. . . . It seems to me, in short, that what we have done here is to engage our closest neighbor and friend, compromise our efforts to limit inflationary pressures, reduce the efficient flow of an important commodity to a large portion of the Nation, all at the expense of our consumers, and all in the interests of an industry which makes more profits and pays less Federal taxes than perhaps any other industry.[13]

The APP hearings provided a forum from which Kennedy could express his views on a critical federal policy at a time when that policy was receiving national public attention. According to Joe Onek, who worked on the hearings, Kennedy had intended the investigation to be a "jab" in a broad campaign against the quota system as a whole. And by attacking this system, Kennedy could also discredit the Nixon administration. To Kennedy, "the basic fact seems to be that a secret sudden decision was made within the halls of government that now fixes a strict upper limit on Canadian oil."[14] No names needed to be mentioned.

The oil hearings also illustrate Kennedy's bid for a national constituency. The restriction on Canadian oil affected mainly the northernmost states of the Midwest, for most Canadian oil was directed to their refineries; while the oil import quota system in general discriminated against Massachusetts and the other New England states, they were little affected by this particular change in policy. Onek views the purpose of the hearings as an attempt to mobilize opposition to the quota system in these Midwestern states. Kennedy's constituency—and therefore that of the subcommittee—extends far beyond the borders of Massachusetts.

Staff and Methods

Kennedy has molded the subcommittee staff into a flexible team, poised to respond to a variety of critical issues that may surface. The APP staff, consisting of four majority counsel, inhabits a crowded office on the third floor of the New Senate Office Building. One minority counsel began working with the subcommittee in August 1972. A sixth staff member, Carmine Bellino, is a seasoned investigator long associated with Kennedy family politics.*

APP staff utilize four major sources of information. First are

---

* Bellino, appointed chief investigator for the Senate select committee investigating Watergate, became a subject of investigation himself. A special three-man panel of the Watergate committee studied affidavits alleging that Bellino attempted to hire persons to bug or wiretap Richard Nixon's hotel room during the 1960 presidential campaign.[15] Bellino was subsequently cleared of the allegations.

the complaints and information from diverse areas and sources that Kennedy, because of his national recognition, receives. The subcommittee's investigation into the safety regulations of the Federal Aviation Administration, for example, was prompted by letters of complaint sent by airline pilots to Kennedy.[16]

The so-called public-interest bar provides a most important source of data concerning the functioning of the federal bureaucracy.[17] Hearings on the Federal Trade Commission, for example, were stimulated by the well-publicized Nader Report on the FTC.[18]

A third source is the Administrative Conference, the only agency in the federal government charged with developing improvements in federal administrative processes.[19] The bills to modify the defense of sovereign immunity and to establish a public counsel corporation both originated with the Administrative Conference, as did S.3686, the bill to establish a federal administrative justice center.

Finally, there is the network of "informants," usually employees in federal agencies or ex-government officials willing to "leak like a sieve" to Kennedy.

The flow of data upon which the subcommittee can act is steady, but paltry in comparison to information available to the executive branch. As a result, the subcommittee's monitoring capacity is stretched to its very limits.

APP employs two methods for enforcing agency responsiveness to its investigations. One is to schedule a second set of hearings. Only once in the Ninety-first and Ninety-second Congresses was such a tack taken—on draft reform. According to former staff member Tom Rowe, holding more than one hearing on an issue is rare because it is so time-consuming; each hearing requires painstaking preparation.

The second method—a followup after hearings—is more commonly adopted. Staff members constantly check and recheck with various officials in the agencies to see what changes have been forthcoming; correspondence often continues long after the hearings are concluded. Mark Schneider, a member of Kennedy's personal staff who devotes most of his time to APP matters, says that he has badgered the Selective Service System for several years on agency compliance with the 1971 revision of the Selective Service law.

To achieve wider public input into agency decision-making Kennedy introduced S.343, a bill recommending the establishment of an independent agency to represent the public in proceedings before federal departments. The measure was later incorporated into a bill proposing a Consumer Protection Agency.*

APP is a gadfly to Congress as well as to the bureaucracy. Kennedy permits the aggressive APP staff to poach on other congressional committee jurisdictions where default or passivity justifies intercession. "When a substantive committee has jurisdiction but is not using it," says James Flug, former chief counsel, "we feel free to move in."

One example is the failure of the Senate Interior and Insular Affairs Committee, with jurisdiction over Indian rights to land and water resources, to protect those rights. Kennedy quoted Yellow Wolf of the Nez Perces: "The whites only told one side. Told it to please themselves. Told much that is not true," and held hearings "to hear the other side":

> The taking of Indian land and water and the last infringement of Indian rights did not end in the last century. The lawlessness and immorality perpetuated by the government continues right now, and it will continue tomorrow unless the United States does more than pay lip service to its sacred treaty obligations to the Indian tribes.[20]

Staffers noted that the hearings were instrumental in the establishment of an office of Indian Water Rights (two weeks after the announcement of hearings), the release of a task force report

---

* This latter bill was reported out of the Government Operations Committee but was killed on the Senate floor by a filibuster by Senator Ervin in September 1972. The APP staff spent considerable time fighting to save this bill. In July 1974 its successor in the Ninety-third Congress was facing yet another filibuster, as well as a presidential veto.

on Indian natural resources, and the replacement of Shiro
Kashiwa, the head of the Land and Natural Resources Division
of the Justice Department (whose performance had been so controversial that the White House wanted to prevent him from
testifying before the subcommittee).[21] Like so many of APP's
victories, however, this was short-lived; the second battle of
Wounded Knee eighteen months later left Indians and government
agents dead and wounded, with a solution to Indian problems
no nearer.

Another example of jurisdictional invasion arose over the
refusal of the Labor Subcommittee of the Senate Labor and
Public Welfare Committee to investigate possible violations by
unions of the equal-employment-opportunity requirements applicable to federal contracts, requirements originally established by
President John F. Kennedy. APP scheduled hearings. On the day
of the hearings, President Nixon distributed a memorandum to
the heads of all departments and agencies. "I am determined,"
the President wrote, "that the executive branch of the government lead the way as an equal opportunity employer."[22] Two
direct results of the hearing were a major shakeup in the Office of
Federal Contract Compliance and the issuance of a new set of
nondiscrimination guidelines.

The administration's reaction to a proposed Kennedy hearing
in the summer of 1971 on the Labor Department's new guidelines relating to sex discrimination in employment demonstrated
that the department had at least reduced its reaction time.
"Before the hearings could be held," Kennedy later wrote, "the
Department announced changes in the guidelines that substantially met the subcommittee's concerns and the hearings were
indefinitely suspended pending further developments."[23]

In yet another instance of jurisdiction-jumping, APP laid claim
to an issue—cutbacks in the electrical power supply to the East
Coast—that had already been investigated in January 1970 by the
Senate Commerce Subcommittee on Energy, Natural Resources,
and Environment[24] and which was also within the purview of
the Interior Committee.[25] The hearings were held on three sepa-

rate days in three different parts of the country. The Federal Power Commission bore the brunt of Kennedy's ire for its failure to implement the recommendations of its own June 1967 report to President Johnson entitled "Prevention of Power Failures."[26]

Tom Susman, who staffed the hearings, feels that apart from the publicity that they attracted they were not particularly effective. And the followup correspondence between the FPC and the APP staff proved to be rather inconclusive, demonstrating the inherent limitations of APP oversight. Susman wrote to the Commission sporadically, inquiring about matters that came to his attention, and in response received inch-thick documents describing in detail FPC's policy on the particular point in question. Comprehension of these reports, as Susman readily admits, required a far higher level of expertise in energy matters than he or any other staff member has, whereas Interior Committee staff members had the background necessary for a thorough understanding of the technical issues involved. The subcommittee reluctantly abandoned the effort to conduct a truly thorough study.

Soon after the APP hearings the Interior Committee did turn to the question of energy shortages. Whether the APP study prompted this move or not, the APP subcommittee had expended its limited resources investigating a matter best handled by another body.

The Problem of Priorities

The APP subcommittee's reputation as Judiciary's investigative cutting edge was strengthened by its intervention into the byzantine ITT affair. When syndicated columnist Jack Anderson published a memo in 1972 that linked a huge ITT contribution to the Republican National Committee with an out-of-court settlement of a celebrated Justice Department antitrust suit against ITT, the subcommittee staff quickly shelved another investigation in order to concentrate exclusively on the fast-breaking, front-page scandal. Though technically a matter before the full committee, the investigation was largely the handiwork of the subcommittee staff, working almost exclusively with and for Kennedy.

ITT, Watergate, and energy all presented the subcommittee with difficult choices. Should these immediate, high-visibility issues receive top-priority attention of the small APP staff at the expense of longer-term, mundane agency oversight problems? The subcommittee, for better or for worse, seems to have opted for the former. While the ITT crisis preempted all other subcommittee activity and filled the media, what of the less "sexy" but perhaps more wide-ranging abuses within the ICC, CAB, FPC, and other government agencies whose decisions affect the daily lives of millions of Americans?

Systematic oversight of the Justice Department is a particularly heavy casualty of APP fire-fighting. If not monitored by the Judiciary Committee, the Justice Department will not be scrutinized at all. James Flug claims that APP is the "greatest locus of knowledge about the operation of the Justice Department in the entire Congress." The subcommittee, according to Flug, has "unceasing correspondence" with the department, and the APP staff maintains constant contact with Senator Hart's Judiciary Subcommittee on Antitrust and Monopoly in an effort to ensure the maintenance by Justice of a vigorous antitrust program. Flug also points to the staff's effort to monitor Justice's civil rights policies.

Flug claims that although the subcommittee exercises oversight of the Justice Department "on many different specific issues," these issues "really fit into a larger pattern." If so, however, the pattern is an elusive one. The only issues relating to the Justice Department on which Kennedy had held hearings by the end of the Ninety-second Congress were the federal handling of mass demonstrations and electronic surveillance of citizens. These investigations are certainly commendable and necessary, but like most other subjects studied by the subcommittee, attention has tended to be episodic and fragmentary. They do not constitute a systematic and integrated oversight process.

It is probably inevitable that the APP subcommittee has come to be, in Flug's words, "the fire brigade for liberal causes" in the Senate, racing feverishly from one conflagration to another, leaving the rebuilding and analysis of source and solutions to others. Perhaps that is as it should be. If Chief Kennedy's brigade is seen racing toward the Federal Power Commission today, neither the Department of Labor nor the congressional committees that are supposed to oversee it may rest easy. APP's sirens may be shrieking at them tomorrow, with Walter Cronkite and Company close behind.

10

Judicial Nominations: Whither "Advice and Consent"?

The importance to the American political system of a federal judiciary of high competence, integrity, and independence can scarcely be exaggerated. It is not simply that federal judges are appointed for life terms and daily decide questions of great political significance and legal complexity. As de Toqueville noted long ago, our system is distinctive in the extent to which the most fundamental political, social, and philosophical issues are eventually passed upon by judges. To list but a few of the subjects of judicial decisions in recent years—racial equality, procedural rights in criminal cases, the rights of the poor, legislative reapportionment, relationships between religious and secular

NOTE: This chapter was prepared by Peter H. Schuck and Dr. Martha Joynt Kumar.

authority—is to affirm what the authors of *The Federalist* predicted, that the quality of the federal judiciary and the quality of American legal institutions are indissolubly wedded. The Senate Judiciary Committee's performance of its constitutional duty to advise and consent on judicial nominations, then, is a critical test of its responsiveness to the most fundamental needs of the American polity. And by almost any standards, Judiciary fails that test.

Judicial nominations amount to a considerable portion of the Senate Judiciary Committee's workload. (The House plays no role in the nomination process.) The number of nominees, of course, varies from one Congress to another, depending upon the number of vacancies caused by death and retirement, and the number of new judicial positions created by legislation. The fluctuation can be seen in the number of nominations the committee has considered since the Eighty-seventh Congress.

Justices of the United States Supreme Court, judges of the United States circuit courts of appeals, United States district court judges, United States attorneys (i.e., federal prosecutors), United States marshals (i.e., officials who execute federal court orders)—all these nominations are considered by the Senate Judiciary Committee. Since the processing of Supreme Court nominations by the Senate Judiciary Committee and the full Senate has been a subject of some study,[1] and since most articles concerning judicial nominations have stressed consideration by

TABLE 6.
Executive Nominations Considered by Senate Judiciary Committee

Congress	Nominations
92nd	169
91st	344
90th	140
89th	284
88th	84
87th	354

SOURCE: The Calendars of each Congress published by the Senate Judiciary Committee.

the president and the Justice Department, we shall focus our analysis on the circuit court, district court, U.S. attorney, and U.S. marshal nominations, and on their consideration by the Senate and particularly the Judiciary Committee, constitutional partners—but often silent ones at that—in the process.

The Constitution provides that the president shall make appointments by and with the advice and consent of the Senate. Article II, Section 2 provides:

> He shall have power, by and with the advice and consent of the Senate, to make treaties, provided two-thirds of the Senators present concur; and he shall nominate, and by and with the advice and consent of the Senate, shall appoint ambassadors, other public ministers and consuls, judges of the Supreme Court, and all other officers of the United States, whose appointments are not herein otherwise provided for, and which shall be established by law: but the Congress may by law vest the appointment of such inferior officers, as they think proper, in the President alone, in the courts of law, or in the heads of departments.

The president clearly was to initiate the nominating process; the Senate would enter at a later phase. Alexander Hamilton elaborated in *Federalist* No. 66 on the meaning of the president's role in this process:

> It will be the office of the President to *nominate* and with the advice and consent of the Senate to *appoint*. There will, of course, be no exertion of *choice* on the part of the Senate. They may defeat one choice of the Executive and oblige him to make another; but they cannot themselves *choose*— they can only ratify or reject the choice of the President [emphasis in original].[2]

In short, the president would send names to the Senate, which would either accept or reject these appointees.

The Senate, Justice, and the ABA

Tradition has constructed a different nominating process from that envisioned by the Constitution and by Hamilton. The president no longer initiates the process; it starts in the Senate and in the Department of Justice. The Senate is instrumental in selecting the nominees for the position of U.S. marshal, U.S. attorney, and U.S. district court judges, and, to a lesser extent, U.S. circuit court judges.

When a vacancy occurs, the senators from the states involved send names to the Justice Department. How senators determine which names to forward depends upon idiosyncratic factors, partisan considerations, and the nature of the position that is vacant. Senators of the president's party play particularly important roles. If only one senator is of the president's party, then his role is central; a senator from the opposing party can expect only that the president will not nominate someone particularly odious to him. He is in no position to name the person he wants; he only has veto power.[3] Occasionally, senators from the same state cannot reach agreement on nominees from their state. For example, Senator Clifford P. Case, a Republican, and Senator Harrison A. Williams, Jr., his Democratic colleague, are, according to Martin Tolchin of the *New York Times*, "barely on speaking terms" over New Jersey nominations to the federal bench. "When Senator Williams was recommending to a Democratic President, he didn't consult me," Senator Case told Tolchin, adding, "Today, recommending to a Republican President, I don't consult him."[4] Senators Jacob Javits and James L. Buckley of New York, both Republicans but with little else in common, also have great difficulty in agreeing on nominees, only to find that some of their nominees received "unqualified" ratings by the bar association.[5]

Senators use various methods to develop names to submit to the Department of Justice. Some senators confer with local party officials, and, in a few cases, with informal boards of lawyers created to evaluate potential nominees. Some even rely upon the Department of Justice for names:

> Many senators, who find judicial patronage an embarrassment and a bother, approach the Justice Department

privately and ask that they remove the onus by picking the judges for them. This leaves immense discretionary power in the hands of the Attorney General, who is, by tradition, a political arm of the President. Other senators tell the Attorney General what candidates they have chosen, but request that he publicize that the intiative for the appointment came from the Justice Department, not from them. While reluctant to give up their power over judicial selection, these senators nevertheless fear that any hint of patronage might harm their carefully cultivated statesmanlike image. In the last category are senators who pick one man and tell the Attorney General and the President: "That's the one I want." When senators are very close to the President, this method works very efficiently, except in cases of notoriously poor candidates.[6]

Senator Javits, who recently stated that half the names of his nominees came from the party organization, has now set up a five-lawyer panel to screen names. He had been severely criticized for his nomination of Mark A. Costantino to be District Judge for the Eastern District of New York. The *New York Times* reported:

> In one instance, the judge cited the wrong criminal statute in making his charge to the jury, which Government lawyers called "an unbelievable error" for a Federal judge. As a result, the conviction of two men for receiving stolen goods was reversed by the Court of Appeals for the Second Circuit on Sept. 5, 1972.
>
> Judge Costantino also has been accused of becoming the business partner of a plaintiff in whose favor he decided a case involving the sale of land for a cemetery.[7]

Senators Charles H. Percy and Adlai E. Stevenson III of Illinois submit names to a "blue ribbon" panel of lawyers which they have informally created to consider such nominations. Many senators solicit nominees from local party leaders.[8] Some senators who use panels do so because of their unfortunate experiences in relying upon state party leaders.

Sheldon Goldman, in a seminal article on the judicial nomination process, observes:

> When the senator(s) and party leaders from the state scheduled to receive the appointment agree on one candidate who subsequently appears qualified by the Justice Department's and ABA's standards, that candidate's nomination is virtually certain, and confirmation by the Senate is only a matter of time. However, when Justice officials select a man from many submitted names, or have their own candidate to promote and are willing to challenge the senator(s) and state party nominee, extensive negotiations have to be undertaken with these political leaders.[9]

If the nominee is not of the same party as the president, however, the likelihood of his being appointed is seriously diminished. A study of the appointees to federal judgeships since Franklin Roosevelt's presidency shows that presidents essentially select only members of their own party (see Table 7).

When senators submit several names for consideration and/or when the senators are not from the president's party, the decisions of the Justice Department become critically important. Professor Goldman notes:

> The first reality—and an obvious one to casual observers of the process—is that the President's men in the Justice

TABLE 7.

Appointees to Federal Judgeships by Party

Administration	Appointees	
	Democrats	Republicans
Roosevelt	188	6
Truman	116	9
Eisenhower	9	165
Kennedy	111	11
Johnson	159	9
Nixon (1969–1970)	3	86

SOURCE: Congressional Quarterly Service, *CQ's Guide to the Congress of the United States* (Washington: Congressional Quarterly, Inc., 1971), p. 237.

Department, i.e., the Attorney General and especially the
Deputy Attorney General and his assistants, are primarily
responsible for judicial selection. Thus, our attention must
focus on the Justice Department rather than the White
House. . . . It is hard to determine the number of appeals
court judges who are initially selected and promoted by the
Justice Department officials on their own or at the instigation
of the President. The difficulty is that for political reasons
the department prefers its suggestions to become the recommendations of the senators of the President's party from the
appointee's state. However, it is probably no exaggeration to
suggest that close to one out of five Eisenhower or Kennedy
appeals court appointees had his nomination initiated by the
Justice Department.[10]

Although concerned with the quality of nominees, the Department of Justice tailors its expectations to what the senators concerned will accept. In appointing judges to the district and circuit
courts in the South, for example, the Kennedy administration
decided that it would never be able to win confirmation for black
lawyers or civil rights advocates. Accordingly, they never tried. In
the words of their Attorney General Katzenbach:

> We do not expect to find or to be able to obtain confirmation
> for militant civil rights advocates in the South. What we
> seek is to assure ourselves that nominees will follow the law
> of the land. We are satisfied with that much.[11]

Victor Navasky, in his study of the Justice Department under
Robert Kennedy, states that Justice officials never even advocated
challenging the southern senators. At the end of Robert Kennedy's tenure as Attorney General,

> . . . in the principal Southern states there were no Negro
> circuit court judges (twelve white ones), no Negro district
> court judges (sixty-five white ones), no Negro U.S. Com-
> missioners (253 white ones), no Negro jury commis-
> sioners (109 white ones), and no Negro U.S. Marshals
> (twenty-nine white ones). As a study of the Southern Re-

gional Council concluded, "A Negro involved in a federal court action in the South could go from the beginning of the case to the end without seeing any black faces unless they were in the court audience, or he happens to notice the man sweeping the floor."[12]

Thus, indirect senatorial influence in the nominating process extends their given power of suggesting nominees. Every participant in the nominating process realizes that senators have the last say; few outside the Senate are willing to exceed limits that senators appear to impose concerning a nominee's acceptability.

Both the Justice Department and the Senate have recently come to rely heavily on one nongovernmental source in determining who should be nominated for district and circuit court vacancies: the American Bar Association. Since the end of the Truman administration, the ABA's role in the nominating process has grown to approach that of the president and the Senate: each has a veto power over nominations initiated elsewhere.

Today, the ABA has a twelve-member standing committee on the federal judiciary which considers persons for vacancies. Bernard Segal, former chairman of the committee, testified how the ABA committee, now headed by the former Attorney General, Lawrence Walsh, determined judicial "fitness":

> When Judge Walsh became the Deputy Attorney General and Mr. Rogers, the Attorney General, we finally evolved the system we had requested so that we received as many as 17 names for a single vacancy; also a system whereby each prospective nominee was sent an exhaustive questionnaire we drafted going into his entire background, literally from his pre-college days to the present, and the nature of his practice, his legal training, his experience, his extracurricular activities. . . . To effectuate the practice of submitting several names per vacancy, rather than only one, Judge Walsh and I set up the system of informal reports. What occurs is that the Deputy Attorney General will advise the ABA committee chairman that the following individuals are

under consideration. The chairman and the member of the circuit only—not the whole committee—will then conduct an exhaustive investigation, the reason being that, at that point, neither the Senator, in most cases, nor the Attorney General wants to have too much talk triggered by an investigation. They want a completely off-the-record survey.[13]

The full ABA committee, in the case of a formal recommendation, and the chairman and the relevant circuit members, in the case of an informal one, meet and confer one of four possible ratings: "exceptionally well-qualified," "well-qualified," "qualified," or "not qualified."[14] The lowest, an "unqualified" rating, virtually assures that the person will not be nominated or, if nominated, will not be confirmed.* The ratings, according to Senator Abraham Ribicoff (D., Conn.), are by "one man's" fiat—the full committee stamp is "rubber"[15]—and encourage participants in this process to name the most qualified persons it can find. Often they don't. But once these names are referred to the committee and a recommendation is made, the committee strains to award at least a "qualified" rating:

> Where the committee says a man is not qualified, I need not say to you, Senator, as a lawyer, that there is no more unpleasant task than for a group of lawyers to pronounce as not qualified another lawyer who has probably aspired to the position all of his life and suddenly has the support which at least makes him get serious consideration and perhaps, absent this decision, would be appointed. So that no one is called "not qualified" except after a vast amount of soul-searching by the committee. . . .[16]

The Justice Department will usually accept the ABA ratings. The Kennedy administration did nominate a few persons who were rated "unqualified" by the ABA, but the Nixon administration has not. Apparently, the ABA has finally established an absolute veto power over federal judicial nominations.

* There are exceptions to this rule. See pp. 236–237.

Committee Consideration of Nominees: *Rush to Judgment*

Once the full record (including an FBI check) has been assembled and the president has nominated an individual, the appointment is sent to the Senate. All appointments to judicial posts are automatically and immediately sent to the Senate Judiciary Committee. In the case of U.S. district and circuit court nominations, the names generally remain in the committee for about a month before hearings are held. Nominations for U.S. marshal and U.S. attorney are usually disposed of more swiftly. And at the end of a Congress, all nominations move far more rapidly than they do at the beginning.

No nominees for judicial posts in the Ninety-second Congress were rejected by Judiciary, nor were any defeated on the Senate floor. No names for such posts were withdrawn from consideration by the President. The only nominations drawing public and media attention were those for Supreme Court vacancies and that of Richard Kleindienst as attorney general. All other nominations were routinely accepted or held over without action.

Eastland appoints an *ad hoc* subcommittee of senators to consider district court nominations (seventy-two in the Ninety-second Congress) and circuit court nominations (eighteen).[17] The full-committee staff generally processes nominations for U.S. marshal (ten in the Ninety-second) and U.S. attorney positions (twenty-two); none of the staff specializes in particular positions. Certain senators, however, do specialize in court nominations. In the Ninety-second Congress, Senator Eastland appointed the same members to the *ad hoc* subcommittee to consider almost all of the court nominees—except for Supreme Court positions, which are handled by the full committee. The *ad hoc* subcommittee includes Eastland, Senator McClellan (the second ranking Democrat on the full committee), and Senator Hruska (the ranking Republican). These three are not simply the ranking members of the Senate Judiciary Committee; they are also the committee's most conservative members. No other committee members have formally served on this rather permanent *ad hoc* subcommittee in the Ninety-second Congress. No senator or staff member interviewed could recall ever having heard any of the liberals on the Judiciary Committee complain to the chairman about this "stacking" of the subcommittee. Several observers echoed the common refrain: the liberals rarely attend the public hearings on these nominations, although they are free to do so.

The Judiciary Committee staff commences the process of Senate consideration by sending a "blue slip" to the senators from the state in which the vacancy arose, informing them of the nomination. This is "senatorial courtesy." The slip, under Eastland's signature, says:

> Dear Senator:
> Will you kindly give me, for use of the Committee, your opinion and information concerning the nomination of [name, district, name of former judge]. Under a rule of the Committee, unless a reply is received from you within a week from this date, it will be assumed that you have no objection to this nomination.[18]

In practice, however, the committee waits as long as it takes the senator to reply.[19] The staff also sends similar letters of inquiry to the ABA and state and local bar associations. Once the slips are returned, hearings are scheduled for district and circuit court nominations. No hearings are held for U.S. attorney and U.S. marshal nominations unless formally requested. Generally, the staff prepares the information on nominees for these positions for the consideration of the full committee. If a senator disapproves by blue slip, the nomination is halted unless and until an accommodation can be worked out with the Department of Justice. Disapproval at this point is almost unheard of, however, since names are only sent to the committee after the appropriate senators have been consulted.

The Senate Judiciary Committee indulges a very strong presumption that the president's nomination should be confirmed.

Because the committee must deal with so much legislation, members do not seriously scrutinize appointments unless compelling questions are raised by other senators or by interest groups. Neither senators nor interest groups, however, raise questions about nominations to the district or circuit courts or to the U.S. attorney and U.S. marshal positions. According to one senator who led a challenge and lost, "You don't get involved in these nominations because you rarely can win a fight on lower court nominations and you just make enemies. Senators take a challenge to their nominee as a personal affront."[20]

After a district or circuit court nomination has lain in the full committee for about two weeks, Senator Eastland typically announces in the *Congressional Record* that the *ad hoc* subcommittee will consider the nomination. One week after the announcement, the subcommittee holds hearings on the nomination and reports back to the full committee, which in turn submits its report to the full Senate. No individual announcements or accounts of hearings are sent to committee members. The time lag between the hearing and full Senate approval is generally no more than a few weeks, depending upon when the full committee meets.

The hearings on district and circuit court nominations before the *ad hoc* subcommittee are regarded by almost everyone as a formality; certainly they do not represent any serious, independent investigation by the Judiciary Committee into the merits of the appointments. The full committee is only too ready to accept the "findings" of the subcommittee, and the full Senate is equally uncritical of the determinations of the Judiciary Committee. *Hearings, subcommittee approval, full committee approval, and Senate confirmation frequently occur all on one day.* Of the ninety district and circuit court nominations sent to the Senate in the Ninety-second Congress, forty-one went from hearings to full Senate confirmation in one day. In addition, several nominees were considered together on the same day. Almost all of those nominees confirmed on one day were treated in conjunction with

as many as seven other circuit and/or district court nominees.*
On five separate days, thirty-two such nominees were considered.
Consider one day, April 21, 1971. On that day, the nominees
for four circuit and three district court vacancies were considered.
Only one member of the full committee, Senator Roman
Hruska, was present throughout the hearings on these seven
nominees. The then chief counsel, John Holloman III, also
attended. Other senators, not on the Judiciary Committee, presented testimony in favor of nominees from their states. Senator
McClellan appeared for consideration of a nominee from his circuit, but the Judiciary Committee was not otherwise represented.

Senator Hruska conducted individual hearings on each nominee. *The seven hearings took a total of fifty-five minutes to complete, an average of six minutes per nominee.* The format was as
follows: Hruska opened each hearing with a statement that senators had approved the nomination by blue slip and that the ABA
and state bar association had rated the appointee. Senators from
the nominee's state read a biography of the nominee in a perfunctory manner. Hruska's main question was whether the nominee was aware of the rule of the Judicial Conference prohibiting
judges from having conflicts of interest by reason of membership
on corporate boards of directors or other official corporate ties.
The nominee was asked if he had any conflicts of interest and,
if so, what provisions he had made to remove that conflict.
Hruska asked if anyone in the room wished to speak on behalf of
or against the nominee. The subcommittee then moved on to the
next nominee. Six minutes had elapsed from start to finish.
Another federal judge had been appointed to a life term on the
bench. This format was typical of the processing of all the district or circuit court nominees in the Ninety-second Congress;
none aroused any controversy.

Senators do occasionally interrogate a nominee at a hearing,

---

* April 21, 1971 (seven); May 26, 1971 (three); September 21, 1971
(five); November 23, 1971 (six); December 1, 1971 (three); December 2,
1971 (six); December 4, 1971 (two); June 28, 1972 (eight).

but they rarely press the nominee even if their questions remain unanswered. Senator John J. Williams (R., Del.), for example, closely questioned David Bress, nominee for U.S. attorney for the District of Columbia, in a September 21, 1965, hearing. Senator Williams asked about Bress's previous representation of Bobby Baker's Serv-U Corporation; the Justice Department had just instituted suit against Baker. Although his questions were never answered satisfactorily, Williams did not fight against confirmation.* During the Ninety-first Congress, Senator Hart and the other Democratic liberals on the committee forced fuller hearings over the nomination of James Gorbey to a district court judgeship in Pennsylvania. As mayor of Chester, Pennsylvania, the nominee had arrested twenty-eight persons in a 1964 civil rights demonstration that lasted sixty-nine days. In two days of hearings, significant questions concerning Gorbey's role were raised by University of Pennsylvania law professor Paul Bender on behalf of the ACLU. Liberals dropped the matter when they found that Senator Hugh Scott, who had just entered the hearing room, was continuing to support the nominee from his state. Minutes later, the hearing terminated and Gorbey was confirmed.

The case of Judge Costantino is another excellent illustration of the inadequacy of Judiciary Committee hearings on judicial nominations. Public hearings were held to consider the nominations of Costantino and four other men to fill three district and two circuit court vacancies. The nomination hearings of the five men, which were attended only by Senator Hruska and then chief counsel John Holloman III, took a total of fifteen minutes. With less than three minutes devoted to the consideration of Costantino's fitness for a position on the federal bench for life, few words were uttered on his behalf. Senator Javits, Costantino's sponsor, told the committee:

---

* While Bress's nomination as U.S. attorney was confirmed, he was not confirmed when President Johnson later nominated him to be U.S. district judge for the District of Columbia on January 10, 1969. President Nixon withdrew the nomination on January 23, 1970.

I take particular pleasure in the fact that the President has
named Judge Costantino because it took some looking into
because he comes from Staten Island and a painstaking review of his judicial and legal career convinced us all that
he should be advanced to the District Court and that he
would bring to it the qualities of heart and mind that were
extremely desirable.

I think that in a sense that it is a great vindication of the
American system that we could so much go out of our way
to find the man who so much deserves preferment, which
I hope he will receive.

Costantino got his preferment, and Staten Island its recognition,
but what sort of justice do the people get who must appear before
him?[21]

When interest groups, particularly the ABA, raise a question
about a nominee's fitness, hearings are also held but rarely result
in a nominee's defeat. The ABA is the most active group pressing
for more than perfunctory hearings. When the ABA Committee
on the Federal Judiciary gives an "unqualified" rating to a person,
hearings usually last more than the normal six minutes—but not
necessarily. The hearing for Luther Bohanon, nominated by
President Kennedy for a district judgeship in Oklahoma, lasted
only fifteen minutes in spite of his "unqualified" rating. No one,
including Senator Olin Johnston who was presiding, even asked
the nominee about the rating. Strong support for Bohanon by the
powerful Senator Robert Kerr (D., Okla.) probably deterred
questions.

In the case of David Rabinowitz, who was nominated for a
district judgeship in Wisconsin despite an "unqualified" rating
from the ABA, the hearing lasted only fifty-five minutes. No
witnesses other than the nominee and the senators from Wisconsin were heard from. The ABA position in the Rabinowitz case
was stated only in a conclusory letter dated September 24, 1963,
to the chairman from Robert W. Meserve, chairman of the ABA
committee: "I regret to advise you that the members of our

committee are unanimously of the opinion that Mr. Rabinowitz is not qualified for this appointment." The Judiciary Committee members did not inquire as to the reasons for the ABA rating, and Rabinowitz was confirmed. A similar letter to Eastland regarding Bohanon was sent August 22, 1961.

If the ABA is willing to openly agitate against a nominee, it can bring about exhaustive hearings. The difference between the perfunctory Bohanon and Rabinowitz hearings and the six-month hearings held for Irving Ben Cooper, nominee for a district judgeship in New York, was the ABA's readiness to actively fight the Cooper nomination.[22] Representatives of the New York City Bar Association came to Washington to testify against Cooper on the ground that as a state court judge he "lacked judicial temperament." Witnesses testified that Cooper called youths who appeared before him in open court "punks," "bums," "flotsam and jetsam," and "slime of the earth."[23] Cooper had been sponsored for the nomination by Emanuel Celler, chairman of the House Judiciary Committee. Celler had written to the attorney general:

> "I submit this name to you because I believe him to be the best-qualified. . . . I would be less than frank if I did not tell you that I would be greatly disappointed were he not nominated."[24]

The National Association for the Advancement of Colored People (NAACP) and other interest groups have fought lower-court nominations before the Senate Judiciary Committee—the NAACP battle against the appointment of former Mississippi Governor James Coleman to the Fifth Circuit Court of Appeals is a notable instance—but have rarely, if ever, won there. The long string of failures in such campaigns has bred a self-fulfilling fatalism about Judiciary Committee deliberations.

The ABA as Judge and Jury

The assumption on the part of many Judiciary Committee members that a nominee has been adequately investigated elsewhere along the line[25] is highly dubious. Although the ABA rating is very influential on members, the ABA's investigatory findings and even its final decisions are not disclosed. The ABA does not publicly explain its ratings to the Justice Department or the Senate Judiciary Committee but simply informs the chairman of the rating by brief letter. The sources of the ABA's information, the nature of the discussions preceding the final vote, the vote by particular members, the reasons for the division of opinion—all of these data are hidden in the final rating. And members of Judiciary have shown no interest in requiring the ABA to make its reasons public, even when an "unqualified" candidate is before them, as with the Bohanon and Rabinowitz nominations. The ABA's role in the nomination process has been criticized on other grounds as well. Senator Marlow Cook has detected an ABA bias in favor of corporation lawyers. In a 1970 speech delivered to the Louisville Bar Association, Cook said:

> "First, let us begin with a few facts of life about ABA of which we are all aware but only seldom discuss. The ABA is essentially large-firm oriented and these large firms across the United States tend to represent defendants in personal injury cases, i.e., insurance companies, and do corporate work in general. Now certainly no one in this room would object to the representation of these types of clients, many of you represent corporations.
>
>   In fact, I did a lot of corporate work myself when I was still actively engaged in the practice of law. But I know and you know that there is a certain bias which all lawyers develop in favor of their clients and against their adversaries. This is basic human nature. Our legal system is after all an adversary system which encourages this and there is nothing wrong with it. And I contend, and you know it's true, that there is a certain condescension which many corporate, big-firm lawyers exhibit toward plaintiff-oriented practitioners.
>
>   Since the American Bar Association is essentially dominated by this type of lawyer, it is only logical that their judgments might be colored when asked to pass upon the

fitness of certain lawyers for appointment to the federal bench who represent plaintiffs and practice either alone or in small firms."[26]

Another member of Judiciary complains that one of his nominees for a district judgeship, a black lawyer who was practicing law alone in a poor neighborhood, was given an "unqualified" rating due to his unglamorous practice. This attorney was nevertheless confirmed and has since rendered significant decisions as a federal judge and has been acclaimed by the legal community.[27]

While the ABA can be criticized for being too secretive in its deliberations, failing to explain its decisions, and favoring particular types of lawyers, the ABA committee has also been accused of not being selective enough. Victor Navasky charges that the ABA committee was too often willing to accept nominations put forward by the Justice Department.[28] Citing an unpublished study by Professor Harold Chase of the University of Wisconsin, Navasky contends that the ABA committee often changed its ratings between the first informal and the formal rating (without, of course, publicly stating the justification for such changes). Professor Chase found that during a two-year period in the Kennedy administration,

> almost 29 percent of 101 informal ratings differed from the formal ratings. Seventy-two ratings (by the ABA) showed no change; 7 which looked not qualified on the informal were qualified on the formal; 1 went from qualified to not qualified; 1 from well-qualified to qualified; 3 from well-qualified to qualified; 3 from well-qualified to exceptionally well-qualified.[29]

If the ABA is to continue as a central participant in the nominating process, it should institute an appeals process from adverse ratings which nominees might invoke, as well as full explanation by the committee of its rating in each individual case. Nominees should be able to confront the evidence against them. The Judiciary Committee and the Senate need to have the full case before them prior to the presentation of informal as well as formal reports. Rather than accommodating its ratings to the Justice Department's wishes, the ABA should hold fast to its own ratings, leaving it to the president and the Senate to determine what factors other than professional competence should be weighed in the appointment process. The ABA should not exercise a veto over nominations, because its rating represents the views of only a few of the nominee's peers concerning his professional competence. Until the ABA committee makes public its rationale for particular ratings, these ratings should not be a determinative factor in the nomination process.

If the ABA is to have the privilege of partnership in the nominating process—an extraordinary delegation of public power to a private organization—other interest groups should also be encouraged to participate, for their views of the nominee's qualifications may be at least as informative and relevant as those of the ABA. The only group besides the ABA that is consistently interested in nominations is the NAACP, but even this group rarely gets involved in nominations for positions below the Supreme Court level. At the very least, the Judiciary Committee should notify groups other than the ABA and the state bar associations concerning nominations. Until the committee can convince such groups that its nomination deliberations are not simply *pro forma* and sham, however, widespread participation by such groups will not be forthcoming.

Part of the inadequacy of the process of consideration can be explained by the inherent difficulty of scrutinizing nominees. The Judiciary Committee must exploit independent sources of information about nominees if it is to perform its investigatory function. Committee staff can be used to compile data concerning the qualifications and criticisms of nominees, rather than simply putting together one-page biographies to be read at a six-minute hearing. The committee should also encourage the formation of an investigative, research network of lawyers, law school professors, and journalists, similar to the group that developed such devastating evidence concerning the judicial fitness of Judge G. Harrold Carswell, to investigate the qualifications of lower court nominees. It is essential that an adversary, independent, fact-finding capability and mechanism be built into the nomination process to replace the one the Founding Fathers relied upon, but which has atrophied from disuse.

That the Senate Judiciary Committee has utterly failed to discharge its independent responsibility in the nomination process for district and circuit court positions is evident from the committee's performance in confirming the nomination of Carswell to the Fifth Circuit Court of Appeals in 1969. Although the same information that later defeated Carswell's nomination to the Supreme Court was available to the committee then, Carswell was confirmed for the Fifth Circuit in the same hasty and desultory fashion typical of the committee's deliberations on almost all judicial nominations. The *ad hoc* subcommittee heard data on Carswell as only one of three nominations on the morning of June 5, 1969, and apparently the session was of informal brevity.* The full committee approved his nomination along with those of twenty-eight other judicial nominees on June 18. On June 19, the Senate confirmed Carswell and eighteen other nominees. At every stage in this process, every major participant —the senators from Florida, the Department of Justice, the ABA, the *ad hoc* Judiciary subcommittee, the full Senate Judiciary Committee, and the full Senate—relied upon every other participant to perform the necessary investigation. In the end, *none* assumed the responsibility.

* Since the committee's file on Carswell is unaccountably missing from its repository in the National Archives, information concerning the duration of the 1969 hearing was necessarily based upon an interview with Richard Wambach of the Judiciary Committee staff.

11

Private Bills:
The Gravy Road

Dorothy Kilmer waited on the street corner for her fiancé. Absorbed, she did not notice the commotion down the street. Suddenly a shot punctured the evening air. Kilmer never met her fiancé that evening, for the shot, fired by a District of Columbia policeman, severed her spinal cord and paralyzed her. The District of Columbia refused to compensate her, arguing that the policeman had been off duty at the time of the incident.

It took an act of Congress—a private bill—to pay her medical fees.* [1]

Sondra D. Shaw opened her mail one morning and found a demand from the Internal Revenue Service for $12,608.73 in back taxes. It was the final outrage in a string of calamities.

* She was awarded $15,000. In any other municipality, of course, the federal government would not have been involved.

NOTE: This chapter was prepared by Peter H. Schuck and Dr. Martha Joynt Kumar.

242

Unknown to Shaw, her estranged husband had embezzled funds from his company. Then, one Sunday, he had taken the two Shaw children for an outing, and they never returned. The disturbed husband had killed them and himself. Because she had filed a joint federal income tax return with her husband, the IRS imposed the tax liability on the distressed and grieving mother and widow for the funds embezzled by her late husband.

It took an act of Congress—a private bill—to discharge Mrs. Shaw from this debt.[2]

Fully two-thirds of the bills referred to the Senate Judiciary Committee in the Ninety-second Congress had no particular bearing on the great social issues that crowd the committee's agenda. These are private bills,* directed at relief for one or a few specified individuals who seek protection against the rigor of federal statutes or against harmful administrative actions or inactions. One classic definition is:

> The line of distinction between public and private bills is so difficult to be defined in many cases that it must rest on the opinion of the Speaker and the details of the bill. It has been the practice of Parliament, and also in Congress, to consider as private such [bills] as are for the extent of individuals, public companies, or corporations, a parish, city, or county, or other locality. To be a private bill it must not be general in its enactment, but for the particular interest or benefit of a person or persons.[3]

Examining the process of handling private bills affords a glimpse of a few members of Congress dispensing valuable favors and funds to private individuals or groups under circumstances far removed from public consciousness, scrutiny, participation, or concern. And that combination always spells trouble.

There are two major types of private legislation: claims bills

---

* Much of the data in this section is taken from Martha Joynt Kumar, "Private Bills and the Legislative Process" (Ph.D. dissertation in Political Science, Columbia University, 1972). (Cited as "Joynt.")

and immigration bills. A claims bill seeks to recover from the U.S. Treasury money that an individual believes the federal government owes him, or seeks permission to sue the federal government in the U.S. Court of Claims.* An immigration bill seeks a waiver of the requirements for citizenship or for residence in the United States prescribed by the immigration and naturalization statutes.

When considering private bills, Congress acts as a court of last resort. Persons seeking relief by private bill are required to have already exhausted their efforts and failed to secure relief from government agencies or from the courts. Such persons are in effect petitioning Congress to make an exception for them by means of direct legislation. Private bills, then, seek to accommodate the rigor and inflexibility of general, impersonal legal rules with the ethical demands for justice and equity in the individual case.

Senators and representatives tend to feel somewhat ambivalent about private bills. On the one hand, these bills are unique political assets; the legislator can directly serve his constituent with a knotty problem about which the constituent feels very intensely. If the legislator does no more than introduce the bill, not only the constituent, but his or her family and friends are likely to regard the legislator in heroic dimensions. If the bill passes, the legislator can probably count on undying loyalty from members of the constituent's circle. Best of all, the legislator can do so without using up any of his political "chips," for such bills are rarely controversial, have no ideological overtones, invoke no alliances, and breach no principles. Private bills, in the jargon of the social scientist, confer divisible benefits on small, intensely affected groups of constituents without alienating anyone else. From the politician's point of view, such bills are "pure gravy." They are also excellent log-rolling material. By supporting

* The ancient doctrine of sovereign immunity prevents citizens from suing the United States except as specifically authorized by statute. Jurisdiction over most monetary claims against the United States resides in the U.S. Court of Claims.

private bills introduced by other politicians, the legislator can also build up a stock of favors which he can then trade for these politicians' support on public laws in which he is deeply interested or which are more visible to his larger constituency. And the politician can obtain all these benefits at essentially no personal cost, for he need only introduce the private bill, a meaningless gesture requiring little of the legislator's own time.

Private bills are not, however, an unmixed blessing: requests for private bills are massive; they require considerable staff time to process. Prior to 1970, an estimated 25 percent of the time of members' caseworkers in the House (and only slightly less in the Senate) was expended on private bills.[4] Today, an estimated 10 percent of their time is spent on private bills. Private bills are not particularly interesting, and the ambitious legislator will not want to devote scarce staff resources to them.

Notwithstanding this ambivalence, however, senators and congressmen do introduce much private legislation. Claims bills are only a small proportion of the private bills introduced; immigration bills now dominate. In the Ninetieth Congress, each House member introduced an average of 1.4 claims bills and 14.2 immigration bills.[5] In the entire Ninety-second Congress, 573 claims bills and 2,084 immigration bills were introduced in the House. In the Senate, 476 claims and 1,511 immigration bills were introduced in the Ninety-first Congress, and in the first session of the Ninety-second Congress, 248 claims and 673 immigration bills were introduced.[6] The Ninety-second Congress enacted sixty-seven private immigration bills and eighty-six claims bills.

PRIVATE CLAIMS BILLS: HARDSHIP, FRIENDSHIP, AND SELF-INTEREST

Three major factors impel members to introduce private claims bills: a case of hardship or injustice; the imperatives of friendship; or the prospect of financial support from the beneficiary.

Typical hardship cases were those of Dorothy Kilmer and Sondra Shaw described above. Another type of hardship bill involves persons inadvertently overpaid by the federal government. Such persons are legally liable for the amount of the overpayment, even though the money may already have been spent by the time the error is discovered. When it is particularly difficult for a person to repay the money, a private bill is sometimes introduced to relieve the individual of the obligation.

Although most private claims bills seek to mitigate cases of inequity and hardship, friendship sometimes motivates introduction of a bill. The late Senator Everett Dirksen introduced a bill in the Eighty-seventh Congress to grant $100,000 to the widow of Gregory L. Kessenich, civilian head of the patent section of the Army Ordnance Department during World War II.[7] Kessenich had been denied special compensation for his part in the development of the bazooka rocket on the ground that the invention was developed while he was a government employee. The importance of Kessenich's role in the project had been questioned: in a 1944 article, the journal *Army Ordnance* indicated that only a few of the developments on the bazooka were made by Kessenich.[8] In 1957 the secretary of the army, Wilber M. Brucker, concluded that there was no reason to single out Kessenich for any special compensation.[9] In 1962 Pentagon official Cyrus Vance also refused to award any money for the same reason.[10]

What proved to be of "special significance" in the Kessenich case was his widow's well-placed connections.[11] Mrs. Kessenich had become a friend of the Dirksens and had purchased a home in De Bary, Florida, adjacent to the Dirksens. A congressional staffer, asked if he was aware of the friendship, said: "Aware of it? Senator Dirksen made it very clear that was why he was introducing the bill."[12] Dirksen's devotion was great indeed. After the bill to award Mrs. Kessenich $100,000 was signed into law, it was discovered that approximately $65,000 would be taken in taxes. Rising to the challenge, Senator Dirksen simply sponsored and won enactment of another private bill in the next

Congress to relieve her of the necessity of paying taxes on the money.[13]

Dirksen did not confine his generosity—with the taxpayers' money—to personal friends. In the Eighty-ninth Congress, Dirksen introduced a private bill for the relief on the Erman-Howell Division of the Luria Steel and Trading Co.[14] The firm's attorney, Sidney J. Hess, later contributed $500 to Senator Dirksen's 1968 reelection campaign.[15] The private bill paid the company $129,919 in expected profits on a government contract bid which it had lost through an alleged error by the Justice Department.

Another private claims bill that benefited an apparent campaign contributor was introduced by Senator Quentin Burdick in 1967.[16] The Swanston Equipment Company, headed by William Swanston, received $21,376 that it had paid in duty on farm machinery equipment imported from Canada. Swanston claimed that that particular kind of machinery was exempt from duty, although the Treasury Department report opposed the exemption.[17] Swanston, who had reportedly contributed $100 to Burdick's 1964 campaign,[18] received his money back.

Members who have introduced private claims bills because of factors such as friendship or money do not necessarily press for the bill's passage. As noted above, the member can often satisfy the constituent simply by introducing the bill, knowing that it will be killed by the Senate or House Judiciary committees. As members well know, criteria that induce members to introduce private bills are not always the same ones by which the Judiciary committees evaluate them. Individual members are concerned neither with how their bills affect the total number of private claims bills introduced nor with the precedents that the bills might establish. The Judiciary committees, however, faced with an enormous volume of bills, must consider both these factors.

Committee Procedures

All private claims bills in the House are routinely referred to Judiciary Subcommittee No. 2. The subcommittee rules stress equity in extending relief to individuals who have no recourse to administrative or judicial remedies under existing law. . . . The right to petition for such redress is guaranteed by the Constitution. The task of the subcommittee is to determine whether the equities and circumstances of a case create a moral obligation on the part of the government so that an individual merits relief.[19]

William Shattuck, chief counsel of the subcommittee, lists additional criteria considered by the House subcommittee in approving claims bills: (1) No other remedy can exist; all administrative and judicial remedies must have been exhausted. (2) The situation must be singular, with few or no other individuals in the same distress; passing a bill relieving only one is an injustice to others similarly situated. (3) The United States government, or federal personnel or property, must be involved. (4) In the case of technical bills referred to the Court of Claims, the chief commissioner of the court must approve the claims.[20]

The smaller the amount of money, the easier it is to get bills through the subcommittee with a favorable report. Rule 8 of the House Judiciary Subcommittee No. 2 provides that bills with favorable departmental reports and amounting to less than $500 may be reported by the subcommittee chairman without subcommittee discussion. When larger sums of money are involved, hearings must be held in the subcommittee, and strong forces must be marshaled to win approval.

The Senate Judiciary Committee considers claims bills in a quite different way. No permanent subcommittee handles these bills and no formal rules govern their disposition.* The Senate keeps claims bills in the full committee and refers them to the professional staff for consideration. If a private claims bill is controversial, the Senate committee appoints an *ad hoc* subcommittee of three members to consider the bill. Usually no more than five or ten such subcommittees are created during one Congress,

---

* The absence of formal rules characterizes Senate Judiciary Committee operations generally (see Chapter 2).

and any senator who wishes to may be on one. It is not surprising, then, that Senator Tunney was on the special subcommittee that considered the cyclamates bill;* he was also a sponsor of the bill. Senator Dirksen was often on subcommittees that considered his private claims bills.

An important factor in the fate of a private bill in the Senate (but not in the House) is whether the sponsor of the bill is a member of the Senate Judiciary Committee and is willing to push his bill. Committee members often succeed in having their bills favorably reported under circumstances in which non-Judiciary senators might fail. Of the 47 claims bills reported by the Senate Judiciary Committee in the Ninetieth Congress, 17 were sponsored by members of the committee. In the House, however, only 30 of the 164 claims bills reported were sponsored by committee members.[21]

A Sweet Giveaway—Almost!

Not all private claims bills are for widows and orphans, and not all are considered only in the subcommittee offices. During the Ninety-second Congress, the House passed, and the Senate Judiciary Committee held hearings on, a bill (H.R.13366)† to authorize the payment by the Court of Claims of hundreds of millions of dollars of private claims by farmers and food processors for losses occasioned by the federal government's 1969 ban of cyclamates, widely used artificial sweeteners.

In less than a decade, cyclamate consumption in the United States had grown astronomically, reaching approximately 20 million pounds a year by 1968. Cyclamates had become standard ingredients in canned soups, chewable vitamins, cough syrups, jams, jellies, and canned fruits, in addition to their well-publicized use in soft drinks. So widespread had their use become that cycla-

---

* The handling of this controversial bill is discussed at length below.

† Strictly speaking, this was not a private bill; it sought to confer jurisdiction on the Court of Claims to consider a specific class of private claims. In all other respects, it was tantamount to a private bill.

mates were placed on the Food and Drug Administration's list of food additives "Generally Recognized As Safe" (GRAS).

Yet scientific reports during the 1960s increasingly linked cyclamates and their sometime metabolite, CHA (cyclohexylamine), with myocardial and circulatory strains, chromosome damage, skin rashes, and cancer. When the largest manufacturer of cyclamates, Abbott Laboratories, documented an association between cyclamate ingestion and bladder cancer in laboratory mice, pressure mounted within the Food and Drug Administration to invoke the Food, Drug, and Cosmetic Act's so-called Delaney clause requiring the banning of carcinogenic food additives. After a scientist at the FDA, refusing to permit the suppression of the Abbott findings any longer, made them public, Secretary of Health, Education, and Welfare Robert Finch was obliged to announce a ban on the further use of cyclamates in October 1969.

Shortly thereafter, a steady stream of private claims bills designed to reimburse industrial users and farmers for cyclamate losses began to flow through the Judiciary Committees. H.R.13366 almost made it all the way in the Ninety-second Congress. According to the majority report on the bill in the House Judiciary Committee:

> The court would be directed to determine the amount of loss resulting from each claimant's good faith reliance to his detriment on the safety of cyclamic acid and its salts by virtue of its inclusion and continuance on the list of substances generally recognized as safe for their intended use as promulgated under the Federal Food, Drug, and Cosmetic Act (GRAS list). The Court would be directed to include as the basis of its judgments, direct and indirect costs and damages but not including lost profits.[22]

The proponents of the bill claimed that farmers and processors acted "in good faith" when, prior to the ban, they packed their fruits and other foods using cyclamates; that these producers were left with heavy inventories; and that many were nearly wiped out financially. Proponents of the bill believed that the government was morally obligated to indemnify those hurt by the ban, since cyclamates were on the FDA's GRAS list, a designation which, they insisted, signified government approval of their use and upon which they had relied.

The sponsors further emphasized that the FDA could have moved sooner and thus minimized the financial ruin suffered by small farmers and producers. Congressman Robert L. Leggett (D., Cal.) cited a highly critical report made by the L. H. Fountain (D., N.C.) subcommittee on FDA oversight, a unit of the House Government Operations Committee:

> It was evident at least as early as 1966 that there was a genuine difference of opinion among qualified experts as to the safety of the cyclamate sweeteners. Consequently, FDA had an obligation at that time to remove cyclamates from the GRAS list, to declare them to be a "food additive" within the statutory definition, and to ban their use until industry had established their safety. But despite the mounting evidence in the ensuing years, FDA did not act. . . .

Leggett continued:

> The Fountain Committee found that the FDA at the very least should have acted on July 26, 1969, when a work was published in *Nature*—pages 406-407—describing myocardial lesions associated with cyclamates.[23]

Opponents of the bill viewed it as a benefice for businesses that knowingly used cyclamates despite long-held and substantial questions concerning its safety. In her testimony on behalf of Ralph Nader's Public Interest Research Group, Anita Johnson stated:

> I oppose the bill. The bill, if passed, would reward manufacturers for bad business judgment and for wanton indifference to the public health. The diet food industry had notice, long before the 1969 ban, of cyclamate safety doubts. They continued, despite that notice, to market in spite of a possible ban. They made a calculated human judgment to

supply cyclamate to consumers even if dangerous to their
health.
The industry had had notice of cyclamate safety doubts
for over 15 years. In 1950, the FDA cleared cyclamate for
use as a drug for diabetics who could not eat sugar. In 1951,
FDA scientists published a study of artificial sweeteners which
concluded that cyclamate was safe, but reported unexplained
tumors in their cyclamate test rats.[24]

Johnson and others cited additional warnings of possible health
hazards presented by cyclamates: in 1955 the Food and Nutrition
Board of the prestigious National Academy of Sciences warned
that cyclamate use should not be expanded because long-term
safety was not known; in 1962 the board reiterated its warning;
in 1967 the World Health Organization recommended a restriction on the ingestion of cyclamates; in 1968 the Food Protection
Committee of the National Academy of Sciences reviewed the
evidence for FDA and declared that "totally unrestricted use of
the cyclamates is not warranted at this time."[25]

Opponents of the legislation insisted that both users and manufacturers of cyclamates were not caught by surprise when the
FDA banned the sweeteners. In fact, two soft-drink giants, Cott
and No-Cal, had a substitute on the grocery shelves within a
week of the ban. The bill's opponents on the House Judiciary
Committee said in their minority report:

> Was this and much other evidence . . . not sufficient to put
> the industry on notice . . . ? Some producers were ready. . . .
> Pepsi-Cola had readied a new diet drink without cyclamates
> one year before the ban. Coca-Cola told the New York Times
> that it was equally well prepared. "Taking out insurance,"
> was the way Coca-Cola President Charles Adams described
> the readiness of Coke's new diet product. "We've been
> working with alternative artificial sweeteners since the early
> sixties," he stated.[26]

One provision of the bill instructed the Court of Claims to permit payment in cases where cyclamates had been used in "good
faith reliance" on their inclusion on the GRAS list. Opponents

argued that this "good faith" proviso would in fact create a yawning loophole. James R. Mann (D., S.C.) pointed out:

> How does one rely on the GRAS list in bad faith? . . . If I walk into that Court of Claims with a bill that says, if I relied on the GRAS list, I am paid my direct and indirect costs, I will say, "Your Honor, I relied on the GRAS list and certainly I relied on it in good faith." What kind of knowledge would have to be charged to me to make me not rely on the GRAS list in good faith? There is no such thing.
>
> The bill is an automatic payment upon your appearance on your day in court and your proof of damages—and I assume that anyone will know how to do that.[27]

Opponents also debunked the argument that inclusion of a substance on the GRAS list signified government approval. Edward P. Boland (D., Mass.) noted:

> The [GRAS] list was simply a notice to industry—and to the public, as well—that the 600 substances went exempt from the testing demanded by the food additives amendment [rigorous testing of additives for toxicity].
>
> It did not award FDA sanction to any of these additives.
>
> On the contrary, the list should have been interpreted as a warning to industry and consumer alike, a warning that special vigilance should be exercised in using any of the 600 GRAS substances.[28]

The implications of this legislation were staggering. The minority report posed the question:

> Are we prepared for the new departure in governmental responsibility that adoption of this legislation represents? In our tradition, private individuals and commercial interests have not been recompensed when suffering economic injury as a result of the reasonable regulation of the public welfare. . . . The ramifications that come from an effort to have the government indemnify the individual from the financial consequences of a proper exercise of Federal regulatory power are almost too vast to contemplate. Let's not open that Pandora's box.[29]

Ordinarily, claims bills are approved only if there is little or no opposition. In this instance, however, members of Congress were subjected to unprecedented lobbying from economic interests, led by the National Canners Association (NCA) and the National Soft Drink Association, and from other members. In fact, NCA had developed the "good faith" language in the bill.[30] Many of the fruit farmers, processors, and distributors using cyclamates were located in California; of the thirty-eight members of the California delegation, twenty-five eventually voted for the bill on the House floor, while six opposed it, two voted present, and five members did not vote.[31]

Although hearings were held by Subcommittee No. 2 in September and October 1971, it was not until May 1972 that the bill reached the House floor. Chairman Harold Donohue delayed approval by the subcommittee until March 8. Full-committee chairman Celler also opposed the bill—certain death for any ordinary claims bill—but the committee nevertheless voted (17 to 7, with three members voting "present") to report the bill. At the end of June, it passed the House by a vote of 177–170. The outcome in the House had been in doubt, but as the roll call neared the end, the California delegation went to work. The *Washington Post* reported:

> The bill appeared beaten at the end of the House roll call. But then California members began "cashing chips" as Representative B. F. Sisk (D., Cal.) put it, and changed enough votes to win.[32]

Indeed, so great was the pressure that six members—William Harsha (R., Ohio), Sherman Lloyd (R., Utah), William Dickinson (R., Ala.), Robert Mollohan (D., W.Va.), Harley Staggers (D., W.Va.), and John Brademas (D., Ind.)—actually changed votes from nay to yea, while a few others were persuaded to support the legislation as their names were called.

The bill died because the Senate Judiciary Committee failed to act on the House-passed bill.[33] The final returns, however, are not all in. A similar bill (H.R.7252) was introduced by Congressman John A. Blatnik (D., Minn.) in the Ninety-third Congress.*

PRIVATE IMMIGRATION BILLS

In the processing of private immigration bills, Congress comes closest to degrading legislation to the status of a mere commodity, an article of trade. Commerce in this particular commodity is brisk, for the price is low and the payoff is often high. In the process, the Judiciary committees have been demeaned into little better than legislative flea markets.

The reason is not difficult to find. The mere *introduction* of a private immigration bill is distinctive in that, when accompanied by a request for an Immigration and Naturalization Service report, it grants a certain measure of relief: the automatic suspension of deportation proceedings.† Accordingly, many immigrants seek only the introduction of a bill and do not press for disposition by Congress. (If the House has already rejected such a bill, however, the introduction of another in the Senate will not stay deportation.) The availability of this relief, devoid of cost to the politician, has—like any free good—stimulated an inexhaustible demand, and immigration bills now dominate private-bill introductions.

Since introduction rather than final disposition of immigration bills is the critical step, at least in the Senate Committee,‡ there has been little pressure to move the bills along. For example, in House Judiciary Subcommittee No. 1 (immigration and naturali-

---

* And cyclamates may yet be resurrected to sweeten a new generation of food products. In early 1974, Abbott Laboratories filed a petition with the FDA to permit Abbott to market cyclamates once again, citing studies purporting to cast some doubts on the earlier Abbott findings.

† See *U. S. ex. rel. Knauff* v. *McGrath*, 181 F. 2d 839 (2nd Cir. 1950), cert. denied, 340 U. S. 940 (1951). As a result of this case, the attorney general may not deport an alien whose report has been requested by the subcommittee, at least while the bill remains active.

‡ See below.

zation) during the Ninetieth Congress, 4,846 private bills (over three-quarters of those introduced) were still pending at the end of the session.

In an effort to reduce the number and length of outstanding deportation stays, the House Judiciary Committee modified its rules several years ago. Rule 4 of the subcommittee now limits the applicability of the stay procedures:

> The subcommittee shall not address to the Attorney General communications designed to defer deportation of the beneficiaries of private bills who have entered the United States as nonimmigrant stowaways, in transit or deserting seamen, or by surreptitiously entering through the land or sea borders of the United States.
>
> Exemption from this rule may be granted by the subcommittee in cases where the bill is designed to prevent extreme hardship. However, no such exemption may be granted unless the author of the bill has secured and filed with the subcommittee full and complete documentary evidence in support of his request to waive this rule.[34]

The subcommittee has further stiffened its rules to provide that members must demonstrate hardship in the case of all private bills introduced. These changes have dramatically reduced the number of private immigration bills with which the House subcommittee must deal. The 6,278 bills and resolutions introduced in the House in the Ninetieth Congress fell to 4,932 in the Ninety-first Congress, and to a low of 2,084 in the Ninety-second Congress. And only 88 of those bills were still pending at the end of that Congress.[35]

On the other hand, the Senate subcommittee, which eschews rules, has not similarly limited its consideration of immigration bills, and its workload has not materially changed. Moreover, the full Senate Judiciary Committee, according to subcommittee staff member Drury Blair, "feels that every person should have the right to petition the government and it wants to keep down rules excluding bills."[36] This expansive outlook is tempered by the fact that many such bills languish indefinitely in the Senate subcommittee rather than being sent to the House, where they would surely be killed.

While a member's influence often counts for much in the treatment of an immigration bill, the existence of hardship is usually even more important. Thus a bill introduced to grant posthumous citizenship to an alien killed fighting with the U.S. forces in Vietnam is almost certain to get a favorable report from the committees, regardless of who introduced it, while a bill for the relief of a ship-jumping crewman is just as likely to fail to obtain committee approval, regardless of who sponsors the bill, what the Justice Department finds, or what the staff says.

Table 8 indicates the range of beneficiaries of private immigration bills in the Ninetieth Congress.* Waivers of naturalization requirements benefiting 150 persons were enacted; many sought to allow Cuban doctors, scientists, and lawyers to work in states with laws permitting only citizens of the United States to practice. The waiver typically provided that the Cuban professional could apply the time spent here as a visitor toward the five-year residency requirement for immigrants. Only 3 of the 3,924 bills filed for visitors whose visas had expired were enacted; under the House subcommittee's new rules, such bills cannot be considered without a special exemption.

Assembly-Line Law: The Chinese Ship-Jumpers

In 1965, under the leadership of Emanuel Celler in the House and Edward Kennedy in the Senate, a *public* immigration bill, the landmark Immigration and Naturalization Act, was passed. Among its many provisions was a requirement for the automatic deportation of alien crewmen jumping their ships in the United States. The new law met immediate legal challenges which delayed deportations for two years. During this two-year period,

---

* The mix of bills had changed somewhat by the 93rd Congress. For example, the number of permanent-resident bills is greatly reduced. Bills for orphans comprise the largest category. Unfortunately, the Immigration and Naturalization Service no longer publishes this table.

TABLE 8.

Beneficiaries of Private Bills, 90th Congress

Purpose of Bill	Bills Introduced	Beneficiaries of Bills Introduced	Beneficiaries of Bills Enacted	Beneficiaries of Bills Pending
To grant permanent residence status to aliens deportable due to:[1]				
(1) subversive activities	10	10	0	8
(2) narcotic activities	24	40	3	33
(3) illegal entry or visa fraud	123	138	1	100
(4) mental defect	5	5	0	2
(5) tuberculosis	7	7	0	6
(6) violation of nonimmigrant status as:				
crewman	217	428	0	350
exchange visitor	846	1,109	1	1,026
student	451	555	6	417
visitor	3,924	4,901	3	4,192

Subtotal	6,230	8,276	16	7,118
To cancel deportation proceedings	4	7	0	6
To permit entry for permanent residence although inadmissible due to:				
(1) criminal activities	18	16	1	13
(2) illegal entry to visa fraud	29	30	0	25
(3) quota not available—orphan ineligible under general law	134	145	47	80
(4) illiteracy	19	23	2	116
Subtotal	304	364	56	243
To confer citizenship benefits by:				
(1) waiver of naturalization requirements	614	568	150	355
(2) restoration of lost US citizenship	27	23	1	8
(3) waiver of cause for expatriation	3	3	0	3
(4) bestow citizenship posthumously	3	3	3	0
Subtotal	647	597	154	366
Totals[2]	7,293	9,355	229	7,828

[1] Totals larger than categories listed indicate other unlisted purposes.

[2] The final totals include *all* bills or beneficiaries of bills in the 90th Congress.

SOURCE: U.S. Department of Justice, Immigration and Naturalization Service, "Private Bills and Beneficiaries of Private Bills, 90th Congress, by Type of Bill and Action." Table 57.

fewer than ninety-five private bills for crewmen were introduced. But when the New York Court of Appeals upheld the 1965 act, and the Supreme Court in 1967 refused to grant review, a flood of private bills descended on Congress: in the Eighty-ninth Congress and in the first session of the Ninetieth Congress, over seven hundred private bills were introduced in the Senate to aid aliens who had jumped their ships.

An investigative reporter for the *Miami Herald*, James Batten, chronicled the series of events that had generated this flood.[37] First the attorney general had initiated massive deportation proceedings. Then immigration lawyers for Chinese sailors who had jumped ship decided to try private bills as a stopgap, while seeking an administrative remedy to halt deportations. The lawyers first sought House members to introduce their bills, but had to bypass them because Rule 4 of Subcommittee No. 1 precluded their consideration of such bills. Since private immigration bills are allowed to remain active in the Senate Judiciary subcommittee for long periods, and no rules hamper its members, the Senate was a natural haven for such bills. The lawyers first went to Senators Jacob Javits and Charles Goodell of New York, since most of the crewmen and their lawyers lived, if only temporarily, in New York. They could not induce either senator to sponsor the bills.

Unable to use members of the House or the senators from New York, the lawyers consulted lobbyists to place many of their bills. The most enterprising lobbyist assisting the immigration lawyers was Charles Murray, son of and administrative assistant to the late Senator James E. Murray (D., Mont.), who was chairman of the Interior and Insular Affairs Committee from 1934 to 1960. When the senator died, Charles Murray stayed on in Washington as a lobbyist, although he was not officially registered as one in the Ninetieth Congress.

The senators who were induced to sponsor large numbers of the Chinese crewmen bills were all Democrats and, like Murray himself, from the Midwest or West: Gaylord Nelson (Wis.) introduced ninety-eight of the bills; Daniel Brewster (Md.)

seventy-five, Harrison Williams (N.J.) seventy; Daniel Inouye (Ha.) seventy; Lee Metcalf (Mont.) thirty-five; Frank E. Moss (Utah) thirty-five; Joseph M. Montoya (N.M.) twenty-five; George S. McGovern (S.D.) twenty; Gale W. McGee (Wyo.) eighteen; and Alan Bible (Nev.) eighteen.[38] Most of these senators were liberals, came from areas with relatively few immigrants, and knew Charles Murray personally or through members of their staffs.

When the *Miami Herald* broke the story of the Chinese crewmen bills in the summer of 1969, one of the most surprised people was Senator Gaylord Nelson, who had introduced the largest number of bills—almost a hundred. He insisted that he did not know that he had done so:

> All immigration cases are routinely handled by the chief caseworker along with other casework. None of these cases was called to my attention because they were considered as routine humanitarian measures to afford the alien involved an opportunity to seek administrative relief prior to summary deportation.[39]

Warren Sawall, then head of Senator Nelson's office staff and the man responsible for the introduction of the bills, claimed that several of those introduced under Nelson's name in fact came from Senator George McGovern's office. McGovern had been absent during most of the summer of 1968 while campaigning for the presidential nomination and his legislative assistant, Benton Stong, referred bills to Sawall. Stong, who had previously worked on the Senate Interior and Insular Affairs Committee chaired by Senator James Murray, and who had obtained his job through Charles Murray, indicated that some of the bills he referred to Nelson's office had originally come from Charles Murray. Since there is no rule that a senator must write his own name on each bill, Sawall had simply written or typed Nelson's name on the bills himself.[40]

Senators Brewster, Williams, and Inouye (who, with Nelson, accounted for almost half the bills introduced) each had difficulty remembering *anything* about their bills. Senator Brewster, who was later convicted of accepting a bribe to influence a vote on another bill, explained:

> I should be casually aware of many of these bills but we had such a routine . . . when I would walk over to the [Senate] floor, I'd be given a handful of papers. There are a lot of extraneous things put in the *Congressional Record* . . . we put them [the bills] in without looking at them.[41]

Staff members—many of whom have been in Congress longer than their senators—have a network of friends in the Capitol who owe them favors. Sometimes, they explained, pity was a factor. Senator Inouye's administrative assistant, Henry Giugni, said that quite a few of the bills introduced by Inouye came from Stephen DeBurr, a lobbyist pushing crewmen bills. Giugni confided: "I introduced them for him because I felt sorry for him."* [42]

Lobbyists were also linked directly with some of the senators themselves. Senator Harrison Williams, for example, confirmed that several of the crewmen bills which he had introduced came directly from Charles Murray. "Murray," he said, "comes with good credentials."[43] Murray said of his own activities: "I'm as clean as a hound's tooth. I can go before anyone and justify any bill I've ever asked a senator to put in. I know senators and staff who've been my friends over the years, and I go up and ask for a favor. . . . I've got nothing to hide."†[44]

Numerous staff members reported being offered money. Robert J. Keefe, administrative assistant to Senator Birch Bayh, told James Batten of the lobbying tactics:

> They call in and say, "Are you in the market for any Chinese bills?" It's like they're selling a bag of beans. They tell me it would be worth, say, $500 to Senator Bayh. But the going

---

* Giugni felt sorry for DeBurr, he said, because DeBurr was a struggling lawyer. In fact, DeBurr was in real estate, though he had once attended law school.

† Murray died in March 1974.

rate is lower than that. The minimum is $100 and the average would be higher—$200 and $250.[45]

Two years earlier, the price for a private immigration bill was reported to have been at least as high as $2,000. The price apparently fell because the bills were being processed more quickly by the Senate subcommittee staff, and thus deportation was being delayed for a relatively short period of time.

Several senators called for an investigation of the matter, a sure sign that word of the scandal was reaching the public's attention. The Senate Select Committee on Standards and Conduct held an inquiry in September 1969.[46] On May 28, 1970, the select committee released a three-page report on its investigation of the crewmen bills, concluding, "The committee did not find any evidence that any senator or any employee of the Senate received or accepted a bribe, the promise of a bribe, or anything else of value in consideration of the introduction or attempted introduction of any bill."[47] The report noted that the select committee had not investigated the merits of any bills, nor the motives of lawyers and lobbyists involved in the cases. They did find violations by lobbyists and lawyers who were paid for having bills introduced. They recommended blandly:

> The House of Representatives has escaped these consequences through the adoption of a rule by its Judiciary Committee which severely limits private immigration bills for deserting seamen. Although the Committee on Standards and Conduct does not suggest that access to meritorious private legislative relief be closed, the Senate Committee on the Judiciary might wish to review the practices disclosed by this investigation and consider some alternative to its present system of handling these bills.[48]

The report of the select committee was sham, shallow, and inconsequential, consistent with the prior practice of other Senate investigations of questionable behavior by members of "the Club."[49] Interviews with staff members confirmed what the *Miami Herald* articles had clearly demonstrated: that Senate staff members were offered money and other things of value in return for the introduction of private bills, and that immigration lawyers hiring lobbyists to have bills introduced had charged their clients exorbitant sums said to be necessary to pay senators for this service.

Beyond the Gravy Road

Because the select committee failed to discharge its public responsibilities, it is incumbent upon the Senate and House Judiciary committees or appropriate subcommittees to investigate the private-bill process, and to report their findings publicly. Private bills have a legitimate place in the legislative system. They can temper the rigor of law with a responsiveness to individual cases of injustice, permitting a result-oriented flexibility of which administrative agencies often seem incapable. Yet private bills also constitute particularly valuable and unique political currency: each bill is a matter of supreme importance to one or a few petitioners, often desperate and willing to pay a considerable price for it; yet each is also a matter of supreme indifference to the legislator and to everyone else. Private bills provide good logrolling material, lending valuable fluidity to the legislative bargaining process. Under the circumstances, however, it is tempting for the legislator to treat private bills casually and/or to exact money or improper favors in return for supporting them.

When one considers the "bazooka bill" of Senator Dirksen, the cyclamates bill, and the Chinese ship-jumper bills, one discerns a common thread. In each case, a well-connected person or well-organized (but often tiny) group was able to exploit the low visibility of the private-legislation process, the lack of formal criteria or rules (particularly in the Senate), and the apathy and indifference of the Congress to raid the United States Treasury or, as in the case of the ship-jumping crewmen, to obtain preference by lining the pockets of lawyers, lobbyists, and legislators. There is no way of knowing whether such travesties on law-making are rare or common. What *is* known is that the existing process of private-bill legislation is almost entirely uncontrolled and subject to grave abuse. Indeed, it is the very antithesis of justice: random, unprincipled, and easily manipulated.

It should be possible to impose some discipline over the private-legislation process without bureaucratizing it or otherwise vitiating its laudable purpose. It should also be possible to improve upon a system that squanders much of the precious staff time available to members with little discernible benefit to the public. One minimal reform is to formalize procedures and criteria for handling private bills in the Senate to conform, more or less, with those in the House. Another, more ambitious innovation would be the creation, on a trial basis, of a congressional arm, analogous to the General Accounting Office, that would process all private bills, investigating their merits and making recommendations to the full Judiciary committees of each chamber, which would then vote on each bill. This office would be mandated to develop explicit criteria of "hardship" which, if approved by Congress, would govern the deliberations and recommendations of the office, creating over time a flexible but predictable body of equitable principles.

V

CRIME AND PUNISHMENT

12

Criminal Laws
and Criminal Justice

In fashioning a criminal justice system, Congress confronts one
of its most challenging tasks. It must not only make the most
delicate social and philosophical choices, but it must make these
choices in the absence of much factual information bearing on
the most basic questions. What are the various causes of crime
and what is their relative importance? Which kinds of crimes can
be deterred and which cannot? Why do juveniles commit such a
large proportion of major crimes? What effects do procedural
safeguards in the courtroom have on the incidence of crime in
the streets? What is the precise relationship between reported
crime and actual crime? What methods of rehabilitation work?
Will pouring more money into the criminal justice system materially affect the crime rate, and if so, what are the critical points
of leverage?

NOTE: This part was prepared by Peter H. Schuck and Michael E. Ward.

For answers to these questions, Congress—and the nation— look to the Judiciary committees. In the Senate, the criminal justice system lies principally within the domain of three sub- committees: the Subcommittee on Criminal Laws and Procedures, the Subcommittee to Investigate Juvenile Delinquency, and the Subcommittee on National Penitentiaries. The work of a fourth, the Subcommittee on Constitutional Rights, bears directly on the procedural aspects of the criminal justice system. It is the first of these subcommittees, however, that clearly predominates in criminal matters; its work is considered in this chapter.*

The House Judiciary Committee tends to be far less active in the criminal justice area than its Senate counterpart. During the Ninety-second Congress, Subcommittees Nos. 3, 4, and 5 handled legislation relating to criminal law and procedure.† In the Ninety- third Congress, no fewer than *five* House Judiciary subcommit- tees considered such legislation, a diffusion of effort and expertise which has further strengthened the primacy of the Senate in this legislative field.

THE SENATE SUBCOMMITTEE ON CRIMINAL LAWS AND PROCEDURES: McCLELLAN COUNTRY

Senator John McClellan of Arkansas is the recognized "crime- fighter" of the Senate. As chairman of the Judiciary Subcommittee on Criminal Laws and Procedures, McClellan rides shotgun in the federal anticrime effort. The metaphor would please him.

In the criminal law field, McClellan casts his long shadow far beyond the subcommittee hearing room onto the Senate floor. Senators often ask McClellan how to vote on criminal issues; they know that he can control thirty to forty votes on such issues,

---

* The work of the Subcommittee to Investigate Juvenile Delinquency is discussed in Chapter 13, that of the Subcommittee on National Peni- tentiaries in Chapter 14, and that of the Subcommittee on Constitutional Rights in Chapter 8.

† Some of this legislation is discussed in Chapters 13 and 14.

and when these are combined with the fifteen to twenty votes controlled by Senator Hruska, the ranking minority member of the subcommittee, a majority is almost assured.[1] One Judiciary staff member has explained McClellan's power:

> McClellan's real power in the criminal area comes when he stands on the floor and waves his hands and gets red in the face, and screams about coddling criminals. . . . Many a liberal senator thinks twice about the headlines at home and voting against him. . . . Of course, the often simplistic structure of public debates and the headlines on law and order are hardly attributable to McClellan's efforts alone. The Nixon Administration is also responsible. But McClellan is able to raise to a fever pitch on the floor his colleagues' fear that they won't be able to adequately explain criminal justice reform to their constituents.

McClellan and Hruska lead a remarkably bipartisan coalition in the subcommittee, which actively cooperates with the Nixon administration. Most administration proposals are introduced jointly by McClellan and Hruska, and the majority and minority staffs enjoy frequent and close contact with the Department of Justice.[2] The subcommittee is divided along philosophical rather than traditional party lines. Democrats McClellan, Eastland, Ervin, and Byrd and Republicans Hruska, Scott, and Thurmond— the "conservatives"—tend to attribute crime to permissiveness, inadequate sanctions, and the Warren Court decisions on criminal procedure; they see the remedy in stricter law enforcement, harsher penalties, and fewer rights for the accused. The "liberals"—Hart, Kennedy, and Republican Marlow Cook—tend to see crime as environmentally caused; they seek large social solutions and are jealous of the civil liberties and rights of the accused.*

Liberal groups such as the ACLU depend upon Senators

---

* Interestingly, "conservatives" tend to oppose, and "liberals" to support, gun control, a law-and-order issue strongly supported by "conservative" police groups.

Kennedy and Hart to advance their causes on the subcommittee,[3] but the senators, although sympathetic, seem to lack the time to follow through on these issues. Although McClellan and Hruska attended sixteen and eighteen, respectively, of the twenty-three days of hearings in the Ninety-first and Ninety-second Congresses for which there was a printed record at the time this was written, Kennedy was present on only six, and Hart on two. Moreover, Kennedy and Hart were not formally represented by counsel on the days they were absent.

The Federal Criminal Code

The conservatism of the subcommittee, its close cooperation with the Nixon administration, and Senator McClellan's dominance caused great concern among many liberals when the subcommittee began the protracted, Herculean task of reforming the Federal Criminal Code. A draft of a new code had been prepared by the National Commission on Reform of Federal Criminal Laws (the "Brown Commission") which had been established in November 1966 and included three subcommittee members—McClellan, Hruska, and Ervin. At first, McClellan and Hruska attended few meetings of the commission, and then only for short periods. During the closing days of the commission's work, however, they began to make their presence felt. A study draft of the code prepared by the commission staff and published in June 1970 was too reformist and "liberal" for McClellan. In November 1970, Robert Blakey, then McClellan's chief counsel, submitted a list of vigorous objections and demanded many changes. After a long, bitter "showdown" session on these issues, many provisions were returned to the two staffs for further work and negotiation. Because of the rapidly approaching deadline, a desire not to extend the commission work indefinitely, and the value of preserving unanimity in the major part of the commission's work, the final commission report, issued on January 7, 1971, merely presented alternatives where disagreements could not be resolved and left terms undefined where consensus could not be reached.[4]

TABLE 9.

Classification and Sentencing in Brown Commission Report and S.1 (93rd Cong.)

Brown Commission Category	Sentence	S.1 Category	Sentence
Infraction	No imprisonment	Violation	30 days
B Misdemeanor	30 days	Misdemeanor	6 months
A Misdemeanor	1 year	E Felony	1 year
– – –	– – –	D Felony	3 years
C Felony	5 years	C Felony	5 years
B Felony	10 years	B Felony	10 years
A Felony	20 years	A Felony	20 years

Selected Crimes: Categories and Sentences

Offense	Brown Commission Category	Equivalent S.1 Category	Actual S.1 Category
Marijuana Possession	Infraction (no imprisonment)	Violation (30 days)	Misdemeanor (6 mo.)
Possession of Abusable Drug[1]	B Misdemeanor (30 days)	Misdemeanor (6 mo.)	E Felony (1 yr.)
Engaging in Riot	B Misdemeanor (30 days)	Misdemeanor (6 mo.)	E Felony (1 yr.)
Prostitution	B Misdemeanor (30 days)	Misdemeanor (6 mo.)	D Felony (3 yr.)
Other work in House of Prostitution	A Misdemeanor (1 yr.)	E Felony (1 yr.)	D Felony (3 yr.)
Dissemination of Obscene Material	A Misdemeanor (1 yr.)[2]	E Felony (1 yr.)	D Felony (3 yr.)
Misuse of Flag	no offense	– – –	Violation (30 days)
Criminal Contempt of Court	6 mo. maximum	– – –	No maximum

[1] Drugs under Schedule III or IV of the Comprehensive Drug Abuse Prevention Act.

[2] Unless "carried on in reckless disregard of risk of exposure to children under eighteen or to persons who had no effective opportunity to choose not to be so exposed," in which case it is a Class C Felony (5 years).

SOURCE: Compiled by Michael E. Ward.

In the Ninety-second Congress draft legislation was developed by the subcommittee staff to implement the commission recommendations, and hearings covering general policy areas were held in 1971 and 1972. Some liberal staff members had earlier expressed concern that the draft would embody the more conservative, "hard-line" opinions of the commission minority—with which McClellan agreed—but would nevertheless be presented as implementing the commission report. They also feared that the draft would be pushed through Congress with only superficial hearings, due to the close cooperation between the Justice Department and Senator McClellan.*[5]

The subcommittee bill was introduced at the opening of the Ninety-third Congress as S.1, the Criminal Justice Codification and Reform Act. The bill did in fact adopt many of the minority views of the commission: the death penalty was retained;[6] possession of marijuana was classified as a misdemeanor, rather than a less serious "infraction";[7] the requirement for corroboration in perjury cases was eliminated;[8] and a ban on handguns and registration of all firearms, supported by a majority of commissioners, was omitted.[9] While the commission report omitted a definition of obscenity, probably because of an inability to reach consensus, the draft legislation included a broad definition.[10] In the commission report, intent was the necessary element for the crime of aiding a deserter; in the draft, only "knowledge" was required.[11]

One of the most innovative parts of the proposed code, a systematic grading and sentencing system, was altered in the subcommittee draft (see Table 10). Many crimes carrying a one-year sentence were considered misdemeanors in the commission report, whereas under the draft they were felonies, with all of the serious

---

* These staff members believed that they were misled by the Department of Justice once before; the department supposedly informed Senator Ervin that the District of Columbia crime bill would just be a routine court reorganization, while it actually contained some of the preventive detention provisions that Senator Ervin was actively opposing at that time.

consequences of a felony conviction. In addition, some crimes were placed in more serious categories in the subcommittee draft than in the commission report. Both versions called for longer sentences for "special dangerous offenders."[12]

Many of the changes in the subcommittee draft, however, might surprise liberal critics of McClellan's subcommittee. The draft replaces the commission's new definition of treason with the Constitution's narrower definition.[13] Other national security offenses are "liberalized": the draft omits the commission-proposed offense of "recklessly impairing military effectiveness," listing only the offense of sabotage, which requires intent;[14] publication of classified information, a felony under the commission report,[15] is not mentioned in the draft; the draft bill follows the suggestion of an ACLU report rather than the commission in accepting improper classification as a defense to the misuse of classified information.[16] Not only are the crimes against "civil rights" as defined by the commission preserved under the draft, but the conspiracy requirement—which necessitated two or more persons participating in the crime—is eliminated, and protection is extended to all persons, not only citizens.[17] Perhaps most significant, the draft eliminates the strict requirement in 18 U.S.C. Section 242 that a deprivation of the privileges and immunities guaranteed citizens by the Constitution must be "under color of law" to be illegal. The proposed draft also creates the offenses of environmental spoliation and unfair commercial practices,[18] neither of which was mentioned in the commission report. Finally, the draft code enters fields not considered by the commission, recodifying the law in such areas as interception of communications and immunity of witnesses.[19] As one close observer noted, "McClellan and Blakey were willing to accept reforms in relatively non-controversial areas, where the law professors all seemed to agree."

When the administration's more conservative bill (S.1400) was introduced in 1973, serious bargaining began in an effort to merge the two bills. Hearings were completed in 1974.

Input and Hearings

A number of bills are reported out of the subcommittee without hearings. These, however, are generally routine bills, or ones on which the House has already held hearings. The major work of the subcommittee involves more complex and substantial matters. In these cases, the subcommittee will hold public hearings. This process operates in fixed cycles. When hearings are held on an area, such as organized crime, all related legislation is considered at the same time, or not at all. Such a procedure reduces the subcommittee's ability to respond to new issues as they arise. If a particular concern does not receive full consideration in the hearings, or is introduced after the hearings, it must wait until the field is reopened, which may be a long time. This is particularly true with regard to legislation amending Title I of the Omnibus Crime Control and Safe Streets Act of 1968.

For example, the Law Enforcement Assistance Administration (see below) will not be closely scrutinized until the agency requires a reauthorization of funds. Meanwhile, the subcommittee has ignored the many difficulties with LEAA operations that have come to public attention and has given short shrift to important bills seeking to expand LEAA programs.

Another result of this procedure is that each set of hearings covers a broad range of topics, making adequate discussion of any specific legislation very difficult. The Organized Crime Control Act, for example, as first submitted by Senator McClellan, contained eight substantive parts (or "titles"). Relatively few witnesses not connected with the federal government were heard, and four of these nonfederal witnesses were questioned superficially or not at all. Senator McClellan hurried some witnesses because of lack of time. In March 1970 the subcommittee crammed ten witnesses into two days of hearings on seven largely unrelated bills.[20] Clearly, none of these bills received the attention it deserved, although some of these measures became titles of the Omnibus Crime Control Act of 1970.[21]

The limited nature of the hearings on the Omnibus Crime

Control Act is discussed below in the case study on the Law Enforcement Assistance Administration. While the subcommittee did have access to the extensive hearings that had already been held in the House Judiciary Committee, it was considering bills that would have fundamentally altered the block-grant approach of LEAA—some of them in a manner not considered by the House—and more extensive hearings would have been appropriate.

As the foregoing suggests, the hearings have not constituted a major source of outside input for the subcommittee. Approximately one hundred witnesses were heard during the Ninety-first and Ninety-second Congresses, an average of only twenty-five per year, and considerably less than most other major Judiciary subcommittees. Senator McClellan has been absent from 30 percent of the hearings for which printed records are available. The hearings have been fairly balanced, however, in terms of witness affiliations. Malcolm Hawk, then minority counsel of the subcommittee, expressed the view that "liberal" witnesses are always given full opportunity to testify.[22] But a number of such witnesses felt that their testimony was little more than a *pro forma* exercise that did not affect the substance of the subcommittee's work.* Another frequent Senate witness stated that, while most congressional committees handle dissent openly and honestly, the Criminal Laws and Procedures Subcommittee members simply cut off the testimony of witnesses with whom they do not agree.[23]

The criminal law field, like some of the others within Judiciary's jurisdiction, lacks a significant number of active, well-

---

* For example, Senator McClellan was absent during the fourth set of hearings on the criminal code. Senator Hruska, who was presiding, informed witnesses that they would have to limit testimony to thirty minutes because of pressing Senate business. Two of the witnesses whose testimony was thus limited, and missed entirely by the chairman, represented the National Council on Crime and Delinquency and the ACLU. The testimony of the former, which has expended considerable time in the drafting of model acts in the criminal field, was received with minimal questioning. The ACLU had prepared a 144-page evaluation of the commission report. Its report was received, but it might just as well have been submitted by mail; its witness had no time to make any significant contribution.[24]

organized groups economically motivated to provide the critical subcommittees with opinions, ideas, and information on a continuing, systematic basis. As a result, subcommittees in the field must attempt to initiate contact with private groups themselves and seek to develop extragovernmental sources of communication. The Subcommittee on Criminal Laws and Procedures has relied extensively on governmental sources and congressional investigations for its information. Although both are undeniably valuable sources and compensate to some degree for the lack of public input, the result is nevertheless an excessive and undesirable concentration of influence over legislation by Senator McClellan and the executive branch.

In developing legislation, the staff may study work by organizations in the field, but it only occasionally contacts nongovernmental groups—such as the International Association of Chiefs of Police—for information during the drafting process. The ten sections of the Organized Crime Control Act of 1970, which passed the Senate in essentially the form reported by the subcommittee, were developed largely from proposals of the National Commission on Law Enforcement and the Administration of Justice, although model acts and recommendations of other organizations, including the National Council on Crime and Delinquency and the American Bar Association, played a part.[25] Some of the measures were derived from the organized crime hearings conducted by Senator McClellan's Government Operations Committee in the early sixties.[26]

The Victims of Crime Act, which was processed by the subcommittee and passed the Senate in the Ninety-second Congress, was an amalgamation of four bills*—one of which was drafted by the subcommittee in response to a suggestion of the American Bar Association made at the House hearings on the Organized

---

* The four bills covered the compensation of the victims of violent crime; public safety officers' life insurance; death and dismemberment benefits for public safety officers; and the expansion of the civil remedies provided to the victims of racketeering under Title IX of the Organized Crime Control Act.

Crime Control Act. Two others were submitted by senators other than McClellan, and the fourth was an administration proposal. If the subcommittee's overwhelming influence in the criminal justice area is to be exercised responsibly, fresh air must be allowed into the subcommittee. The subcommittee staff should make a greater effort to directly contact more groups and interested individuals prior to the drafting of legislation. Drafts should be circulated among a wide audience, and modifications should be made to accommodate legitimate criticism before the legislation is introduced and hearings are held.

The subcommittee should also hold more frequent, and more extensive, hearings. The subject matter of each set of hearings should be limited to one or two specific types of legislation and hearings should be extended and witnesses afforded more time when necessary. Witnesses should also be questioned closely on their testimony. The subcommittee should be prepared to hold hearings on a subject whenever it becomes an issue, whether or not an authorization has expired.

To explore all sides of an issue adequately, the liberals on the subcommittee should ensure the presence at every hearing of either a senator or a staff member authorized to interrogate witnesses.

Finally, in revising the Federal Criminal Code, the subcommittee should continue to hold two separate types of hearings. The first should deal with policy issues, such as the death penalty and marijuana. The second should address the considerable technical problems of drafting an entirely new criminal code, to prevent the necessity of too much patchwork after the code is enacted.

CRIMINAL JUSTICE IN THE
HOUSE JUDICIARY COMMITTEE

No subcommittee of the House Judiciary Committee has achieved the stature and primacy in the criminal justice field enjoyed by the Senate Subcommittee on Criminal Laws and Procedures, and legislation concerning criminal justice has been parceled out to several subcommittees. Subcommittee No. 5, headed by the full-committee chairman, retained control over the expansive LEAA legislation during the Ninety-second Congress, but no other subcommittee had a well-defined role in the criminal justice area.

This pattern has continued in the Ninety-third Congress, with five of the seven subcommittees significantly involved in criminal justice legislation. The Subcommittee on Courts, Civil Liberties, and the Administration of Justice (formerly No. 3) has received legislation on corrections, capital punishment, amnesty, the taking of hostages in federal prisons, and various measures affecting criminal procedure. The Subcommittee on Civil Rights and Constitutional Rights (formerly No. 4) has considered legislation dealing with the treatment and rehabilitation of narcotics addicts and with criminal records and data systems. The Subcommittee on Monopolies and Commercial Law (formerly No. 5) processed the extension of LEAA's authorization and amendment of its governing legislation. The Subcommittee on Crime (which had been created as Subcommittee No. 6 early in the Ninety-third Congress prior to the "reform" of the subcommittee structure) was given responsibility for oversight of LEAA and has considered a "community anti-crime assistance" bill. Finally, the Subcommittee on Criminal Justice (newly created in the Ninety-third Congress) considered the Federal Rules of Evidence, reform of the Federal Criminal Code, special prosecutor legislation, and various measures relating to the Watergate prosecution.

During the Ninety-second Congress, and to a lesser extent during the Ninety-third as well, most criminal justice legislation considered by the House Judiciary Committee and its subcommittees was not drafted by committee or subcommittee staff—a sharp contrast with the Senate Judiciary Committee, where new legislation is often developed by staff at the request of the subcommittee chairmen. Various factors account for this difference. The House Judiciary Committee has more members, fewer chairmen, more bills, lower budget, and a smaller staff. Since no member has subcommittee staff at his command, the subcommittee

chairmen must permit other members greater access to the staff—
leaving the staff less time to devote to the development of bills.

When simple or routine legislation is referred to the committee, a congressman will find it either acceptable or unacceptable
in principle. Changes will be designed primarily to perfect the
bill. In these cases, members and staff appear to rely primarily
on their own knowledge, based mainly on readings of law reviews
and court cases, in evaluating the legislation.[27]

On more complex bills, which are generally a response to a
nationally felt need, individual members are seldom completely
"for" or "against"; rather, the controversy centers around the
content of the particular provisions of the bill. Compromises are
usually necessary. Thus legislation may be almost completely
rewritten by the subcommittee. The version of the Omnibus
Crime Control Act of 1970 reported out of the committee was
drafted primarily by Benjamin Zelenko, then chief counsel for
Subcommittee No. 5, and Franklin Polk, minority counsel.[28]
Neither the congressmen nor the staff persons indicated any
extensive use of outside information resources even in rewriting
legislation. Former Congressman McCulloch stated that, while
the minority consistently draws upon the expertise of the Department of Justice, it seldom turns to private groups. He agreed with
Jerome Zeifman, counsel to Subcommittee No. 4, that congressmen can too easily become dependent on such groups.*[29]

The House Judiciary Committee often operates to "liberalize"
Senate measures, for the Senate Subcommittee on Criminal Laws
and Procedures is dominated by conservatives, while most of the
House Judiciary subcommittees are predominantly liberal. One
lobbyist opines that most of the House Judiciary Committee's
efforts are actually expended resisting Senate measures, often on
civil libertarian grounds.[30] The committee held extensive hearings on the Organized Crime Control Act, for example, and to
the consternation of Senator McClellan,[31] spent eight months

---

* Representatives of some private groups confirmed the infrequency of subcommittee contacts other than requests for testimony.

considering—or delaying, according to one's viewpoint—its enactment. The bill reported, however, did not make any changes so significant as to be unacceptable to Senator McClellan or the Senate.

The House committee must also bargain with the Senate when legislation originates on the House side. Franklin Polk believes that the Senate is generally reluctant to pass House-originated legislation;[32] this reluctance is magnified by the striking ideological differences in the two committees with jurisdiction over criminal justice legislation. Although staff members have denied it,[33] at least one close observer suggests that the House Judiciary Committee sometimes anticipates Senate reaction by compromising on criminal justice bills before reporting out legislation.[34] If this is true, then when the committee moves toward the Senate position on conference, it is compromising for a second time. A similar deference to the Senate occurs when the House waits while the Senate takes action, as when the House committee took no action on handgun control because of a belief that the Senate would limit the scope of possible action.[35]

The House committee exercises little oversight of federal agencies in the criminal justice field.* Instead, House committee hearings appear to provide a much-needed source of outside information when legislation is being rewritten, and more information may then be obtained by staff follow-ups on testimony.[36] When legislation is being evaluated, the hearings arc directed at the education of the public and other members of Congress. But hearings are seldom held simply to affect agency policy.

LEAA: THROWING MONEY AT THE PROBLEM

All of these themes of subcommittee substance and style—the colossal dominance of McClellan and his conservative, prosecu-

* An investigation of the Department of Justice's handling of the Kent State prosecutions by the staff of the Subcommittee on Civil Rights and Constitutional Rights in July 1973 was a notable exception.

torial approach to crime control; the hurried, desultory mode of legislation; the narrow range of inputs from which it draws; the reluctance to correct past error; a "hardware" approach to crime control—converge in the case of the Law Enforcement Assistance Administration, McClellan's most awesome and expensive legislative creation.

In the late 1960s, it became obvious that the control of crime was among the foremost concerns of the American people. The Kefauver and McClellan investigations of the fifties and early sixties had revealed the extent of organized crime in the United States. A president had been assassinated. Barry Goldwater had made crime a major issue in his 1964 presidential bid. Our cities had been torn with riots in the middle of the decade, and campuses were in turmoil. Many Americans had been shocked by Supreme Court decisions expanding the rights of those accused of crimes. In 1968, Robert Kennedy and Martin Luther King, Jr., were assassinated. By the latter part of the year, the concern reached a peak, and "law and order" became the primary domestic issue of the November campaigns.

Congress prepared to invest large sums of money in a desperate effort to stem the rising tide of crime. Former Attorney General Ramsey Clark has described the dangers of this course:

> Misused, the system of criminal justice can destroy liberty and cause crime. A national police, false arrest, invasions of privacy, the intimidation of dissent, wrongful prosecution, denials of due process, corrupt officials, excessive use of force, failure to enforce the law, police brutality, denial of rights—all threaten freedom and all cause crime. The American people must understand the limitations of law enforcement and criminal justice and the great danger of exceeding those limits.[37]

Ignoring these warnings, Congress developed its programs with minimal deliberation. The result was the creation of the Law Enforcement Assistance Administration, beset by problems from its first days but nourished by its loving and uncritical parent, the Senate Subcommittee on Criminal Laws and Procedures. Five years and $1.5 billion after the enactment of the legislation, LEAA, with all its warts, is here to stay.

How It All Began

Alarmed by the increase in the crime rate,[38] President Johnson on July 23, 1965, established the National Commission on Law Enforcement and the Administration of Justice,[39] whose 1967 final report called for a massive federal spending program administered by the Department of Justice.[40] In response to this recommendation, the Johnson administration developed a bill to establish a grant-in-aid program to states and local governments, operated under the attorney general, for the purpose of funding programs to develop "new approaches and improvements in law enforcement and criminal justice."

Grant-in-aid programs are of particular concern to the American citizen, for such programs use tax money to pursue social goals. Congress has two duties regarding these programs: to assure that the goals are selected and defined in accord with the needs of the American people and to see that the money is spent lawfully in pursuit of those goals. These duties are fulfilled by developing programs carefully and monitoring their operations to prevent abuse. In the case of LEAA, neither duty was discharged.

The administration bill was introduced by Emanuel Celler in the House and John McClellan in the Senate. The House Judiciary Committee hearings, held in April and May 1967,[41] also covered other proposed legislation. As a result, the bill did not get the complete consideration it should have had: relatively few addressed themselves to the grant-in-aid provisions of the administration bill, which essentially was the one the House Judiciary Committee adopted.

A number of Republican members, however, while supporting the bill, called for significant amendments. Congressmen Tom Railsback and Edward G. Biester, Jr., recommended that the grants be made to the states, which would decide how to disburse the funds among their local communities; if a state were not committed to a statewide effort, local communities could be funded directly.[42] This plan for "block grants" to the states was offered as an amendment on the floor by William Cahill of New Jersey. Supporters of the amendment feared that the federal government would control local police forces through its grants, giving excessive power to the attorney general.[43] Opponents stressed their belief that law enforcement was a local, not state, responsibility, and that state governments and bureaucracies would hinder the implementation of the program through apathy, politics, inexperience or red tape.[44] The Cahill amendment passed the House 246–147; the final vote on the bill was 378–23. Thus the House legislated a new form of federal assistance—a form of revenue sharing, whereby all major decisions and allocations of federal money would be made at the state level, with minimal federal control—*without ever having held hearings on, or debated the proper methods of, implementing such a program.*

The administration proposals faced a more tortuous journey in the Senate. The bill was referred to the Judiciary Subcommittee on Criminal Laws and Procedures chaired by Senator McClellan, who was preoccupied with other measures. As the hearings on anticrime legislation began in March 1967, McClellan pointed out that three bills of particular significance (to him) would be considered by the subcommittee: proposed legislation to overturn the *Miranda* decision (on the inadmissibility of confessions at trial), to "regulate" the use of wiretapping, and to outlaw organized-crime syndicates. In his view, the administration proposal was simply "another of the bills to be considered."[45] As in the House, the vast majority of witnesses did not even address themselves to the administration bill, and those that did were seldom questioned on it. The subcommittee reported out the administration proposals with several changes, including the establishment of a three-person, bipartisan administering board, independent of the Department of Justice[46] (the subcommittee feared allowing too much control to the liberal Ramsey Clark, then attorney general).

McClellan realized he could not get full committee approval

of his own titles on confessions and wiretapping because of the absence at that time of committee member Hugh Scott, whose vote McClellan needed. As a result, McClellan delayed consideration of the bill, through parliamentary maneuvering, until Congress adjourned. When Congress reconvened in 1968, McClellan was able to have the bill reported with the additional titles he had proposed, although the three-person governing board of the LEAA was now placed under the control of the attorney general.[47]

Knowing that his own titles might very well be subject to a presidential veto, McClellan struck a bargain with the administration, which was most concerned with the creation of LEAA (Title I) in the form it desired. McClellan would not support a block-grant approach if the President would not veto the bill because of McClellan's titles on confessions and wiretappings, or oppose those titles too vigorously.[48] The block-grant idea, then, was mentioned only in the separate views of Senators Scott, Dirksen, Hruska, and Thurmond, who stressed their fears of federal control and a national police force.[49]

In order to ensure that the administration held to its part of the bargain, when the bill came to the Senate floor Senator McClellan delayed the votes on Title I until after consideration of his measures. When, after heated battles on the other titles, Title I became the pending business on the floor, Senator Dirksen offered a slightly modified version of the Cahill amendment. True to his word, Senator McClellan did not support the amendment; but he did not actively oppose it, either. Without McClellan's opposition, the Dirksen amendment passed, forty-eight to twenty-nine. Final passage of the bill was merely *pro forma*.

A strong possibility remained that the content of the bill would be changed in the Senate-House conference, depending upon the selection of the conferees. Perhaps some of the difficulties that later arose in the administration of LEAA might then have been resolved. Before the conference could be held, however, Senator Robert F. Kennedy was assassinated. On June 7, 1968, the House, caught up in the frenzy of the moment, agreed to the Senate bill without requiring a conference. On June 19, President Johnson signed the Omnibus Crime Control and Safe Streets Act of 1968 into law.

Title I of the Act established the Law Enforcement Assistance Administration. The agency was empowered to make two types of grants. Planning grants were to be given to states for the establishment of State Planning Agencies (SPAs) and for the development of comprehensive plans for the improvement of law enforcement. After the states had submitted the plans and LEAA had approved them, LEAA would make "action" grants to implement the plans. Eighty-five percent of the action grants were to be distributed among the SPAs on the basis of state population, and the allocation of the remaining 15 percent was to be within the discretion of LEAA. The federal government would pay from 50 to 75 percent of program costs. Seventy-five percent of all block-grant funds were to be passed on by the states to local governments. Funds were also authorized for a research arm, the National Institute of Law Enforcement and Criminal Justice, which could make grants and conduct in-house research. A funding level of over $100 million was authorized for fiscal years 1968 and 1969, with $300 million for 1970.

What Went Wrong

LEAA commenced operations in October 1968. Difficulties, many of which continue to plague LEAA today, surfaced almost immediately. But when they did, the Judiciary committees had already turned their attention elsewhere.

Administrative problems were the first to become apparent. Because of the potentially massive funding involved and the fear of partisan, federal control of local law enforcement, Congress had hoped to insulate the program from political pressures[50] and to that end had set up the bipartisan tripartite administration. But the issue of how decisions were to be made under such a structure had never been thoroughly discussed, much less resolved, and the general counsel of LEAA interpreted the "troika" provision to mean that all decisions had to be unanimous.[51] For the first few months, under the Johnson appointees, the system seemed to work. The new Nixon-appointed administrators, however, did not find consensus so easy to reach. The LEAA administrator, Charles H. Rogovin, resigned after fifteen months, explaining that the arrangement was unworkable. For the next eleven months the agency was run by the associate administrators. Jerris Leonard was appointed administrator in May 1971, by which time Congress had removed the requirements for unanimity.

Misuse of funds first came to public attention in the spring of 1971, but not because of the Judiciary committees. LEAA's own audit disclosed irregularities in the fiscal operations of Alabama and Florida. Auditors disallowed close to $600,000 of Alabama's expenditures.* The Florida audit turned up $500,000 of questionable expenditures.†[52] These disclosures prompted *not* the Judiciary committees, charged with the creation and oversight of LEAA, but the Legal and Monetary Affairs Subcommittee of the House Government Operations Committee to hold extensive hearings in July and October 1971 on the operations of LEAA. The investigations of this subcommittee disclosed further misuse of LEAA funding. Contracts had been awarded for communications equipment without competitive bidding in Arkansas (estimated excess cost to the American taxpayer: $200,000) and Wisconsin ($175,000).[53] In both cases, the Motorola Corporation received over 90 percent of the communications-equipment contracts. Specifications for equipment required had sometimes been drawn up with Motorola assistance. In one instance, the same individual served on the SPA communications task force and represented Motorola before a county

* The audit included such items as a thousand McDonald's hamburgers for a conference unrelated to the state's LEAA program and a $15,000 film that was never used.
† It cited compensation of individuals who performed no services for the SPA, rent on unoccupied office space, and dinners for 1000 at a banquet attended by only 641.

board.[54] One congressional staff member has commented, "Some people say LEAA has never accomplished anything, but if you want to see what they've done, just look at Motorola stock."*

In Indiana, $84,000 of LEAA funds were applied toward a $140,000 all-weather aircraft to be used for investigative and other law-enforcement purposes. Instead, of the first forty-six hours of flight time, 65 percent were spent transporting non-law-enforcement personnel, including the governor, around the country. In Alabama, $117,247 were used to establish a "police cadet college training program." There were twenty-six enrollees in the program, nine of whom were sons of high government officials. In nineteen instances enrollees received double pay for their attendance, through funds from two different LEAA sources. The city of Heflin, Alabama, purchased a car with LEAA funds. The car turned out to be primarily for the use of the mayor.[55]

LEAA funds were also misspent in more subtle ways. Any excess cash balances held by states under federal grants are costly to the taxpayer. The government must borrow the money before giving it to the states, and must therefore pay interest on it. A system of letters-of-credit was developed to minimize this excess. Nonetheless, from July 1969 to June 1971 the average semiannual cash balance of SPAs was $18.5 million, which cost the federal government an estimated $4 million in interest and finance charges. In some cases, the government even ended up paying interest twice: the excess funds were sometimes invested in U.S. Treasury bonds![56]

LEAA took some steps to correct these deficiencies in its program. The national audit staff was increased. In congruence with the block-grant approach, however, the emphasis of LEAA is on state auditing, and it conducted a program in 1972 to train state

---

* Some of the Republican members of the Government Operations Committee argued that there were valid reasons for the success of Motorola. They said that in some cases Motorola servicing was more readily available than its competitors, while in others Motorola was the only bidder with solid-state equipment.

auditors.[57] LEAA contracted for the development of a grant-management information system, but this was not expected to be in operation until 1974. LEAA has also required that cash balances not exceed the funds required to support one week's activities.[58]

While the Government Operations Committee report complained about misspent funds, it also—somewhat inconsistently, since pressure to spend often results in unnecessary and unwise allocations of funds—complained about the *under*expenditure of funds, the issue of fund flow. It found that no more than twenty-five cents of every dollar awarded to states as "action funds" had been disbursed to local governments as of the end of fiscal 1971. The states had obviously been unable to absorb the funds awarded by LEAA. As the report stated:

> The reasons why LEAA's block grant programs have become afflicted by this semi-paralysis are many, but none do much to mitigate the obvious conclusions.
>   . . . LEAA has asked for, and the Executive Office of Management and Budget has approved, more block funds than States are effectively and efficiently able to spend.[59]

The report might have added that Congress had continued to appropriate these funds.

This pressure to absorb funds has resulted in hastily prepared state plans and projects. A 1971 memorandum from the director of the Arkansas SPA illustrates this dramatically:

> We have about $484,000 in 1970 funds. We need to spend all these funds plus a sizable chunk of 1971 funds. . . . It will be difficult to justify requests for significant amounts of 1972 funds if we still have large amounts of 1970 and 1971 funds remaining to be obligated.
>   Therefore, we need increased efforts at "stimulating the community" to design programs or projects that will facilitate the control and prevention of crime and delinquency.
>   If an appropriate project is designed for a valid need we would consider several different funding approaches. . . .[60]

This type of program development is at least partly responsible for the "shopping list" approach and the emphasis on hardware discussed below.

The minority of the Government Operations Committee felt that nondisbursement of funds was justified: to attempt to disburse the money within the fiscal year would "ignore the principles of sound planning and utilization." The minority also pointed out that Congress authorized the disbursement of action funds for the two years following the grant award.[61] In any event, however, through proper planning both Congress and LEAA might have assured that funds not be awarded to states until they would be effectively used.

In order to address many of these problems, LEAA reorganized its structure shortly after Jerris Leonard took office in May 1971. A regionalization added staff capability for program and fiscal monitoring; its impact remains to be seen. An advisory commission was also created. Leonard argued that the Government Operations Committee was criticizing an entire program on the basis of fifteen states where there were difficulties, ignoring the forty jurisdictions where the program was working effectively.[62] Hardly a persuasive defense, to be sure, but it was the only one available.

Yet the most serious problems of LEAA have been less obvious than these fiscal difficulties. They involve questions of policy and have not yet been resolved by either LEAA or Congress. Although the Omnibus Crime Control and Safe Streets Act requires states to develop "comprehensive plans," it does not assist the states in discerning what type of plan qualifies as "comprehensive." The original act lists only twelve criteria, mostly procedural; the only significant substantive requirements are that the plan "take into account" the needs and requests of local governments, provide for a balanced distribution of funds, and contain a "comprehensive outline of priorities," including descriptions of

(A) *general* needs and problems; (B) existing systems;
(C) available resources; (D) organizational systems and ad-

ministrative machinery for implementing the plan; (E) the *direction, scope,* and *general types* of improvements to be made in the future; and (F) *to the extent appropriate,* the relationship of the plan to other relevant state or local law enforcement plans and systems [emphasis added].[63]

LEAA has failed to fill this vacuum. LEAA could, under the vague language of the act, have chosen to exercise almost any degree of supervision in the approval of state plans; it chose to exercise almost none. The "comprehensive plans" of states have often been far from comprehensive. *Law and Disorder III,* a nongovernmental report on LEAA prepared by the Lawyers Committee for Civil Rights Under Law, has concluded that too often the plans produce mere "shopping lists" of equipment to be purchased. LEAA has often advanced funds before plans have been approved, exercising no oversight to see that the funds are being expended in accordance with the plans. Inconsistent grants have often been made.[64]

LEAA has even failed to supply states with the assistance and information needed to formulate comprehensive plans. One of the major problems may have been the rapid growth of funds, without a corresponding growth in LEAA's knowledge of what works. Yet LEAA does not even provide an informational clearinghouse; SPAs have no means of learning of the successes and failures of other states, or of gaining access to research information.[65] The work of LEAA's research arm, the National Institute of Law Enforcement and Criminal Justice, has not been coordinated with the grant process.

LEAA has not developed any standards by which the effectiveness of programs can be measured. The agency has developed no goals for its program. As the National League of Cities–U.S. Conference of Mayors commented, "LEAA has yet to clearly define its mission and priorities." The Government Operations Committee report pointed out that the 1968 Act authorized LEAA "to conduct evaluation studies," yet four years after its birth LEAA has not evaluated its own performance; it has not evaluated the performance of its grantees; but short of that, it has neither established the standards by which effectiveness and performance are to be measured nor provided SPAs with any meaningful assistance in the evaluation process.[66]

LEAA has taken some belated steps to remedy these deficiencies. It awarded a contract for the design of a criminal justice information system. SPAs are now required to include an evaluation component in state plans; guidelines or criteria, however, are still lacking. LEAA contracted with the Brookings Institution to develop evaluation procedures, and has established a National Advisory Commission on Criminal Justice Standards and Goals. The Committee for Economic Development, however, concluded that this commission "has constructive possibilities but no real power."[67]

The lack of direction in the early years, and the need to spend ever-increasing amounts of money, has led to an emphasis on hardware in state programs. Police were the most organized of the recipients of LEAA largesse, and equipment manufacturers were quite willing to help SPAs spend their money. Helicopters, weapons, communications systems, vehicles, computers, alarm systems, closed-circuit television, and photographic equipment were among the more popular purchases. In some cases, this equipment was developed or purchased without any real study of its efficacy. LEAA's research institute, for example, spent $50,000 to develop a sophisticated viewing instrument which was of no apparent usefulness in law enforcement. Martin Danziger, director of the institute, ruefully confessed:

It was a $50,000 investment and we don't know what to do with it. We gave the money, the contractor produced exactly what we asked for. It works. But we don't know what kind of a problem it can solve. We're looking for a problem now.[68]

Some of this hardware can, of course, have a beneficial impact on the criminal justice system; in Dallas, for example, an LEAA-funded command and control unit reduced the response time of police from thirteen to three minutes.[69] The minority of the Government Operations Committee argued that law enforcement agencies were, and still are, lacking in the necessary physical tools to get the job done properly.[70] It is unclear, however, what part of these expenditures for hardware was a response to a real criminal justice need, and what part was attributable to a fascination with technology, a need to spend "free" money, and the availability of the equipment industries anxious to help absorb the funds now and find a problem to solve later.

LEAA funds have also been used in ways that raise serious constitutional questions. Ignoring the requirements of Title VI of the Civil Rights Act, the agency has failed to examine the racial impact of programs funded by the states and to require, until recently, nondiscrimination in hiring practices and the composition of SPAs.* Decisions to provide twenty-four-hour surveillance of downtown areas through closed circuit systems[71] raise serious First Amendment questions at a time when government surveillance of private citizens is being widely criticized in the press and in Congress. LEAA funds have also been used to assemble data banks. A most egregious example was the maintenance of files, through the Oklahoma Office of Inter-Agency Coordination, on "individuals/organizations engaged in dissident activities." The project collected information on, among others, antiwar protesters and members of an Afro-American group at a state college. A regular weekly report covered a meeting of a welfare rights group, the Oklahomans for Indian Opportunity formed by then Senator Fred Harris's wife, and the activities of a peace candidate. The project was abolished by the newly elected state governor in early 1971,[72] but its funding by LEAA raises doubts about LEAA's concern for individual rights.

LEAA has invested in the establishment of a national computerized file of criminal history records, controlled by the FBI

---

* See the reports of the Lawyers Committee for Civil Rights Under Law, *Law and Disorder*.

and fed by LEAA-supported state information systems. According to *Law and Disorder III*, this has been done without any examination of the necessity, usefulness, or constitutional implications of the program.[73] No federal laws regulate this system; access to the state systems is on terms defined by the state itself.*
LEAA imposes no protective standards as a condition of its grants, requiring only that states establishing information systems with LEAA funds ensure that adequate provisions are made for security, individual privacy, and the accuracy of the data collection. The scope of data in the national file is determined by the FBI. At the national level, federal agencies are able to obtain information for clearing federal employees and employees of federal contractors. In the past, federally chartered banks have also had access to such information, although there is presently debate in Congress over whether such practices should continue. The use of these records for employment purposes, particularly when they include arrests without convictions, raises clear constitutional issues that should be addressed by Congress.

Many of these policy issues arise from a basic confusion about the fundamental purposes of LEAA. Is LEAA primarily designed to improve the criminal justice system—the police, the courts, and the correctional system—or was it created to reduce crime? The two, of course, are not unrelated; the latter may be an indirect result of the former. The inadequacy of the criminal justice system, however, is only one element in reducing crime. The incidence of crime is also highly correlated with low income, unemployment, poor housing, and poor health conditions. The tradeoffs and relative emphases between these two purposes has considerable impact on the types of programs that LEAA should be funding. Some criminal justice system improvements, such as improvement in public defender services, would promote justice but probably would not reduce crime. Alternatively, if the purpose is to reduce crime, then some grants only tenuously related

---

* Massachusetts has refused to permit the FBI access to some of its information systems, citing the dangers to rights of privacy.

or completely unrelated to the criminal justice system would be appropriate. SPAs have funded such programs. In San Mateo, California, funds were granted to enable the county board of education to assist kindergarten pupils with chronic learning problems. One city in New York State was funded to sustain a youth employment project. The report of the House Government Operations Committee is replete with further examples of efforts to address the social and economic correlates of crime that do not necessarily affect the criminal justice system.[74] A crucial question is whether, as socioeconomic programs, they should be reviewed and approved by SPAs largely or wholly dominated by representatives of the criminal justice system.

The Omnibus Crime Control and Safe Streets Act is by no means clear with regard to LEAA's objective. While the statutory language does mention the reduction of crime, the emphasis is clearly on pursuing that goal through improvements in the criminal justice system. The Nixon administration tacitly admitted as much when, in an exchange of letters between Attorney General John Mitchell and Secretary of Health, Education and Welfare Elliot Richardson, LEAA agreed to limit its efforts in the juvenile delinquency area to those services provided through the criminal justice system.*[75] More explicitly, LEAA stated in its December 1970 official newsletter:

> LEAA does not seek to solve social and economic problems which contribute to crime. This is the responsibility of other Federal and State agencies. The purpose of LEAA is to give large-scale financial and technical aid to strengthen criminal justice at every level throughout the Nation.[76]

The Government Operations Committee concluded in its report:

> The real issue is whether, given the broad mandate of the act and the existence of other Federal programs which address the underlying causes of crime, the direct assault on

* See pp. 310–311.

crime should be dissipated in programs which may indirectly tend to reduce crime. The Safe Streets Act was not intended to be a comprehensive answer to the social ills of America, but rather a strong Federal response to the specific needs of State and local criminal justice systems. The impact of block grant funds on the criminal justice system is dissipated by the diversions discussed here.[77]

Yet at other times, LEAA stresses the broader goal of crime reduction. Jerris Leonard responded to the Government Operations Committee study with the assertion that the majority

appear to be unable to come down hard against crime.
Rather, they talk about such academic things as improving the criminal justice system, forgetting that the point of the program is to reduce crime.[78]

In accordance with this philosophy, Leonard announced on January 13, 1972 a new program to be funded through discretionary grants. This "High Impact Program" would concentrate efforts in a limited number of cities to reduce the rates of specific crimes. Guidelines urged such broad objectives as a decrease in institutionalization of offenders, a restructuring of police departments, adequate treatment of addicts, and reducing unemployment, but failed to give specific directives on expenditures. A sudden enormous influx of funds created planning problems in some cities. The "crime specific" program orientation raised some question whether these funds should be integrated with other LEAA moneys and was strongly criticized for lack of guidelines on administration, planning, and program integration, and lack of evaluative techniques which would permit an eventual isolation of the factors that might actually lead to crime reduction.[79]

Broad policy questions such as whether the populace is to be subjected to ever-increasing amounts of surveillance, whether arrest records are to be freely circulated among the states, whether federal law enforcement funds should be spent on weapons and helicopters or on probation and parole programs, or whether programs to address the causes of crime are to be designed by boards dominated by representatives of the criminal justice system, should be resolved after due deliberation by the elected representatives of the people, not by an appointed bureaucracy. To be sure, Congress endows executive agencies with a significant degree of discretion, but the failure to provide adequate goals and guidelines for the exercise of that discretion, and the failure to monitor agency operations for compliance with statutory standards, constitute a grave abdication of responsibility by the Judiciary committees.

The First Opportunity for Reform

Congress had an excellent opportunity to address some of the problems of LEAA and to clarify some of the confusions of purpose when the agency's authorization expired in 1970. The House was the first to act upon the authorization and proposed amendments. Hearings were held by Subcommittee No. 5 in February and March 1970. The issue mentioned most often was the amount of funds that were being passed on to the cities. Only the representatives of the Urban Coalition Action Council pointed out the lack of leadership, priorities, and evaluation; the insufficiency of plans; and the stress on police expenditures.[80] The full Judiciary Committee reported out a bill making a number of substantive changes in LEAA. The three-person administration was replaced by a single administrator; a new grant program for corrections was added; the federal government was permitted to make discretionary grants for up to 90 percent of the cost of programs; and states were required to pay at least one-quarter of the nonfederal share for programs funded under the state plan. A requirement was added that LEAA approve only state plans that allocate an adequate share of assistance to high crime areas. The committee also noted, but did not resolve, questions about LEAA procedures for extending technical assistance, enforcing nondiscrimination laws, and providing means for a review of state fund distribution.[81]

The bill passed the House and was referred to Senator McClellan's subcommittee during the period when it was holding hearings on the subject. Senator McClellan's hearings were desultory, consisting of the statements of twelve witnesses, only one of whom did not represent some level of government.[82] Although even this somewhat cursory examination disclosed many of LEAA's difficulties, the bill reported out by the Senate subcommittee and full committee contained no fundamental changes in the structure of the agency. The House provision for states contributing a portion of the nonfederal share—the "buy-in" provision—was eliminated, and the provision in the original act requiring states to pass 75 percent of their funds on to local governments was weakened.[83] The Senate Judiciary Committee report on the bill noted that there had been criticism of the lack of funds going to cities and the disproportionate funding of police projects, but dismissed these as the result of the first year of the program, when only limited funds were available and police were the only component of the criminal justice system ready to take advantage of the funds.[84] Senators Bayh, Hart, and Kennedy, however, filed minority views, noting that "disproportionate funds have been scattered on grants to purchase basic equipment and support basic law enforcement for low crime areas."[85] The senators offered two alternative approaches for correcting deficiencies; a system of block grants to urban areas and a revision of the block-grant approach. The latter, offered as an amendment on the floor of the Senate by Hart, would have reduced block grants to 60 percent of the action grants, and raised discretionary grants to 40 percent. The amendment lost forty-two to twenty-eight. The block-grant system had apparently lost very little support since its casual acceptance in 1968.

The bill passed the Senate on October 8, 1970, with a number of other titles attached; after the differences in the bills were worked out in conference, the final bill was passed by both houses on December 17. Title I, which constituted the amendments to the 1968 act, made some changes in LEAA. The funding situation of the cities, which generally have a higher incidence of crime than rural and suburban areas, was improved in several respects: state plans were required to assure that areas of high crime incidence received adequate funds; the "buy-in" provision was included, i.e., states were required to provide one-quarter of the local share of action programs; and the federal share of most action programs was raised to 75 percent. Other changes, however, hurt the cities: LEAA was permitted to waive the requirement that 40 percent of planning funds be passed on to local governments; states were no longer required to pass 75 percent of action funds to local governments; and by fiscal year 1973, 40 percent of the local share was required to be in cash.*

Other provisions of the 1970 amendments gave the administrator sole "administrative" powers, including the appointment and supervision of personnel, with all "other" powers to be exercised by him with the concurrence of at least one of the associate administrators; required SPAs to include representatives of public agencies maintaining crime-control or -reduction programs, as well as the original law enforcement agencies; expanded action grants to include the establishment of Criminal Justice Coordinating Councils and community-based delinquency prevention programs; and instituted a new grant program for corrections, to be split evenly between block and discretionary grants. Funds were authorized in the sums of $650 million for fiscal year 1971, $1.5 billion for 1972, and $1.75 billion for 1973. Thus, while making significant changes in the operations of LEAA, but failing to address the basic problems of lack of direction and goals, the Congress continued to authorize rapidly escalating funds. The congressional liberals, who have traditionally been the most critical of LEAA operations, were the strongest proponents of the swollen authorization.

What Might Have Been Done

A number of options were open to Congress in 1970 by which it might have improved the operations of LEAA without abandoning the block-grant approach. A congressional mandate to increase audit capability and operations might well have prevented some

---

* Interestingly, LEAA has never ruled that the states, through the buy-in, must contribute *pro rata* to the cash share.

of the more blatant misuses of federal funds. A one-year extension might have been granted with a warning to "shape up, or else." However, most grant programs depend on more than one year's authorization. Local subgrantees might be reluctant to undertake projects if they could not be assured of funds to complete the effort. According to a Senate staffer, a one-year authorization also produces a high degree of instability, and instability, resulting from the hiatus without a director and the former requirement for unanimity among the three directors, was one of LEAA's greatest difficulties.[86] While these might be valid arguments against such a measure, however, one cannot help but wonder why such arguments did not prevent short-term authorizations for other agencies, such as the now defunct Office of Economic Opportunity.

Congress might have used the opportunity provided by the 1970 amendments to impose statutory goals and standards of evaluation upon the agency. Although this might have been incompatible with the block-grant approach, and excessive detail should not normally be written into a statute, Congress might alternatively have dictated that LEAA itself develop such goals and standards within a certain specified period.

As mentioned above, the description of the "comprehensive plan" requirement in the 1968 act was sufficiently general to be used either to require very specific analysis of needs, resources, goals, and operative steps, or to permit a mere *pro forma* recitation of these factors, with a list of planned expenditures. Some critics believe that LEAA has acquiesced in the latter.[87] Congress could have taken the opportunity in 1970 to clarify the requirements for a comprehensive plan, compelling LEAA to exercise more oversight of state plans.

Most important, Congress could have clearly delineated the purposes of the LEAA grant program. The resolution of the crime reduction—criminal justice system improvement issue has been ripe for congressional action since the original passage of the act.

Why Congress Did Not Act

Congress chose none of these actions. Program changes were made, but none of the basic problems was addressed. One explanation given is that the program was too new and had not been given a chance to "shake down." Former LEAA Administrator Charles Rogovin has suggested that, while newness might have been a reason not to examine too carefully the questions of fund use, Congress should still have reviewed the fund flow, inquiring as to why so few of the appropriated funds had been expended.[88] (Congress did address one facet of the fund-flow problem in questioning the lack of funds being passed on to the cities.) Congress might also have sought to learn what measures LEAA was taking to prevent fund misuse. The argument that it was too early to try to deal with the basic direction of LEAA has some merit. The administrative difficulties resulting from the "troika" and unanimity requirements had prevented LEAA from operating efficiently. And in many cases, states were still in the process of determining priorities and addressing basic problems, such as antiquated equipment, which needed to be resolved before new and innovative programs could be effectively implemented.

Rogovin, acknowledging the constraints on what might have been done in the 1970 amendments, raised the more critical question: why was nothing done in the succeeding years as the problems of LEAA became even more apparent?[89] Why did the Judiciary committees, with jurisdiction over the agency, wait for the Government Operations Committee to take action? One explanation, particularly applicable to the Senate Subcommittee on Criminal Laws and Procedure, is that a committee that finishes work on a subject or reauthorizes an agency is reluctant to reexamine it until the authorization expires. Since the 1970 amendments authorized funds for three years, extensive hearings and investigations were not held again until early 1973. As we shall see, however, Senator McClellan, for reasons of his own, chose not to wait until 1973 to renew LEAA's authorization.

Perhaps the most significant factor in the failure of the Juciciary committees to pay sufficient attention to these problems, either in 1970 or later, is the lack of any well-organized groups, with well-defined economic interest in the legislation, to force LEAA reform onto the committees' political agendas. The only significant dispute in the 1970 deliberations involved the grants to cities, where a powerful lobby group did exist: the National League of Cities–U.S. Conference of Mayors. No powerful private group was there to represent the victims of crime, the citizens subjected to invasions of privacy, the taxpayer supporting Motorola and paying double interest on federal grant funds. No one, except the Urban Coalition Action Council, had the motivation to do the investigation necessary to uncover many of these problems and force Congress to scrutinize them. A congressional aide wonders if the results might have been different if the report of the Committee for Economic Development, a prestigious organization of powerful businessmen and educators, which was highly critical of federal efforts in the criminal justice field, had been published at that time instead of in the summer of 1972.[90]

The Almost-Missed Opportunity

Many legislators anticipated that, despite the many improvements made by Jerris Leonard, such as the regionalization, increased audit staff, and creation of the National Advisory Commission on Criminal Justice Standards and Goals, fundamental changes would have to be made in the 1973 extension of LEAA. Congressman Railsback, for example, commented:

> As one of the architects of the block grant approach, I'm afraid I'm of the opinion that we need some kind of better guidelines for federal oversight to see that the money is better spent.[91]

The hope of these legislators, however, was very nearly frustrated by the combined forces of the chairman and ranking minority member of the Senate Subcommittee on Criminal Laws and Procedures. In September 1972, the House enacted a bill amending the Omnibus Crime Control and Safe Streets Act to require the development of treatment programs for narcotics addicts as a condition for LEAA corrections grants. During the Senate debate on this bill, other measures compensating victims of crime and establishing an insurance program for public safety officers to be administered by LEAA—bills that had been reported from the Subcommittee on Criminal Laws and Procedures—were added as amendments. Senator Hruska then suddenly and without warning offered an amendment extending the authorization of LEAA for another year, until June 30, 1974, arguing that the agency needed the time to "adjust itself to a working basis, taking into consideration the several amendments" giving LEAA additional administrative responsibilities for the narcotics and insurance programs.[92] Judiciary Committee liberals were stunned by this extraordinary maneuver concerning a major program. By this time, Congress could no longer claim ignorance of LEAA's problems, or that the program needed more time to "shake down." Nonetheless, Senator McClellan immediately supported the amendment. He explained that the subcommittee would certainly need more than the first five months of the new Congress to study any proposed amendments to LEAA, and that the Hruska amendment would give it a full eighteen months. McClellan threatened that if the act were not extended now, it would expire before all the amendments could be considered.[93] Senators Tunney, Bayh, and Kennedy spoke vigorously against the extension; Kennedy offered a compromise extension of six months. McClellan responded to all three senators that there was nothing to prevent their offering bills to amend the Omnibus Crime Control and Safe Streets Act at any time,[94] knowing full well that such legislation would be referred to his subcommittee—where it would languish until he saw fit to consider it. Indeed, two of Senator Bayh's bills amending the 1968 act were already gathering dust in McClellan's subcommittee.[95] A senator's opportunity to get such an amendment considered—unless Senator McClellan favored it—would come only when the subcommittee chairman was obliged, because of the need for reauthorization, to open up the issue. The three liberals were particularly concerned because the

Hruska amendment had never been considered by the committee,[96] a technique that effectively prevented any consideration of the many complex issues involved in an extension of LEAA.

When the roll was called, the Kennedy compromise lost, twenty-eight to forty-three, and the Hruska amendment was passed, sixty-three to nine. It cannot be known how many senators knew exactly what they were voting on; senators often depend on staff aides to tell them what the issue is, and how they should vote. In this case, the amendment came without warning, and the choice presented to the senators may have been in terms of "for" or "against" LEAA. In addition, senators frequently depend on another senator's advice in a particular field, and McClellan's influence in the criminal field is awesome. Finally, many senators may have known what they were voting on, but may have been afraid of "voting against law enforcement" in an election year.

Despite these advantages, the McClellan-Hruska maneuver failed. Congress adjourned before a Senate-House conference could be held on the bill.

Stalemate and Status Quo

When the Ninety-third Congress assembled, the House Judiciary Subcommittee No. 5 (now called the Subcommittee on Monopolies and Commercial Law) held extensive hearings on the future shape of LEAA. The Nixon administration pressed to transform LEAA into a prototype for "special revenue sharing," giving the states virtually total discretion over the use of the federal funds without the necessity of conforming to state plans. Others, including most liberal Democrats, wished to see LEAA's block-grant approach curtailed in favor of increased control from Washington over program content, at the expense of the SPAs. In the end, neither of these forces prevailed: the "special revenue sharing" was defeated, and no significant changes in the structure of LEAA (such as block grants directly to the cities) were adopted. The House did change the formulas for federal and state shares and made some significant changes in emphasis. The words "and criminal justice" were added after each reference to "law enforce-ment"; the audit, accounting, and coordination requirements for state plans were tightened; and data-gathering to permit federal evaluation was required. But a political stalemate blunted any major structural changes. The opposition of existing program constituencies at the state and local level to changes in LEAA, the increase in Democratic control of the state houses, and the hostility to revenue sharing by urban areas conspired to maintain the status quo. A two-year extension was voted.

In the Senate, two days of hearings were held by McClellan's subcommittee. Recognizing that a similar standoff would occur in the Senate, the chairman offered a substitute to the House bill incorporating most of its changes but providing for a five-year extension, thus ensuring that Congress would not reevaluate LEAA until at least 1978. The McClellan substitute was adopted with a few amendments, including one introduced by Bayh (requiring that a certain percentage of block grants be spent on juvenile delinquency) and two by Kennedy (providing individu-als access to their criminal history files, and providing urban areas the opportunity to formulate criminal justice plans and to receive block-grant funds to implement them).

In conference, chairman McClellan did not fight very hard for the Bayh·amendment, perceiving it as a Trojan horse that would weaken the basic block-grant structure of LEAA by open-ing the gates to categorical programs. When Congressman Seiber-ling decided to vote against the Bayh amendment, breaking the solid Democratic front in the House delegation, the conferees deleted it, while retaining the Kennedy amendments. A three-year extension was agreed upon, and the measure was enacted. LEAA, with which everyone seems to be dissatisfied—but for dif-ferent reasons—has thrived on scandal, failure, drift, and waste. And it is safe until 1976.

13

Youth, Drugs, and Guns: Keeping up with the Headlines

Two-thirds of the serious crimes in America are committed by persons under twenty-one. Drugs are considered a major cause of crime. Over one-fourth of all violent crimes involve firearms. These are the three critical problems which the Senate Judiciary Subcommittee to Investigate Juvenile Delinquency, in a highly bipartisan effort, has sought to attack since Birch Bayh assumed command at the beginning of the Ninety-second Congress.* Although one close observer suggested that the choice of much

* House Judiciary Committee activity on gun control and drug policy is discussed later in this chapter. House Judiciary does not have jurisdiction over the major juvenile delinquency legislation discussed in this chapter; it is referred instead to the Education and Labor Committee. The Subcommittee on Courts, Civil Liberties, and the Administration of Justice (formerly Subcommittee No. 3), however, is considering measures to establish a Juvenile Justice Institute.

of the subcommittee's work is prompted by Senator Bayh's "presidential ambitions,"[1] both majority[2] and minority[3] staff and representatives of organizations involved with the subcommittee's work disagree with this contention. They point out the political hazards and lack of political benefit in the juvenile delinquency, drug abuse, and gun-control fields, expressing a belief in Bayh's genuine commitment to ameliorating these problems. Indeed, during the Ninety-second Congress, Bayh devoted more of his time to this subcommittee than to any of the others on which he serves, including Constitutional Amendments.

The membership of the subcommittee is decidedly more liberal than that of the full Judiciary Committee. The Democrats—Bayh, Hart, Burdick, and Kennedy—are all liberals, and the Republicans—Hruska, Cook, Fong, and Mathias—are, with the exception of Hruska, generally moderates. Subcommittee legislation has nevertheless fared quite well in the conservative-dominated full committee.

The minority members and staff of the subcommittee play an active role in its work, sharing the responsibility for its productivity. Senator Marlow Cook, the ranking minority member, had considerable experience in the juvenile area before coming to the Senate, and maintains contact with many Kentuckians who work in the field.[4]

Cook does not strictly adhere to partisan lines in his work on the subcommittee. In hearings on the 1971 extension of the Juvenile Delinquency Prevention and Control Act of 1968, for example, Cook interrogated and criticized administration witnesses just as intensely as Senator Bayh.[5] He also supported Bayh's "Saturday night special" bill (discussed below) in the face of strong administration opposition, apparently spearheaded by Senator Hruska, the second-ranking minority member.

Although Senator Cook does not attend many hearings in person,* both he and the other minority members generally send

* Through May 1, 1972, Cook had attended only two days of subcommittee hearings in the 92nd Congress. Senator Hruska had attended four, Senator Mathias, three. The only majority member other than Chairman

staff members who report to them on the proceedings. The staffs of Senators Cook and Mathias often work with the majority staff on juvenile justice matters.

JUVENILE DELINQUENCY AND JUVENILE JUSTICE

The subcommittee held hearings in March 1971 to consider the various federal efforts to deal with juvenile delinquency, and the information developed was very disturbing. Representatives of the Departments of Labor and Housing and Urban Development stated that the primary responsibility for the fight against juvenile delinquency rested with the Department of Health, Education, and Welfare, in its Youth Development and Delinquency Prevention Administration (YDDPA).

YDDPA, whose functions have since been assumed by HEW's Office of Youth Development, administered a grant program under the Juvenile Delinquency Prevention and Control Act of 1968. The Act provided for block grants to states, upon the submission of a comprehensive state plan, for 90 percent of the cost of planning, 60 percent of the cost of preventive services, and 75 percent of the cost of rehabilitative services. The program was authorized for $25 million for fiscal 1969, $50 million for 1970, and $75 million for 1971.

The program, however, had never quite gotten under way. No director was appointed until February 1970. Until June 1970, the agency was just an "office," a fairly subordinate position within the HEW hierarchy. Furthermore, only one state plan had been approved. States preferred to seek funds from the Law Enforcement Assistance Administration in the Department of Justice, which imposed a lower matching requirement, a lesser "buy-in" provision (none at all until 1970), and a requirement to pass

---

Bayh to attend a single day of hearings in the 92nd Congress through May 1, 1972, was Senator Kennedy. In the Senate, it is not uncommon for only the subcommittee chairman to attend hearings.

on only 75 percent of the funds to local programs. States also knew that Congress was far more liberal, if not profligate, in appropriating funds to LEAA. The House appropriated less funds to YDDPA in its first two years than the administration requested, perhaps with good reason—the program did not even have a director. In fiscal 1971, Congress did grant the budget request of YDDPA. Throughout the period, however, YDDPA sought funding well below its authorization, HEW cut the YDDPA requests, and the Office of Management and Budget reduced the departmental request. The President's budget requested from Congress only $19.2 million in fiscal 1969, $15 million in 1970, and a like amount in 1971.

At the oversight hearings of the subcommittee, HEW responded to the suggestion that it bore primary responsibility for delinquency efforts by noting that the bulk of funding went to LEAA, which had been authorized in 1970 to fund community-based delinquency programs. But it turned out that LEAA had no specific juvenile delinquency unit, and had spent only 14.3 percent of its funds in fiscal 1971 on juvenile delinquency. According to Senator Bayh:

> The legislative oversight hearings . . . and the investigation of the Subcommittee staff revealed that [YDDPA] had not fulfilled the goals of the Juvenile Delinquency Prevention and Control Act of 1968, and by their own admission, had not successfully provided either the national leadership or the coordination necessary for an effective Federal approach to the problems of juvenile delinquency.[6]

The Juvenile Delinquency Subcommittee was clearly dissatisfied, and the federal agencies knew it. Hearings were scheduled on legislation to extend the 1968 Act. Between these two sets of hearings, Attorney General John Mitchell and Secretary of HEW Elliot Richardson reached an agreement by an exchange of letters (on May 25, 1971, the day before the hearings) delineating the responsibilities of LEAA and YDDPA in the juvenile field. YDDPA would be administered

> to complement the Law Enforcement Assistance Administration block grant program and encourage more comprehensive planning for juvenile delinquency prevention and control by defining the funding authority of YDDPA as the area of prevention and rehabilitation administered outside the correctional system while the focus of LEAA is within the correctional system.[7]

HEW also agreed to coordinate federal efforts in the juvenile delinquency field.

The bill to be considered by the Juvenile Delinquency Subcommittee called for only a one-year extension of YDDPA. The subcommittee was willing to give the agency an opportunity to improve its operation, and the administration agreed with this approach.[8] When the representatives of HEW and YDDPA testified before the subcommittee, they offered amendments to the extension that embodied the Richardson-Mitchell agreement: YDDPA would be limited to developing alternative or supportive systems outside the juvenile justice system. The administration also wanted an authorization of "such funds as may be necessary," rather than the proposed $75 million.[9]

The subcommittee was not entirely satisfied with the suggested modifications to the extension measure. Some of them, such as the amended fund authorization, seemed to institutionalize the very characteristics of YDDPA—the lack of expenditures and the limited scope and number of programs—which had disturbed the subcommittee. Bayh and Cook severely criticized the appropriations approach of the agency, arguing that YDDPA had not made any significant effort to obtain adequate funding from the appropriations committees, and in fact had reduced its requests each year. John D. Twiname, administrator of HEW's Social and Rehabilitation Service (in which YDDPA is located), responded that the new approach would obviate the need for more funds.

The administration, however, insisted that, since HEW already spent much more on juvenile delinquency through other programs than the $75 million authorized for YDDPA, often with insufficient coordination of efforts, the creation of an additional, large funding program at that time would be unwise.[10]

In the end, the subcommittee refused to agree to the amendments affecting the basic programs. Both Bayh and Cook opposed the division of functions between HEW and LEAA.[11] As Senator Bayh stated:

> YDDPA's recommendations to limit the scope of its activities to programs "outside of the juvenile justice system" were opposed . . . primarily because we believe that this would be a reduction in the total federal delinquency effort. Furthermore, it did not seem appropriate for YDDPA to abdicate such an important part of its responsibility in favor of LEAA, an agency which has not demonstrated any great commitment in the juvenile delinquency area.[12]

The act was extended for one year. To have allowed it to lapse would have been to make LEAA the only significant granting agency for juvenile delinquency funds, and the subcommittee was not enamored of LEAA's "hardware," prosecutorial, law enforcement, and adult crime approach.[13] The subcommittee also insisted upon the $75 million authorization.

In its report to the Senate, the Judiciary Committee explained that the simple extension would both allow Congress to complete its overview of the program and indicate to the administrators that their performance was being evaluated.[14]

The subcommittee's actions clearly had some effect. That the Mitchell-Richardson letters were exchanged the day before the hearings on the extension of the act obviously was not coincidental. YDDPA continued through fiscal 1972 to concentrate on prevention rather than rehabilitation. Through technical assistance and an "institutional" approach, it stressed Youth Services Systems—the integration of the operations of various institutions and agencies in the community with the involvement of youth.[15]

When YDDPA came before the subcommittee in 1972 seeking another extension, it once again requested changes in its statutory direction and purpose. Both the administration and Senator Cook had bills before the subcommittee that would limit the focus of the agency to the Youth Services Systems.[16] Cook called for an authorization of $75 million. The administration wanted "such sums as may be necessary"; YDDPA saw its new role as a *coordinator* of services, and as such did not plan to request more than a $10 million appropriation. YDDPA argued that a heavily funded federal agency would only be seen as a competitor by other agencies and could not effectively coordinate their activities.

Bayh was clearly disturbed by YDDPA's requests. He expressed concern that such youth service systems, which could be operated at the local as well as state level, would not have any access to assistance. He could not understand how YDDPA could expect to fund ever-increasing numbers of systems, as the agency planned, without increasing its appropriation. He disputed the assertion that an agency with a strong program of its own could not coordinate the efforts of others.[17] Bayh concluded that the purposes of the original Juvenile Delinquency Prevention and Control Act could not be fulfilled through YDDPA, but the subcommittee felt it was important to maintain a juvenile delinquency component in HEW pending enactment of broader, more effective legislation—which was already in the works.[18] Senator Mathias submitted legislation to establish a broader program within HEW itself, with the administrator directly responsible to the secretary. Senator Cook's bill, with some modifications, was reported to the Senate;[19] a somewhat amended bill passed the House, and the Senate accepted the House bill.

The Comprehensive Approach

The subcommittee also continues to reshape the existing federal anti-juvenile-delinquency effort. When the extension and reauthorization of LEAA came to the floor in the early summer of 1973, Senators Bayh, Cook, and Mathias, dissatisfied with LEAA's contribution to that effort, introduced an amendment drafted by majority staff that would require states to spend 20 percent in the first year and 30 percent in subsequent years of their block-grant funds on a comprehensive juvenile delinquency program.[20] The subcommittee staff alerted the many private groups with which it has contact to the pending proposal, and the groups initiated an effort by their local organizations to contact senators. By the time the measure was called up, cosponsors were being added too rapidly to keep count. The amendment passed the Senate by unanimous consent, Hruska and McClellan having failed to galvanize an opposition. Despite a similar effort by private organizations to reach the House conferees, the percentage requirements were eliminated in the conference. The result was that state plans are now required to include a program for the improvement of juvenile justice, though not necessarily funded with LEAA moneys.

Bayh had directed the subcommittee staff to begin work on a comprehensive bill on juvenile delinquency shortly after the 1971 hearings. The staff turned to many outside sources for input: the American Parents Committee, the National Council of Juvenile Court Judges, and the YMCA and YWCA were among the most prominent.[21] The subcommittee staff, along with some of the private organizations and the authors of this legislation, had become convinced that HEW had proved itself unwilling or unable to properly administer a large-scale juvenile delinquency program. The staff instead developed legislation that would set up a National Office of Juvenile Justice and Delinquency Prevention in the Executive Office of the President. The agency would be responsible for the administration of two types of grant funds: a traditional categorical-grant program to public and private nonprofit agencies, and a block-grant program. The block-grant program was designed to anticipate—and avoid—the difficulties that had plagued YDDPA and LEAA.

Hearings on the comprehensive bill were held in May and June 1972 and in February, March, and June 1973. Private

groups involved with youth and juvenile justice policy participated actively in the hearings. The Nixon administration, believ-
ing that existing federal efforts sufficed, strongly opposed the
measure.[22] To accommodate legitimate suggestions and criticism,
the staff then drafted appropriate modifications.

In March 1974 the subcommittee approved a comprehensive
bill placing administration of juvenile delinquency programs in
HEW, under the aegis of an assistant secretary. In May, however, the full Judiciary Committee, under McClellan's prodding,
amended the bill, placing the program under LEAA control and
requiring LEAA to expend considerably more money on juvenile
delinquency. That bill passed the Senate on July 25, 1974, by a
vote of eighty-eight to one. Earlier, on July 1, the House had
passed an Education and Labor Committee bill that adopted the
HEW approach and also incorporated Bayh's Runaway Youth Act
as Title IV. The Senate-House conference is expected to maintain
LEAA control.

DRUGS

Most Americans know that "smack" is heroin and "grass" is
marijuana, but few know the street names for the "uppers" and
"downers," the amphetamines and barbiturates, the abusable drugs
that are in millions of medicine chests. In the Senate, laws
regulating the production and distribution of both types of
drugs are within the jurisdiction of the Juvenile Delinquency
Subcommittee.

In the Ninety-second Congress, Senator Thomas F. Eagleton
(D.,Mo.) introduced legislation that would have reclassified
amphetamines into the tightly controlled Schedule II of the Controlled Substances Act, thereby prohibiting the refilling of pre-
scriptions and allowing production quotas to be established by the
federal government. The subcommittee decided to hold hearings
on the bill. Immediately prior to the hearings, the Bureau of
Narcotics and Dangerous Drugs decided to reclassify the drugs

administratively. The subcommittee nevertheless decided to hold the hearings, since two related drugs, Ritalin and Preludin, had not been rescheduled, and the manufacturer of Escatrol, an amphetamine-barbiturate compound, was still requesting an administrative hearing to have the drug exempted from the rescheduling.[23] The subcommittee was also concerned about the levels of the quotas administratively placed on the manufacture of amphetamines.[24]

The first round of subcommittee hearings produced publicity about the potential dangers of amphetamine abuse. A second set of hearings dealt with the use and abuse of amphetamines in the treatment of obesity. After the first hearings, Ritalin and Preludin were moved to Schedule II[25] and the manufacturer of Escatrol withdrew its request for a hearing. Following the second set of hearings, production quotas for amphetamines were reduced to 20 percent of the previous year's production.[26]

In the course of preparing the hearings the staff had consulted a number of persons who stressed the dangers of barbiturate abuse,[27] and several witnesses made the same point. A report on amphetamines by Congressman Claude Pepper's House Select Committee on Crime, which recommended the study of barbiturate diversion, further convinced the subcommittee that these questions required exploration.[28] The subcommittee sought additional information. It sent out a questionnaire to over six hundred persons, primarily people involved with law enforcement, regarding barbiturates.

This information, the testimony at the hearings, and a General Accounting Office report on drugs resulted in the development of legislation to reclassify the drugs into the more tightly controlled schedule into which amphetamines had been moved, and to require each dosage unit to be labeled in a manner that identified the manufacturer. Hearings were held. Another bill was developed requiring manufacturers to incorporate inert "tracer" elements into stimulants and depressants to aid investigations into their illegitimate use, and requiring the Department of Justice to take further specific steps to control the diversion of these drugs. The extensive collection of data on the "downers" also resulted in a significant staff report, "Barbiturate Abuse in the U.S."[29]

No action was taken on the barbiturate bills, and they were introduced again in the Ninety-third Congress. Meanwhile, the subcommittee's concern forced the administration to act: in the spring of 1973 the Food and Drug Administration proposed that barbiturates be moved to the tighter controls of Schedule II.

Hearings in the Ninety-second Congress on the abuse of methadone, the synthetic substitute often used in heroin treatment, were continued in various parts of the country. A subcommittee bill imposing tighter controls on methadone required registration by individual operators of methadone maintenance and detoxification programs with the attorney general and compliance with certain health and security standards. It was signed into law in May 1974 as Public Law 93-281.

When the Nixon administration's package of drug legislation was referred to the subcommittee in 1973, Bayh strongly opposed its Procrustean provisions on preventive detention and casual drug use. The subcommittee failed to hold hearings on the proposals, but Bayh sponsored an amendment to the Controlled Substances Act increasing criminal penalties for high-level, nonaddicted drug entrepreneurs. Adopted by the Senate as part of the Compensation to Victims of Crime bill (S.800) in April 1973, the measure still rests in the Crime Subcommittee of House Judiciary.

Hearings were also held in the Ninety-third Congress on the highly controversial use of drugs in sports. In hearings on the "love drug" Methaqualone (Sopors, Quaaludes), the major manufacturers refused to appear and were subpoenaed. As a result of these hearings, the FDA, which had delayed the formation of an expert panel on Methaqualone, suddenly announced a decision to move the drug to the more restrictive Schedule II. In the drug area, at least, the subcommittee has demonstrated that the bureaucracy can—with difficulty—be moved.

In the House, legislation concerning drug abuse is normally referred to the Subcommittee on Civil Rights and Constitutional Rights (Subcommittee No. 4 in the Ninety-second Congress), chaired by Don Edwards. During the Ninety-second Congress, the subcommittee held hearings on various pieces of legislation pertaining to the treatment and control of narcotics addiction. Two bills, amending the Narcotics Addicts Rehabilitation Act of 1965 to permit methadone treatment in federal institutions and amending the Omnibus Crime Control and Safe Streets Act of 1968 with regard to treatment programs under corrections grants, were reported out of the committee and passed the House. Versions of both bills also passed the Senate, but, due to the many amendments added by that chamber, the second one never became law.

GUN CONTROL:
PLAYING RUSSIAN ROULETTE

America, as has often been noted, is a violent society, and guns are the instruments of much of its violence. More than 25 percent of all violent crimes in the United States involve firearms.[30] During the last decade alone, six national political figures have been killed, maimed, or critically wounded by the blast of a gun: John F. Kennedy, Martin Luther King, Jr., Robert Kennedy, Malcolm X, George Wallace, and John Stennis.

The relationship between crime and gun control, however, is complex. Those areas of the country where guns are most plentiful and the gun laws least restrictive have the highest murder and gun-murder rates.[31] Within each area, though, there is not always a clear correlation between gun control and murder rates.[32] Gun-control legislation has, through identification of the owner of a weapon involved in a crime, helped in the solution of crimes. Prevention of some crimes also results from arrests on the basis of gun violations; many of the persons so apprehended have doubtlessly obtained the gun in preparation for a more serious crime.[33]

Despite the obvious need for some type of legislation addressing the gun problem, Congress has consistently evaded a resolution of the issue. Over 70 percent of the American people favor gun-control legislation,[34] yet it has always required a national tragedy to move gun legislation to the floor of either chamber. Many attribute the cause of this congressional paralysis to one organization—the National Rifle Association of America (NRA). The influence of this organization and the inertia of Congress were amply demonstrated in the enormous effort that was required to win Senate approval of a very limited bill designed merely to close a loophole in the 1968 Gun Control Act. In the failure of the Judiciary committees of Congress to act decisively on gun control—despite the support of the vast majority of the American people and the opportunity for reform generated by a tragic series of gun-related national crises—we see the Congress in marasmus: debilitated, unable to respond to a widely perceived but poorly organized public interest, incapable of generating and assimilating valuable information, and subject to the veto of a powerful, intense minority.

History of Recent Gun-Control Legislation

Shortly after the late Senator Thomas J. Dodd of Connecticut assumed the chairmanship of the Subcommittee to Investigate Juvenile Delinquency of the Sentate Judiciary Committee in the early 1960s, he ordered the staff to investigate the problem of the interstate mail-order purchase of guns. It was discovered that 25 percent of the mail-order gun purchasers in Washington and Chicago had prior criminal records. As more information continued to be uncovered, Senator Dodd quickly became convinced of the need for federal firearms legislation. Representatives of the firearms industry, sporting groups, including the National Rifle Association, and government agencies participated in the development of a bill regulating mail-order purchase of handguns. Dodd introduced the bill in 1963, but it languished in the Commerce Committee, to which it was referred.[35]

As has become an all-too-familiar pattern in America, an assassin's bullet was required to force Congress to take any action. The murder of President Kennedy generated a national outcry for gun control. Franklin Orth, executive director of NRA at that time, worked with the Juvenile Delinquency Subcommittee to amend Senator Dodd's bill to include rifles, and the Commerce Committee held hearings. Despite several concessions to sportsmen and Orth's personal support, however, NRA position statements opposed the bill,[36] and many other sportsmen and a representative of the firearms industry testified in opposition to the controls.[37] As a result, the bill died in committee.

Early in 1965 Dodd introduced a new, stronger bill at the request of the Johnson administration. This bill restricted interstate and foreign traffic in firearms to licensed dealers, prohibited sales to juveniles and felons, and required authorization by the secretary of the treasury for importation of firearms. Opposition from the NRA was immediate; a newsletter warning that the bill would lead to total confiscation of guns was mailed to the membership. Members of Congress were deluged with letters stating that the newsletter contained incorrect information.* The NRA later said these mistakes resulted from the "susceptibility" of the language to such interpretations, and were not made with "intent to mislead."[38]

The association, along with other organizations such as the National Wildlife Federation, the National Shooting Sports Foundation, the Wildlife Management Institute, and the Sporting Arms and Ammunition Manufacturers Institute, testified during the eleven days of hearings held in the Juvenile Delinquency Subcommittee in mid-1965 on their concern about undue interference with the legitimate, primarily sporting uses of guns. Support for Dodd's bill came from federal and state officials and police organizations.[39] Hearings were held in the House Ways and Means Committee as well, but no further action was taken.

Again, outside events intruded. In August 1965 riots broke out in the Watts section of Los Angeles. Senate Juvenile Delinquency Subcommittee investigators discovered that, contrary to

* The letter listed the manufacturer's license fee at twice its actual amount, neglected to mention exceptions from the bill's prohibitions, and stated that the bill would prohibit the interstate transportation of firearms by the owner for lawful purposes.

the pronouncements of the NRA that the guns involved had been stolen, and that gun laws could therefore have had no effect on the riots, most of the arms had in fact been in the possession of the residents before the rioting and looting broke out; they were purchased, not looted, guns.[40]

By May 1966 the subcommittee was able to report the bill to the full Judiciary Committee. Opposition by a minority of the committee led by Senator Roman Hruska, however, delayed action on the bill. In order to get the bill to the floor, Senator Dodd agreed to report a weaker version, proposed by Hruska and similar to Dodd's original measure.[41] The bill restricted controls to handguns and did not address the importation of foreign surplus firearms. The committee report included a statement expressing the support of eight committee members for Dodd's stronger measure.[42] As the bill was reported only three days before adjournment, no action was taken.

The bill was reintroduced in the next Congress. Senator Hruska demanded that the subcommittee hold hearings on his gun-control bill, which he had not yet introduced. The NRA again sent out a letter to its members about the Dodd bill; this letter also contained misinformation.[*43]

In the middle of hearings held in July 1967, riots broke out in Newark and Detroit. Once again, subcommittee investigators determined that the guns had been in the possession of the rioters prior to the riots. Yet the NRA continued to contend that there were only three or four snipers in Detroit, and that they were using stolen guns. More delay ensued.[44]

In April 1968, however, the full Judiciary Committee met to consider the Omnibus Crime Control and Safe Streets Act. Although the House Judiciary Committee had heard testimony on firearms legislation,[45] the bill passed by the House had no firearms provisions. Senator Dodd argued for the inclusion of gun control as a title of the bill. Only after restrictions on the inter-

---

* The letter stated that the interstate sale of guns to individuals would be prohibited, whereas the bill did not then contain such a provision.

state sales of long guns were removed did the committee approve Dodd's amendment, by a vote of nine to seven. The primary effect of the resulting title was thus to limit the interstate sale of handguns. Once again, outside events overcame congressional inertia. While the full committee was considering the measure, Dr. Martin Luther King was killed in Memphis. Despite a strong letter campaign from the NRA, the Senate finally passed the title.

Another national tragedy had to intervene before the bill became law. On June 5 Robert Kennedy was shot in Los Angeles. The House, without conference, very quickly passed the bill, including the handgun limitation, as sent over from the Senate. Even the NRA, through Congressman Robert L. F. Sikes (D.,Fla.) (formerly on its board of directors), informed the House that it would not object.[46]

For once, public concern did not subside. Senator Dodd introduced both his own bill to control the sale of long guns and an administration bill that would require registration of firearms and licensing of gun owners. Controversy centered upon the registration and licensing provisions.[47] To break the deadlock, Dodd urged that the committee report the bill extending the interstate sales restrictions to long guns, and consider registration and licensing separately. The committee reported out the bill as Dodd recommended. The Senate passed the bill, and Senate language was retained in the Senate-House conference. The Gun Control Act of 1968, signed by President Johnson on October 22, 1968, forbade the mail-order sale, and the sale to nonresidents of a state, of all firearms; prohibited any sale of guns to juveniles, felons, addicts, and the mentally retarded; and forbade the importation of military surplus and nonsporting firearms. The Secretary of the Treasury was to develop criteria for determining whether a gun was suitable for sporting purposes.

The NRA: Drawing a Bead on Congress

Many sportsmen's and conservation groups have opposed gun-control legislation and have testified against it at hearings.

Nevertheless, it is the NRA that is associated in the public—and congressional—mind with unrelenting hostility to gun-control measures and with the political influence to work its will on Congress. Where does the NRA derive its extraordinary—and politically enviable—reputation?

The NRA is an organization of approximately one million members. Its official purposes include:

> the improvement of its members in marksmanship . . . and to promote social welfare and public safety, law and order, and the national defense; to educate and train citizens of good repute in the safe and efficient handling of small arms . . . and generally to encourage the lawful ownership and use of small arms by citizens of good repute.[48]

The organization has no official connection with the arms industry. Nevertheless, four of the twenty-two members of its executive committee in 1970 were directly involved in the sale and manufacture of firearms.[49] That industry also advertises heavily in its magazine, the *American Rifleman.*

Political neutrality is required by the NRA bylaws but is drawn into question by many of its activities. For many years, the NRA refused to acknowledge its role as a lobby; only in late 1968 did Franklin Orth, then executive vice president of the organization, register as a congressional lobbyist.*[50]

The NRA maintains a Legislative Information Service, which reviews and analyzes firearms legislation that comes before Congress and the state legislatures. A section of the *American Rifleman* is devoted to informing members on the status of such bills. The NRA also occasionally sends out special legislative bulletins to members, analyzing a bill and urging that they write to their representative in opposition.

It is through this technique of encouraging letter-writing campaigns that the NRA exercises most of its power. It is not uncom-

---

* Even today, if one calls the national headquarters and asks to speak to the lobbyist, the switchboard operator will state that the NRA does not have a lobbyist.

mon for tens of thousands of letters to be received by congressmen or senators in response to a plea by the association. The NRA disavows any more than infrequent direct contacts with congressmen, except when information is requested or testimony solicited.[51] Yet the following statement by Representative Sikes was reported in the *American Rifleman*:

> It is essential, however, that [the NRA] and all organizations which seek to preserve sanity in legislation affecting weapons maintain the same close contacts with members of the House and Senate that you maintained last year.[52]

The NRA carefully refrains from endorsing, or opposing, any political candidate. It does not, however, hesitate to clearly and conspicuously delineate the gun-control stands of various senators and congressmen in the *American Rifleman*. The defeat of Senators Dodd and Joseph D. Tydings (D.,Md.), both strong gun-control advocates, in the 1970 senatorial election, was given considerable exposure in the publication.

Few would credit the NRA with the defeat of Dodd, who ran in a three-way race and was tainted by front-page scandals, but the notion that the NRA was responsible for Tydings' upset has flourished. Senator Tydings himself remarked after his defeat, "I suppose this will discourage others from taking on the gun lobby."[53]

The NRA has certainly done nothing publicly to discourage this view of its political potency. In announcing the results of the 1970 election, the *American Rifleman* discussed each candidate's gun-control views along with his fate at the polls. The connection was not stated, but seemed compelling. The article also mentioned the "wide margin" by which the senator from Maryland lost, which was in actuality only 2 percent.[54] (In contrast, the victory of Senator Hruska in Nebraska, where, the magazine reported, gun control was not involved, was described as "narrow," when the difference was 5 percent.)[55] Abandonment of support for gun-control legislation was implicitly suggested as a determining factor in the senatorial races in Pennsylvania, Wisconsin, and Minnesota. The paradox that support for gun control could work against a candidate when over 70 percent of the American population favors such controls may perhaps be easily resolved: gun control is not a major issue for the majority of Americans; a candidate's stand on that one question will not determine their votes. The gun groups, on the other hand, while small, are intensely interested—as evidenced by the NRA's mail campaigns. Their votes may perhaps be determined on that one issue. Thus, an "anti-gun" stand would hurt the candidate among the latter groups, but not help him among the former.

But if one defines the "gun lobby" as the NRA, the potential of these voters to swing an election is not so clear. Such a limitation would not be entirely unreasonable. The *American Rifleman* and the NRA legislative bulletins are the primary sources by which people learn of their legislators' stand on firearms legislation, and their circulation is largely limited to the NRA membership. It is unlikely that a voter without ready access to information on a candidate's gun-control stance would base his vote entirely on that issue. It thus seems plausible to assume that most persons whose vote may be determined by the single issue of gun control are probably members of the NRA. Yet even if all NRA members in a state had cast their vote for the winner in 1970, the switch of that entire membership to the loser would have affected the outcome of only one Senate race— Senator Vance Hartke's narrow victory over Richard Roudebush in Indiana—and the victory of J. Glenn Beall, Jr., in Maryland would have been reduced to a few hundred votes.[56] NRA members might, of course, form citizens' groups in an effort to influence other voters, but they would have to base their arguments on more than the gun issue. House races could, of course, be more significantly affected if gun supporters are geographically concentrated. This, however, would reduce the number of House seats so affected and therefore the magnitude of any generalized ability on the NRA's part to defeat its enemies.

This view—that the NRA cannot itself "swing" an election—is

reinforced by the subjective judgment of both the NRA and a congressional staff member familiar with gun-control politics.[57] Both believed that Senator Tydings would have lost regardless of the gun issue; Maryland voters were tired of his personality; he had been accused by *Life* magazine of a conflict of interest;[58] he was a prime target of the Nixon administration; and he was a liberal in a state that gave George Wallace 40 percent of the vote in the 1972 presidential primary.*

The actual role of the NRA in the Tydings defeat can never be known for certain, but if this thesis is true (and since by its rules the NRA cannot provide any candidates with financial support), one might well conclude that the NRA exercises influence well beyond what its actual ability to deliver votes would warrant. Members of Congress and the press believe that NRA wrath carries more potential for harm than it does, and because they believe this, the belief becomes something of a self-fulfilling prophecy.

The NRA contends that it advocates "reasonable" gun-control measures, mentioning in this regard its cooperation with Senator Dodd in 1963.[59] The fact remains, however, that since that time, the NRA has never supported a measure actively considered by Congress. The NRA would like to replace the Gun Control Act of 1968 with more "moderate" legislation, but disavows any desire or intention to have the act repealed without replacement. The NRA argues, by comparing crime and homicide rates in the least and most restrictive states, that the act has been ineffective in reducing crime.† Such statistics, of course, fail to consider the

---

* Efforts to interview Tydings with regard to these and other issues during the summer of 1972 proved fruitless.

† The homicide rate in three of the seven states that the NRA considers the least restrictive (Arizona, Arkansas, Kansas, Kentucky, Minnesota, Vermont, and Wisconsin) is less than in any of the states the NRA classifies as most restrictive (California, Massachusetts, Michigan, New Jersey, New York, Oklahoma, and West Virginia). The average for the least restrictive states is 4.8 per 100,000, compared with 5.7 in the most restrictive.

many other variables involved in the crime rates. Proponents of gun control similarly choose states to prove that gun control reduces the homicide rate and percentage of gun murders.* Such comparisons are crude; if one examines the rates, the homicide rate appears to be more highly correlated with variables such as geographical location than with gun laws. Another traditional but legally fatuous argument—that gun control violates the Second Amendment's guarantee of the right to bear arms—has largely been abandoned by the NRA.[60]

The NRA found succor in the Nixon administration. Several conferences were held at the White House, prior to May 1971, to discuss the issue of gun control. After the first of these conferences, Maxwell Rich, who had represented the NRA, commented:

> It has become quite evident that the views of the nation's law-abiding gun owners are to be given, and are being given, full consideration within the present administration. This can be taken as a hopeful sign for the future.[61]

Nonetheless, while the administration opposes gun or ammunition registration and owner licensing, it has not joined the NRA efforts to dilute the 1968 act.

Russian Roulette on the Judiciary Committee

One purpose of the 1968 Gun Control Act was to prohibit the importation of the "Saturday night special," the cheap, snub-nosed, easily concealed handgun that is responsible for 43 percent of the gun murders in the United States.[62] The act accomplished this by prohibiting the importation of handguns unless they were recognized as "particularly suitable for or readily

---

* Senator Tydings, for example, pointed out that the percentage of gun murders and the overall homicide rate was lower in five states with strong laws (Pennsylvania, New Jersey, New York, Massachusetts, and Rhode Island) than in any of six states with weak laws (Florida, Arizona, Nevada, Texas, Mississippi, and Louisiana).

adaptable to sporting purposes." The secretary of the treasury was authorized to prescribe regulations governing that determination.

When the Treasury Department announced its criteria for the importation of handguns, even the NRA seemed satisfied. An article in the *American Rifleman* said:

> [In the past] one excuse assigned for doing nothing [about the importation of Saturday night specials] was that it would be impossible to work out a system which would admit legitimate target and similar handguns while excluding the riffraff of the firearms world.
> Yet, since the change in the U.S. Administration early this year, such a system has been devised although it may not work perfectly. . . . The new IRS point system tends to give importations priority to large, target-type pistols with safety requirements and to shut out crude, stubby, easily concealed .22s and .25s.[63]

Nevertheless, purveyors of cheap handguns soon found a means of circumventing the 1968 act. Since 80 percent of such guns had been of foreign origin, Congress in 1968 had not regulated domestic production.[64] The industry began to manufacture the frames domestically and import the parts, cut the barrels off legally imported handguns, or manufacture the entire gun domestically.[65] After having reduced the importation of handguns from an annual rate in 1968 of over 1.2 million[66] to less than 300,000 in 1970,[67] Congress was faced with a domestic industry geared up to produce a million cheap guns annually and authorized to import parts for another 1.4 million.[68] The Justice Department directed the Juvenile Delinquency Subcommittee's attention toward this problem, expressing the administration's concern.[69] G. Gordon Liddy, then of the Treasury Department, more lately of Watergate, and a man columnist Jack Anderson has described as having a "fantastic passion for guns," informed the NRA at its annual conference that the administration felt compelled to make a scientific inquiry into the area of handgun safety:

> Among other things, we feel that anyone purchasing a hand-gun for legitimate purposes is entitled, just like the pur-chaser of any other machine or instrument, to know that it will operate safely and reliably.[70]

This perverse emphasis on the safety to the gun user, rather than on its availability to criminals and unstable persons, was to prove significant in the ensuing efforts to legislate regulation of cheap handguns. The Treasury Department soon contracted for a series of safety and reliability tests.

The Juvenile Delinquency Subcommittee drafted a bill, intro-duced in September 1969, to close the loophole that exempted domestic production from the restrictions of the 1968 act. The bill would have simply extended the restrictions to domestic sales and manufacture. Senator Dodd was defeated for reelection before any action was taken. The new subcommittee chairman, Birch Bayh, despite his liberal voting record, had not been known as a strong advocate of gun control. During the first months of Bayh's chairmanship, however, the subcommittee staff briefed him on the subject, analyzing mail in favor of the legis-lation (particularly support from law enforcement agencies) and materials prepared by the National Council for a Responsible Firearms Policy. Bayh developed a keen interest in the legisla-tion.[71] In May 1971, Congressman John M. Murphy (D.,N.Y.), with considerable publicity, introduced a bill similar to Senator Dodd's, prohibiting the domestic manufacture of most handguns, on the House side. In September Bayh introduced a slightly revised bill and commenced hearings.[72]

The NRA had advocated such a bill a few years earlier in the *American Rifleman.* It had argued:

> It would seem possible for Congress to prohibit the importa-tion of parts for barred handguns and possibly to restrict the interstate sales of handguns corresponding to those that cannot be legally imported. . . .

It will be interesting to see whether the Congressional "crusaders" who backed the Johnson Administration's confiscation slanted gun controls—crying out all the meanwhile that the NRA opposed all controls—will support this relatively simple and effective form of control.[73]

When the NRA had the opportunity, however, it executed a swift *volte face*. While professing a desire to see crudely made handguns removed from the market, and pointing out that such guns were never advertised in the *American Rifleman*, Maxwell Rich stated:

Another approach is to apply to domestic handguns those standards applicable presently to firearms importation. The difficulty is that the criteria established . . . in 1969 are largely subjective and have resulted in highly questionable decisions.[74]

These were the same criteria the NRA had in 1969 argued should be applied domestically.

The administration also waffled. While agreeing that the "Saturday night special" must be eliminated, administration witnesses did not believe the "sporting purposes" test in the 1968 act was proper. They argued, without much evidence, that this test would ban guns that could be useful for police and self-protection.[75] Meanwhile, the Treasury Department tests were seeking feasible, objective criteria that would measure safety and reliability.

These hearings strengthened Bayh's convictions about the value of the legislation he had introduced,[76] and he strongly contested the administration position. Police weapons, he pointed out, were already excepted by the 1968 act. More important, he was less concerned with the safety of the "criminal" firing the gun than with that of the victim or police officer in front of it, and safety and reliability would not protect the latter. The administration had pointed out the loophole permitting the domestic production of "Saturday night specials" to the subcommittee earlier but had taken no action to develop a bill until early 1971, when tests were commissioned. The attorney general and the secretary of the treasury were unavailable to testify on the Bayh bill. Donald E. Santarelli, then an associate deputy attorney general* did testify, however, that the administration would soon have a bill, possibly within forty-five days.[77] That proposal was a great deal more than forty-five days in coming.

During the hearings, the completed report on the administration tests was released. It states that while some "safety" criteria could be developed, there was no correlation between safety and the cost of the handgun; the "Saturday night special" was not significantly less safe than other handguns.[78] The administration was left without the criteria desired for its bill.

The *American Rifleman* then editorialized that the quest for safety criteria should be taken from the Treasury Department and conducted in the National Bureau of Standards, in the Commerce Department.[79] Shortly afterward, the magazine reported that the administration bill was ready, and that it would permit the criteria to be developed by the secretary of commerce.[80] No such bill was ever introduced.

The hearings ended in November 1971. The subcommittee took no immediate action on the Bayh bill. Perhaps it felt that any efforts at passage would be futile at that time. Or perhaps it was awaiting the promised administration bill. In any case, one more national tragedy was required to energize Congress. On May 15, 1972, Governor George C. Wallace of Alabama was shot and maimed—with a "Saturday night special." When the subcommittee met in executive session on May 17 to consider the Bayh bill, consensus could not be reached. One congressional staff member has suggested that, although Senator Bayh had the votes to report out the bill, Senator Hruska and other opponents were determined to debate its merits at great length—the subcommittee equivalent of a filibuster.[81] Others believe that

---

* Santarelli was appointed to succeed Jerris Leonard as administrator of LEAA in the spring of 1973. He was ousted in mid-1974 after being quoted as having called for President Nixon's resignation.

Hruska wanted a "Saturday night special" bill reported to the Senate.[82] Whatever the cause of the impasse, it was resolved through a compromise suggested by Senator Philip Hart.[83] The subcommittee would report the Bayh bill to the full committee after adding specific criteria to be developed by Senators Bayh and Hruska. If they could not reach agreement, both versions would be reported to the full committee.[84]

Negotiations proved unsuccessful. Bayh reported his bill to the full committee, incorporating the specific criteria developed by the Treasury Department to regulate imports of handguns under the 1968 act. Hruska chose not to report a bill at that time.

The full Judiciary Committee first met to consider the bill on June 20. At that time, Hruska presented an amendment consistent with administration policy that would replace the "sporting purposes" test with a safety and reliability test to be developed by the secretary of commerce and the chief of army ordnance. Such criteria would not address the problem of eliminating cheaply available and easily concealable handguns but would simply ensure the safety of the user.

The committee put off consideration of the bill until the following week,[85] with a vote on Senator Hruska's substitute scheduled for June 27. During the interim, feverish efforts were made to convince the committee members of the value of Senator Bayh's bill. Numerous staff memoranda were distributed explaining the differences between the Bayh and Hruska bills, and the deficiencies of the latter.*

When the subcommittee reconvened, Senator Sam Ervin, who is always influential on such matters, announced that he had

---

* The Bayh bill, which Hruska had criticized as being too subjective and leaving too much to the discretion of the secretary of the treasury, now incorporated very specific criteria. The Hruska bill, on the other hand, left the development of such criteria to the secretary and included such vague phrases as standards "appropriate for the particular model" and safety and reliability for "normal usage." The Hruska bill also permitted the importation of certain classes of military surplus guns, formerly prohibited. It set up a new testing system, under licensed testing facilities, which would be more complex than the existing system, and possibly very costly.

studied both bills in depth and had decided to support the Bayh bill.[86] From that point on, passage was almost assured. Hruska's amendment was defeated, five to nine. Amendments calling for registration and licensing offered by Senator Kennedy were also defeated. The final vote was twelve to two to report the Bayh bill, with only Senators Eastland and McClellan dissenting.[87]

The fate of the legislation on the floor of the Senate was far from certain. On August 3, 1972, the NRA gave the lie to its claim that members of Congress are not directly contacted by the organization. The NRA addressed a letter to all senators expressing its strong opposition to the bill.[88] (This legislation was, of course, very similar to that earlier *proposed* in the *American Rifleman.*) The NRA apparently also got in touch with senators individually the weekend before consideration of the measure.[89]

On the Friday prior to Senate deliberation on the bill, the subcommittee staff decided to brief a member of each senator's staff about the Bayh bill. As the legislation was being debated on the floor, three subcommittee staff members remained with Bayh to help him deal with the issues; three other staff persons stayed on the telephone. As each amendment to the act was brought up for debate, the subcommittee staff would contact the staff of other senators to supply information about the amendment.

In addition to the NRA and the National Council for a Responsible Firearms Policy, a new group had entered the fray by the time the bill came to the floor: a coalition of thirty-three groups under the leadership of the Americans for Democratic Action, including labor unions, the American Civil Liberties Union, Common Cause, the American Friends Service Committee, and the National Council of Churches.[90] None of these groups would individually have made gun control its top priority, but the formation of a coalition permitted the expression of support without detracting from the other concerns of the organizations. An amendment by Senator Hart to prohibit the possession of handguns by all civilians except licensed pistol clubs, and one by Senator Kennedy calling for forms of licensing or registration, were defeated. Finally, Senator Theodore F. Stevens (R.,Alaska) offered an amendment similar to Hruska's, substituting a safety and reliability test for the existing criteria in the Bayh bill. This, the crucial vote, was not nearly as close as some had feared: the amendment was defeated, thirty-five–fifty-seven. The Handgun Control Act of 1972 was then passed by the Senate, sixty-eight–twenty-five, and sent to the House.

During the entire period that the Senate Judiciary Committee was struggling with the Bayh bill, the House Judiciary Committee waited. Chairman Emanuel Celler introduced legislation stronger than Bayh's bill but did not direct his committee to take any action. The staff, however, wrote letters to police around the country to assess the support for the legislation. The committee was apparently reluctant to bring gun control before the House for fear that existing legislation would be weakened rather than strengthened.[91] Finally, in late June 1972, Celler's own Subcommittee No. 5 held hearings on gun control.[92] Following the hearings, however, the subcommittee did not push the legislation, even though there was sufficient support to have the bill reported out of subcommittee.[93] One aide justified this inaction by asserting that the Senate would not pass House-initiated legislation in the criminal field; he explained that the committee was waiting because the Senate would circumscribe the field within which the House could act.[94] Finally, in late summer, the Bayh bill was referred to the House Judiciary Committee.

The "Saturday night special" lives. The Bayh bill was rapidly reported out of House Judiciary Subcommittee No. 5 on a vote of five to four.[95] Congressmen Celler, McCulloch, Jacobs, Mikva, and McClory supported the Bayh bill, and Brooks, Abourezk, Hungate, and Hutchinson were opposed. It died in the full committee, however, when the Ninety-second Congress expired.

Waiting for the Next Shot

The arduous journey of gun-control legislation through Congress demonstrates the ease with which a well-organized lobby can create a facade of power and transform the facade into reality, exercising effective veto power over urgent reforms. Congressional inertia and the lack of effectively organized and well-financed countergroups strengthen this veto power.

Intensity of public opinion is undoubtedly a valid criterion for legislators to use in determining their votes. Indeed, the ability of an intense minority to protect its vital interests is a *sine qua non* of a meaningful pluralism. Nevertheless, a majority that is seriously concerned by an issue, but unable to give it first priority, must create *ad hoc* coalitions of groups whose main concerns lie elsewhere. If such coalitions fail to act, control by the intense minority will be assured, except when Congress hastily responds to crisis—a response that is generally too little and too late.

Finally, the history of the "Saturday night special" should suggest to the House Judiciary Committee the dangers of waiting for Senate action. Perhaps if Subcommittee No. 5 had reported stronger gun-control legislation earlier, and had attempted to educate the full committee and the House to the urgent need for action, the full committee would have been ready to accept, as a compromise, the Bayh bill. It did not, and the "Saturday night special" still flourishes.

In late January 1973, shortly after the Ninety-third Congress convened, Senator John Stennis of Mississippi, chairman of the Senate Armed Services Committee and one of the most senior members of the Senate, was shot and seriously wounded—with a handgun—by two young men in front of his Washington, D.C., home. The response of Congress suggests that a decade of assassinations has dulled its ability to respond decisively to such events, much less exercise vigorous initiative and leadership. The *Washington Post* captured the lethargy of the moment:

> In the Congress, much of the thought [on gun control] is also too narrow. Sen. Hugh Scott, the leader of the President's party in the Senate, commented that the Stennis shooting "does highlight the fact that Washington is a very dangerous city in which to live." Around 10,000 Americans are murdered every year by gunfire and thousands more take their own lives with firearms or are wounded in accidents

involving guns. Until we begin to understand that it is the United States in which it is dangerous to live, we are not apt to make Washington or any place else very much safer for us all.[96]

The Ninety-third Congress has not altered this dour prognosis. The subcommittee chairman has remained conspicuously silent. Up for reelection in gun-loving Indiana in 1974, Bayh did not reintroduce his "Saturday night special" bill or even hold hearings on gun control during the Ninety-third Congress. Senator Kennedy reintroduced his registration and licensing bill, while Senator Hart reintroduced his measure to prohibit civilian possession of most handguns. Senator Stevenson has also reintroduced a bill combining registration with prohibition of certain handguns, and Senator McClure has introduced a bill to repeal the 1968 act. Congressman Pepper has introduced a measure similar to the Bayh bill. Congressman John D. Dingell (D., Mich.) has taken a novel approach: his bill would ban handguns that melt below a certain temperature, effectively eliminating the cheaper guns.

Action on these bills, however, appears unlikely: with no legislative focus and with Bayh busily mending fences back home, the loose coalition of private organizations that were active toward the end of the Ninety-second Congress appears to have disintegrated. A newly formed *ad hoc* group of House members spearheaded by Michael J. Harrington (D., Mass.), are planning to lobby for reform. They have new ammunition—an August 1973 report of the National Advisory Commission on Criminal Justice Standards and Goals that calls for the total banning of handguns.

Six months after the Stennis shooting, the *Washington Post* reviewed the bold pledges of early action on handgun legislation by President Nixon and others, noting that "so far, nothing has happened on this score from Congress, and nothing more has been heard from President Nixon on the subject." The editorial concluded:

> To be sure, six months isn't a long time in the legislative process. But experience suggests that it's enough time for

some 5,000 Americans to be murdered by gunfire and for thousands more to be wounded in gun accidents. In a real sense, the cause of sound gun controls would be better served if public officials would forego these empty statements about "senseless shootings" and "tragic events" each time one of the victims happens to be someone a lot of people know. This would at least spare us the false hopes raised by these false promises. Only when public officials come to realize that the same senseless tragedies are occurring every day to ordinary people are we likely to see the enactment of effective controls on deadly weapons.[97]

STAFF WORK AND HEARINGS

The majority staff of the Subcommittee to Investigate Juvenile Delinquency researched and drafted most of the legislation considered by the subcommittee. The minority and majority staff cooperate well, frequently achieving a truly bipartisan effort. According to the minority counsel, the majority is accommodating in the development of witness lists and in the drafting of bills.[98]

The subcommittee's openness to outside sources of information, its careful preparation for hearings, and extensive oversight activities are notable in a Congress where these practices are unfortunately the exception rather than the rule. The subcommittee draws from a number of sources in developing bills—particularly various nongovernmental groups interested in the areas of its jurisdiction,*—seeking opinions, leads, additional contacts, and data from them. Figures on the expenditures of LEAA in the juvenile delinquency field, for example, were supplied by the National Council on Crime and Delinquency. These figures proved to be more detailed and better suited for analysis than

---

* Among the most important of these are the National Council on Crime and Delinquency, the National Council of Juvenile Court Judges, the American Parents Committee, the YMCA, the YWCA, the National Council of Churches, and the National Council for a Responsible Firearms Policy.

those supplied by the agency itself. Drafts of legislation are sometimes circulated among groups for comments.[99] The subcommittee also appears willing to seek information directly from unconventional (for Congress) sources. In February 1972, for example, Senator Bayh and staff members (other subcommittee members had been invited) traveled to California to view treatment programs for barbiturate addicts and to talk to the addicts themselves in closed sessions.[100]

The original impetus for some of the legislation developed by the subcommittee comes from outside groups, as in the case of the Runaway Youth Act, which would provide $10 million in grants for facilities established to assist runaway youths. In this case, a number of houses for runaway youths contacted the committee to stress the need for such legislation.* Other legislation has grown out of information disclosed at hearings, as in the hearings on YDDPA, in which the subcommittee learned of the deficiencies of the Juvenile Delinquency Prevention and Control Act and as a result developed new, more comprehensive legislation.

Substantial research by the subcommittee staff prior to the drafting of legislation and the holding of hearings has two distinct advantages. A record is developed on the specific legislation being considered, so that other senators and their staffs may more effectively evaluate the bill, and the needs of many groups unable to attend the hearings receive consideration.

The subcommittee staff makes the same extensive use of outside groups in structuring hearings. At least twelve witnesses have represented individual "projects," such as runaway houses and halfway houses, dealing with juvenile delinquency or drug abuse. The subcommittee also seeks to hear from those directly affected by its legislation: twenty present or former juvenile delinquents or drug abusers appeared before the subcommittee as witnesses. This allows hearings to be used to perfect a bill, to

---

* The measure passed the Senate in the 92nd Congress, but the House did not act. It has passed the Senate again in the 93rd Congress.

accommodate criticisms directed at specific methods embodied in legislation, and to resolve basic policy issues.

Hearings are most often used to educate the public or the senators themselves on particular legislation. The deficiencies of present federal programs, the runaway youth problem, and domestic production of "Saturday night specials" are examples. Because the subcommittee staff is already steeped in the various dimensions of the problem, the draft legislation reflects this sophistication.

Education of the public is often advanced by the subcommittee's confrontation of executive agencies at the public hearings. This confrontation serves an oversight function as well. The hearings on the extensions of the Juvenile Delinquency Prevention and Control Act, for example, prompted some improvement in the operations of YDDPA, and the hearings on amphetamines directly affected FDA policy decisions.

The subcommittee often confronts agency policy and achieves public education through nonlegislative hearings. Neither the second set of hearings on amphetamines nor the first investigations into the role of the federal government in the juvenile delinquency field involved any proposed legislation. Hearings on juvenile confinement institutions served to publicize the present state of juvenile corrections, as well as to apprise the subcommittee of some of the areas in which legislation was most needed.[101]

The subcommittee has exercised some oversight of drug company compliance with the drug-abuse laws. The staff, occasionally accompanied by Senator Bayh, occasionally visits the companies to view their procedures.

These efforts at careful drafting and oversight are shared by few other Judiciary subcommittees, particularly in the criminal law field. The failures of the Subcommittee on Criminal Laws and Procedures and the House subcommittees to identify the defects in the administration of LEAA, the lack of serious agency oversight activities by those subcommittees (except for Subcommittee No. 4 with respect to civil rights), and the inadequate oversight of the Bureau of Prisons by the House subcommittee are examples of subcommittee derelictions in the criminal justice field which only serve to underscore the relative effectiveness and conscientious performance of the Subcommittee to Investigate Juvenile Delinquency.

There are still improvements to be made in the juvenile delinquency area. The subcommittee might seek to expand its sources of information by developing an advisory committee of young people, at least a majority of whom would be former delinquents, although it must be conceded that motivating them and bringing them together on any regular basis would not be easy.

The subcommittee might also increase the flow of unsolicited information, as well as keep members informed on the many staff investigations, by preparing a periodic staff newsletter to be distributed to members and to organizations and individuals with an interest in the subcommittee work. Such a technique is used successfully by the Subcommittee on Constitutional Rights.

14

Corrections:
The Legacy of Attica

It is no accident that prison reform became one of the new pre-occupations of the Judiciary committees in the Ninety-second Congress. The war that raged for days between inmates at the state penitentiary in Attica, New York, and prison officials in September 1971 captured the fickle and fleeting attention of the American public as only a natural or human disaster can. The nearly forty deaths at Attica, the dramatic presentation of the events on national television each night, the political recrimina-tions that preceded and followed the battle, and the riots that soon erupted in other penal institutions meant that America had christened a new "crisis."

The tensions that produced Attica were ancient and chronic, and the tragic result surprised no one familiar with prison condi-

NOTE: This chapter was prepared by Peter H. Schuck and Michael E. Ward.

tions. Yet few in Congress, and even fewer members of Judiciary, had taken much notice until Attica made prison reform a front-page issue. While Subcommittee No. 3 had held hearings on corrections practices in May and June of 1971, that had been a rather isolated event. During the Ninety-first Congress, for example, the entire field of corrections policy did not even merit a separate heading in the index of the House Judiciary Committee calendar, and only a few corrections bills were to be found under other headings. Between January and September 9, 1971 (the date of the Attica uprising), a total of 3 bills, with a total of 43 sponsors, were referred to Subcommittee No. 3. In the four months following Attica, 4 bills with a total of 129 sponsors were referred to the subcommittee. Within a year, 19 corrections bills had been referred. Of the 111 bills pertaining to criminal justice introduced in the House since January 1971, 93 were submitted after the disturbances at Attica.

Attica was not the only reason for increased congressional interest. In the late 1960s, several commissions dealt with the subject of prison reform. Chief Justice Warren E. Burger and Attorney General John Mitchell expressed concern over the mounting problems in the nation's prisons. Litigation in federal courts has also begun to focus on the problems of prisoners. Until Attica, however, most recommendations concerning prison reform were verbal pronouncements, not legislative or regulatory actions. As in so many policy areas, only crisis could make Congress act.

SENATE SUBCOMMITTEE ON NATIONAL PENITENTIARIES

The Senate Judiciary Subcommittee on National Penitentiaries was created in 1948, but existed in name only; prior to 1960, it had no legislative jurisdiction and operated on an annual budget of less than $3,000. Subcommittee funds were used primarily to finance trips by senators to penitentiaries. Prior to 1969, the Subcommittee employed no professional staff whatsoever. Appropriations did not increase substantially until after Senator Quentin Burdick became subcommittee chairman in 1969. In the Ninety-first Congress, the subcommittee received an authorization of $40,000. During the Ninety-second Congress, its budget more than tripled, reaching $134,800; in the Ninety-third, it will reach $167,000. If there is a bright side to Attica, it must be the increased public concern about corrections policy that this growth manifests.

Yet the subcommittee's power remains decidedly limited. Constitutionally, Congress can legislate directly only in matters concerning the federal prison system, administered by the Bureau of Prisons,* and federal grants to state corrections systems are primarily administered by the ever-expanding Law Enforcement Assistance Administration, whose programs fall under the jurisdiction of Senator McClellan's Subcommittee on Criminal Laws and Procedures. Amendments to LEAA programs are therefore sent to that subcommittee instead of to the National Penitentiaries Subcommittee. "LEAA is simply too big for us to compete with," says one Burdick aide, "and the result is that corrections policy tends to be lumped together with law enforcement programs. The special problems associated with corrections policy receive very little attention." Appropriations for the Bureau of Prisons and for grant for state corrections programs are buried in the appropriations for State, Justice, Commerce, and related agencies, thus lowering their visibility still further.

Quentin Burdick is a lawyer and a former Republican who switched party affiliation in 1946, later becoming the first Democratic member of Congress in North Dakota's sixty-nine-year history, winning the 1972 election by a margin of 22 percent.[1] Burdick represents a primarily agricultural state whose population is 56 percent rural, and only four percent black—a

---

* The subcommittee can conduct oversight of local and state penal systems that are under contract to the federal government to house federal prisoners. The eight hundred institutions presently under federal jurisdiction are required to meet minimum federal standards.

constituency that is decidedly underrepresented in the U.S. prison population.

Burdick became interested in corrections policy while a member, but before becoming chairman, of the National Penitentiaries Subcommittee. He informed himself about prison problems through personal visits to penitentiaries and instructed Jim Meeker, then his administrative assistant and now the subcommittee staff director, to answer letters received from prisoners by the subcommittee. Burdick's frequent visits to penal institutions, both federal and state,* and his successful escalation of subcommittee appropriations, manifest his enthusiastic leadership in the area of corrections. He introduced much new legislation concerning penitentiaries (four bills during the Ninety-second Congress) and has chaired numerous hearings since taking control of the subcommittee in 1969.

By his own assessment,[2] Burdick pursues prison reforms in an unobtrusive, incremental manner, shunning the controversy and publicity that envelop more politically ambitious members of Congress. Lacking higher political goals, Burdick need not cultivate the national media and large interest groups with dramatic and controversial actions. One observer believes that Burdick's deliberate, piecemeal, almost plodding approach reflects a passive nature.[3] Meeker sees Burdick's low-key style as idiosyncratic but also effective.[4] A Burdick bill in the Ninety-first Congress, for example, which created a system of halfway houses to provide community treatment for federal prisoners had, by April 1974, spawned over eighty such facilities.

Subcommittee members take an interest in current prison conditions to varying degrees. During the Ninety-second Congress, Chairman Burdick introduced four bills in the corrections area, while Senator Bayh introduced three. Senator Cook was responsible for three, Senator Mathias for two, and Senator Hart, in part, for four. According to Meeker, Hart also allocates valuable

---

* He has now visited every federal institution, except for two newly constructed ones.

staff resources to the subcommittee's work in the person of his aide, Burton Wides.

As is common in the Senate, members' attendance at hearings is sporadic. Burdick attends all sessions, the only member to do so. The only hearings with high attendance rates were those at which famous—or infamous—personalities, such as James Hoffa and Johnny Cash, testified.* Early in the Ninety-second Congress, the subcommittee held crucial oversight hearings regarding the controversial so-called Ten-Year Plan of the Bureau of Prisons. The plan raised for consideration the fundamental policies and future directions of the Bureau of Prisons, yet only Senators Burdick and Mathias attended.⁵

Professional staff was not hired by the Subcommittee on National Penitentiaries until 1970, when Sheldon Krantz, an authority on correctional justice, was hired as a consultant. Four staff people currently work for the subcommittee. Meeker, who was appointed staff director in 1971, has a background in journalism. He worked as a reporter for a Fargo, North Dakota, newspaper and taught part-time at the Pennsylvania State University School of Journalism.⁶ Meeker hired an assistant in May 1972. The majority staff now includes one lawyer, and there is one minority counsel.†

Legislation and Input

The keystone of the subcommittee's reform program is a series of bills to modify the parole system for federal prisoners. The most important of these bills was introduced by Burdick in the Ninety-second Congress, during which hearings were held. Entitled the Parole Commission Act, the bill (S.1463 in the Ninety-third

* Hoffa testified before the subcommittee in June 1972 and Cash appeared in July of the same year.

† Ron Meredith, who was minority counsel during the last half of the 92nd Congress, works closely with the majority staff in drafting legislation. At the close of the 92nd Congress, he left his position on the subcommittee to become Cook's legislative assistant. Robert Fearing, Senator Cook's former legislative assistant, is now minority counsel.

Congress) would replace the existing Parole Board with a Parole Commission composed of commissioners and a national appeals board. The bill would require procedural safeguards for all prisoners with respect to both parole determination and parole revocation, such as formal hearings, access to certain documents, written justifications for commission decisions, and the right to an "advocate" (but not necessarily an attorney). The subcommittee approved the bill in May 1974, but Senator McClellan has delayed full committee action, insisting that the president have the power to designate the appeals board and that initial decisions on parole cases be made by the commissioners, who would be political appointees, rather than by hearing examiners, who would be career civil servants.

The subcommittee's pretrial diversion bill (S.798 in the Ninety-third Congress) would authorize the Bureau of Prisons to implement a program for channeling certain persons facing minor criminal charges to employment, educational, and other alternatives possibly leading to dismissal of the charges. Modeled on the Manhattan Court Employment Project and Project Crossroads in the District of Columbia, the bill had widespread support, particularly after the Department of Justice dropped its insistence that participants in the program must have pleaded guilty prior to diversion. S.798 passed the Senate unanimously in October 1973, after hearings in July 1972 and March 1973. The House Judiciary Subcommittee on Courts, Civil Liberties, and the Administration of Justice held hearings on pretrial diversion legislation in February 1974.

The Federal Prisoners Furlough Act, broadening the reasons for which federal prisoners can be granted furloughs, was reported by the subcommittee, passed by both houses, and signed into law in January 1974. It permits furloughs in order to establish or reestablish family and community ties and for any other reasons in the public interest. This bill won the support of the Bureau of Prisons and the American Bar Association.

Hearings were held by the subcommittee during the Ninety-second Congress on a criminal records bill. Burdick, its principal sponsor, reintroduced it as S.1308 in the Ninety-third Congress. Despite Meeker's protests, Chairman Eastland referred it to two other subcommittees—Criminal Laws and Procedures and Constitutional Rights. After McClellan and Ervin took opposing views on this bill, Senator Hruska sided with Ervin and McClellan lost control of the bill. If enacted, it would greatly restrict the use of arrest or indictment records that did not result in a conviction, and would permit a one-time federal offender to nullify his criminal record after serving his sentence and completing a period of parole or probation. The bill would permit the court to determine as a matter of discretion whether nullification of the record would serve the public interest, and the attorney general could challenge this determination. The bill would allow the use of such records, however, in future court proceedings, in law enforcement investigations, and in specified classes of employment situations involving security risks.*

Ideas for legislation, and supporting data, come to the subcommittee from several sources. Some of the provisions of the criminal records bill, for example, were suggested by a presidential task force on prisoner rehabilitation and by the American Bar Association. The staff also drew upon information from the Department of Justice and the American Civil Liberties Union in order to develop a workable procedure acceptable to a broad spectrum of interests.[7]

In the case of the pretrial diversion bill, Meeker researched the policy questions with the assistance of the Library of Congress, the American Bar Association, and the Chamber of Commerce, and drafted the basic bill. Final drafting was done with the assistance of the Office of the Senate Legislative Counsel,[8] which performs drafting services for Senate subcommittees and members upon request.

The subcommittee also routinely acquires information from the American Correctional Association, the National Council on Crime and Delinquency, and the Bureau of Prisons. According

---

* This and related bills are discussed in Chapter 8.

to Justis Freimund of the National Council on Crime and Delinquency, the subcommittee staff often solicits opinions on existing bills but seldom contacts the council for suggestions about new areas for legislation.[9] Finally, Burdick and Meeker both observe that prisoner mail has also been particularly valuable in determining areas of study.[10]

The subcommittee has consistently drawn for hearings upon a wide range of witnesses with a great variety of backgrounds, including current and former inmates and staff of experimental corrections projects. The hearings during the summer of 1972, for example, involved ten former inmates.

Oversight—The Subtle Approach

The National Penitentiaries Subcommittee conducts little regular or formal oversight of the Bureau of Prisons, in part because the bureau enjoys a permanent authorization. Indeed, hearings on bureau operations have been held only three times since the subcommittee's inception in 1948: in 1964, when James Bennett was director of the bureau; in 1971, and in 1972. In 1971, the subcommittee investigated the "Ten Year Plan" that the bureau had prepared in response to a presidential request. The plan directed itself to the preparation of federal offenders for reintegration into society, maintenance and custodial care of federal offenders, and upgrading the level of correctional practices.[11] According to the plan, only the most hardened criminals would be imprisoned. Actual methods to implement the plan, however, were not discussed during the hearings.

Sometimes, the mere introduction of a bill has an effect on the bureau. In 1972, ranking minority member Cook, who favors more oversight of the bureau,[12] requested hearings on an administration bill that provided the occasion for limited oversight. The legislation introduced by Senator Burdick established pensions for correctional employees and set minimum and maximum age limits for their hiring. At the time the bill was introduced, the average age of prisoners was twenty-eight, while the average hiring age of corrections personnel was thirty-five. The American

Federation of Government Employees initially objected to the inclusion of age limits. The bill was not reported out of the subcommittee because, according to Cook, the combined opposition of the American Federation of Government Employees and the Department of Justice (because of the pensions) made passage unlikely.[13] Since then, the Bureau of Prisons has voluntarily raised the average age of its employees to within the limits set by Burdick's proposal.

Burdick and Meeker conduct informal oversight of the bureau through personal communications with bureau officials. Burdick utilizes a characteristically subtle approach in dealing with the bureau, seeking to alter its policies through informal conversations with its officials, and resorting to hearings only when absolutely necessary. The subcommittee staff also attends some policy-making meetings held within the bureau.

Burdick's lack of urgency concerning formal oversight has much to do with his confidence in Norman Carlson, the bureau's director. According to Meeker, "Carlson is very enlightened, given the constraints which he operates under. He is way ahead of the public even if he is not as liberal as some of the reformers. We feel he ought to be supported."

The subcommittee's sympathy for Carlson's problems extends to the bureau's "Ten Year Plan," its blueprint for the future. "Sure it contained plans for constructing and remodeling facilities, which the liberals didn't like," notes Meeker, "but it also stressed basic skills, vocational education, replacement of penitentiaries with smaller facilities, and greater program resources. The bureau feels that so long as the courts continue to send them prisoners, they must house them. It's not their job to convince the courts not to lock people up." Whether it is the bureau's job to be more candid and forceful with *Congress* about the failures of its "rehabilitation" programs, however, does not seem to be an issue of great concern to the subcommittee.

Mail from prisoners offers a unique and effective method of maintaining oversight of federal and state penal institutions as well as providing a source of ideas for legislation. The subcommittee receives, on the average, fifty pieces of mail a week from prisoners. When a letter cites a problem that must be handled legally, the staff refers it to state ACLU offices or other public-defender projects dealing with prison problems. When a problem relates to the Bureau of Prisons, it is referred directly to bureau officials. After a reply is received from the bureau, the case is further analyzed by the subcommittee staff. In most cases, problems are resolved directly by the bureau's intervention with officials at the institution in question. If the inmate presents a better explanation of the facts than does the bureau after the initial interchange, the staff may again review the case.[14] In any event, staff members rely on the explanation provided by the bureau; they do not conduct independent investigations.

Chairman Burdick, ranking minority member Cook, and subcommittee staff members personally visit prisons in order to gather information and conduct on-the-spot oversight. However, prison officials are notified in advance of all visits. According to Meeker, subcommittee members and staff have never been denied access to any parts of the prison or to any inmates or prison staff.

Burdick believes that his subcommittee has been successful in making the need for prison reform a part of the conventional wisdom among liberals and conservatives alike. He points with pride to the unanimous Senate approval of the pretrial diversion bill, the quadrupling of the subcommittee's budget in only five years, the expansion of the Bureau of Prisons programs and budget, and the new interest of the blue-ribbon American Bar Association and Chamber of Commerce in corrections legislation. Presumably, the better evidence of success—a decline in recidivism rates—lies somewhat farther in the dim future, well beyond the almost commonplace inmate insurrections of the 1970s.

CORRECTIONS IN THE HOUSE COMMITTEE

During the Ninety-second Congress, Subcommittee No. 3, chaired by Robert Kastenmeier of Wisconsin, had jurisdiction over patents, trademarks, copyrights, and revision of laws. Like all other subcommittees, however, it also possessed "general jurisdiction over judiciary bills as assigned," a device by which, as we have seen, former full-committee chairman Emanuel Celler kept the power to refer important legislation as he saw fit. It is through this general jurisdiction that Subcommittee No. 3 concentrated much of its efforts in the Ninety-second Congress on corrections legislation. In October 1971, its professional staff of one (Herbert Fuchs) was expanded with the addition of a special counsel, Howard Eglit, to concentrate on corrections matters. In the Ninety-third Congress, Subcommittee No. 3 became the Subcommittee on Courts, Civil Liberties, and the Administration of Justice, with jurisdiction over a variety of subjects, including patents, trademarks, and copyrights, criminal procedure, certain constitutional amendments, amnesty, capital punishment, and corrections. Eglit left the subcommittee during 1973* and no special counsel for corrections was named to replace him. The professional staff was expanded to three counsel, however, and all perform some corrections work. Corrections now consumes approximately one-third of the staff's time, and is the largest single area of subcommittee activity.[15]

Kastenmeier takes his subcommittee responsibilities seriously. During the Ninety-second Congress, he attended all subcommittee meetings and hearings, while failing to attend seven meetings of his other committee, Interior and Insular Affairs. Most other members are quite active in terms of attendance and participation at subcommittee meetings, particularly Tom Railsback, the ranking minority member. The most inactive member is Charles W. Sandman, Jr., who ran (unsuccessfully) for governor of New Jersey in 1973. The subcommittee is unusually unified, often cosponsoring legislation as a group and/or passing measures out of subcommittee unanimously. It was the only Judiciary subcommittee to hold open markup sessions in the Ninety-second Congress.

During the Ninety-second Congress, the subcommittee con-

---

* He now works for the American Civil Liberties Union in Chicago.

centrated its legislative efforts on parole reform, holding twenty days of hearings on the subject.[16] Howard Eglit explained this preoccupation with parole on the ground that inmates who wrote to the subcommittee, as well as correctional reformers, particularly criticized the federal parole system. Since it had not been investigated for at least forty years, the system was also considered by many subcommittee members to be a high priority. According to Eglit, parole was regarded as a relatively "safe" area to pursue.[17] Although Kastenmeier regarded the parole issue as important, and Tom Railsback believed the subcommittee's parole legislation, which would have made parole for federal prisoners automatic unless an independent parole board could justify denial of parole, was the most important work of the subcommittee,[18] the bill (H.R.16276) was never reported out of the full Judiciary Committee.

Until impeachment intruded, the Ninety-third Congress was somewhat more fruitful for the subcommittee; it has held almost twice as many days of hearings on corrections as in the previous Congress. Not much legislation has been reported, however. The Parole Reorganization Act (H.R.13826), similar to the Senate bill, was still pending in the subcommittee in July 1974, despite close consultation with Meeker of the Senate subcommittee staff and with the existing Federal Parole Board.

In January 1974 the subcommittee heard testimony on a series of bills promoted by Kastenmeier which would prevent states from denying most ex-offenders the right to vote in federal elections. After numerous changes were made, a clean bill (H.R. 9020) was prepared. In February 1974 the subcommittee finally held hearings on pretrial diversion legislation (H.R.9007), a related bill having already passed the Senate unanimously months earlier. Unlike the Senate-passed pretrial diversion bill, Congressman Railsback's measure would entrust administration of the program only to the U.S. Probation Service. Railsback has also sponsored a bill (H.R.9433) to reform the Federal Prison Industries and provide more meaningful vocational training opportunities. As of July 1974 each of these bills was still pending in the subcommittee.

The legislative record is not wholly barren. The Federal Prisoners Furlough Act, enacted in late December 1973,[19] was originally a Kastenmeier bill and resulted from hearings in July 1973. The Senate approved the measure, which greatly liberalizes the availability of furloughs, without holding hearings of its own.

Oversight

In the past, the subcommittee exercised little systematic oversight of the sprawling federal prison system. To help fill this void, Railsback has pressed for annual appearances before the subcommittee by the director of the Bureau of Prisons to report and answer questions. In April 1974, no hearings had ever been held on the Bureau's "Ten Year Plan," already several years old.

An important exception to the lack of oversight, however, was the subcommittee's January 1974 report on the bureau's Special Treatment and Rehabilitative Training (START) Program.[20] As a result of more than two hundred letters from inmates of Leavenworth Penitentiary and the Medical Center for Federal Prisoners in Springfield, Missouri, complaining about the conditions at Leavenworth and the START program at Springfield, the subcommittee personally visited the facilities in October 1973. Although critical of many of Leavenworth's shortcomings, including crowded cells, persistent homosexual rapes, and primitive vocational training, the subcommittee report raised particularly pointed questions about the START program. An extremely controversial innovation, START is an involuntary "behavior modification" program which is intended as a forerunner of future such experiments in federal facilities and which is directed at the most refractory inmates. The subcommittee report described START:

> The program description of START issued by the Federal Bureau of Prisons states that the program is based on a system of rewards. An inmate begins at the most severe level of

incarceration and from there his conditions can improve through rewards as he moves upward through eight different levels of confinement. The progress of an inmate is supposed to depend on his willingness to adjust his behavior to the rules of the program. At the first level the inmate is allowed out of his cell two hours a week for exercise and twice for showers. The rest of the week he sits in a cell 6-by-10 feet behind a steel door with a small window. The window can be covered with paper blocking all light by the staff if it so desires. In one case an inmate alleged his window was covered for 42 straight days. When asked about this allegation, the staff said it was for no longer than two weeks but that the records concerning this could not be located at the time of our visit. All the inmates supported the 42 day version as being the truth. After 20 consecutive "good days" the inmate moves to the second level. At this level the inmate is allowed to work three hours a day, eat meals out of his cell and have one and one-half hours of recreation a day. Gradually, the inmate is allowed more privileges until he is graduated from the program and returned to the general population of the penitentiary.

Of the 22 admissions to START since September 1972, only two had graduated to open population at the time of our visit. Two more were adjudged psychotic and sent to a mental ward, two finished their sentence and were released and four were removed from the program early, either because they were too disruptive or for other reasons. Of the remaining prisoners in the program, nearly one half of them were refusing to cooperate at the time of our visit. The Subcommittee met with the inmates who were still in the program in a group, and individually. To the man, the inmates distrusted and were suspicious of the program. They felt that even if they did graduate that they will be singled out for retribution by other inmates because of the stigma of having been associated with a program that is hated and feared throughout the Federal prison system.[21]

The subcommittee noted that the START program raised "serious constitutional questions," was susceptible to abuse, and did not appear to work, and it announced its intention to hold a public hearing on the program.[22] One week before the hearing was to have been held, the bureau discontinued START. While the bureau cited "economic reasons" for the program's demise, the subcommittee staff is convinced that its oversight, together with an ACLU lawsuit challenging the program, constituted START's *coup de grâce.*

The START imbroglio was unusual for the subcommittee. More typically, the staff communicates with the bureau on a regular basis over a wide range of corrections issues, from the handling of prisoner mail to the transfer of inmates to community-based facilities. The staff receives some seventy-five letters from prisoners, corrections officials, guards, and others.

Replies to all such letters are drafted and forwarded to Kastenmeier for his signature. When a legal problem arises, the prisoner is referred to an attorney in his area, often a government or ACLU lawyer who has demonstrated expertise in dealing with prisoners in the past.[23]

In problems pertaining to the federal prison system, the staff may contact the information officer of the Bureau of Prisons. The bureau then reviews the problem and advises the staff as to whether or not the situation can be rectified. Investigations are rarely pursued further by the subcommittee staff.

As in the Leavenworth tour, congressional visits to federal and state prisons are announced well before the visit takes place. Subcommittee members talk privately with groups of prisoners, guards, and administrators in an effort to compensate for the prearrangement.

Input

The number of outside groups contributing expertise and legislative ideas to the subcommittee's corrections work is surprisingly small. The National Council on Crime and Delinquency, the American Bar Association, the ACLU National Prison Project, the Center for Correctional Justice, the NAACP Legal Defense Fund, and constitutional law professors are the most important constituency groups. Eglit rarely contacted correctional organizations such as the American Correctional Association or sheriffs' and police chiefs' organizations because these groups did not share his philosophy toward correction, which is highly skeptical concerning the role prisons can play in rehabilitation.[24] Although this bias still informs the subcommittee's work, these groups are invited to testify at hearings.

With the exception of the National Council on Crime and Delinquency, groups seldom approach the staff on their own initiative to offer information or opinions on legislation. Conservative "law and order" groups show very little interest in the subcommittee's activities and play no significant role in influencing the shape of corrections legislation. Comments received after subcommittee hearings, however, are taken into account at the subsequent markup sessions.[25]

Hearings on corrections have frequently been held outside Washington. In selecting witnesses for hearings, the staff tries to ensure that certain groups are represented, including prisoners, litigating attorneys, correctional workers and officials, representatives of organizations in the field, and university faculty members. During the Ninety-second Congress, witnesses were drawn from a wide variety of sources, including individuals involved in the operation of innovative corrections-related projects, who constituted 18 percent of those testifying. Nineteen former or present inmates testified. Controversial defense lawyers such as Fay Stender, George Jackson's attorney, also appeared. The hearings on parole reform involved more than forty witnesses drawn from a broad spectrum. Four former offenders appeared.

The subcommittee seems not to regard publicity as an appropriate legislative weapon. "When Attica erupted," confides one subcommittee aide, "we didn't go up there or play an active role because we didn't want to seem to be publicity-seekers, even though we had held hearings on corrections three months earlier. We let Claude Pepper [chairman of the House Select Committee on Crime] get all the publicity."

Yet the publicity that Attica and other prison insurrections generated during the early 1970s achieved what the Judiciary subcommittees have never even attempted to do. It alerted the American public to the utter failure of traditional corrections policies and to the potential social dynamite that lies behind prison walls. What goes on—and does *not* go on—behind those walls is nicely summarized in the results of a new study released by the Bureau of Prisons in April 1974. One out of every three federal offenders commits a new crime within two years after his release from prison, according to the study, and the recidivism rate is about the same as that reported ten years ago.[26] The director of the Bureau of Prisons, Norman Carlson, managed to extract some pleasure from these grim statistics: "It certainly refutes the charges we keep hearing about a 70 or 80 percent recidivism rate for all prison systems. In the past ten years, the prison population has gotten tougher but the success rate for offenders has improved. I think that says something for corrections at the federal level."[27]

That the chief federal corrections officer can, with some justification, regard such high recidivism rates as "progress" suggests how much remains to be done. For a brief moment—until Attica fades from our collective consciousness—corrections reform may have a potential constituency in America. It remains to be seen whether the Judiciary committees will seize the day or let it pass.

VI

FUTURES

15

Recommendations for Change

One does well to approach the reform of complex organizations with considerable humility. Such organizations are, after all, *institutions,* venerable products of a delicate and often irrational process of historical evolution, social adaptation, and political necessity. And in the case of Congress and its committees, of course, the institution must function in a context in which the very goals and values implicit in any evaluation or recommendation for change are themselves the subject of intense disagreement and conflict.

Nevertheless, to say that institutions such as the Judiciary committees have evolved into distinct and unique forms is not to say that they cannot be improved, at least marginally, by the infusion of "rational" considerations. Similarly, to say that there is wide disagreement over the particular policies that these committees should pursue is not to say that there are no criteria by which they may be fairly evaluated and appropriate changes tentatively

NOTE: This chapter was prepared by Peter H. Schuck, Michael E. Ward, and Dr. Martha Joynt Kumar.

361

suggested. The representative character of congressional committees, the nature of the pluralistic polity for which they legislate,
and the moral imperatives of a democratic society provide certain
minimal standards.

The Judiciary committees should be responsive to as diverse an
assortment of interests, values, and sources of information as possible. They should be capable of acquiring and assimilating a
broad spectrum of information, as well as generating such information by their own initiative, and they should be able to independently evaluate such information without undue reliance
upon its source. The Judiciary committees should operate efficiently, without unnecessary delay, and with a due regard for the
virtues of expertise, flexibility, and innovation. Resources for
legislative functions—funds, staff, analytical capability—should be
commensurate both with their great responsibilities and with
those available to the executive branch. Such resources should
not be squandered on activities whose constitutionality and/or
usefulness is highly dubious. Oversight of executive-branch activities should be vigorous, independent, and systematic. The formal
and informal deliberations of the committee and the reasons for
their actions and inactions should be open to public scrutiny
and accountability. The powers of the full committee and subcommittee chairmen should be great enough to facilitate efficient
operations, but not so great as to negate the broad representative
character of these bodies, and such powers should be circum-
scribed by formally adopted rules.

One may certainly cavil at the formulation of these criteria or
their application in particular cases. Yet one must begin some-
where, and these criteria would almost certainly command the
support of most Americans and of the Congress itself. Nevertheless, this study has demonstrated that the House and Senate
Judiciary Committees, when judged by even these minimal, non-
controversial standards, are seriously deficient in a number of
respects. The following recommendations, then, as well as others
explicit or implicit in the foregoing chapters, are offered in a
constructive spirit and with these modest objectives in mind.

THE SENATE JUDICIARY COMMITTEE

1. Adopt formal rules

The Legislative Reorganization Act of 1970 requires that all standing committees publish rules governing their operations. Only the Senate Judiciary Committee has failed to comply with this mandate.

It is axiomatic that members must know when their committee is to meet, yet executive sessions of the Judiciary Committee, particularly at the end of a session, are often called on only a few hours' notice. Meetings should be scheduled at regular times, as in the House committee, rather than at the chairman's discretion. Procedures should exist whereby a majority of the members may convene meetings under certain conditions. An agenda should be published at least two days before all meetings so that members may prepare for discussion and decision.

Committee rules should also include a time limit on debate to prevent committee filibusters, such as that waged on February 4, 1970, by Senator Strom Thurmond against Birch Bayh's motion to consider the nomination of G. Harrold Carswell to the U.S. Supreme Court. As Thomas Jefferson recognized, a filibuster is designed to enable an intense minority to protect its vital interests against a "lukewarm" majority. There must be limits, however, to its exercise if majority rights are not to be trampled in the process.

The practice of disposing of bills by informal polling of subcommittee opinion, rather than at formal meetings, should be restricted or prohibited. When subcommittees poll on legislation, staff opinion is a much more important factor than it is when subcommittees meet formally. The Immigration and Naturalization Subcommittee has apparently not met as a subcommittee since the 1965 act was approved by it, and important legislation, such as the bill to penalize employers who knowingly hire illegal aliens, has died without subcommittee action as a result.

The absence of formal rules has produced relatively few abuses (with some important exceptions discussed in Chapter 1) because of the generally fair and temperate chairmanship of Senator Eastland. But Judiciary should not have to rely on the good will of its chairman to ensure its equitable and efficient operation.

2. Restructure the procedure for consideration of judicial nominations

In light of the profound importance to our constitutional system of a federal judiciary of the highest quality, the present procedures for disposing of judicial nominations for U.S. district courts and courts of appeals are shockingly inadequate. A permanent subcommittee to consider judicial nominations should replace the *ad hoc* subcommittee appointed by the chairman, which now performs this function so poorly. The permanent subcommittee should be far more representative of the diversity of value systems in the Senate and among the American people.

The committee should reassert its coordinate constitutional role in the confirmation of the president's nominees. In order to accomplish this, the committee must vastly augment its independent investigatory activity with respect to judicial nominees, rather than relying upon the unreasoned, narrowly oriented, and often partisan recommendations of the Justice Department and the American Bar Association. Members should closely scrutinize and interrogate nominees at the confirmation hearings, instead of engaging in the perfunctory, mass-approval rituals that have characterized the committee's performance in the past. Confirmation should be withheld whenever substantial questions are raised concerning the nominee's fitness to serve.

3. Rationalize the procedures for processing private legislation

This recommendation is discussed below in connection with the recommendations for the House Judiciary Committee.

4. Abolish unnecessary subcommittees and scrutinize subcommittee budgets for waste

The Senate Judiciary Committee receives a budget double that of any other Senate committee. Yet, with some notable exceptions (including Antitrust and Monopoly, Juvenile Delinquency,

Separation of Powers, Constitutional Rights, and Administrative Practice and Procedure), Senate Judiciary subcommittees give the taxpayers remarkably little for their money in the form of hearings, public education, legislation, or oversight of executive agencies. If one excludes private bills from consideration, the record of Senate Judiciary is one of monumental inactivity, even by Senate standards.

A serious and critical review of the Judiciary budget is long overdue. One might begin such a review by asking why the Revision and Codification Subcommittee should receive $62,300 in 1973 alone, when it held no hearings, had no legislation referred to it, filed no report with the full committee, and apparently did nothing but provide Senator Ervin with additional personal staff. One might also ask why the Immigration and Naturalization Subcommittee received $473,500 in the Ninety-second Congress, about 60 percent of what the *entire* House committee and its subcommittees received—yet never met, held no hearings, produced no public legislation, and processed only about one-third as much legislation as the House immigration subcommittee.

The Subcommittee on Federal Charters, Holidays, and Celebrations, with an annual budget of $14,500, should be abolished in view of the fact that its legislation is ceremonial and easily handled by a member of the full-committee staff. Numerous observers and senators have advocated the abolition of that wastrel of wastrels—the Internal Security Subcommittee—which holds many lengthy and expensive hearings on the threat to domestic security allegedly posed by left-wing (and occasional right-wing) groups, mostly conducted by the staff counsel, J. G. Sourwine, but reports no legislation. Its budget of $1,152,500 for the Ninety-second Congress could surely be put to better use almost anywhere else.

5. *Increase oversight activities*

The Senate Judiciary Committee, with some notable exceptions (including Administrative Practice and Procedure, Juvenile

Delinquency, and Constitutional Rights), conducts little or no oversight of the bloated federal agencies whose activities it authorizes. The Immigration and Naturalization Service, LEAA, the FBI, the Antitrust Division, and the Civil Rights Division are only some of the agencies of the Justice Department that operate, as we have seen, quite independently of any meaningful surveillance by Senate Judiciary.

The committee should assign to each subcommittee specific responsibility for conducting oversight of particular agencies, and budget should be allocated in part on the basis of subcommittee performance in this area, particularly in view of the paucity of new legislation that Senate Judiciary produces.

6. Improve communications between House and Senate

A Joint Committee on Immigration and Naturalization, without legislative responsibilities, was established in the 1952 Immigration Act, but was abolished by the 1970 Legislative Reorganization Act because it had never met. While the abolition of the joint committee made sense under the circumstances, it also dramatized the existence of an intolerable situation: the widespread lack of communication between the House and Senate Judiciary Committees.

John Holloman III, chief counsel of the Senate Judiciary Committee from 1965 to 1973, noted that in his many years on the Hill, he had *never* been over to the House Judiciary Committee. This is not an unusual situation in the Congress. Members and staff alike develop a loyalty to one chamber and rarely deal with the other, except in conference.

The two Judiciary committees should establish systematic communication with one another in order to facilitate the processing of legislation, maximize investigative resources, and ensure that bills do not die because of poor scheduling or lack of coordination. The two committees do not—and should not—share the same priorities and commitments, but these differences need not preclude improved coordination where possible.

7. *Reorganize jurisdictions over civil rights*

The major failure of the Subcommittee on Constitutional Rights has been its passive, if not hostile, posture toward the civil rights of minority groups and women. Chairman Ervin's ideological predispositions, coupled with the allocation of staff resources to the protection of civil liberties, particularly First Amendment guarantees, suggest that this failure will continue in the future. Accordingly, the Senate or the full Judiciary Committee should remove from the Subcommittee on Constitutional Rights jurisdiction over rights deriving from the equal-protection clause of the Fourteenth Amendment, and from the Thirteenth and Fifteenth Amendments. A new committee or subcommittee should be created with legislative jurisdiction over protection and enforcement of those rights. Such a reform will become increasingly necessary if, as suggested in an earlier chapter, the Subcommittee on Constitutional Rights accepts enlarged responsibilities in the areas of criminal and prisoner rights. In addition to any such reforms, the Judiciary Committee should encourage the Senate Appropriations Committee to use its greater leverage to ensure civil rights compliance by federal agencies.

THE HOUSE JUDICIARY COMMITTEE

1. *Energize the committee*

The House Judiciary Committee in the Ninety-second Congress generally performed as if its legislative duty were simply to process legislation referred to it. The Senate committee takes a much broader view of its functions: not only does it process legislation; it generates and develops many bills of its own. The Senate subcommittees often investigate new areas where little or no legislation has been introduced, while House subcommittees generally do not. The Antitrust and Monopoly Subcommittee in the Senate, for example, developed hearings and legislation on "no-fault" auto insurance. That particular subcommittee investigates perhaps ten major areas in a year, while Subcommittee No. 5 conducted only one major study, on conglomerate mergers, in the last few years.

The Senate Judiciary subcommittees often hold hearings with nonlegislative purposes in mind, such as dealing with what appears to be a recalcitrant, lawless, or inefficient bureau or department. Numerous hearings conducted by the Senate Administrative Practice and Procedure subcommittee, the Separation of Powers subcommittee, the Antitrust and Monopoly subcommittee, and others could provide models for this type of committee activity.

Oversight hearings are desperately needed in the House committee, both to hold agencies more accountable and to augment the committee's information on programing. Such oversight as presently exists is almost always limited to consideration of authorizing legislation, and is rarely done in depth. The only House Judiciary subcommittee consistently discharging oversight responsibilities was Subcommittee No. 4, and those hearings were restricted to civil rights enforcement.

Finally, hearings are needed to dramatize and create public interest in issues requiring the attention of Congress. Again, the Senate Constitutional Rights and Separation of Powers subcommittees can serve as admirable models.

2. Confer more authority upon subcommittee chairmen

Because the jurisdiction of the House Judiciary Committee is so broad, the full-committee chairman cannot possibly administer the committee and still be able to function as a vigorous subcommittee and full-committee chairman. Indeed, Emanuel Celler's desire to control all of the activities of the committee resulted in several incursions by other committees on its jurisdiction.

For subcommittees and their chairmen to function effectively in their assigned legislative areas, they must be allowed to determine, within broad limits, how much money they need, what hearings should be held and how extensive they should be, the number and kind of staff they require, and with whom they can best work. The subcommittees should establish their own procedures and rules, at least to the extent that committee-wide uniformity is not essential.

The full committee should review subcommittee budget requests and operations, but it should presume, in the absence of evidence to the contrary, that the subcommittee knows best what it should be doing. Senator Eastland's dispersion of responsibility to the Senate Judiciary subcommittees provides an excellent operating model for decentralized operations, while avoiding excessive fragmentation.

3 Increase the number of subcommittees and define their jurisdiction

More subcommittees, each with well-defined jurisdictions, are necessary if House Judiciary is to deal effectively with all of the areas within its jurisdiction. Increasing the number of subcommittees would not only permit increased specialization, efficiency, and development of expertise, but would increase the responsibilities and participation of junior members of the committee in subcommittee work. This would probably have the additional benefit, as in Senate Judiciary, of enhancing the prestige of the committee and attracting to it superior members of the House.

The reforms of June 1973 do not go nearly far enough. The subcommittees still have only a very few defined areas for which they are responsible. Matters that are not within these specific areas are ignored unless the chairman refers a particular piece of legislation to a subcommittee. Organized crime, for example, was an area for which no subcommittee had a direct responsibility; hence, none dealt with it. Instead, the House felt obliged to create a Select Committee on Crime to investigate this critical area. Relatively detailed subcommittee jurisdictions would also encourage and permit subcommittees to plan what matters they wish to cover during a Congress; random assignment of bills does not allow this.

Bills within the same subject area should be handled by the same members and staff. Even after the 1973 committee reforms, legislation in the same subject-matter area is often spread among different subcommittees. Thus, for example, no fewer than five subcommittees process crime-related legislation, while three deal with constitutional amendments. Under the circumstances, neither staff nor subcommittees can easily accumulate and exploit subject-matter expertise.

If Judiciary is to be an attractive assignment for House members, it is essential that no one subcommittee monopolize the interesting work referred by the full committee. In the Ninety-second Congress, Subcommittee No. 5 received almost all of the most important bills, and junior members could not serve on it until they had served with the committee for some time. As a result, the Judiciary Committee is not regarded as good an assignment in the House as it is in the Senate. The effect of this fact upon the quality of House Judiciary's work and morale is undoubtedly substantial.

The redefinition of subcommittee jurisdictions in June 1973 did not adequately specify the oversight functions for each subcommittee. House Judiciary seldom holds oversight hearings, in part because its subcommittees are rarely assigned specific responsibility for overseeing particular agencies.

4. Rationalize the procedures for processing private legislation

The different procedures governing the processing of private bills by the Senate and House subcommittees, coupled with the low visibility of such legislation and the utter indifference of almost all members to almost all private bills, have produced grave potential for abuse, a potential realized in the Chinese ship-jumper bills and the Dirksen "bazooka bill."

As long as private bills are processed by subcommittees, these abuses will continue. The House Judiciary Committee, along with its Senate counterpart, should recommend that Congress experiment with the establishment of a joint House and Senate committee on private legislation, a congressional ombudsman, or a congressional agency such as the General Accounting Office to investigate the bills and report them to the floor. Such arrangements would reduce the burden of private bills and ensure some consistency and consideration in their disposition by Congress.

5. *Substantially expand staff and budget*

Perhaps no factor contributes more to the dismal performance of the House Judiciary Committee than the poverty of its staff and budgetary resources. With a staff of 36 (compared to 204 in the Senate committee) and a budget of approximately $800,000 (compared to over $7,500,000 for the Senate committee) during the Ninety-second Congress, House Judiciary simply could not keep abreast of developments within its legislative jurisdiction, much less conduct vigorous investigations or oversight or hold meaningful hearings. House Judiciary's failure to open up substantial new areas of investigation, originate legislation where needed, conduct meaningful oversight outside the civil rights enforcement area, or perform significant data-gathering and public-information functions, attests to the debilitating effects of its severe resource constraints. Such constraints can only perpetuate the committee's passivity and its dependence upon the executive branch, private interest groups, and the Senate committee for information, value assumptions, and ideas. Accordingly, the committee budget should be expanded severalfold, with virtually all of the increase allocated to the subcommittees.

6. *Provide for systematic oversight of agencies and courts*

The committee's past failures in overseeing all agencies within the Justice Department and all other agencies and courts within its jurisdiction and the urgent need for reform have been discussed above.

7. *Provide for the referral and discharge of legislation to and from subcommittees*

The committee should modify its rules to provide that all legislation be referred to subcommittee, except under certain specified conditions, and that jurisdictional conflicts between subcommittees in the consideration of bills be resolved according to prescribed criteria and procedures. At present, the chairman determines by fiat what legislation shall and shall not be referred or retained in the full committee. As a result, more than half the public bills sent to Judiciary in the first session of the Ninety-second Congress remained in full committee, and most of these were not acted upon. The possibility and reality of abuse has been great. Whatever one's views concerning amnesty or school prayer legislation, their fates should not have depended upon the whim of the chairman.

For the same reason, the committee rules should provide that a subcommittee be automatically discharged from further consideration of a bill unless it issues a report on the bill to the full committee within a prescribed period of time. In the case of a proposed constitutional amendment, the time period should probably be a lengthy one, but there can be no justification for a subcommittee's failure to consider legislation simply because the chairman is opposed to it.

8. Restructure the committee's civil rights responsibilities

One subcommittee, preferably Congressman Edwards' unit, should be given formal and exclusive jurisdiction over civil rights legislation as well as civil rights oversight.* This would permit and encourage member and staff expertise in the civil rights field, and facilitate feedback between legislative and implementation functions in this vital field. Such a subcommittee should not have any other legislative or oversight jurisdiction, except in constitution-related areas such as civil liberties. This subcommittee should rely upon an expanded, professionalized investigatory team to perform most of its field work. A special unit in the Civil Rights Commission, increased reliance upon an expanded

---

* The subcommittee jurisdictional reforms of June 1973, described in Chapter 16, move in this direction, but for reasons discussed there, these reforms continue at the whim of Chairman Rodino.

General Accounting Office, or some other investigatory instrumentality might be necessary. In addition, cooperative efforts should be launched with the House Appropriations Committee looking to the increased use of appropriations hearings to ensure civil rights compliance by federal agencies.

16

Postscript:
The Unmaking of House
Judiciary Committee Reform

During the early months of the Ninety-third Congress, the House Judiciary Committee experienced one of the rarest of congressional moments—a spasm of reform agitation. The substantial failure of that effort, coupled with the total absence of any reform effort in the Senate Judiciary Committee, suggest that the committee patterns analyzed throughout this book are deeply institutionalized and will not soon yield to change.

The outlook for reform of a congressional committee was probably never brighter than it was in January 1973 when the

NOTE: This chapter was prepared by Peter H. Schuck and is based largely upon confidential interviews with members and staff of the House Judiciary Committee, conducted in January, February, July, and August 1973, and April 1974.

374

House Judiciary Committee convened for the Ninety-third Congress. The winds of change seemed to be sweeping through Congress, and nowhere more so than in House Judiciary. Members of the committee were deeply dissatisfied. Even those with many years in the House had long chafed under the autocracy of Emanuel Celler. Denied staff, committee leadership positions, and independence, all but the most senior committee members felt restless and resentful. Several brash newcomers had burst on the scene, determined to make the most of their Judiciary assignments.

The pressure for reform had been felt by Celler during the Ninety-second Congress. He had agreed to share significant legislative bounty with subcommittees other than his own, broadening their jurisdictions. But in the end, they got only the crumbs. The immigration subcommittee (No. 1), for example, received a reform proposal for the District of Columbia and the claims subcommittee (No. 2) received a bill authorizing funds for the American Bicentennial Commission. Celler did permit Congressman Kastenmeier, chairman of Subcommittee No. 3, to hold open markup sessions and even to permit television coverage, if approved in advance by the full committee (a condition that rendered this concession of little value). But when the Ninety-second Congress ended, Celler had retained all of the major legislation and perquisites under his control. Nothing of substance had changed after all.

When Celler was unseated and Peter Rodino succeeded to the chairmanship, however, everything became possible. After the November elections, the subcommittee chairmen met with Rodino. They spoke of the importance of defining the subcommittee boundaries, allowing subcommittee chairmen to plan and schedule their own hearings, and allocating adequate funds so that the committee could function effectively. And they urged an end to Celler's practice of requiring subcommittee chairmen to treat with Bess Dick, the staff director, for funds. She had often turned them down peremptorily in the past.

The Ad Hoc Subcommittee

Rodino responded with two actions. First, he "let go" Bess Dick, replacing her with Jerome Zeifman, a staff counsel during the Celler regime. Second, he established an *ad hoc* subcommittee to study the question of committee and subcommittee reorganization. Rodino described the purpose of the subcommittee:

> to make specific recommendations as to how the workload of the committee could be better distributed in order to promote the efficient and expeditious consideration of legislation referred to the committee.[1]

Kastenmeier was named chairman of this body, which included three new members—Wayne W. Owens, Elizabeth Holtzman, who had defeated Celler in a primary election, and Barbara Jordan (D.,Tex.)—and James R. Mann. Rodino was an *ex-officio* member, but generally was represented by Zeifman.

With three of the five members new to Congress and the Judiciary Committee, the *ad hoc* subcommittee at first seemed a remarkable transfusion of new blood into Judiciary's ancient, tradition-encrusted veins. Rodino claimed that "the emphasis in selecting new members to serve on this [sub]committee was designed to insure the effective participation and fresh perspectives of younger Members of Congress."[2] William E. Davis, an aide to subcommittee member Mann, agreed that the new members were an advantage; they could supply novel ideas from a detached perspective.[3] But in retrospect, it appears that Rodino may have seen the transfusion as one of water rather than blood. Aides close to the new *ad hoc* subcommittee stressed that Rodino did not want a reform report submitted by a group of powerful, influential committee members; in their view, he was seeking instead a report that lacked assured acceptability and prestige, one that he could easily manipulate for his own purposes.[4] Whether or not this was Rodino's intention, it was in fact the result.

The *ad hoc* subcommittee met five times from the beginning

of February into the spring and submitted its recommendations to Rodino on April 2, 1973. The subcommittee based its report on a rule adopted by the House Democratic Caucus on January 23, 1973. Section 2(a) of the rule, entitled "Committee and Subcommittee Organization and Procedure," provided:

> *Jurisdiction of Subcommittees.* All subcommittees shall have fixed jurisdiction as determined by the full committee.

Taking this injunction as its theme, the *ad hoc* subcommittee then adopted three premises:

> (1) The inter-relatedness of matters within the jurisdiction of a given subcommittee maximizes the expertise which can be brought to bear on these matters, since a continually growing fund of knowledge and experience can be developed and sustained, rather than being dissipated by the necessity to consider from time to time matters of little or no substantive relationship to each other.
>
> (2) The specific identification of subcommittees with subject areas enhances the ability of the public in general, interested individuals and organizations in particular, and the Congress to recognize and monitor Congressional activities on matters of public concern.
>
> (3) The investing of subcommittees with specified jurisdiction assists new members of the Committee in obtaining assignment to those subcommittees which consider matters of interest and concern to them.[5]

The subcommittee report embraced two major areas; subcommittee reform and Justice Department investigations. On the first, the report recommended that each of the Judiciary subcommittees be named, instead of the former system of numbering followed by vague descriptive titles. Table 10 lists the subcommittee names and chairmen in the Ninety-second Congress and the new subcommittee names and chairmen as recommended (and ultimately instituted) by the Judiciary Committee in the Ninety-third Congress.

TABLE 10.

Subcommittees of the House Judiciary Committee

92nd Congress		93rd Congress	
Subcommittee	*Chairman*	*Subcommittee*	*Chairman*
No. 1 (Immigration)	Rodino	Immigration, Citizenship, and International Law	Eilberg
No. 2 (Claims)	Donohue	Claims and Government Relations	Donohue
No. 3 (Patents, Trademarks, and Copyrights)	Kastenmeier	Courts, Civil Liberties, and the Administration of Justice	Kastenmeier
No. 4 (Bankruptcy and Reorganization)	Edwards	Civil Rights and Constitutional Rights	Edwards
No. 5 (Antitrust Matters)	Celler	Monopolies and Commercial Law	Rodino
— — —	— — —	Crime	Conyers
Special Subcommittee on Reform of Federal Criminal Laws	Hungate	Criminal Justice	Hungate

According to the recommendations, each of the seven newly established subcommittees was to be assigned legislation relating to one or two general areas, and all matters within one subcommittee's jurisdiction were to be related. For example, the report described the work of the proposed subcommittee on Immigration, Citizenship, and International Law:

> The general relationship binding the various matters lodged within this subcommittee's jurisdiction is that of internationalism. Citizenship, immigration, nationality, and passports all center around movement into and out of the United States, whether for temporary purposes or permanently. Included here would be oversight of the Immigration and Naturalization Service and the State Department. The issues of deportation, extradition, and crimes com-

mitted outside the United States also partake of international aspects. While admiralty law applies as to United States waters, it also is very much involved with international commerce in terms of shipping disputes and accidents. So too does the matter of offshore mineral rights partake of international considerations.

The *ad hoc* subcommittee also proposed that the jurisdictions of the subcommittees be fixed so that every legislative matter would be assigned to subcommittees under these jurisdictions. This allocation of jurisdictions was to be binding on the full-committee chairman. The *ad hoc* subcommittee recognized, however, that instances would inevitably arise requiring that the chairman exercise discretion. For example, a bill directed at civil rights abuses by police officers might properly be sent either to the Subcommittee on Civil Rights and Constitutional Rights or to the Subcommittee on Criminal Justice. The report stated:

> We do stress, however, that the proposed Rule is not an essay at pre-empting the discretion of the Chairman, and that it is the Chairman's judgment which will be particularly called into play when these difficulties occur.[6]

The *ad hoc* subcommittee also recommended that committee members be permitted to reselect the subcommittees upon which they chose to sit. This proposal reflected two considerations: the fact that the proposed revised jurisdictions of the subcommittees would otherwise work hardships on existing members, and the reality that many members were assigned to subcommittees that did not maximize their own interests and experience. Finally, the *ad hoc* subcommittee recommended that the subcommittees undertake oversight investigations of the Justice Department. This decision, amply justified by committee passivity in the past, was further spurred by the Watergate revelations implicating top Justice Department officials in criminal activities. The *ad hoc* subcommittee proposed that each Judiciary subcommittee investigate the units within the department that pertained to that sub-committee's jurisdiction. For example, the Monopolies and Commercial Law Subcommittee would exercise oversight over the Antitrust Division of the Justice Department.

Rodino was full of praise for the work of the *ad hoc* subcommittee. It had "worked diligently." Its recommendations embodied "wisdom" and, "with some modifications," would form a basis for reorganization of House Judiciary.[7] And he vowed to follow the jurisdictional guidelines set by the *ad hoc* committee "wherever possible."[8]

Rodino, recognizing that implementation of these recommendations could not be accomplished on the basis of Celler's traditional parsimony, stated:

> It is quite evident that in fulfilling these legislative duties and responsibilities, it will be necessary to expand the personnel of this committee staff and concomitantly it will be necessary to significantly increase the size of this committee's budget.[9]

Rodino and the Democratic Caucus

After the *ad hoc* subcommittee submitted its report to Rodino, the report was sent to the Democratic caucus of the Judiciary Committee, where it was revised, sent back to the *ad hoc* subcommittee, and finally returned to the caucus on June 12. This was the point at which Rodino went to work on the proposed reforms. He submitted his own list of "reforms" to the caucus. This list essentially restored the system of unwritten committee names and jurisdictions—a system that had given Rodino's predecessor as committee chairman enormous discretion and power. Rodino felt that such a plan would effect needed change, while "at the same time preserve a certain amount of discretion in the chairman to obtain a needed degree of flexibility."[10] And exercising his "discretion," the chairman promptly rejected the proposal to permit committee members to reselect their subcommittee assignments. Indeed, Rodino raised the specter of widespread losses of subcommittee seniority and shifts in subcommittee assignments if too many changes were made. The most powerful members stood to lose the most, he suggested, by any thorough-going reforms. "He scared the hell out of those guys," one aide observed.

When the doors of the caucus room opened, Rodino had gotten his way. The final plan retained most, if not all, of the chairman's perquisites.[11] Rodino cited his justification for retaining discretion over the allocation of bills to subcommittees: during his twenty-five years on the House Judiciary Committee, "jurisdiction was never assigned by title."[12] In short, tradition was reason enough.

The chairman of the *ad hoc* subcommittee, Congressman Kastenmeier, had been obliged to accept a "modest compromise plan" which, while adding a subcommittee, rearranging some subcommittee jurisdictions, and replacing numbers with names, left Rodino with virtually the identical powers to allocate bills which Celler had possessed.[13] The specified jurisdictions of the new subcommittees would be advisory only, not binding on Rodino. According to an aide to Congressman Mann, the *ad hoc* subcommittee came to accept Rodino's view that more far-reaching reforms could not be instituted while legislation was being considered by the subcommittee. Yet the *ad hoc* subcommittee had already suggested a way to meet this very objection. It had recommended:

> that upon adoption of the full Committee, the new Rules be implemented by the Committee by or before June 30, 1973.
> That all major bills considered, or in mark-up session before existent subcommittees be identified, and that the present subcommittees continue to exist only until they have pursued these major bills to a legislative conclusion at which time they will cease and the jurisdictions will be properly transferred to the subcommittee specified under [the new rules].[14]

After the Dust Cleared

It is generally recognized on the House Judiciary Committee that the reform effort did not wholly succeed and that Rodino proved every bit as agile and resourceful in defusing it as his wily predecessor would have been. By appointing an *ad hoc* committee dominated by first-termers with a "new and fresh vision"[15] and containing only one subcommittee chairman (Kastenmeier), Rodino assured that its recommendations would lack "clout," particularly with subcommittee chairmen and other senior members of House Judiciary. Rodino must have recognized that with no senior member other than Kastenmeier clearly identified with the insurgency, its staying power would be limited. By stressing the instability which the reforms would create for senior members, he neutralized them as a force for reform. And by replacing Bess Dick, Rodino was able to satisfy the major complaints of the subcommittee chairmen.

The long-run significance of the *ad hoc* subcommittee's efforts remains to be seen. As of April 1974, no subcommittee, including Rodino's, had commenced hearings in connection with the much-discussed major investigation of the Justice Department. And while each subcommittee now had a name, new jurisdictions had neither been formalized in writing nor fully implemented; they are simply guidelines, and remain advisory and precatory only. The first year of the "reforms" has been perhaps the most atypical and frenetic year in the history of the committee. The nomination of Gerald Ford for vice president under the Twenty-fifth Amendment in late 1973 and the impeachment investigation in 1974 have preoccupied the members and staff to an enormous degree. No "normal climate," within which the efficacy of the "reforms" could be fairly evaluated, has yet existed.

According to one outsider who works closely with the committee, however, the jurisdictional reforms, when and if they are actualized, will be modest at best. "When normalcy returns to the Judiciary Committee, we will find that the so-called reforms were essentially cosmetic and impose no meaningful constraints on Rodino's discretion or power."

Nevertheless, members of the *ad hoc* subcommittee are optimistic, feeling that the mere renaming of the subcommittees constituted a major advance for Judiciary Committee reform.[16] What is truly instructive in all this is that by Judiciary Committee—and indeed, congressional—standards, they are probably right.

Appendices

APPENDIX 1.

Interest Group Ratings of Members of the Senate Judiciary Committee, 92nd Congress, 1st Session (1971)

Member	ADA	ACA
Democrats		
James Eastland (Miss.)	7	74
John McClellan (Ark.)	30	64
Sam Ervin (N.C.)	30	87
Philip Hart (Mich.)	96	4
Edward Kennedy (Mass.)	100	5
Birch Bayh (Ind.)	96	14
Quentin Burdick (N.D.)	85	25
Robert Byrd (W. Va.)	26	45
John Tunney (Cal.)	96	5
Republicans		
Roman Hruska (Neb.)	0	91
Hiram Fong (Hai.)	19	50
Hugh Scott (Pa.)	26	45
Strom Thurmond (S.C.)	0	96
Marlow Cook (Ky.)	33	70
Charles Mathias (Md.)	63	21
Edward Gurney (Fla.)	4	95

SOURCE: *Congressional Quarterly*, Vol. XXX, (April 27, 1972), p. 931.

APPENDIX 2.
Committee Ideology: Floor Vote Ratings of Members (1971)

SENATE JUDICIARY COMMITTEE

Rating of	Median	Mean	Standard Deviation	Chairman
Americans for Democratic				
Action (Liberal)	30	44.4	37	7
Average	41	46.6	33.3	XXXX
Americans for Constitutional Action				
(Conservative)	47.5	49.4	32.9	74
Average	39	43.8	30.2	XXXX
Committee on Political				
Education (Labor)	48	52.7	21.5	18.1
Average	56	53.1	27.7	XXXX

HOUSE JUDICIARY COMMITTEE

Rating of	Median	Mean	Standard Deviation	Chairman
Americans for Democratic				
Action (Liberal)	49	51.6	34.4	78
Average	30	39.6	32.2	XXXX
Americans for Constitutional Action				
(Conservative)	38	45.4	33	4
Average	54	51.0	31.8	XXXX

HOUSE JUDICIARY COMMITTEE

Rating of	Median	Mean	Standard Deviation	Chairman
Committee on Political				
Education (Labor)	58	54.3	32.2	100
Average	50	53.2	33.1	XXXX

SOURCE: Data tabulated by Congress Project researchers from ratings for each committee member published by the following three groups:

Americans for Democratic Action: A political action organization of "liberals and the politically aware" dedicated to international cooperation, economic security and freedom. Based on 27 votes in the Senate and 37 votes in the House in 1971.

Americans for Constitutional Action: A political action organization dedicated to the principles of "constitutional conservatism" and opposed to socialism and regimentation. Based on 24 votes in the Senate and 29 votes in the House in 1971.

Committee on Political Education: A political arm of the largest federation of labor unions in the nation, the AFL-CIO. Based on 12 votes in the Senate and 12 votes in the House of 1971.

APPENDIX 3.
Judiciary Committee Rules

HOUSE JUDICIARY RULES
(Adopted February 23, 1971)

RULE I.

The Rules of the House of Representatives are the rules of the Committee on the Judiciary and its subcommittees with the following specific additions thereto.

RULE II. COMMITTEE MEETINGS

(a) The regular meeting day of the Committee on the Judiciary for the conduct of its business shall be on Tuesday of each week while the Congress is in session.

(b) Additional meetings may be called by the Chairman and a

regular meeting of the Committee may be dispensed with when, in the judgment of the Chairman, there is no need therefor.

(c) At least two calendar days (excluding Saturdays, Sundays, and legal holidays) before each scheduled Committee meeting, each Member of the Committee shall be furnished a list of the bill(s) and subject(s) to be considered and/or acted upon at the meeting. Bills or subjects not listed shall be subject to a point of order unless their consideration is agreed to by a two-thirds vote of the Committee.

RULE III. HEARINGS AND BUSINESS MEETINGS

(a) Committee and subcommittee hearings shall be open to the public except when the Committee, by majority vote, determines otherwise.

(b) Committee and subcommittee meetings for the transaction of business, i.e., meetings other than those held for the purpose of taking testimony, shall be closed to the public except when the Committee, by majority vote, determines otherwise.

(c) In all subcommittee proceedings where a vote on a motion to report a bill to the full Committee results in a tie, such bill shall be reported to the full Committee without recommendation.

RULE IV. PROXY VOTING

A vote by a Member of the Committee with respect to any measure or matter being considered in the Committee or in subcommittee may be cast by proxy if the proxy authorization is in writing, designates the person who is to execute the proxy authorization, and is limited to a specific measure or matter and any amendments or motions pertaining thereto.

RULE V. HEARING PROCEDURE

(a) The Committee or any subcommittee shall make public announcement of the date, place and subject matter of any hearing to be conducted by it on any measure or matter at least one week before the commencement of that hearing, unless the Committee or the subcommittee before which such hearing is scheduled, determines that there is good cause to begin such hearing at an earlier date, in which event it shall make public announcement at the earliest possible date.

(b) In the course of any hearing each Member shall be allowed five minutes for the interrogation of a witness until such time as each Member who so desires has had an opportunity to question the witness.

RULE VI. BROADCASTING OF HEARINGS

Whenever the Committee by majority vote so permits any Committee or subcommittee hearing that is open to the public may be covered, in whole or in part, by television broadcast, radio broadcast and still photography, or by any of such methods of coverage under such requirements and limitations as are set forth in Clause thirty-three of Rule XI of the Rules of the House of Representatives and under such other requirements or limitations as the Committee may adopt. Under this rule no subcommittee may authorize the broadcasting or photographing of any of its hearings without the specific permission of the Committee.

SOURCE: Committee Print.

SENATE COMMITTEE RULES

The Senate Judiciary Committee has no rules.

APPENDIX 4.
Duties of the Judiciary Committees

SENATE COMMITTEE ON THE JUDICIARY

". . . To consist of 16 Senators: (1) Judicial proceedings, civil and criminal generally, (2) Constitutional amendments, (3) Federal courts and judges, (4) Local courts in the Territories and possessions, (5) Revision and codification of the statutes of the United States, (6) National penitentiaries, (7) Protection of trade and commerce against unlawful restraints and monopolies, (8) Holidays and celebrations, (9) Bankruptcy, mutiny, espionage, and counterfeiting, (10) State and Territorial boundary lines, (11) Meetings of Congress, attendance of Members, and their acceptance of incompatible offices, (12) Civil liberties, (13) Patents, copyrights, and trademarks, (14) Patent Office, (15) Immigration and naturalization, (16) Apportionment of Representatives, (17) Measures relating to claims against the United States, (18) Interstate compacts generally."

HOUSE COMMITTEE ON THE JUDICIARY

". . . To consist of 38 Members: (a) Judicial proceedings, civil and criminal generally. (b) Apportionment of Representatives. (c) Bankruptcy, mutiny, espionage, and counterfeiting. (d) Civil liberties. (e) Constitutional amendments. (f) Federal courts and judges. (g) Holidays and celebrations. (h) Immigration and naturalization. (i) Interstate compacts generally. (j) Local courts in the Territories and possessions. (k) Measures relating to claims against the United States. (l) Meetings of Congress, attendance of Members and their acceptance of incompatible offices. (m) National penitentiaries. (n) Patent Office. (o) Patents, copyrights, and trade-marks. (p) Presidential succession. (q) Protection of trade and commerce against unlawful restraints and monopolies. (r) Revision and codification of the Statutes of the United States. (s) State and Territorial boundary lines."

APPENDIX 5.
Selected Judiciary Committee Votes, 92nd Congress

---

1. To confirm William Rehnquist as Justice of the United States Supreme Court (Rehnquist confirmation). Vote: Yes 12; No 4.

2. To continue hearings on the nomination of Richard Kleindienst as Attorney General following the testimony of Peter Flanigan (1972) (Motion to continue hearings on Kleindienst nomination). Vote: Yes 6; No 8.

3. To change Bayh bill, which prohibited the manufacture and sale of handguns except for sporting or law enforcement purposes, so as to permit the sale of military surplus handguns and of those handguns meeting safety and reliability tests (1972) (Hruska substitute to S.2507, to amend the Gun Control Act of 1968). Vote: Yes 5; No 8.

4. To compensate victims of crime in areas of primary federal

Voting Record

Democrats	1	2	3	4	5	6		Republicans	1	2	3	4	5	6
Eastland	Y	N	Y	Y	N	N		Hruska	Y	N	Y	N	N	N
McClellan	Y	Y	Y	—	N	N		Fong	Y	N	Y	—	N	N
Ervin	Y	N	N	N	Y	N		Scott, H.	Y	Y	—	Y	N	N
Hart	N	Y	N	Y	N	N		Thurmond	Y	N	Y	—	N	N
Kennedy	N	Y	N	—	N	N		Cook	Y	N	N	Y	N	N
Bayh	N	N	N	Y	N	N		Mathias	Y	N	—	Y	N	N
Burdick	Y	Y	N	N	N	N		Gurney	Y	N	Y	Y	N	N
Byrd, R.	Y	Y	—	—	N	N								
Tunney	N	Y	N	Y	N	N								

jurisdiction and to grant states up to 75 percent of the cost of similar state programs, with recovery limited to a maximum of $50,000 and restricted to hardship cases (Title I, S.750). Vote: Yes 8; No 3.

5. "Neither the United States nor any State shall make any law treating men and women any differently unless the difference in the treatment is based on physiological or functional differences between" (Ervin amendment to H.J. Res. 208, S.J. Res. 8, S.J. Res. 9, the Equal Rights Amendment). Vote: Yes 1; No 15.

6. To provide that the Equal Rights Amendment shall "not impair the validity of any law of the United States which exempts women from compulsory military service" (Ervin amendment to the Equal Rights Amendment). Vote: Yes 3; No 13.

HOUSE COMMITTEE VOTES

1. To permit the use of proxies to votes about which the member has been informed of the legislation on which he is voting and has affirmatively requested that he be so recorded; would strengthen minority opposition (Democratic proposed Rule IV of the Committee). Vote: Yes 14; No 15.

2. To add to the women's rights amendment the provision that the amendment not impair laws exempting women from the draft and laws relating to health and welfare (Wiggins Amendment to H.J.Res. 208, the Equal Rights Constitutional Amendment). Vote: Yes 19; No 16.

3. Do not limit immigration preference to unmarried brothers and sisters of those already citizens, i.e., allow married brothers and sisters preference too (Jacobs amendment to H.R.9615). Vote: Yes 27; No 6.

4. Limit D.C. representation to House of Representatives, i.e., D.C. would be granted no senators (Wiggins amendment to H.J. Res. 253). Vote: Yes 14; No 21.

5. To provide compensation to growers, manufacturers, and retailers who lost money due to the ban on cyclamates (Motion to report H.R.13366, the Cyclamate Ban Compensation Bill). Vote: Yes 17; No 17.

6. To permit use of interstate commerce facilities by state agencies conducting a lottery (Motion to report H.R.2374). Vote: Yes 22; No 17.

7. To provide stricter entrance requirements for immigrants (Dennis amendment to H.R.16188). Vote: Yes 6; No 24.

Voting Record

Democrats	1	2	3	4	5	6	7
Celler	N	Y	Y	N	N	Y	N
Rodino	N	N	Y	N	NV	Y	N
Donohue	NV	NV	Y	N	NV	Y	N
Brooks	N	Y	NV	Y	NV	N	N
Dowdy	NV	NV	Y	NV	NV	NV	NV
Kastenmeier	N	N	Y	N	Y	Y	N
Edwards, D.	N	N	Y	N	Y	Y	N
Hungate	N	N	Y	N	Y	N	N
Conyers	NV	N	Y	N	NV	Y	NV
Jacobs	N	N	Y	N	NV	Y	N
Eilberg	N	N	Y	N	NV	Y	N
Ryan	NV	N	Y	N	N	Y	N
Waldie	NV	N	Y	NV	Y	Y	NV
Edwards, E.	NV	N	Y	NV	NV	NV	**NV**
Flowers	N	Y	Y	Y	NV	Y	N
Mann	NV	Y	Y	Y	N	N	N
Mikva	N	N	Y	N	N	NV	N
Sarbanes	N	N	Y	N	N	NV	N
Seiberling	N	N	Y	N	N	Y	N
Abourezk	N	N	Y	N	NV	Y	N
Danielson	N	Y	Y	N	Y	Y	N
Drinan	N	N	Y	N	N	Y	N

Republicans	1	2	3	4	5	6	7
McCulloch	NV	NV	NV	N	NV	N	Y
Hutchinson	NV	Y	N	Y	Y	NV	Y
McClory	Y	Y	N	N	NV	Y	Y
Smith	Y	N	Y	Y	Y	Y	NV
Poff	Y	Y	N	Y	Y	N	Y
Sandman	Y	Y	Y	N	Y	Y	NV
Railsback	Y	Y	NV	Y	Y	N	NV
Biester	Y	Y	Y	Y	NV	Y	N
Wiggins	Y	Y	N	Y	Y	N	NV
Dennis	Y	Y	N	Y	Y	N	Y
Fish	Y	Y	Y	N	Y	Y	N
Coughlin	Y	Y	Y	Y	Y	Y	N
Mayne	Y	Y	N	Y	Y	N	Y
Hogan	Y	Y	NV	N	NV	Y	N
Keating	Y	Y	Y	Y	Y	N	N
McKevitt	Y	Y	NV	Y	Y	N	N

Notes

CHAPTER 1.   FROM BUSINESS TO BUSING

---

1. U.S., Congress, Senate, Judiciary Committee, *Legislative and Executive Calendars*, 92nd Cong., 1st sess. (June 30, 1972).

CHAPTER 2.   THE SENATE JUDICIARY COMMITTEE: GRAVEYARD FOR LIBERAL LEGISLATION

---

1. Telephone interview with Martin Hamburger, Administrative Assistant to Senator Hugh Scott, April 2, 1974.
2. "James O. Eastland," *Citizens Look at Congress*, Ralph Nader Congress Project (Washington: Grossman Publishers, 1972), p. 13.
3. Ibid., p. 11.
4. Robert Sherrill, *Gothic Politics in the Deep South* (New York: Grossman Publishers, 1968), p. 194.
5. Interview with Senator Philip Hart, July 1972.
6. U.S., Congress, Senate, Judiciary Committee, *Nomination of Thurgood Marshall for the Court of Appeals, 2nd Circuit*, 87th Cong., 2nd sess. (1962), p. 101.
7. Ibid., pp. 55–56.
8. Confidential interview, July 28, 1972.
9. Confidential interview, August 1973.
10. Ibid.

11. Confidential interview, summer 1972.

12. George Goodwin, *The Little Legislatures* (Springfield: Univ. of Massachusetts Press, 1970), p. 60.

13. Quoted in William Morrow, *Congressional Committees* (New York: Charles Scribner's Sons, 1969), p. 192.

14. Mark J. Green, James M. Fallows, and David R. Zwick, *Who Runs Congress?* (New York: Grossman Publishers and Bantam Books, 1972), p. 199.

15. *Congressional Quarterly Weekly Report*, No. 18 (April 29, 1972), p. 931.

16. See "James Eastland," p. 13.

17. Senate Judiciary Committee, *Summary of Activities*, 92nd Cong., p. 2.

18. Ibid.

19. Confidential interviews, summer and fall 1972.

20. Press release, office of Congresswoman Elizabeth Holtzman, Mar. 12, 1973.

21. U.S., Congress, Senate, Committee on Rules and Administration, Expenditures Authorizations for Senate Committees, January 3, 1974, Part II.

22. Ibid., pp. 63, 87.

23. Ibid., p. 58.

24. Ibid., Part II.

25. Aaron Wildavsky, *The Politics of the Budgetary Process* (Boston: Little, Brown, 1964), *passim*.

26. Confidential interview, April 2, 1974.

27. U.S., Congress, Senate, Committee on Rules and Administration, *Senate Inquiries and Investigations*, 93rd Cong., 2nd sess., March 13, 1974 (Committee Print No. 3).

CHAPTER 3.   THE HOUSE JUDICIARY COMMITTEE:
CELLER'S LEGACY

---

1. *New York Times*, Feb. 29, 1972.

2. *Congressional Quarterly*, Aug. 5, 1972, p. 1948. For a review of busing legislation, see *Congressional Quarterly*, July 29, 1972, pp. 1882–1885.

3. Interview with Bess Dick, summer 1972.

4. George Goodwin, *The Little Legislatures* (Springfield: Univ. of Massachusetts Press, 1970), p. 108.

5. *Congressional Quarterly*, June 17, 1972, p. 1387.

6. James C. Kirby, *Congress and the Public Trust* (New York: Atheneum, 1970), pp. 234–235.

7. Mark J. Green, *The Closed Enterprise System* (New York: Grossman Publishers, 1972), pp. 36–37.

8. Interview with Rep. Tom Railsback, July 28, 1972.

9. Telephone conversation with Joseph A. Phillips, Counsel, House Select Committee on Crime, summer 1972.
10. Interview with John Holloman III, Chief Counsel, Senate Judiciary Committee, summer 1972.
11. U.S., Congress, House, Judiciary Committee, *Legislative Calendar*, 92nd Cong., p. 10; U.S., Congress, Senate, Judiciary Committee, *Legislative Calendar*, 92nd Cong.
12. U.S., Congress, House, Judiciary Committee, *Summary of Activities*, 92nd Cong. (1972), p. 1.
13. U.S., Congress, House, *Report of the Clerk of the House*, 92nd Cong., 1st sess. (July 1–Dec. 31, 1971), pp. 156, 168.
14. *Congressional Quarterly*, Oct. 7, 1972, p. 2603.
15. Holloman interview.
16. *Congressional Quarterly*, Oct. 7, 1972, p. 2601.
17. Quoted in the *Washington Post*, Apr. 14, 1974.

CHAPTER 4.   MONOPOLY CAPITOL:
THE ANTITRUST SUBCOMMITTEES

1. William Shepherd, *Market Power and Economic Welfare*, Vol. 212 (1970).
2. David Kamerschen, "An Estimation of the 'Welfare Losses' from Monopoly in the American Economy," 4 *Western Economic Journal* 221 (1966).
3. Comanor and Smiley, "Monopoly and the Distribution of Wealth," Research Paper Series No. 156, Stanford University Graduate School of Business (May 1973).
4. See generally, Mark J. Green, *The Closed Enterprise System* (New York: Grossman Publishers, 1972).
5. See Joseph Gorman, *Kefauver* (New York: Oxford University Press, 1971).
6. *Congressional Record*, Feb. 5, 1958, p. 1739.
7. *Washington Post*, Apr. 11, 1970, p. A14.
8. See Richard Harris, *The Real Voice* (New York: Macmillan, 1964), for an excellent detailed account of the drug amendments.
9. "Philip A. Hart," *Citizens Look at Congress*, Ralph Nader Congress Project (Washington: Grossman Publishers, 1972), p. 16.
10. U.S., Congress, Senate, Judiciary Committee, Subcommittee on Antitrust and Monopoly, *Antitrust and Monopoly Activities, 1962*, 88th Cong., 1st sess. (May 1, 1963), p. 13.
11. Harry Conn, "What's Behind the Handshake?" *New Republic*, June 9, 1952, p. 12.

12. "No Crusades," *Time*, Aug. 30, 1963, p. 17.
13. Douglass Lea, "Senate's Antitrust Watchdog Moves into Environment Consumer Area," *National Journal*, Aug. 22, 1970, p. 1828.
14. Speech of April 8, 1969, to the Lawyers Club, Ann Arbor, Michigan.
15. Speech of April 4, 1969, to the Antitrust Section of the American Bar Association.
16. Speech of March 7, 1970, to the New York Consumer Assembly.
17. For Hart's general sensitivity to the impact of antitrust on consumers, see release of Senator Philip Hart, August 19, 1963.
18. Letter from Ralph Nader to Senator Philip Hart, December 23, 1970.
19. Letter from Senator Philip Hart to Ralph Nader, February 2, 1971.
20. U.S., Congress, Senate, Committee on Rules and Administration, *Senate Inquiries and Investigations*, 93rd Cong. (1973), p. 53.
21. Staff Memorandum from Pat Bario, editorial director, to Senator Hart, January 27, 1971.
22. Ibid.
23. See letter from Ralph Nader to James Eastland, Chairman, Senate Judiciary Committee, Aug. 12, 1970; see also, W. Wallace Kirkpatrick, "Antitrust to the Supreme Court: The Expediting Act," 37 *Geo. Wash. L. Rev.* 740 (1969); Emanuel Celler, "Case in Support of Application of the Expediting Act to Antitrust Suits," 14 *De Paul L. Rev.* 29 (1964).
24. See Green, *Closed Enterprise System*, pp. 145–172 (New York: Grossman Publishers, 1972); William Breit and Kenneth Elzinga, "Antitrust Penalties and Attitudes Toward Risk: An Economic Analysis," 86 *Harvard L. Rev.* 693 (1973).
25. 374 U.S. 321 (1963).
26. Section of Antitrust Law of the American Bar Association, *Antitrust Developments 1955–1968*.
27. Kenneth Elzinga, *The Effectiveness of Relief Decrees in Merger Cases* (Ph.D. diss., Dept. of Economics, Michigan State University, 1967).
28. U.S., Congress, Senate, Judiciary Committee, Subcommittee on Antitrust and Monopoly, *The Failing Newspaper Act: Hearings on S.1312*, 90th Cong., 1st and 2nd sess. (1967–1968), Parts 1–7.
29. Douglass Lea, "Lobbying Overwhelms Opponents of Newspaper Preservation Act," *National Journal*, July 7, 1970, p. 1606.
30. Federal Trade Commission, Bureau of Competition and Bureau of Economics, *Statement on Opposition to Legislation Which Would Legalize Territorial Restrictions in the Soft Drink Industry* (Jan. 17, 1973).
31. U.S., Congress, Senate, Judiciary Committee, Subcommittee on Antitrust and Monopoly, *Exclusive Territorial Allocation Legislation: Hearings on S.978*, 92nd Cong., 2nd sess. (1972), p. 675.
32. *Washington Post*, September 13, 1972, p. E1.
33. Jonathan Cottin, "Antitrust Report/Justice Division, Congress Monitors New Developments in Big Business," *National Journal*, Feb. 10, 1973, pp. 177, 183.
34. Lea, "Senate's Antitrust Watchdog," p. 1828.
35. Ibid.

36. U.S., Congress, Senate, Judiciary Committee, Subcommittee on Antitrust and Monopoly, *Economic Concentration: Hearings*, 88th Cong., 2nd sess. (1964).

37. Morton Mintz and Jerry Cohen, *America, Inc.* (New York: Dial Press, 1971), p. 69.

38. U.S., Congress, Senate, Judiciary Committee, *Antitrust Aspects of the Funeral Industry: Hearings*, 88th Cong., 2nd sess. (1964).

39. U.S., Congress, Senate, Judiciary Committee, *Antitrust Aspects of the Funeral Industry*, Views of the Subcommittee on the Antitrust and Monopoly, 89th Cong., 2nd sess. (1966), p. 2.

40. Ibid., p. 54.

41. U.S., Congress, Senate, Judiciary Committee, Subcommittee on Antitrust and Monopoly, *Alleged Price Fixing of Library Books: Hearings*, 89th Cong., 2nd sess. (1966), p. 6.

42. Ibid., p. 1.

43. U.S., Congress, Senate, Judiciary Committee, Subcommittee on Antitrust and Monopoly, *Prices of Quinine and Quinidine: Hearings*, 90th Cong., 1st sess. (1967).

44. U.S., Congress, Senate, Judiciary Committee, Subcommittee on Antitrust and Monopoly, *Government Intervention into the Market Mechanism: Hearings*, 91st Cong., 1st and 2nd sess. (1969–1970), Parts 1–5.

45. Letter from Ralph Nader to Senator Philip Hart and Rep. Emanuel Celler, Dec. 23, 1970.

46. Letter from Senator Philip Hart to Ralph Nader, Feb. 2, 1971.

47. James Ridgeway, "Antitrust Doldrums," *New Republic*, Mar. 18, 1967, p. 13.

48. *Washington Post*, Mar. 11, 1973.

49. Richard Barber, *The American Corporation* (New York: Dutton, 1970), p. 70.

50. The memoranda referred to hereinafter are all located in the Emanuel Celler file at the manuscripts room at the Library of Congress.

51. *New York Times*, Apr. 23, 1950.

52. *Congressional Record*, Jan. 29, 1951, pp. A474–475.

53. *Wall Street Journal*, May 15, 1950.

54. 374 U.S. 321 (1963).

55. U.S., Congress, House, Judiciary Committee, Subcommittee No. 5, *Current Antitrust Problems: Hearings*, 84th Cong., 1st sess. (1955).

56. U.S., Congress, House, Judiciary Committee, Subcommittee No. 5, *Activities of Peter A. Strobel, Public Buildings Service, General Services Administration: Hearings*, 84th Cong., 1st sess. (1955).

57. U.S., Congress, House, Judiciary Committee, Subcommittee No. 5, *Monopoly Problems in Regulated Industries—Airlines: Hearings*, 84th Cong., 2nd sess. (1956); *Monopoly Problems in Regulated Industries—Television: Hearings*, 84th Cong., 2nd sess. (1956).

58. U.S., Congress, House, Judiciary Committee, Subcommittee No. 5, *Consent Decree Program of the Department of Justice (Oil Pipelines): Hearings*, 85th Cong., 1st sess. (1957); *Consent Decree Program of the Department of Justice (American Telephone and Telegraph Co.)*, 85th

Cong., 2nd sess. (1958); *Consent Decree Program of the Department of Justice*, Report, 86th Cong., 1st sess. (1959).
59. *Washington Post*, Feb. 2, 1969.
60. U.S., Congress, House, Judiciary Committee, Subcommittee No. 5, *Index of Antitrust Subcommittee Publications*, staff report, 92nd Cong., 1st sess. (1971). The computation does not include reports that merely list all of the antitrust laws or all hearings; it counts the 1969–1970 conglomerate hearings as seven separate hearings, and includes two hearings held in 1972 but not yet published.
61. For an expanded discussion of this incident, see Green, *Closed Enterprise System*, pp. 74–75.
62. *Washington Post*, Feb. 2, 1969.
63. House Judiciary Committee, *Legislative Calendar*, 90th Cong. (1969), p. 20.
64. *I. F. Stone's Bi-Weekly*, Sept. 20, 1971.
65. *Washington Post*, Feb. 2, 1969.
66. Ibid.
67. Ibid.
68. Robert Sherrill, "We Can't Depend on Congress to Keep Congress Honest," *New York Times Magazine*, July 19, 1970, p. 20.

CHAPTER 5.   ACRES OF DIAMONDS:
PATENTS AND COPYRIGHTS

---

1. See Irene Till, "The Legal Monopoly," in Mark J. Green, ed., *The Monopoly Makers* (New York: Grossman Publishers, 1973) pp. 294–298.
2. "Two Patent Studies Pending," *Science*, May 11, 1973, p. 573.
3. *Daily News Record*, July 9, 1972.
4. National Science Foundation, *National Patterns of R & D Resources, 1953–1972*, Report No. 72–300 (1972).
5. "Two Patent Studies," p. 573.
6. U.S., Congress, Senate, Judiciary Committee, Subcommittee on Patents, Trademarks, and Copyrights, *Hearings on S.2, S.1042, S.1691*, 90th Cong., 1st sess. (May 17 and 18, 1967), Part 1, p. 86.
7. Ibid., p. 204.
8. See, for example, the following reports of the Subcommittee on Patents, Trademarks, and Copyrights: Fritz Machlup, *An Economic Review of the Patent System*, Study No. 15; Seymour Melman, *The Impact of the Patent System on Research*, No. 11; Morris Friedman, *The Research and Development Factor in Mergers and Acquisitions*, No. 16; Victor Abramson, *The Patent System: Its Economic and Social Basis*, No. 26.
9. See list of members and employment background in Memorandum of

Law by Department of Justice, May 11, 1967 in Appendix to *Hearings on S.643, S.1253 and S.1255*, by the Subcommittee on Patents, Trademarks, and Copyrights of the Senate Judiciary Committee, 92nd Cong., 1st sess. (May 13, 1971), Part 2, p. 499.

10. U.S., Congress, Senate, Judiciary Committee, Subcommittee on Antitrust and Monopoly, *Administered Prices in the Drug Industry,* (1959–1961), Parts 14–26.

11. *U.S.* v. *Glaxo Group Ltd.,* Civil No. 558–68 (D.D.C. filed 3/4/68); *U.S.* v. *Ciba Corp. and C.P.C. International,* Civil No. 792–69 (D.N.J. filed 7/9/69); *U.S.* v. *Ciba Corp.,* Civil No. 791–69 (D.N.J. filed 7/9/69); *U.S.* v. *Fisons, Ltd.,* Civil No. 69 C 1530 (N.D. Ill., filed 7/23/69); *U.S.* v. *Bristol-Myers,* Civil No. 822–70 (D.C.C. filed 3/19/70).

12. *U.S.* v. *Westinghouse Electric Corp.,* Civil No. 70 C 852, (N.D. Calif., filed 4/22/70).

13. *Hearings on S.643, S.1253, and S.1255,* Parts 1 and 2.

14. Ibid., p. 229.

15. Ibid., p. 483.

16. List not made public but referred to in U.S., Congress, Senate, Judiciary Committee, Subcommittee on Patents, Trademarks, and Copyrights, Report 92–935, 92nd Cong., 2nd sess. (June 29, 1972), p. 9.

17. See, for example, letter sent to Senator Eastland and other members of the Senate Committee on the Judiciary by Edward J. Brenner, Executive Director, Association for the Advancement of Intervention and Innovation, published in its journal, *ACTION,* Mar. 1972, p. 72.

18. Ibid., inside front cover.

19. Ibid., inside back cover.

20. *U.S.* v. *Minnesota Mining and Mfg. Co.,* Criminal Action No. 61–73D, filed Dec. 13, 1961.

21. Letter of solicitation for members dated Sept. 19, 1972.

22. Bureau of National Affairs, *Patents, Trademarks and Copyright Journal,* Mar. 29, 1973, p. A–1.

23. *Congressional Record,* Apr. 17, 1973, p. H.2866.

24. See Till, "Legal Monopoly," p. 293.

25. These included H. G. Henn, *The Compulsory License Provisions of the U.S. Copyright Law;* W. M. Blaisdell, *Commercial Use of the Copyright Notice;* G. D. Cary, *Joint Ownership of Copyrights;* W. S. Strauss, *The Damage Provisions of the Copyright Law;* A. Latman and W. S. Tager, *Liability of Innocent Infringers of Copyrights;* B. A. Ringer, *The Unauthorized Duplication of Sound Recordings;* A. Bogsch, *Protection of Works of Foreign Origin;* C. Berger, *Copyright in Government Publications.*

26. Report of the Register of Copyrights on the General Revision of the U.S. Copyright Law, House Committee Print, July 1961, p. XI.

27. Ibid., pp. 119 ff.

28. *Copyright Law Revision,* Part 2, "Discussion and Comments on Report of the Register of Copyrights on the General Revision of U.S. Copyright Law," House Committee Print, Feb. 1963.

29. Ibid., Part 3, "Preliminary Draft for Revised U.S. Copyright Law and Discussions and Comments on the Draft," Sept. 1964; Part 4, "Further Discussions and Comments on Preliminary Draft for Revised U.S. Copyright Law," Dec. 1964.

30. Ibid., Part 5, "1964 Revision Bill with Discussions and Comments," Sept. 1965.

31. Ibid., Part 6, "Supplementary Report of the Register of Copyrights on the General Revision of the U.S. Copyright Law: 1965 Revision Bill," May 1965.

32. U.S., Congress, House, Judiciary Committee, Subcommittee No. 3, *Hearings on H.R.4347, H.R.5680, H.R.6831, H.R.6835* (all identical), 89th Cong., 1st sess. (1965).

33. U.S., Congress, House, Judiciary Committee, *Copyright Law Revision, accompanying H.R.2512,* Report 83, 90th Cong., 1st sess. (Mar. 8, 1967).

34. Ibid., p. 100.

35. Ibid., p. 134.

36. Ibid., p. 43.

37. Ibid., p. 21.

38. Ibid., p. 85.

39. *Williams & Wilkins Co. v. U.S.,* No. 75–68, in the U.S. Court of Claims, 1968.

40. 42 U.S.C. Par. 275.

41. Report of Commissioner to the U.S. Court of Claims, *Williams & Wilkins Co. v. U.S.,* filed Feb. 16, 1972.

42. *Washington Post,* Nov. 28, 1973.

43. U.S., Congress, Senate, Judiciary Committee, Subcommittee on Patents, Trademarks, and Copyrights, *Hearings on S.597,* 90th Cong., 1st sess., (Mar. and Apr. 1967).

44. U.S., Congress, Senate, Judiciary Committee, Subcommittee on Patents, Trademarks, and Copyrights, *Patents, Trademarks, and Copyrights,* Report 92–935, 92nd Cong., 2nd sess. (June 29, 1972).

45. *Congressional Record,* Mar. 26, 1973, p. S.5615.

46. U.S., Congress, Senate, *Copyright Protection in Certain Cases,* Report 92–934, to accompany S.J. Res. 247, Sen. McClellan from the Committee on the Judiciary, 92nd Cong., 2nd sess. (June 29, 1972).

47. U.S., Congress, House, *Copyright Protection in Certain Cases,* Report 92–605, Dissenting Views, to accompany S.J. Res. 132, Mr. Celler from the Committee on the Judiciary, 92nd Cong., 1st sess. (Nov. 3, 1971), p. 4.

48. U.S., Congress, House, *Copyright Protection in Certain Cases,* Report 92–1449 with Dissenting Views, to accompany S.J. Res. 247, Mr. Celler from the Committee on the Judiciary, 92nd Cong., 2nd sess. (Sept. 30, 1972), p. 6.

CHAPTER 6. SEPARATION OF POWERS: FINDING THE FOUNDING FATHERS

1. Quoted in James M. Naughton, "Constitutional Ervin," *New York Times Magazine*, May 13, 1973, p. 80.
2. U.S., Congress, Senate, Judiciary Committee, Subcommittee on Separation of Powers, *A Study of the Separation of Powers Between the Executive, Judicial and Legislative Branches of Government: Hearings*, 90th Cong., 1st sess. (July 19–20, Aug. 2, and Sept. 13–15, 1967), pp. 2, 3.
3. Kevin Phillips, "Our Obsolete System," *Newsweek*, Apr. 23, 1973, p. 13.
4. Telephone interview, Joel M. Abramson, Minority Counsel, Separation of Powers Subcommittee, Sept. 15, 1972.
5. U.S., Congress, Senate, Judiciary Committee, Subcommittee on Separation of Powers, *Executive Privilege: The Withholding of Information by the Executive: Hearings on S.1125*, 92nd Cong., 1st sess. (July 27, 28, 29; Aug. 4, 5, 1971).
6. Abramson interview.
7. Interview with Tom Farrar, Special Counsel to Senator Gurney, Sept. 13, 1972.
8. Interview with Rufus L. Edmisten, Chief Counsel and Staff Director, Separation of Powers Subcommittee, Sept. 13, 1972.
9. Abramson interview.
10. Edmisten interview.
11. Interview with Arthur S. Miller, Professor of Law, George Washington University Law School, Sept. 15, 1972.
12. U.S., Congress, Senate, Judiciary Committee, Subcommittee on Separation of Powers, *Constitutionality of the President's "Pocket-Veto" Power: Hearings*, 92nd Cong., 1st sess. (Jan. 26, 1971), pp. 219–233.
13. Ibid., pp. 13, 18, 20.
14. Ibid., pp. 10, 11.
15. Ibid., p. 21.
16. Ibid., pp. 23–24.
17. Edmisten interview.
18. Telephone interview with Carey Parker, Sept. 25, 1972.
19. *Albertson* v. *SACB*, 382 U.S. 70.
20. *Boords* v. *SACB*, 421 F 2d 1142 (D.C. Cir. 1969).
21. U.S., Congress, Senate, Judiciary Committee, Subcommittee on Separation of Powers, *President Nixon's Executive Order 11605 Relating to the Subversive Activities Control Board: Hearings*, 92nd Cong., 1st sess. (Oct. 5, 7, 1971), p. 9.
22. Edmisten interview.
23. *Hearings on E.O. 11605*, p. 13.
24. Ibid., pp. 15, 16, 19.

25. Ibid., pp. 50, 51.
26. Ibid., p. 9.
27. Ibid., pp. 24–27.
28. Ibid., p. 25.
29. Telephone interview with John Marks, Sept. 26, 1972.

CHAPTER 7. CONSTITUTIONAL AMENDMENTS: LEGISLATING FOR THE AGES

1. Arthur E. Sutherland, Jr., *Constitutionalism in America* (New York: Blaisdell, 1965), p. 203.
2. U.S., Congress, Senate, Judiciary Committee, *Amending the Constitution Relating to Electoral College Reform: Hearings*, 91st Cong., 2nd sess. (1969), p. 5.
3. Letter from Senator Birch Bayh to Michael E. Ward, Sept. 15, 1972.
4. Ibid.
5. Interview with Jason Berman, Staff Director, Subcommittee on Constitutional Amendments, July 25, 1972.
6. U.S., Congress, Senate, Judiciary Committee, Subcommittee on Constitutional Amendments, *Hearings on S.J. Res. 4, etc., Relating to the Election of the President*, 89th Cong., 2nd sess., 90th Cong., 1st sess. (1968).
7. Berman interview.
8. U.S., Congress, Senate, Judiciary Committee, Subcommittee on Constitutional Amendments, *Hearings on S.J. Res. 1, etc., To Amend the Constitution Relating to Electoral College Reform*, 91st Cong., 1st sess. (1969).
9. Confidential interview, summer 1972.
10. *Hearings on S.J. Res. 1* (1969), p. 6.
11. Confidential interview, summer 1972.
12. *Hearings on S.J. Res. 1* (1969), p. 7.
13. S. Rept. 91–1123, 91st Cong., 2nd sess. (1970), p. 9.
14. U.S., Congress, House, Judiciary Committee, *Hearings on H.J. Res. 179, H.J. Res. 181 and similar proposals*, 91st Cong., 1st sess. (1969), Ser. no. 1.
15. H. Rept. 91–253, 91st Cong., 1st sess. (1969).
16. Interview with Bess Dick, Staff Director, House Judiciary Committee, July 14, 1972.
17. Interview with Franklin Polk, Minority Counsel, House Judiciary Committee, Aug. 9, 1972.
18. Interview with Paul J. Mode, Chief Counsel, Subcommittee on Constitutional Amendments, July 25, 1972.

19. U.S., Congress, Senate, Judiciary Committee, Subcommittee on Constitutional Amendments, *Hearings on S.J. Res. 61, To Amend the Constitution So As to Provide Equal Rights for Men and Women*, 91st Cong., 2nd sess. (1970).
20. Mode interview.
21. U.S., Congress, Senate, Judiciary Committee, *Hearings on S.J. Res. 61, and S.J. Res. 231, Proposing an Amendment to the Constitution of the United States Relative to Equal Rights For Men and Women*, 91st Cong., 2nd sess. (1970).
22. S. Rept. 92–905, 92nd Cong., 2nd sess. (1972).
23. Votes supplied by the Judiciary Committee to the Ralph Nader Congress Project.
24. U.S., Congress, House, Judiciary Committee, Subcommittee No. 4, *Hearings on H.J. Res. 25, 208, and Related Bills, and H.R. 916 and Related Bills*, 92nd Cong., 1st sess. (1971), Ser. no. 2.
25. H. Rept. 92–359, 92nd Cong., 1st sess. (1971).
26. Mode interview.
27. *Oregon v. Mitchell*, 400 U.S. 112 (1970).
28. Mode interview.
29. U.S., Congress, Senate, Judiciary Committee, Subcommittee on Constitutional Amendments, *Lowering the Voting Age to 18*, Committee Print, 91st Cong., 1st sess. (Feb. 1971).
30. S. Rept. 92–26, 92nd Cong., 1st sess. (1971).
31. H. Rept. 92–37, 92nd Cong., 1st sess. (1971).
32. U.S., Congress, Senate, Judiciary Committee, Subcommittee on Constitutional Amendments, *Hearings on S.J. Res. 52, S.J. Res. 56*, 91st Cong., 2nd sess. (1970).
33. *Congressional Record*, Vol. 117, pp. D1085, D1094 (daily eds., Oct. 28 and 29, 1971).
34. *Congressional Record*, Vol. 118, pp. D712, D719, D759 (daily eds., June 21, 22, and 29, 1972).
35. *Congressional Record*, Vol. 118, p. D575 (daily ed., May 22, 1972).
36. U.S., Congress, House, Judiciary Committee, Subcommittee No. 1, *Hearings on H.J. Res. 46, H.J. Res. 253, H.J. Res. 374, H.J. Res. 470, and Similar Resolutions*, 92nd Cong., 1st sess. (1971), Ser. no. 10.
37. U.S., Congress, House, Judiciary Committee, Subcommittee No. 5, *Hearings on Proposed Amendments to the Constitution and Legislation Relating to Transportation and Assignment of Public School Pupils*, 92nd Cong., 2nd sess. (1972), Parts I, II, and III, Ser. no. 32.
38. Mode interview.
39. Berman interview.
40. *Hearings on S.J. 52*, pp. 10–11; Berman interview.
41. Confidential interview, summer 1972.

CHAPTER 8. CONSTITUTIONAL RIGHTS:
ACID TEST FOR CONSERVATIVES

1. Interviews with Lawrence Baskir, Chief Counsel, Subcommittee on Constitutional Rights, June 26 and July 5, 1972.
2. Ibid.
3. Interview with Senator Sam J. Ervin, Jr., June 26, 1972.
4. Ibid.
5. S. Rept. 92–524, 92nd Cong., 1st sess. (1971).
6. Letter from Senator Sam Ervin to Michael E. Ward, Aug. 25, 1971.
7. Letter to Judge Spencer Roane, September 6, 1819, in Ford, ed., *The Writings of Thomas Jefferson* (1899), Vol. 10, p. 140.
8. Veto Message, July 10, 1832, in Richardson, ed., *Messages and Papers of the Presidents* (1900), Vol. 2, pp. 581–583.
9. Proposed Speech on Gold Clause Cases, February 1935, in E. Roosevelt, ed., *FDR—His Personal Letters, 1928–1945* (1950), Vol. 1, pp. 459–460.
10. Ervin letter.
11. "Sam J. Ervin, Jr.," *Citizens Look at Congress*, Ralph Nader Congress Project (Washington: Grossman Publishers, 1972), pp. 34, 38.
12. Confidential interview, summer 1972.
13. Baskir interviews; interview with Hope Eastman, Acting Director, American Civil Liberties Union Washington Office, July 10, 1972.
14. Baskir interviews.
15. Ibid.
16. U.S., Congress, Senate, Judiciary Committee, Subcommittee on Constitutional Rights, *Hearings on S.818, S.2456, S.2507 and Title IV of S.2029, Bills to Amend the Voting Rights Act of 1965*, 91st Cong., 1st and 2nd sess. (1970).
17. Baskir interviews.
18. U.S., Congress, Senate, Judiciary Committee, Subcommittee on Constitutional Rights, *Hearings on Preventive Detention*, 91st Cong., 2nd sess. (1970).
19. Baskir interviews.
20. Confidential interview, summer 1972.
21. Baskir interviews.
22. U.S., Congress, Senate, Judiciary Committee, Subcommittee on Constitutional Rights, *Hearings on S.895*, 92nd Cong., 1st sess. (1971), pp. 94–121.
23. *Washington Star-News*, Apr. 18, 1973.
24. Ibid.
25. Baskir interviews.
26. S. Rept. 92–524.
27. Baskir interviews.
28. Aryeh Neier, "Have You Ever Been Arrested?" *New York Times Magazine*, Apr. 15, 1973, p. 16.

29. Interview with Jerome Zeifman, Counsel, Subcommittee No. 4, July 18, 1972.

30. Ibid.

31. Telephone conversation with Marvin Caplan, Leadership Conference on Civil Rights, Aug. 11, 1972.

32. Interview with Rep. William McCulloch, July 24, 1972.

33. U.S., Congress, House, Judiciary Committee, Subcommittee No. 5, *Hearings on H.R.4249, H.R. 5538, and Similar Proposals,* 91st Cong., 1st sess. (1969), Ser. no. 3, pp. 218–306.

34. U.S., Congress, House, Judiciary Committee, Civil Rights Oversight Subcommittee, *Enforcement of the Civil Rights Act of 1965: Report,* 92nd Cong., 2nd sess. (1972).

35. U.S., Congress, House, Judiciary Committee, Civil Rights Oversight Subcommittee, *Enforcement and Administration of the Voting Rights Action of 1965: Hearings,* 92nd Cong., 1st sess. (1971), p. 1.

36. Interview with Rep. Don Edwards, July 19, 1972.

37. *Voting Rights Enforcement Report.*

38. Zeifman interview.

39. Confidential interview, summer 1972.

40. U.S., Congress, House, Judiciary Committee, Civil Rights Oversight Subcommittee, *Federal Employment Problems of the Spanish Speaking: Hearings,* 92nd Cong., 2nd sess. (1972), Ser. no. 35.

41. U.S., Congress, House, Judiciary Committee, Civil Rights Oversight Subcommittee, *Report of the U.S. Commission on Civil Rights on the Education of the Spanish Speaking: Hearings,* 92nd Cong., 2nd sess. (1972), Ser. no. 35.

42. U.S., Congress, House, Judiciary Committee, Civil Rights Oversight Subcommittee, *Responsibilities of the Federal Power Commission in the Area of Civil Rights: Hearings,* 92nd Cong., 2nd sess. (1972), Ser. no. 24.

43. U.S., Congress, House, Judiciary Committee, Civil Rights Oversight Subcommittee, *The Role of the Farmers Home Administration in the Achievement of Equal Opportunity in Housing,* Committee Print, 92nd Cong., 2nd sess. (Apr. 1972).

44. Interview with George Dally, Assistant Counsel, Civil Rights Oversight Subcommittee, July 18, 1972; Edwards interview.

45. Edwards interview.

46. Comptroller General of the United States, *Compliance with Antidiscrimination Provision of Civil Rights Act by Hospitals and Other Facilities Under Medicare and Medicaid,* Report to Committee on the Judiciary, House of Representatives (July 13, 1972).

47. Edwards interview.

48. Ibid.

49. Confidential interview, summer 1972.

50. U.S. Commission on Civil Rights, *The Federal Civil Rights Enforcement Effort: A Reassessment* (1973), pp. 2, 9.

51. 42 U.S.C. §2000d (1970).

52. *Adams* v. *Richardson*, Civ. Action No. 73–1273 (D.C. Cir., June 12, 1973), slip opinion, pp. 2–3.
53. U.S. Commission on Civil Rights, *The Federal Civil Rights Enforcement Effort* (Oct. 1970); *Six Months Later* (May 1971); *One Year Later* (Nov. 1971); *A Reassessment* (Jan. 1973).
54. Figures supplied by HEW in a letter of Oct. 26, 1972 to Michael E. Ward from Theodore Miles, Assistant General Counsel, Civil Rights Division, Office of the General Counsel, HEW.
55. Joint statement of Attorney General John Mitchell and Secretary of Health, Education, and Welfare Robert Finch, June 3, 1969, p. 9.
56. HEW data supplied in letter of Oct. 26, 1972.
57. Lawyers' Review Committee to Study the Department of Justice, *Report* (Aug. 6, 1972), p. 8.
58. U.S. Commission on Civil Rights, *The Federal Civil Rights Enforcement Effort* (1970), p. 238.
59. 372 F.2d 836, 852–53 (1966).
60. *Adams* v. *Richardson*, 480 F.2d 1159, 1163 (D.C. Cir. 1973).
61. *Adams* v. *Richardson*, 356 F. Supp. 92, *affirmed* 480 F.2d 1159 (D.C. Cir. 1973).
62. Ibid.
63. 351 F. Supp. 636, 642, *affirmed* 480 F.2d 1159 (D.C. Cir. 1973).
64. U.S. Commission on Civil Rights, *Federal Civil Rights Enforcement Record: One Year Later.*
65. For a more complete discussion of these issues, see testimony of Peter H. Schuck before the Subcommittee on Migratory Labor of the Senate Committee on Labor and Public Welfare, June 19, 1972, and Peter H. Schuck, "Black Land-Grant Colleges: Discrimination as Public Policy," *Saturday Review*, June 24, 1972, p. 46.
66. *Reassessment*, pp. 262–263.
67. Confidential interview, summer 1972.
68. 331 F. Supp. 836 (M.D. Ala. 1971).
69. Ibid.
70. *Reassessment*, p. 245, n.11.
71. Office of Equal Opportunity, U.S. Department of Agriculture, *OEO Annual Report* (July, 1972), p. 5.
72. *Reassessment*, p. 240.
73. Ibid., p. 273.

CHAPTER 9.   ADMINISTRATIVE PRACTICE AND
             PROCEDURE: KENNEDY'S FIRE BRIGADE

---

1. U.S., Congress, Senate, Judiciary Committee, Subcommittee on Administrative Practice and Procedure, *Presidential Commissions: Hearings*, 92nd Cong., 1st sess. (1971), p. 6.

2. *Newsweek*, Oct. 2, 1972, p. 98.

3. John Chancellor, NBC News (Washington: WTOP, Apr. 23, 1973).

4. Telephone interview with Thomas Susman, Assistant Counsel, Subcommittee on Administrative Practice and Procedure, Jan. 19, 1973.

5. Ibid. See also U.S., Congress, Senate, Judiciary Committee, Subcommittee on Administrative Practice and Procedure, *Sovereign Immunity: Hearings*, 91st Cong., 2nd sess. (1970).

6. *Hearings on Presidential Commissions*, pp. 12, 90, 155, 165, 234.

7. Ibid., pp. 291–292.

8. Interview with Jim Flug, Chief Counsel, Subcommittee on Administrative Practice and Procedure, Sept. 9, 1972.

9. Ibid.

10. *Congressional Quarterly Weekly Report*, Feb. 27, 1970, p. 603; Mar. 13, 1970, p. 738.

11. *Congressional Quarterly Weekly Report*, Mar. 13, 1970, p. 738; Apr. 10, 1970, p. 959.

12. U.S., Congress, Senate, Judiciary Committee, Subcommittee on Administrative Practice and Procedure, *Administration of Oil Import Program: Hearings*, 91st Cong., 2nd sess. (1970), p. 2.

13. Ibid., pp. 40–42.

14. Ibid., p. 42.

15. *Washington Post*, Aug. 4, 1973.

16. Susman interview.

17. Ibid.

18. Robert Fellmeth, *The Nader Report on the Federal Trade Commission* (New York: Grove Press, 1969); U.S., Congress, Senate, Judiciary Committee, Subcommittee on Administrative Practice and Procedure, *Federal Trade Commission Procedure: Hearings*, 91st Cong., 1st sess. (1969), p. 3.

19. Susman interview.

20. U.S., Congress, Senate, Judiciary Committee, Subcommittee on Administrative Practice and Procedure, *Federal Protection of Indian Resources: Hearings*, 92nd Cong., 1st sess. (1971), Part I, pp. 1–5.

21. Susman interview.

22. *Congressional Quarterly Weekly Report*, Apr. 4, 1969, p. 466.

23. U.S., Congress, Senate, Judiciary Committee, Report No. 92–558, 92nd Cong., 1st sess. (1971), p. 16.

24. *Congressional Quarterly Weekly Report*, Feb. 13, 1970, p. 417.

25. Susman interview.

26. U.S., Congress, Senate, Judiciary Committee, Subcommittee on Administrative Practice and Procedure, *Electric Power Reliability: Hearings*, 91st Cong., 2nd sess. (1970), p. 40.

CHAPTER 10. JUDICIAL NOMINATIONS:
WHITHER "ADVICE AND CONSENT"?

---

1. See, for example, Richard Harris, *Decision* (New York: Ballantine Books, 1971); Joel Grossman, *Lawyers and Judges: The ABA and the Politics of Judicial Selection* (New York: John Wiley & Sons, 1965); Richard Richardson and Kenneth Vines, *The Politics of Federal Courts* (Boston: Little, Brown, 1970), Martin and Susan Tolchin, *To The Victor. . . .* (New York: Random House, 1971); Sheldon Goldman and Thomas Jahnige, *The Federal Courts as a Political System* (New York: Harper and Row, 1971).
2. *The Federalist*, No. 66 (New York: Modern Library), p. 433.
3. Richardson and Vines, *Politics of Federal Courts*, p. 61.
4. *New York Times*, July 29, 1973.
5. Ibid.
6. Tolchin, *To The Victor*, pp. 163–164.
7. *New York Times*, July 29, 1973.
8. Confidential interview, summer 1972.
9. Sheldon Goldman, "Judicial Appointment to the United States Courts of Appeal," *Wisconsin Law Review*, Winter 1967, pp. 190–191.
10. Ibid., pp. 188–189.
11. Quoted in Victor Navasky, *Kennedy Justice* (New York: Atheneum, 1971), p. 244.
12. Ibid., p. 243.
13. Bernard Segal, Testimony before the Subcommittee on Improvements in Judicial Machinery of the Senate Judiciary Committee, *Judicial Fitness*, 89th Cong., 2nd sess. (Feb. 15, 1966), Part I, p. 48.
14. Ibid., p. 50.
15. *New York Times*, July 29, 1973.
16. *Judicial Fitness*, p. 50.
17. U.S., Congress, Senate, Judiciary Committee, *Summary of Activities*, 92nd Cong., p. 8.
18. Richardson and Vines, *Politics of Federal Courts*, p. 61.
19. Interview with John Holloman III, Chief Counsel, Senate Judiciary Committee, July 1972.
20. Confidential interview, July 1972.
21. Transcript of hearing on Mark A. Costantino, National Archives, May 13, 1971, p. 7.
22. U.S., Congress, Senate, Judiciary Committee, *Nomination of Irving Ben Cooper: Hearings*, 87th Cong., 2nd sess. (1962).
23. Tolchin, *To the Victor*, p. 144.
24. Ibid.
25. Holloman interview.
26. Press release, Sept. 29, 1970, pp. 2–3.

27. Confidential interview, July 25, 1972.
28. Navasky, *Kennedy Justice*, p. 263.
29. Quoted in ibid., pp. 263–266.

CHAPTER 11.   PRIVATE BILLS: THE GRAVY ROAD

1. John A. Reynolds, "Private Laws for Private Citizens," *American Mercury*, Feb. 1956, p. 63.
2. U.S., Congress, House, *A Bill for the Relief of Sondra D. Shaw*, H. Rept. 2760, 90th Cong., 2nd sess. (1970), Private Law 90–362.
3. Asher Hinds, *Precedents of the House of Representatives* (Washington: U.S. Govt. Printing Office, 1907), IV. 3285.
4. Interviews with a sample of twelve caseworkers in the House and twelve in the Senate.
5. Martha Joynt, "Private Bills and the Legislative Process," (Ph.D. diss., Columbia University, 1972), p. 25.
6. Compiled from House and Senate calendars by Martha Joynt Kumar.
7. U.S., Congress, Senate, *A Bill for the Relief of the Estate of Gregory L. Kessenich*, S. Rept. 449, 87th Cong., 2nd sess. (1962), Private Law 87–578.
8. Colonel L. Skinner, "Birth of the Bazooka: The Genesis of a Powerful Portable Antitank Weapon," *Army Ordnance*, Vol. 26 (Sept.–Oct. 1944), pp. 283–285.
9. Letter to Chairman James Eastland from Wilber M. Brucker, H. Rept. 445, 85th Cong., 1st sess. (July 15, 1957), p. 6.
10. U.S., Congress, House, *A Bill for the Relief of the Estate of Gregory L. Kessenich*, H. Rept. 2261, to accompany S.149, p. 12.
11. Charles Roberts of *Newsweek* discovered this material through confidential interviews.
12. Confidential interview, Mar. 1972.
13. Private Law 88–32.
14. U.S., Congress, Senate, *A Bill for the Relief of the Luria Steel and Trading Co.*, S. Rept. 1176, 89th Cong., 1st sess. (1965). See also William Eaton, "Dirksen Pushes Firm's Claim," *Washington Daily News*, June 10, 1969.
15. Eaton, "Dirksen Pushes Firm's Claim."
16. U.S., Congress, Senate, Judiciary Committee, *A Bill for the Relief of the Swanston Equipment Company*, S. Rept. 86, to accompany S. 471.
17. Mar. 14, 1967, letter to Senator James Eastland from Fred Smith, general counsel to the Treasury Department, S. Rept. 86 (1969).
18. Campaign contributions as reported to the Clerk of the Senate.
19. U.S., Congress, House, Judiciary Committee, *Subcommittee No. 2 Rules*, p. 1.

20. Interview with William Shattuck, Mar. 1970.
21. Joynt, "Private Bills and the Legislative Process," pp. 107–108.
22. U.S., Congress, House, Judiciary Committee, H. Rept. 92–1070 to accompany H. Rept. 13366, 92nd Cong., 2nd sess. (1972), p. 2.
23. *Congressional Record*, June 24, 1972, p. H. 6807.
24. Testimony of Anita Johnson, Hearings before Subcommittee No. 2 of the House Judiciary Committee, 92nd Cong., 1st sess. (Sept. 30, 1971).
25. Minority Views on H. Rept. 13366. H. Rept. 92–1070, p. 16.
26. Ibid., p. 17.
27. *Congressional Record*, July 24, 1972, p. H. 6811.
28. Ibid., p. H. 6819.
29. H. Rept. 92–1070, p. 20.
30. *Congressional Record*, July 24, 1972, p. H. 6811.
31. Ibid., p. H. 6823.
32. *Washington Post*, July 25, 1972.
33. For a fuller account of the cyclamates bill, see James Fallows, "Picking Up the Tab," *Washington Monthly*, Nov. 1972.
34. U.S., Congress, House, Judiciary Committee, Subcommittee No. 1, Rule No. 4.
35. U.S., Congress, House, Judiciary Committee, *Summary of Activities*, 92nd Cong. (Nov. 1972), p. 5.
36. Quoted in Joynt, "Private Bills and the Legislative Process," p. 85.
37. James Batten, "Ship Jumper Bills Offense to Senators," *Miami Herald*, Aug. 3, 1969.
38. Ibid.
39. *Congressional Quarterly Weekly Report*, Aug. 15, 1969, p. 1481.
40. Batten, "Ship Jumper Bills."
41. Ibid.
42. Ibid.
43. Ibid.
44. *Miami Herald*, Aug. 4, 1969.
45. Ibid.
46. News release by the Senate Select Committee on Standards and Conduct. Statement by Senator John Stennis, Chairman, Sept. 29, 1969.
47. U.S., Congress, Senate, Judiciary Committee, Report 91–911, 91st Cong., 2nd sess. (1970), p. 1.
48. Ibid., p. 3.
49. See, for example, Mark J. Green, James M. Fallows, and David R. Zwick, *Who Runs Congress?* (New York: Grossman Publishers and Bantam Books, 1972), pp. 149–50.

CHAPTER 12.   CRIMINAL LAWS AND
CRIMINAL JUSTICE

1. Confidential interview, summer 1972.
2. Confidential interview, summer 1972.
3. Interview with Hope Eastman, Acting Director, American Civil Liberties Union Washington Office, Aug. 15, 1972.
4. Confidential interviews and telephone conversations, summer 1972.
5. Confidential interview, summer 1972.
6. *Final Report of the National Commission on Reform of the Federal Criminal Law*, §3601; S.1, 93rd Cong., §1—4E1.
7. *Report*, §1824; S.1, §2—9E1.
8. *Report*, §1351; S.1, §2—6D1.
9. *Report*, p. 246.
10. S.1, §2—9F5.
11. *Report*, §1119; S.1, §2—5B10.
12. *Report*, §3202; S.1, §1—4B2.
13. *Report*, §1101; S.1, §2—5B1.
14. *Report*, §1106; S.1, §2—5B4.
15. *Report*, §1114.
16. U.S., Congress, Senate, Judiciary Committee, Subcommittee on Criminal Laws and Procedures, *Reform of the Federal Criminal Laws, Part IIIb: Hearings*, 92nd Cong., 2nd sess. (1972), p. 1430; *Report*, §1115, Comment; S.1, §2—5B4.
17. S.1, §2—7F1.
18. S.1, §2—8F3; S.1, §2—8F4.
19. S.1, Chap. 10, Subchap. C; S.1, Chap. 10, Subchap. D.
20. Titles I, II, IV, V, and X of the final bill involved recommendations of the Commission. U.S., Congress, Senate, Judiciary Committee, Subcommittee on Criminal Laws and Procedures, *Hearings on S.30, S.974, S.975, etc.*, 91st Cong., 1st sess. (1969), pp. 503, 505, 508, 510–511; U.S. Congress, House Judiciary Committee, Subcommittee No. 5, *Hearings on S.30 and Related Proposals*, 91st Cong., 2nd sess., Ser. no. 27, pp. 98, 100, 104. Title VIII was an administration bill. The American Bar Association and the National Council on Crime and Delinquency were among those whose proposals were studied for Title X. (House hearings, p. 108.) Title II also drew from recommendations of the Brown Commission in its preliminary work. (House hearings, p. 98.)
21. See, for example, S. Rept. 72, 89th Cong., 1st sess. (1965), pp. 55, 125–126.
22. *Congressional Record*, Vol. 116, pp. D114–5, D119 (daily digest, 1970).
23. S. Rept. 92–100, 92nd Cong., 1st sess. (1971), pp. 4–5.
24. Interview with Malcolm Hawk, Aide to Senator Hruska, Aug. 10, 1972.

25. Confidential interview, summer 1972.
26. Hearings on Reform of Federal Criminal Laws, pp. 1393–1394, 1427 ff., 1537 ff.
27. Interview with Jerome Zeifman, Counsel, Subcommittee No. 4, July 18, 1972; interview with Tom Mooney, Minority Counsel, House Judiciary Committee, Aug. 4, 1972; interview with Franklin Polk, Minority Counsel, House Judiciary Committee, Aug. 9, 1972.
28. Interview with Ben Zelenko, Chief Counsel, House Judiciary Committee, July 19, 1972; Polk interview.
29. Interview with Rep. William McCulloch, July 24, 1972.
30. Confidential interview, summer 1972.
31. *Congressional Record*, Vol. 116, p. 36393 (1970).
32. Polk interview.
33. Interview with Bess Dick, Staff Director, House Judiciary Committee, July 14, 1972.
34. Confidential interview, summer 1972.
35. Polk interview.
36. Zelenko interview.
37. Ramsey Clark, *Crime in America* (New York: Simon and Schuster, 1971), p. 100.
38. *Congressional Record*, Vol. 111, p. 4363 (1965), Presidential Message.
39. 30 Fed. Reg. 9349 (1965), Executive Order 11236, signed July 25, 1965.
40. President's Commission on Law Enforcement and Administration of Justice, *The Challenge of Crime in a Free Society*, p. 285.
41. U.S., Congress, House, Judiciary Committee, Subcommittee No. 5, *Anti-Crime Program: Hearings on H.R.5037, H.R.5938, H.R.5384, H.R.5385, and H.R.5386*, 90th Cong., 1st sess. (1967), Ser. no. 3.
42. H. Rept. 488, 90th Cong., 1st sess. (1967), p. 46.
43. *Congressional Record*, Vol. 113, p. 21081–104 (1967).
44. *Congressional Record*, Vol. 113, pp. 21819, 21821, 21824, 21825 (1967), remarks of Messrs. Celler, Rodino, and Eilberg.
45. U.S., Congress, Senate, Judiciary Committee, Subcommittee on Criminal Laws and Procedures, *Controlling Crime Through More Effective Law Enforcement: Hearings on S.674, S.675, S.678, S.917, etc.*, 90th Cong., 1st sess. (1967), p. 2.
46. S. Rept. 1097, 90th Cong., 2nd sess. (1968).
47. Richard Harris, *The Fear of Crime* (New York: Praeger, 1969), pp. 58–72.
48. Ibid., pp. 76, 97; confidential interview, summer 1972.
49. S. Rept. 1097, pp. 221–222, 227–228.
50. *Congressional Record*, Vol. 114, p. 14777 (1968); remarks of Senators McClellan and Hruska.
51. U.S., Congress, Senate, Judiciary Committee, Subcommittee on Criminal Laws and Procedures, *Federal Assistance to Law Enforcement: Hearings on S.3, S.964, S.965, etc.*, 91st Cong., 2nd sess. (1970), p. 518.
52. *National Journal*, Jan. 29, 1972, pp. 181, 183.
53. U.S., Congress, House, *Block Grant Programs of the Law Enforcement*

Assistance Administration, H. Rept. 92–1072, 92nd Cong., 2nd sess. (1972), pp. 19, 27.
54. Ibid., pp. 27, 33–34.
55. Ibid., pp. 42, 100, 49.
56. Ibid., pp. 78–80.
57. *National Journal,* Jan. 29, 1972, p. 183.
58. H. Rept. 92–1072, pp. 8, 154.
59. Ibid., pp. 12, 14.
60. Ibid., pp. 15–16.
61. Ibid., p. 145.
62. *National Journal,* Jan. 29, 1972, p. 183.
63. Public Law 90–351, Sec. 303; 82 Stat. 20.
64. Lawyers Committee for Civil Rights Under Law, Sara Carey, *Law and Disorder III* (prepublication draft, 1972).
65. H. Rept. 92–1072, pp. 74–75.
66. Ibid., p. 70.
67. Committee for Economic Development, *Reducing Crime and Assuring Justice* (1972), p. 68.
68. "Justice Report/Congress holds past criticism in check as it considers revenue-sharing role of LEAA," *National Journal,* Mar. 31, 1973, pp. 450, 452.
69. *Washington Post,* July 23, 1972.
70. H. Rept. 92–1072, p. 154.
71. *Law and Disorder III,* pp. 12–17.
72. *A Report by the Lawyers' Review Committee to Study the Department of Justice,* Aug. 6, 1972, Appendix, pp. 9–11.
73. *Law and Disorder III,* p. 1.
74. H. Rept. 92–1072, pp. 61, 64–65.
75. Letter of John Mitchell to Elliot Richardson, May 25, 1971; Letter of Secretary of Health, Education and Welfare to John Mitchell, May 25, 1971; in S. Rept. 92–220, 92nd Cong., 1st sess., pp. 6–8.
76. H. Rept. 92–1072, p. 64.
77. Ibid., pp. 62, 63.
78. *Washington Post,* July 23, 1972.
79. *Law and Disorder III,* pp. 56–58. This report contains an extensive critique of the LEAA program, with full consideration of the questions of privacy, civil rights, the police-industrial complex, etc.
80. U.S., Congress, House, Judiciary Committee, Subcommittee No. 5, *Hearings on H.R.14341, H.R.15947 and Related Proposals,* 91st Cong., 2nd sess. (1970), Ser. no. 17, pp. 724–761.
81. H. Rept. 91–1174, 91st Cong., 2nd sess. (1970), pp. 2, 3, 5.
82. *Hearings on S.3* (1970).
83. S. Rept. 91–1253, 91st Cong., 2nd sess. (1970), pp. 1–7.
84. Ibid., pp. 24–25.
85. Ibid., p. 87.
86. Confidential interview, summer 1972.
87. Interview with Sara Carey, Lawyers Committee for Civil Rights Under Law, July 20, 1972.

88. Interview with Charles Rogovin, former administrator of LEAA, June 27, 1972.
89. Rogovin interview.
90. Confidential interview, summer 1972.
91. Interview with Rep. Tom Railsback, July 28, 1972.
92. *Congressional Record,* Vol. 118, p. S.15128 (daily ed., Sept. 18, 1972).
93. Ibid.
94. *Congressional Record,* Vol. 118, p. S.15130–1 (daily ed., Sept. 18, 1972).
95. S.2148 (with Senator Mathias, et al.) and S.2535, 92nd Cong.
96. *Congressional Record,* Vol. 118, pp. S.15129, S.15131 (daily ed., Sept. 18, 1972).

CHAPTER 13. YOUTH, DRUGS, AND GUNS: KEEPING UP WITH THE HEADLINES

1. Confidential interview, summer 1972.
2. Interviews with Mathea Falco, Chief Counsel and Staff Director, Subcommittee to Investigate Juvenile Delinquency, June 21 and Aug. 16, 1972.
3. Interview with David Huber and Ron Meredith of Senator Marlow Cook's office, July 18, 1972.
4. Interview with Senator Marlow Cook, July 28, 1972.
5. U.S., Congress, Senate, Judiciary Committee, Subcommittee to Investigate Juvenile Delinquency, *Hearings on S.1732,* 92nd Cong., 1st sess. (1971).
6. Letter from Senator Birch Bayh to Michael Ward, Sept. 15, 1972.
7. Letter from Elliot Richardson, Secretary of HEW, to John Mitchell, Attorney General, May 25, 1971.
8. Ibid.
9. *Hearings on S.1732,* pp. 20–25.
10. Interview with Robert Gemignani, Commissioner of YDDPA, Aug. 4, 1972.
11. *Hearings on S.1732,* p. 31.
12. Bayh letter.
13. Falco interviews.
14. S. Rept. 92–220, 92nd Cong., 1st sess. (1971), p. 2.
15. Gemignani interview.
16. The administration bill was also introduced by Senator Cook.
17. U.S., Congress, Senate, Judiciary Committee, Subcommittee to Investigate Juvenile Delinquency, *Hearings on S.3148, S.3443, S.3521, and S.3555,* 92nd Cong., 2nd sess. (1972), pp. 88–89, 94, 102, 110, 112–113, 117.
18. Bayh letter.

19. S. Rept. 92–867, 92nd Cong., 2nd sess. (1972).
20. Bayh letter.
21. Falco interviews.
22. Ibid.
23. U.S., Congress, Senate, Judiciary Committee, Subcommittee to Investigate Juvenile Delinquency, *Hearings on S.674, Amphetamine Legislation, 1971,* 92nd Cong., 1st sess. (1972), pp. 72, 76.
24. U.S., Congress, Senate, Judiciary Committee, Subcommittee to Investigate Juvenile Delinquency, *Hearings on the Efficacy of Amphetamines for the Short-Term Treatment of Obesity and the Related Issue of Production Quotas,* 92nd Cong., 2nd sess. (1972).
25. 36 Fed. Reg. 20686 (1971).
26. 37 Fed. Reg. 3195 (1972).
27. Falco interviews.
28. Telephone conversation with John Rector, Deputy Chief Counsel, Subcommittee to Investigate Juvenile Delinquency, Jan. 9, 1973. See also H. Rept. 91–1807, 91st Cong., 2nd sess. (1971)
29. Falco interview.
30. Ramsey Clark, *Crime in America* (New York: Simon and Schuster, 1971).
31. Ibid., pp. 85–86.
32. *American Rifleman,* Oct. 1969, pp. 54–55.
33. See letter to Congressman John Murphy from Ralph Alkire, Acting Director, Alcohol, Tobacco and Firearms Division, Internal Revenue Service, May 12, 1971.
34. Gallup polls cited by Senator Edward Kennedy in Additional Views, S. Rept. 95–1004, 92nd Cong., 2nd sess. (1972), p. 33.
35. Senator Thomas J. Dodd, with the assistance of Carl Perian, "Federal Firearms Legislation—1961–1968," unpublished report, pp. 3–11.
36. Ibid., p. 14.
37. U.S., Congress, Senate, Commerce Committee, *Hearings on S.1975 and S.2345,* 88th Cong., 2nd sess. (1964), Ser. no. 45, pp. 1–28.
38. U.S., Congress, Senate, Judiciary Committee, Subcommittee to Investigate Juvenile Delinquency, *Hearings on S.1592, S.14, S.1180, S.1065,* 89th Cong., 1st sess. (1965), pp. 207–214.
39. Ibid., pp. 1–721.
40. Dodd, "Federal Firearms Legislation," p. 21.
41. Ibid., pp. 21–27.
42. S. Rept. 1866, 89th Cong., 2nd sess. (1966).
43. Dodd, "Federal Firearms Legislation," pp. 27–28.
44. Ibid., pp. 31, 35.
45. U.S., Congress, House, Subcommittee No. 5, *Hearings on H.R.5037, H.R.5038, and Related Bills,* 90th Cong., 1st sess. (1967), Ser. no. 3.
46. *Congressional Record,* Vol. 114, p. 16077 (1968).
47. U.S., Congress, Senate, Judiciary Committee, Subcommittee to Investigate Juvenile Delinquency, *Hearings on S.3691, S.3604, S.3634, S.3637,* 90th Cong., 2nd sess. (1968).
48. Articles of Incorporation, National Rifle Association of America, filed

New York County, New York, Nov. 17, 1871; extension of purposes certified Mar. 22, 1956, Washington, D.C.

49. Jonathan Cottin, "Washington Pressures National Rifle Association," *National Journal*, May 2, 1970, p. 950.

50. *Congressional Quarterly Almanac*, 1968, p. 563; 1969, p. 1109.

51. Interview with Jack Basil of the Legislative Information Service of the National Rifle Association, Washington, July 12, 1972.

52. *American Rifleman*, Aug. 1969, p. 47.

53. Ibid., Dec. 1970, p. 22.

54. Ibid., pp. 22–23.

55. Election results from *Congressional Quarterly Almanac*, 1970, pp. 1085–1092.

56. Based on state membership figures for April and May 1972 supplied by the National Rifle Association and the results of the 1970 senatorial races as reported in *Congressional Quarterly Almanac*, 1970, pp. 1085–1092.

57. Basil interview, and confidential interview, summer 1972.

58. *Life*, Sept. 28, 1970, p. 27.

59. Basil interview.

60. Ibid.

61. *American Rifleman*, Mar. 1971.

62. U.S., Congress, Senate, Judiciary Committee, Subcommittee to Investigate Juvenile Delinquency, *Hearings on S.2507*, 92nd Cong., 1st sess. (1971), p. 29.

63. *American Rifleman*, July 1969, p. 7.

64. S. Rept. 92–1004, p. 9.

65. *Christian Science Monitor*, June 1, 1971.

66. Firearms Task Force Report to National Commission on the Causes and Prevention of Violence, p. 173.

67. Letter to Senator Birch Bayh from William Dickey of Treasury Department, May 26, 1972.

68. *Christian Science Monitor*, June 1, 1971.

69. U.S., Congress, Senate, Judiciary Committee, Subcommittee to Investigate Juvenile Delinquency, *Hearings on S.100, S.977, S.2433, S.2667*, 91st Cong., 1st sess. (1969), p. 46.

70. Quoted in *American Rifleman*, May 1971.

71. Interview with Lawrence Spieser, former Staff Director and Chief Counsel, Juvenile Delinquency Subcommittee, June 16, 1972.

72. *Hearings on S.2507* (1971).

73. *American Rifleman*, May 1969, p. 10.

74. *Hearings on S.2507* (1971), pp. 315–316.

75. Ibid., 131–162, 258–280.

76. Letter from Senator Birch Bayh to Michael Ward, Sept. 15, 1972.

77. *Hearings on S.2507* (1971), pp. 26–27, 134–162, 263–278.

78. *American Rifleman*, Dec. 1971, pp. 18–19.

79. Ibid.

80. *American Rifleman*, Feb. 1972, p. 48.

81. Confidential interview, summer 1972.

82. Confidential interview.

83. Confidential interview, summer 1972.

84. S. Rept. 92–1004, 92nd Cong., 2nd sess. (1972), pp. 7–8.

85. Ibid., pp. 8, 18.

86. Falco interview.

87. Votes supplied to the Congress Project by the Judiciary Committee.

88. Letter from Maxwell Rich, Executive Vice President of the National Rifle Association, to Senator Birch Bayh, Aug. 3, 1972.

89. Confidential interview, summer 1972.

90. Telephone conversation with Lynn Perle, Americans for Democratic Action, Aug. 15, 1972.

91. Interview with Ben Zelenko, Chief Counsel, House Judiciary Committee, July 19, 1972.

92. U.S., Congress, House, Judiciary Committee, Subcommittee No. 5, *Hearings on H.8828 and Related Bills*, 92nd Cong., 2nd sess. (1972), Ser. no. 33.

93. Interview with Franklin Polk, Aug. 9, 1972.

94. Ibid.

95. *Congressional Record*, Vol. 118, p. S.15075 (daily ed. Sept. 18, 1972).

96. *Washington Post*, Jan. 1973.

97. *Washington Post*, July 28, 1973, p. 14.

98. Huber and Meredith interview.

99. Ibid.

100. Rector conversation.

101. U.S., Congress, Senate, Judiciary Committee, Subcommittee to Investigate Juvenile Delinquency, *Hearings on Juvenile Confinement Institutions and Correctional Systems*, 92nd Cong., 1st sess. (1971).

CHAPTER 14. CORRECTIONS: THE LEGACY OF ATTICA

1. "Quentin Burdick," *Citizens Look at Congress*, Ralph Nader Congress Project (Washington: Grossman Publishers, 1972), p. 2.

2. Confidential interview.

3. Confidential interview, summer 1972.

4. Interviews by Congress Project researchers with James Meeker, Staff Director, National Penitentiaries Subcommittee, summer 1972.

5. U.S., Congress, Senate, Judiciary Committee, Subcommittee on National Penitentiaries, *Hearings on the Future Role of U.S. Bureau of Prisons*, 92nd Cong., 1st sess. (March 2–3, 1971).

6. Congressional Staff Directory, 1972 and 1973, Charles B. Brownson (Washington, D.C.); see staff biography, p. 670 of 1972 edition or p. 681 of 1973 edition.

7. Meeker interviews.

8. Ibid.

9. Interview with Justis Freimund, National Council on Crime and Delinquency, summer 1972.

10. Confidential interview.

11. U.S. Department of Justice, Bureau of Prisons, "Long Range Master Plan," May 1972.

12. Interview with Senator Marlow Cook, July 28, 1972.

13. Ibid.

14. Meeker interviews.

15. Ibid.

16. U.S., Congress, House, Judiciary Committee, Subcommittee No. 3, *Hearings on Bills Related to Parole, H.R.12908, 13118, 13230, 13293,* 92nd Cong., 1st and 2nd sess., (1971–1972), pp. 142, 144, 145.

17. Interview with Howard Eglit, special counsel for corrections, summer, 1972.

18. Interview with Congressman Tom Railsback, July 28, 1972.

19. Public Law 93–209, December 28, 1973.

20. U.S., Congress, House, Judiciary Committee, "Inspection of Federal Facilities at Leavenworth Penitentiary and the Medical Center for Federal Prisoners" (Washington, D.C.: Government Printing Office, Jan. 1974).

21. Ibid., pp. 10–11.

22. Ibid., p. 11.

23. Interview with Eglit, summer 1972.

24. Ibid.

25. Interview with William Dixon, Staff Counsel, Subcommittee on Courts, Civil Liberties, and the Administration of Justice, April 1, 1974.

26. *New York Times,* April 14, 1974, p. 21.

27. Quoted in *Washington Post,* April 12, 1974, p. A3.

CHAPTER 16.   POSTSCRIPT: THE UNMAKING OF HOUSE JUDICIARY COMMITTEE REFORM

---

1. Remarks by Rep. Peter W. Rodino, *Congressional Record,* June 30, 1973, p. H.5799.

2. Ibid.

3. Telephone interview with William E. Davis, Legislative Assistant to Rep. James Mann, Aug. 22, 1973.

4. Telephone interviews with Gordon Kerr, Legislative Assistant to Rep. Barbara Jordan, and Colin Mathews, Legislative Aide to Rep. Wayne Owens, Aug. 22, 1973.

5. U.S., Congress, House, Judiciary Committee, "Report of the *Ad Hoc* Subcommittee on Committee Reorganization," Apr. 2, 1973.

6. Ibid., p. 3.

7. Statement of Peter W. Rodino before House Select Committee on Committees, May 10, 1973, p. 9.
8. Quoted in *Washington Post*, June 20, 1973.
9. Remarks by Peter W. Rodino, *Congressional Record*, June 20, 1973, p. H.5799.
10. Ibid.
11. Kerr interview.
12. *Washington Post*, June 20, 1973.
13. "House Judiciary Unit Makes Changes in Its Subcommittees," *Washington Post*, June 20, 1973.
14. "Suggested Procedure for Adoption of Reorganization Plan," Addendum to the Report of the *Ad Hoc* Subcommittee on Committee Reorganization.
15. Rodino statement, May 10, 1973.
16. Davis interview.

Index